No Job for a Woman

Hearts and Sails Book 2

Alina Rubin

Every effort has been made to ensure this book is free from errors or omissions. This is a work of fiction. Characters, names, businesses, places, events, and incidents are either the products of the author's imagination or have been used in a fictitious manner.

Publisher: Alina Rubin

ISBN: Paperback 979-8-9855378-3-3

Cover Design: GetCovers

Editor: Kirsten Rees| Book Editor and Author Coach

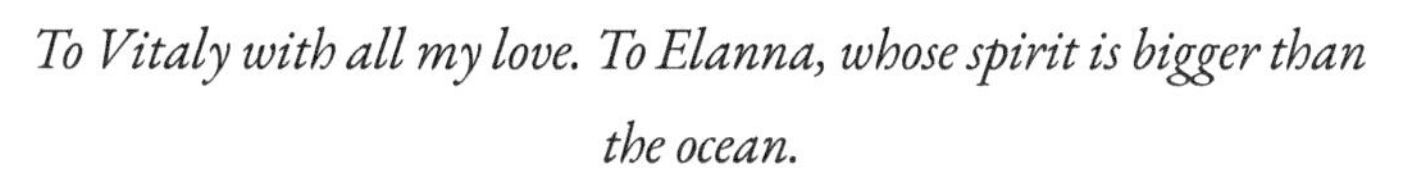

To Vitaly with all my love. To Elanna, whose spirit is bigger than the ocean.

To all the angels who whisper to me as I write.

Leave a Review!

I would love to know what you thought of *No Job for a Woman*!

You can write a review at:

Amazon

Goodreads

BookBub

Join the crew! Be the first to know of new adventures by subscribing to the newsletter at alinarubinauthor.com

I love hearing from my readers! Please connect with me!

Instagram: Alina.Rubin.Author

Facebook: Alina Rubin Author

Email: alina@alinarubinauthor.com

Table of Contents

Chapter 1

London, 1810

The answer would be 'no' once again. Dr. Willis's hazel eyes revealed a kind soul. He was civil enough to invite Ella inside his exam room, give her a chair, and offer her a glass of water to relieve her thirst. Among the other eighteen practices she'd visited, there were physicians who laughed at her. Three slammed the door in her face. Two said she was breaking the law. One said she dishonored her sex. Another suggested she was mad. Finally, there were a few, like this physician, who read Dr. Pesce's letter, but their faces remained unmoved.

With a bewildered expression, Dr. Willis handed the letter back to her. "I'm sorry, Miss Parker. I don't understand why Dr. Pesce sent you here. I can't hire you as an apprentice."

Ella tilted her head. Her logic hadn't worked on other physicians, but she had to try. "Do you have many female patients, Doctor?"

"Yes, about half of my practice are women."

"Don't you think they would be more comfortable with a lady doctor? Especially when their complaints are about feminine issues?"

Dr. Willis scratched his bearded chin. "Most ladies bring someone with them when coming to see me. A few times, my wife stepped in to make them feel more comfortable."

Ella suppressed the urge to roll her eyes. "I'm not speaking of simply holding a patient's hand through the exam, although I've offered such comfort as well. Women may be more open with me about their symptoms, and more comfortable letting me view their bodies or examining them. I'm able to treat their maladies. It may surprise you, but I've studied at a medical school and passed my exams."

The doctor's eyes bulged. "That's unbelievable! Medical schools in England forbid female students. Could you show me your diploma?"

"Well, no." Ella bit her lip. "I passed the exams, but the professors refused to give me a degree."

He scoffed and stood. "I don't want to hear any more of this. It's impossible for me to employ a woman in my practice, no matter the circumstances. Excuse me, Miss, but I have much work to do."

With a proud expression that masked the heaviness in her chest, Ella swept out of the doctor's house. Dr. Willis was the second to last entry on her list. Her mentor, Dr. Joseph Pesce, could not accuse her of a lackluster effort.

Her legs dragged for several blocks to the last address. The July sunshine heated the strands of her cropped raven hair that escaped her bonnet. The hem of her skirt brushed on the grime and soot of the street. She missed the loose shirt and trousers she had worn to university two months ago. Those clothes were comfortable, easy to care for, and granted an enthusiastic reception to the promising medical student who wore them. Where her alter ego, Alan Parker, strolled in with ease, Ella Parker was not welcomed.

As Ella turned onto the street of the address she was looking for, the rustle of leaves on trimmed hedges and the aroma of summer flowers replaced the clap of hooves and the stench of manure of busy London roads. The houses in this neighborhood pleased the eye with fresh paint, large windows, and decorative columns. She stopped outside a four-floor house of a pleasant yellow color. The prominent sign in a window announced the doctor's residence. Even less likely to find success at such a thriving practice. While waiting at the back door, she bent to smell the tea roses.

"How may I help you, Miss?" A young man's voice inquired. "And please keep that rose if you like it so much. I'll cut it off for you."

"No need." She took a moment to collect herself and make her expression confident before straightening to face him. His tall frame and red hair caused her to stiffen as his friendly smile changed to the mean grin of a medical student she knew well.

"William Jeffers," she said slowly.

His eyes studied her, resting first on her face, then on her bosom that she went to great lengths to hide when she was a student in the university. "Parker. Although, obviously not Alan Parker. What's your real name?"

"It doesn't matter. What are you doing here?"

Jeffers advanced and stood nose-to-nose with her. Or rather nose to chin because he was taller. "I should be asking that question. This is my uncle's practice. He specializes in midwifery. He's out right now, but I'll be happy to see you." He chuckled and lowered his tone. "Very happy to see you undressed on the exam table. When I learned you were a girl, I was terribly sorry for missed opportunities to get to know you better. Looks like we can make up the lost time."

He put his hand on her waist, but she smacked it away. "Keep your hands off me," she hissed. "I had some business with your uncle, but since he's not here, I'm leaving. You have no right to be a doctor, especially caring for female patients. I heard you plagiarized your thesis paper. How can you be practicing medicine?"

"It's incredible what money and connections can do. All kinds of faults can be forgiven. I'm my uncle's apprentice, gain-ing experience at his prestigious practice. And what are you?" He snapped his fingers. "Ah, a colleague of my uncle mentioned that a young woman asked him for a job and made an outrageous claim she received training in a medical school. So that was you. Well, I will be sure to tell him, and any other doctor I know, who you are and how you received your knowledge."

Her cheeks heated. "I made no false claims. Unlike you, I worked hard, authored my own thesis, and answered every question on my exam. I may not have a diploma, but I'm much more capable of treating patients than you. But let that be your and your uncle's problem. Goodbye."

She spun on her heel to leave.

"If you change your mind, I have the exam table ready," he called after her, laughing.

***

Matilda Pesce was stirring a heavy pot on the stove when Ella burst through the door. Dr. Pesce's sister gave her a questioning gaze.

Ella's whole body ached from weariness, and her spirits slumped from the sting of rejections and the disgust of the encounter with Jeffers. She had expected such responses, but the reality proved far worse.

"I've visited every doctor practice on the list. None of them want a woman assistant," Ella announced.

Matilda snorted. "No surprise there. Did you believe some-one would hire you?"

"No," Ella admitted, sitting at the table to rest her feet. "I only did it to satisfy Dr. Pesce. Of course, when he made the list, he thought I would present myself in men's clothing. He imagines I can pull off such a disguise day after day. I can't play a man forever. Nor do I want to."

"He hasn't seen you since you were a pubescent girl. In the past two years, you've blossomed into a woman. Seventeen is a beautiful age. Even the short hair suits you." Matilda gave an amused smile.

A red apple in the bowl called to Ella, so she picked it up and bit into its sweet flesh. The aroma of the meaty broth simmering on the stove made her even hungrier.

The kitchen, and the entire house, looked much like when Ella first left it two years ago for medical school. Except Dr. Pesce's bedroom, exam room, and dissection room downstairs now stood empty. The doctor took a posting as a surgeon on a warship the same day that Ella left for the university and had not visited his sister since.

The bell chimed at the backdoor, and Matilda hurried away. A baby cried, and an uneven woman's voice asked how to treat her daughter's rash. While Matilda led the mother to the herb room, Ella stirred the soup and chopped some parsley. A smile touched her lips, hearing the baby coo as the midwife sang something soothing. After the mother and baby left with a rustling package that smelled of marigolds, her friend returned to the kitchen with a dreamy expression.

"That baby girl gave me a scare at her birth. She was breech, and the doctor was late. I delivered her with one hand supporting her shoulders, and my other hand inside the birth canal, on her cheekbone, to free her head." She demonstrated the movement with her arms. "Did you learn this in medical school?"

Ella frowned. "I believe so. My instructor called it the Mauriceau maneuver. We spent little time on it though because he advocated for using forceps instead."

"Of course." Matilda rolled her eyes. "Women helped other women give birth from the beginning of time. Then men invent some device and declared that midwives are too weak and too dim to use it. Forceps do help at times, but I managed without the doctor to deliver that child. And now she's getting so big."

Ella grinned at her friend, energetic and able in her fifties. Matilda traversed the city delivering babies, ran her herb shop, and kept the house spotless, all without help.

Matilda stirred the soup and minced garlic. Ella stood next to her, placing out a cutting board and knife to slice carrots. If she was barred from wielding a scalpel, at least she could do some cutting in the kitchen—for now.

"So now what?" Matilda asked. "Do I get you as my assistant? Or are you going to fret to death before each birth?"

Ella avoided the midwife's gaze. Despite watching many successful deliveries in medical school, the memory of her mother dying in labor made her pulse race to the verge of fainting. Even if she overcame her fear, delivering babies wouldn't satisfy her ambition. After all, Alan Parker had assisted famous professors in innovative surgeries and was promised a great future in medicine. "I delivered the maid's baby with only the landlady to assist me. It's just... what was the point of going to medical school if I'll never be a doctor?"

Matilda shook her head. "I never understood my brother's plan. Joseph is such a dreamer."

Ella's knife made even slices at great speed, channeling her frustration into her work. "He wants me to give midwifery a chance. Only if I'm sure the profession isn't for me, then he will let me join him on the *Neptune* as his assistant. If you ask me, I'm ready to go to Plymouth now. I even bought a book about various sea creatures. The sea is full of wonder."

Matilda stopped cutting and threw up her hands. "Wake up, Ella. A woman on a warship? Living among seamen who drink and cuss?"

Ella tossed the chopped carrots into the soup. "I won't drink. Maybe I'll teach the seamen some manners."

The midwife rolled her eyes. "That should go well. A well-bred lady doesn't belong in such a place. Or do you plan to disguise yourself as a man again?"

"No, my body has changed, and I've learned from my mistakes. Even as a woman, I'll find a way to fit in somehow."

"Fit in?" Matilda left the room and returned a minute later with a pair of shoes. "These are Joseph's shoes. Can you fit into them?"

Ella laughed as she slid her foot into the large shoe. "No, that's not going to work."

Matilda nodded. "You see it yourself. You can't make yourself 'fit' into what's not for you."

"Now let me try on your shoes."

The midwife frowned but removed her low-heeled boots. Ella attempted to slide them on. "Too narrow. They're not for me either."

"They can expand with wear." Matilda winked. "But you see the point. Fitting in is painful. People should be where they belong."

"And where do I belong?"

Matilda gave her a pat on the back. "In my shop. Caring for women in labor, for sick children, for working people struggling with pain and disease. Business isn't as good as it used to be before medical men turned on female herb healers in their press campaigns, urging people to seek only qualified physicians, but clients still come. They know they are better off buying my remedies than trudging to a charity hospital."

As confirmation of Matilda's words that clients have not abandoned her, the bell once more chimed from the back door.

From a corner of her eye, Ella caught a glimpse of the customer who wore a thick veil that completely hid her face. The client didn't reply to Matilda's greeting but followed the midwife to the herb room. Curious, Ella stepped in after them, but the woman halted at the sight of her.

"Is she your assistant? Is she trustworthy? My request is... delicate."

"You can trust Ella as much as me," the midwife answered. "I've been in the business for over thirty years. What's ailing you?"

The woman did not answer.

"Spit it out. I've seen and heard it all."

The woman still did not speak. Her posture was rigid as she stared at the jars in the cabinets. Matilda gestured for her to sit on the sofa, but she remained standing in the middle of the room, glancing at the labels on the containers: sage, lavender, valerian root...

Matilda cleared her throat. "By your mysterious silence, I will guess you want me to get rid of a baby you carry. I despise such work. It's dangerous to your health and is against the law. I would much rather help you deliver the infant secretly and find a family to raise it. If you undress, I will look at your belly."

"No." Her voice was raspy and sharp. "There is no baby."

"Ah, trouble conceiving. Why didn't you say so? I have plenty of treatments for that. Red clover, black snakeroot, and more." She turned her gaze to Ella. "Well, don't just stand there, twirling your thumbs. Find those remedies."

Ella scanned the shelves for the right herbs.

The veiled woman grabbed Matilda's hand. "No. That's not what I need. Do you have herbs to make a man love me? You know, a love potion? If I become pregnant, even better."

Ella gaped. This customer was nothing like the ones she'd met.

The midwife withdrew her arm. "What do you think I am? A medieval sorceress?"

"The papers say that's what herb healers are. I have plenty of money, and I will do anything. Make my dream man love me."

Matilda shook her head. "There are no such herbs. If anyone tries to sell you any love potions, run the other way. You need to calm your nerves. I can sell you teas to help you sleep better or increase your appetite."

"Forget it. If you can't make him love me, give me something else. I'll make you rich."

She leaned in and whispered something into Matilda's ear. The midwife recoiled, as if from an invisible slap. "Get out of my house! Never come here again."

When the door slammed behind the strange woman, Matilda returned to the kitchen, covering her mouth with a trembling hand. "I thought I'd seen it all, but nothing like this. I must thank the medical papers for this madness. She believed me a witch! If it's in the paper, it must be true."

"What did she whisper in your ear?" Ella asked.

"The man she pines for loves someone else. She wanted a poison for his sweetheart, something hard to detect."

Ella drew air between her teeth. "We should report her to the constable. She may get that poison somewhere else."

Matilda's shoulders slumped, and she rested her hand on her heart. "I would, but I'm afraid. Not a word I ever thought I would use."

Puzzled by Matilda's anxiety, Ella touched her friend's shoulder. "What is it?"

Matilda teared up, sobbing. "Two of my dear friends, herb healers like me, sit in jail. They did their best for their patients, but sometimes disease can kill despite their efforts. The grieving families blamed the healers. The medical community gave the accusers their full support, happy to rid themselves of the competition. Sometimes I think of closing the shop. I would've if not for my loyal customers who depend on me." She wiped her eyes with the back of her hand.

Ella patted Matilda on the shoulder. "Good heavens, that's awful. What if you only work as a midwife?"

Matilda sighed and turned to the simmering soup to salt it. "Midwives are still in demand, but men got into the business as well. Male midwives, called accoucheurs, are all the rage. And, as before, we must work with doctors in case of a difficult delivery, since we aren't allowed to use the forceps."

"I've learned how to use the forceps at medical school."

The midwife put her hands on her hips. "Then unlearn. You know perfectly well that only barber-surgeon guild members use them, and their membership excludes female midwives. We must be careful. A month ago, I was a thread away from arrest."

Ella drew a sharp breath. "What?"

"Finish cutting, or we'll never eat." When Ella's knife rhythmically sliced vegetables, Matilda continued, "Do you remember Mrs. Kelley?"

Ella nodded, recalling the nervous woman she met at the herb shop before.

"She's been a frequent customer, now pregnant with her third child, and buying remedies for herself and the children. A couple of months ago, her daughter Violet came down with a cough and a fever. Mrs. Kelley summoned a physician, who bled the child and eventually the fever broke. The cough remained though, and the girl couldn't sleep, so the mother came to me for a remedy. I sold it to her, and carefully told her the dosage, but the fool gave Violet too much."

"Oh my!" Ella covered her mouth with her hand.

"Calm yourself. The child is fine. Herbs are not as dangerous as the apothecary's remedies. She developed a rash and a bellyache. Bad, I know, but it would have gone away. The mother panicked, summoned the doctor again, and when he learned what she gave the girl, blamed me and my herbs. Said that I'd poisoned the child."

"But surely Mrs. Kelley realized her mistake and told the doctor the truth?"

Matilda tasted the soup, shaking her head. "Brace yourself, there's more. At the time I didn't know what happened to Violet, but I learned the details later. The next day after Mrs. Kelley's visit, a constable showed up and took me to the station. Turns out, Mrs. Kelley's husband is in a prominent position with the police and his men oversaw the cases of many herb healers, including my jailed friends. I thought I was done for. My record book saved me, as well as the note I gave to the wife. When Mr. Kelley showed me the bottle as the evidence, I asked how it could be half-empty if I instructed the mother to give the child only a couple of spoonfuls."

"Thank goodness you had the presence of mind to say this."

"Yes. He was livid with me and with his wife, but he let me go. Mrs. Kelley arrived the next day, all teary-eyed and apologetic, but I had it with her. The fool jeopardized everything I built. She pleaded with her husband to close the case, but he would not, and his people will keep their eyes open for any misdeeds from me. Ever since that visit to the station, I can't sleep at night." Matilda's head slumped as she finished the story.

"I am so sorry." Ella opened her arms to embrace her friend. "How awful and unfair."

"Well, now you know what you are getting into." Matilda straightened her apron and peered into Ella's face. "We must be careful and know our limits. You understand?"

"Yes."

"Now let's have our supper and a pear tart to celebrate you becoming my assistant."

She sauntered to the silverware drawer, but before she opened it, a loud knocking came from the door.

"Matilda, open the door! I know you are home." The voice belonged to a woman.

Ella startled and stared at Matilda. The midwife's face blanched.

"Maybe someone's in labor," Ella suggested.

Matilda shook her head. "Let's hope so." She sighed and crossed herself.

Chapter 2

Matilda stepped to the door, muttering to herself. Ella bristled from the premonition, but the midwife's bellow made her jump.

"You dare to show your face here?"

"Matilda, calm yourself. Is this any way to treat me?"

Ella hastened to the door. The visitor was a woman of Matilda's age, stout, and plainly dressed in a brown coat and a gray bonnet. She regarded Ella with curiosity.

"You've taken an assistant, Matilda? It's about time. You can't spend your life grieving for Lindsey, and you're not young."

A shadow passed over Matilda's face at the mention of her adopted daughter who'd died several years ago. "None of your business, Ada. We've nothing to discuss."

"You think I would come if there was not a need? You are the last midwife in the city I would call on but here I am."

"Well, you wasted your time. Go home."

Ella had never seen her friend so incensed, with her hands trembling, and eyes blazing with rage. Yet what Ada said worried her.

"Did you say you need a midwife?" Ella asked.

"No." Matilda barked.

"Yes!" Ada answered at the same time.

Ella raised her palms in a peaceful gesture. "Matilda, you must hear this woman out. Someone needs your help."

Her friend's face squeezed. "If there's a woman in labor, Ada can go and deliver the baby. She's been a midwife as long as I have. But she can't ask me for help. Not after she turned into Judas and testified against the other healers. My friends are rotting in jail because of her lies."

"I had to do it, or I would've joined them!" Ada burst into tears.

"Shame on you, coward." Matilda hissed and turned away from her.

Ella raised her hands, trying to get the attention of both women. "As important as that story is, I want to know if someone needs our help."

Ada nodded. "Yes, thank you, dear. There's a mother in labor, and she is asking for you, Matilda. That's why I'm here."

Matilda pivoted on her heel. "Then why didn't she call me in the first place?"

The other midwife sighed. "The client is Mrs. Kelley. I've been with her since last night. She's all frightened, and her labor halted several times. She could've birthed that baby hours ago, but she keeps fretting and calling for you. You delivered her other two children—you know how to talk to her. She's mad with fear. Please, I know you are livid with me, and with her too, but she needs you."

Matilda made a step towards the door. "Who did you leave her with?"

"Flora, my assistant, and Polly, my granddaughter."

"You should've sent one of them for me."

"I feared you wouldn't listen, and they are shy girls. Please, come with me to deliver this baby."

Ella wiped her sweaty hands on her dress and pulled on her boots. Matilda would never abandon a woman in labor, no matter the repercussions. Ella inhaled to steady herself against the creeping chill of fear that enveloped her. *I've studied midwifery. I'm ready to help*, she rallied herself.

Matilda picked up her bag by the door. "One last thing, Ada. You said you were with her since last night, and that's a while. Should we fetch the doctor now? There's a good one living on this street. We could stop by his house first."

Ada rubbed her face. "No, there's no need for that. You'll calm her and all will be well."

"Fine. Let's go, Ella. Time for you to help with a delivery."

Ella threw on her coat and looked towards her own bag with hesitation. When Matilda yelled for her to stop dilly-dallying, she grabbed it. Holding it gave her confidence.

The three of them hurried through the deserted cobblestone streets, illuminated by the wavering light of oil lamps. Ella's heart raced like it wanted to compete with her feet. The midwives panted, both tired by their pace. When they reached a handsome house on a clean street with blooming lavenders, Ada led them to the back door and rang the bell.

"Thank you, Lord!" The servant woman exclaimed, opening the door. "The mistress is worse, and your girls are out of their wits with fright."

Matilda threw Ada a meaningful look as they marched upstairs. As they passed the bedrooms, Ella spotted Mrs. Kelley's children, Violet, and her younger brother, poking their heads out from the nursery. Like these children, Ella once awaited the birth of her brother, only to have her heart broken when he died, and her mother passed as well. She inhaled to ease the pain in the pit of her belly. The memory cut her like a knife.

"In here," Ada pointed to the door at the end of the hall.

No moans or screams came from the mother. Ice ran down Ella's veins. *Are we too late?*

A tear-stricken girl of around thirteen ran from the bedroom and grabbed Ada's hands. "Grandma, she's so pale and quiet. I'm scared she'll die!"

"Polly, have you lost your mind?" Ada barked. "Yelling such things where the mother and her children can hear you! Pull yourself together."

"Wash your face and come back only if you are calm. I don't need a sissy here," Matilda added, and the girl ran towards the back staircase.

Ella entered the bedroom, bracing herself for what she was about to see. Mrs. Kelley seemed a mere child, sprawled on her large four-poster bed, her face white as a sheet. Her chest and large abdomen rose slightly, and her eyes were shut. The burning fireplace across from the bed and the closed windows made the air hot and heavy, so as to prevent the newborn from catching a chill of death. A young woman, about twenty, dabbed Mrs. Kelley's face with a damp cloth. She gave a small smile of relief, seeing the midwives.

Matilda approached the mother, taking her hand. "Hello, my dear."

"Matilda, so good of you to come," Mrs. Kelley whispered. "I'm deathly afraid. "

"Nonsense, it's all your fretting. Just a bit of work, and you will be a mama of three."

Matilda pressed around the woman's belly then checked between her legs. "So close. I can see the baby's head. You just need to push as hard as you can."

Ella helped Matilda prop the mother up with pillows. Mrs. Kelley drew in air and pulled her eyebrows together, but then fell back on the pillow and hung her head like a broken doll.

"I can't," she muttered.

Matilda urged her to try some more, but the woman seemed to weaken with each attempt, until she did not respond to the midwife's voice. Her fists clenched, Matilda marched to Ada, who was huddled in the corner.

When their heads almost touched, she hissed, "I knew you were a dimwit, Ada, but not like that. I asked you if we needed to bring a doctor, and you said no. The baby's not moving, the mother's exhausted. She needs a doctor to get that baby out with forceps!"

Ada sobbed, then shouted to her assistant. "Flora, get Dr. Klein. Do you remember where he lives?"

"I already sent for the doctor. The husband went himself," the assistant replied as she wetted another cloth to revive the mother.

"At least the girl has some sense," Matilda approved.

The midwives consulted among themselves, but Ella had tuned them out. Instead, she approached the bed and lifted the mother's wrist to count the heart rate. The pulse was weak and thready.

Ada gasped. "What's she doing? She's examining like the doctors do."

Matilda scoffed. “Don’t be silly. Just because the girl can find a pulse, it does not make her a doctor.”

“When did the husband leave to fetch the physician?” Ella asked Flora.

“A couple minutes before you came in.” The girl looked towards a wall clock with dancing figurines. “If the doctor’s home, they should be back in ten minutes or so.”

Ella’s mouth dried. A delay put the mother and the baby in peril. She didn’t want to take any chances. *What was the point of going to medical school if not to save lives?* Her jaw set, she opened her bag and removed steel obstetrical forceps.

Ada gasped. “How does she have that thing? She’s not allowed to use them.”

“Why don’t you heat some water, Ada?” Ella asked, but the midwife didn’t move, staring at the forceps with shock and awe. “I need two people to hold her legs. Quickly!”

Polly flew into the room. “I’ll help. I’m calm now.”

Ada pulled her to her side. “Don’t get into this, Polly. Whatever you do, don’t touch the thing this woman is holding.”

Flora positioned herself on the right side of the bed. “I’ll assist.”

“Matilda?” Ella gazed at her friend.

“Ella, you’ll be the death of me,” Matilda said, but took a spot on Ella’s left.

Flora and Matilda lifted the mother’s legs. Ella unhooked the forceps and slid one side of the spoons into the birth canal, trying to place it around the baby's ear. Mrs. Kelley groaned and shifted, but Ella's assistants held her. With bated breath, Ella slipped the other spoon in place and locked the forceps.

Steps boomed, and male voices demanded to know what was going on, but she didn't look up, absorbed by the delicate task. With gentle traction, she worked to bring the baby out. Her shoulders throbbed from the tension. Sweat rolled off her forehead. Mrs. Kelley made infrequent, feeble moans.

The baby's head emerged, followed by the shoulders, and then the rest of the body slipped forth, covered in blood. Ella clamped and cut the cord, then passed the limp, bluish baby to Matilda. While the midwives blew air into the baby's mouth, Ella delivered the afterbirth and stitched the wound between Mrs. Kelley's legs. The baby's whimpering told her that Matilda and Ada succeeded in reviving the baby. Breathing easier, Ella lifted Mrs. Kelley's wrist and checked her heart rate. It strengthened and steadied, and the patient's cheeks regained some color.

"Is that my baby's cry?" Mrs. Kelley whispered with her eyes still closed.

Ella patted her hand. "Yes. You have a baby boy."

Flora wiped the sweat off Mrs. Kelley's face and offered her some water. When the mother perked up, Ella straightened and gazed around the room.

The midwives were washing the infant, a boy of considerable size. His large head was conical in shape and had a purple bruise from the forceps, but his body took on a healthy pink color.

Three men observed. One, tall and mustached, shifted anxious gazes between the mother and the baby, and Ella guessed him to be Mr. Kelley.

She addressed him. "Your wife and son are both fine, sir."

He rushed over to take his wife's hands. Mrs. Kelley gave him a weak smile, and his eyes welled up with tears. Violet and her brother, both in their nightgowns and barefoot, raced into the room, and into their parents' embraces, right when the midwives placed the swaddled baby onto the mother's chest.

Ella's heart swelled with joy for the happy family. As she wiped the forceps before hiding them away in her bag, she felt the study of the two remaining gentlemen who huddled by the door. Her eyes widened when she recognized the younger of the two. Jeffers stood with his arms crossed; the older man he resembled, likely his doctor uncle, observed her with a furrowed brow. Unable to contain herself, she offered Jeffers a triumphant grin, and he returned hers with a menacing one.

***

Matilda marched in silence the whole way home. With her shoulders squared and fists balled, she stomped upstairs. Ella followed, bracing herself for her friend's fury. *The patient had to come first. Surely Matilda will see that once she calms down.* In her bedroom, Matilda flung open her closet and drawers, then reached for her hats. Muttering to herself, she threw a couple of boxes on the bed.

"What are you doing?" Ella demanded.

Matilda tossed a shawl, followed by a cloak. "Packing, of course. You must pack as well. I don't know about you, but I don't want to spend who knows how long in jail. We need to be out of here before dawn."

Her jaw hanging, Ella stepped back. "But the mother and the baby are fine. The father had tears in his eyes when thanking us."

Shaking her finger, the midwife rounded on her. "What were you thinking using the forceps? Where did you even get them?"

"I...," Ella hugged herself. "I was thinking of Mrs. Kelley and her children. The day I played Alan Parker one last time, I passed the Naval Board exams for a ship surgeon, and then I bought a full set of surgical tools, including the forceps."

Matilda crossed her arms. "Midwives are forbidden from using forceps. I told you. Did you know that the men of the Chamberlen family, the inventors of the forceps, used to blindfold the mother and demand for everyone to leave the room, so no one saw their discovery? The secret stayed in the family for a century and a half."

Ella stumped her foot. "One of the most selfish acts in medicine. They saved their own clients and reaped profits, while leaving others to die. Since I had the device, I wasn't willing to wait for a doctor while the mother and the baby were in danger."

Matilda turned back to her packing. Throwing dress after dress onto the bed, she chided Ella. "So, you delivered with the forceps in front of that Judas Ada, and two young women who work for her. Even worse, the father who put my friends in jail and wanted to arrest me. Oh, yes, and the two doctors who looked terribly intrigued by your actions. We would be fools if we stayed in this house another hour. I don't care how many times the husband thanked us. I'm sorry, but your career as a midwife is already over before it started, at least in London. We need to flee."

Ella buried her face in her hands and leaned her back against the wall. Her mind reeled. In her fervor to save the patient, she doomed her dear friend. "I'm sorry too. Not because I won't be a midwife, but for the trouble I caused you." She blinked away the tears that threatened to pour. "You're leaving your home, your herb shop, your beloved clients."

Matilda sighed and swept her into an embrace. "Everything ends, child. Don't fret. I have a cousin out in the country who writes every year, inviting me to visit. Time to surprise her and appear on her doorstep. We'll gather herbs and help her with the harvest."

Ella rested her head on Matilda's shoulder. "I won't go. What good would it be for me to hide in the country, where my skills won't be needed?"

Matilda pinched Ella's cheek. "Then go to your estate. Weren't you planning to check how your lawyer and caretaker are overseeing it? Throw some parties while you're there, find yourself a handsome suitor. Send me an invitation to the wedding."

Ella hugged her tighter, then straightened and looked her friend in the eyes. "Matilda, you know where I'm going. Don't try to dissuade me. *The Neptune* docks at Plymouth next week, according to the naval papers. I will meet Dr. Pesce and join him on the ship as his assistant. I'll write to him on the way. Once you arrive at your cousin's, send a letter to the Cooked Goose Inn at Plymouth. I'll be staying there before the sailing. And speaking of weddings, I'm invited to one at Plymouth."

Chapter 3

"I pronounce you man and wife." The reverend's voice rang like a bell.

The church erupted with applause, and the ladies in wide hats and gentlemen in suits and naval uniforms rose to greet the newly married couple, Veronica and Ernest. Ella stood from the pew and smoothed her ivory gown. The seamstresses demanded a small fortune to make such an elaborate dress in three days, but this was her first formal outing since she ran away from home two years ago. Her allowance from her trust fund, managed by her lawyer until her seniority, allowed for frivolity. To hide her boyish hair, she wore a wig with long black curls. Judging from the admiring glances of young officers, her look suited her.

Touched by the beautiful ceremony, Ella radiated with pleasure. She craned her neck among all those tall officers to catch a glimpse of the bride, her childhood friend from Newcastle. As

Veronica sauntered through the aisle decorated with pink and white roses, on the arm of her new husband Ernest, she gave Ella a dazzling smile.

The church ceremony concluded, and the guests convened at the rented house for a banquet and dancing. In the dining room, Ella spotted her childhood friend Henrietta Fillips from Newcastle and her elder sister Marietta. The weekly meetings of the embroidery circle that consisted of Veronica, these sisters, their mothers, and Ella with her governess, seemed like another lifetime. At the last meeting Ella attended, Lady Fillips announced Marietta's engagement. Now, Marietta's cheeks flushed in a luminous glow; the effect Ella noticed on some pregnant women when she studied midwifery. By contrast, Henrietta's face thinned, and her complexion paled.

As Ella approached the sisters, Marietta gasped, and Henrietta gave her a look of a scared deer.

Ella extended her hands. "I haven't seen you in ages. How are you?"

Marietta's face squeezed, and she shivered. Covering her mouth with her hands, she dashed from the room. Ella froze with her hands outstretched.

Henrietta jumped to her feet, her expression flustered. "I'm sorry. My sister is... unwell. I should go see to her."

Ella dropped her hands and nodded. "I'll come with you. Is Marietta suffering from nausea? I can recommend some remedies."

An audible "arr hrrm" sounded behind them.

Henrietta blanched another shade and put a finger to her lips. With a weighty step, Lady Fillips advanced on them.

"Eloise Parker, did you read my letter where I told you my daughters and I will never speak to you?"

"You're speaking to me now," Ella rebutted.

Lady Fillips knit her brow, as if trying to solve a riddle. Then she smiled as though she found the solution and addressed Henrietta. "Do you see how disrespectful Miss Eloise is to her elders? Her bad influence spreads like influenza." Lady Fillips glanced towards the table where beaming Veronica clinked glasses with Ernest. "I couldn't decline the invitation from Veronica's mother, but I will protect my children from atrocious behaviors, such as running away from their parents or marrying paupers."

Henrietta stooped and stared at the floor. Frustrated by her friend's silence, Ella marched towards the door. Her mood dampened. She still had a great deal to prepare for her sailing. Skipping the rest of the wedding, where she didn't know anyone but the bride and the Fillips family, would be prudent.

A hand caught hers, and she spun to face the bride. Veronica wore a gorgeous rose-colored dress. Her smile was brighter than the diamonds that decorated her swan neck.

"Ella, you can't leave yet. After the breakfast banquet, there'll be dancing."

Ella fidgeted. "I'm sorry, my dear. I don't feel I belong at this gathering. You look incredible, and I wish you and Ernest all the happiness in the world."

The bride threw her hands up. "Don't be silly, you belong here more than anyone else. This wedding would never have happened if not for you. You will have a seat of honor beside me."

Veronica pulled Ella to her table and asked the waiter to bring another chair and a plate. The groom, and both sets of parents, greeted her warmly. Ernest was blue-eyed and fair, and cut a dashing figure in his midshipman uniform. His parents were dressed more simply than the bride's and eyed with hesitation the larded sweetbreads, hare in a creamy sauce, and other extravagant foods they seemed unaccustomed to.

When Ella's glass was filled, and the bride's mother entertained everyone with a story from Veronica's childhood, Ella leaned towards her friend. "Why did you say this wedding wouldn't have happened if not for me? I can't imagine what I could've done."

Veronica beamed. "Remember, the day before you disappeared? We were embroidering together, and I told you that Ernest was wounded, and I was desperate to see him."

Ella nodded, remembering her last embroidery circle meeting with the women. Hours later, her drunk father cut her neck with a broken glass, prompting her to leave home.

"Your governess, Miss Samson, visited us a few days later and told us of your injury and disappearance. She believed you escaped to the port and boarded a ship."

"I did. I thought I'd go to London and become a governess, but I found my calling in medicine instead."

Veronica sipped her champagne. "I was incredibly inspired by your escape. My parents fretted that you'd come to harm, but I told them you would do something great. When Mum sent the maid to prepare my bags for the seaside holiday, hoping to distract me from my worries about Ernest, I refused to go. I told her the only place I was going would be to the Plymouth naval hospital to care for him. To prove my resolve, I refused to eat, and the next day Mum agreed to take me. After he recovered, we insisted on the engagement. I'm so excited about moving to Plymouth and becoming an officer's wife."

Ella clinked glasses with her friend. "Good for you! I'm so proud of your steadfastness. How was Ernest injured? I remember you were distraught because you didn't know."

Veronica bent over to whisper in Ella's ear.

"He was struck by a bullet in the buttocks."

"Oh!" Ella covered her mouth to hide her surprise. "If you changed his dressings, I could see why your parents allowed you to get married. Or even required it of you."

The bride blushed and snickered.

"What are you two giggling about?" Veronica's father asked with a grin. "I want to hear what Eloise has been up to. Sorry,

I heard you're Ella now, but I'm not used to saying your new name." He tapped a finger on his forehead.

Ella grinned. "It's quite alright. Let's just say that I studied medicine but didn't find employment. Luckily, I have a mentor who's a surgeon on a warship. I'll assist him at first, and then I hope to become a full-fledged surgeon myself."

The silence at the table was a bit too long, and Ella's smile dampened. The fathers frowned, the mothers gave each other shocked glances, Veronica gaped, and Ernest coughed into his hand, as if trying not to laugh.

The bride recovered first. "Well, I think that's splendid. Do you know the name of the ship? Is it here at Plymouth?"

"Yes, it's *H.M.S. Neptune*." Ella turned to Ernest. "Have you heard of it?"

"Sounds familiar. I'll ask my friends. Someone would know it. But do you have any idea what life on a ship is like?"

"I sailed from Newcastle to London."

Ernest covered his mouth with his fist to stifle a snicker. "That's a short cruise. And I'm sure you traveled in comfort. Don't expect the same luxuries on a warship."

Ella stiffened her back. "Lack of lavishness doesn't scare me. On that voyage, I helped the surgeon perform an amputation and saved the patient when I found him bleeding."

Veronica gasped, the parents urged Ella to tell more, and Ernest stopped sniggering and gave her a look of respect.

"That's nothing to laugh at," he said. "I'm sorry if I offended you. I just hope the men will treat you well. Seamen come from all levels of society, and not everyone knows how to behave with a lady."

"I have a better idea." Veronica's mother tilted her head. "Ella could stay with Veronica in Plymouth while Ernest is at sea. And we can introduce her to a nice young man. Veronica, where is that Robert Weston I keep hearing about? Two mothers specifically asked me if he was on the guest list, and if their daughters could sit by him."

"That's him." Veronica pointed towards a table where a chestnut-haired young officer gestured with animation, perhaps telling a story of a ship battle. The men at his table listened with mouths ajar. Several young ladies had their faces turned to him like sunflowers to the sun. Ella's eyes stayed on his profile a little too long.

Ernest scoffed. "Weston is a lieutenant on the *Crown*. We aren't exactly friends."

The bride's mother shrugged and touched Ella's hand. "What do you think, my dear? He is obviously handsome. I hear he's also wealthy. Why go on such an ill-advised trip when you can stay with my daughter and be courted by a fine suitor?"

Ella gulped her champagne to relieve the heat that rushed to her cheeks. "I don't think so. My plans are set."

Musicians started playing the polonaise, and Veronica invited everyone to proceed into the ballroom. The gentlemen began inviting the ladies to dance. Ella leaned on the wall, disappointed to be without a dance partner, but then Veronica led three young men in uniforms towards her.

"You must meet my friend Ella. She's about to become a ship surgeon. Ella, these are Ernest's fellow midshipmen from his ship, the *Proud*." She winked at Ella as Ernest swept his bride away to dance.

Scrutinized by the stares from young officers, Ella shifted her feet. The introduction did not have the effect her friend intended. A dark-haired fellow of about twenty broke the silence. "The bride was jesting, right?"

Ella sighed. She only wanted to dance. Yet, she knew her unconventional choices would bring about such conversations. "I'll be the surgeon's assistant on the *Neptune*."

The young men glanced at an officer with a short mustache, who stood apart, nursing his drink with a bored look. "Do you know it, Landon?" One of them asked.

The mustached man rolled his eyes. "It's a large sloop-of-war, twenty-two guns, about hundred and fifty men, led by post-captain Thomas Grey. Time for you to know these things without checking the book, gentlemen."

The dark-haired young man cracked a smile. "That's a little ship compared to the *Proud*. I dare say this pretty lady will be safer with us."

"I agree," a midshipman with a scar on his cheek replied. "If I must spend some time in the sickbay, I would much rather see her face than the carpenter's. He's not much to look at."

The fellows hooted. Ella frowned, about to ask why a carpenter would be attending to the sick, but they quieted as Robert Weston approached the group. He wore a white waistcoat under a blue frock coat that brought out his hazel eyes, and his smile was charmingly mischievous.

"Fellows, you've managed to bore the beautiful lady to death with your ship talk. She's here to dance." He offered Ella his hand and she accepted.

"The *Crown* takes everything, doesn't it, Weston? The prizes, the picks of the crew, and now this lovely woman," the dark-haired man yelled.

The young man winked and revealed a perfect set of teeth. "So it does, and you are well to remember it."

The music changed to a dance Ella didn't recognize. Most dancers left the floor. The few remaining couples glided in quick pace; their bodies scandalously close to each other. Ella watched them, mesmerized. The dance was fast and sensuous, with a one-two-three beat.

Lady Fillips puffed loud enough for all to hear. "It's that indecent dance that came from the Continent, the waltz. Henrietta, stop gawking. It's time for us to leave. Marietta looks ill from such a deplorable display, and I don't blame her."

The music drowned out the swish of their skirts. Ella shook her head, watching Lady Fillips shepherd her daughters out of the room. With a small smile, she turned back to Robert.

"Robert Weston, the third lieutenant of the *Crown*." The young man finally introduced himself. "Have you danced the waltz before?"

"Ella Parker. Um... no, I'm not familiar with this dance. But I would like to try."

"Then give me your hand."

Stares scrutinized her, but she did as he asked and looked into his eyes. He took her right hand into his and put his other hand on her waist. Heat rose to her face. The brush with the buttons of his coat radiated through her. Voices of other people muted in her head. Only the music and the young man's voice sounded.

"Follow my lead," he whispered.

Ella took a few unsure steps but then found her rhythm. He spun her around, and candles flickered in her eyes. Her heart quickened from the pace, and her head reeled. His hazel eyes drew her like magnets.

"Are you the mysterious ship surgeon the place has been buzzing about?" He dipped her gracefully. Blood rushed to her head, making her gasp. When he pulled her up, the smell of sweet wine on his breath pleasantly tickled her nose.

Ella giggled. "The news spread fast. I'll be the surgeon's assistant on the *Neptune*, helping my mentor Dr. Pesce."

He led her into a change step, but his eyes never broke contact with hers. “It’s a bad idea, Miss Parker. If you are in some trouble, please let me help,” he whispered in her ear.

Ella tilted her head. “Thank you, but I can take care of myself. I’m pursuing my chosen profession.”

Robert spun her again. “Can I persuade you to stay at Plymouth? My ship sails tomorrow, but I’d love to see you when I return.”

He held her hand up and guided her into a series of turns, and the beat of the music pulsed through her excited body. She forced herself to breathe.

“I hope to see you again as well, but I’ll board the *Neptune*... It’s my job.”

He shook his head, as if talking to a child. “It’s no job for a woman.”

She laughed and put a hand on her hip. “We’ll see about that.”

The music stopped, and Robert escorted her off the dance floor. He made a bow. “You’re quite a dancer. I hate to leave you, however, I must take care of some boring but necessary ship business. Until we meet again, mysterious Miss Parker. Please be safe.”

Her name on his tongue sounded like a serenade. “You too, Mr. Weston.”

He kissed her hand, and a warmth spread up her arm all the way to her fluttering heart.

After he left, the chatter irritated her ears. There was not enough air to fill her chest. She waved goodbye to Veronica and flew before her friend could stop her.

Enjoying the brightness of the afternoon sun on her face, she gulped the cool air that smelled of the sea. She walked without direction, spinning and twirling along the way. People stared, and she giggled. *What's happening to me? I feel drunk. That dance... so exhilarating. Or maybe it was my dance partner.*

She dashed along one street then another, passing by inns, taverns, and shops. After an hour of aimless meandering, she found the port.

Enormous ships, medium-sized vessels, and small boats came into the view. Dr. Pesce's letter instructed her to board the *Neptune* tomorrow, early in the morning. Robert Weston was likely preparing the *Crown* for sailing. The view gave her a cool awakening. For all she knew, the *Neptune* and the *Crown* would sail in opposite directions, increasing distance between Robert and her with every hour.

He will forget me long before the end of his voyage, she told herself. *I came here to do my job, not to fall for a handsome stranger, like a silly girl.*

Two women stood on the pier and gazed at the ships. One of them, auburn-haired and tall, rocked a whimpering baby in her arms. The other, petite, with her blond hair in a braid, wept into her hands. Their conversation reached Ella's ears.

"I won't bear it," the crying woman sobbed. "Who knows how long he'll be gone."

The other put her baby to her breast, a picture of serenity. "You will bear it like we all do, Nancy. You'll cry a hundred tears, say a hundred prayers, knit... well maybe not a hundred socks, but more than he needs for sure. But then you'll see him again."

Nancy moaned. "Annie, how can you be so stoic? What if they don't come back? Hart is a topman. It must be a dangerous job. And the battles." Her voice broke.

Annie shrugged. "You knew who you are marrying. Why fret now?"

"I married a fiddler. His music stole my foolish heart. Why did he have to be a sailor too?" Nancy wailed.

Ella's heart squeezed. Whether Robert Weston would remember her or not, she wanted him to be safe.

"Hello. Do you know which ship is the *Crown?*" Ella asked, approaching.

Annie studied Ella's dress. "That's the biggest ship here," she said after a pause. "Can't miss it."

The *Crown*, with its many decks, and giant masts, dwarfed the other ships.

"And the *Neptune*?"

"That one." Nancy pointed at a much smaller vessel. It had three masts but was significantly smaller than any other warship. "That bloody ship is taking away my husband from me."

"Mine too," Annie added. "That's the life of a seaman's wife. Are you here to say goodbye to your husband? Must be a fine officer, dressing you so fancy."

Ella smoothed her skirts. "I'm going to sea. On the *Neptune*." She decided not to reveal her profession to avoid another awkward conversation.

Nancy's eyes shined. "Oh, if you meet topman Peter Hart, tell him from me..."

Annie snorted. "Nancy, officers' wives don't mingle with common sailors." She gave Ella a measured stare. "You are a brave one, I give you that. You'll spend months sleeping in a hammock and eating nothing but salted beef. I hope you're not prone to seasickness."

"I..." Ella had given life on a ship little thought before now. "I'm sure I'll endure."

Nancy gazed with admiration. "You must love your husband very much. I love mine too. We married a week ago."

"Mine finally met our son today," Annie piped, kissing her baby. "Proud father grinned ear to ear."

Ella gave the women an encouraging smile. "I'm sure your husbands will return safe and sound."

I will make it my mission to care for these sailors, so they come back to their families. And if it's my fate, I will see Robert Weston again, she vowed.

Chapter 4

On the deck of *H.M.S. Neptune,* First Lieutenant Jack Wyse gazed at the dwindling line of the new recruits. His body was stiff from sitting on the barrel for hours, his throat dry from speaking. Worst of all, his tooth ached with a dull but noticeable pain. From the corner of his eye, he observed the men holystone the deck, supervised by the second lieutenant, Jerrold Van Horn. He'd happily trade places with him to walk around and harass the hands who slacked. Even better, he'd like to be at sea already. The roll of waves would calm his nerves and perhaps, quell the toothache.

"Next." He motioned to the next man to approach. "Wait, I know who you are. Topman Peter Hart? You left to care for your mother?"

The strong-built man chuckled. "Aye, Mr. Wyse, you remember. My mother's better, and I got married, too. The press gang came around, so I thought I'd get back here before they grab me for some other ship."

Wyse chuckled. Good to hear that the man preferred this ship over others. Captain Grey was fair and avoided cruel punishments, like flogging. "Good man. Brought your fiddle?"

"Aye, sir." Hart lifted the case in his left hand. His sea chest was in the other.

"Good. We'll have merriment now and then. I'll assign you to the foretop, as before. You know what to do and where to go."

The seaman signed his name in the book, and Wyse looked to see who was next. Two boys stood before him. The older one, about fourteen, stared at the deck as if he wanted to burn a hole in it with his eyes. Behind him, a boy of about ten, gawked with his mouth open at the men on the yards.

"Are you brothers?" Wyse asked, giving his voice a friendly tone. He was about the age of the younger boy when he came onto the ship, and he never forgot how strange his first days seemed to him.

The younger boy was too distracted to hear, but the older boy answered without lifting his eyes. "No."

"Did the press gang grab you?" He wanted to cuss at the officers who pressed mere children into service. He took a swig from his flask to calm himself.

Instead of answering, the lad dug into his pockets and handed him a crumpled piece of paper. Wyse frowned and read. "Digby

Marks. The Marine Society saved you from jail. Shouldn't you look happier with such a lot?"

Digby scowled and wiped his nose with his hand. "In jail, I'd be with my da. And Ma would visit."

Wyse scoffed. "So you think. Listen boy, there are men here who've been behind bars, and they'll tell you what it's like. Here you can start your sorry life over. Keep your nose clean, and all will be well. You'll be a ship boy. With time, we'll see where we can use you. Understood?"

Digby shrugged. "Where're we goin' anyway?"

"What do you care?" Wyse scoffed. "Ever seen a chart? Keep your head down and mind your business."

That was good advice for any situation. Wyse didn't know their destination. The captain would inform him after opening his dispatches, which sometimes happened after they left the port.

"And now you." Wyse beckoned the younger boy, who risked whiplash from staring in every direction. "Another jailbird? You sure look like a hardened criminal."

"Me?" The boy opened his mouth, revealing gaps among his teeth. "No, sir." He gave Wyse his letter explaining the Marine Society took Tobby Hill, believed to be ten or eleven years old, from the orphanage. The boy grew too old for it and needed employment. Many orphanage graduates ended up working at the mills, but with the need for crewmen, some ended up in the Royal Navy.

Wyse drummed his fingers on the table. "You'll be a ship boy too. Now, listen up, both of you. On Sunday, the captain will read the Articles of War, and you better pay attention. But I'll tell you about Article Thirty. It says that all robbery committed by any person in the fleet shall be punished with *death*. Digby, repeat that."

Digby blinked. "Err... robbery... is that stealing?"

"Exactly. The crime you committed. And if you steal something on the ship, you may find yourself hanging off the mainmast by your scrawny neck. Is that clear?" He gave Digby a hard stare. It should not come to that for a boy, but it didn't hurt to scare the ruffian to steer away from trouble.

The lad scratched his face. "I only stole when I was hungry. And to help my da."

"Here you'll get three square meals and a tot of rum every day. You need something, come to me. But no stealing." He glanced at the younger boy, who was holding his hand on his belly, his expression miserable.

"What's wrong, Tobby? Seasickness getting you already?"

The boy shook his head. "I get bellyaches often."

Wyse scratched his chin. "After we finish, go to the sickbay, and see the surgeon. Don't need you bringing diseases onboard."

The boy shuddered and paled. Wyse shared the sentiment when it came to doctors, but the surgeon had to examine the child for illnesses he could potentially spread to the crew. And maybe the surgeon would fix the boy's bellyache with some potion.

Lifting a pen, Wyse pointed to the ship book. "Sign here, both of you."

The older boy raised his eyes, now wide with fright. "Don't know how."

"Just make an '*x*' like this." Wyse showed the page where half the names had '*x*'s instead of signatures. "The chaplain, Mr. Doolittle, gives lessons to ship boys on Sundays. You'll learn to read and write."

The lad shrugged as if it were the last thing he wished to do with his Sunday and made a crooked '*x*.' Tobby grabbed the pen from him and stuck out his tongue as he carefully wrote out his name. Digby scowled at him, as if accusing the boy of boasting about his schooling.

Wyse directed the older boy to the forecastle and the younger to the sickbay, and was about to call up the next man, but the click of footsteps halted him. The midshipman, George Stafford, had a spring in his gait, showing off his polished shoes with silver buckles. The twenty-year-old's eyes shone as brightly as the buttons on his immaculately fitting uniform. He put his fist to his forehead to greet his superior.

"Mr. Wyse, the captain sends his compliments, and asks you to come by his cabin."

The polish in the midshipman's speech vexed Wyse more than his look. His eager smile irritated him even more. *Was the pup laughing at him and parading how an officer should dress and talk?*

"Sir, I could finish recording the names while you speak to the captain," Stafford offered, gazing at the book with such keenness that Wyse's vexation cooled. Stafford was young and zealous in his duties. It wasn't his fault he came from a well-to-do naval family with excellent connections.

Wyse's back creaked as he rose. He nodded for Stafford to take over and staggered aft towards the great cabin, wondering what Captain Grey wanted.

He knocked on the cabin door. "You wished to see me, sir?"

"Come in, Mr. Wyse."

Wyse stepped inside and saluted the captain, who sat at his desk with stacks of papers before him.

To Wyse's surprise, the captain wasn't alone. The surgeon, Doctor Pesce, stood beside him, shifting from one foot to the other. Wyse's tooth ached at seeing the medical man, but he ignored the pain as he nodded to the doctor.

The doctor gave Wyse a look of concern. "Are you all right, Mr. Wyse? Do you have a toothache?"

Wyse realized that he was holding his cheek. "No need to worry, Doctor, I'm fine. I just sent a new ship boy to the sickbay. An orphanage lad. He has a bellyache."

Dr. Pesce fixed his glasses. "Very good, Mr. Wyse, I'll examine him. Impoverished children often consume a poor diet that spoils digestion. Nothing a potent purgative or an enema can't fix."

Wyse groaned at the medical talk and prayed the captain would change the subject.

The captain obliged and steered the conversation into friendlier waters. "How's it going with the ship roster, Mr. Wyse?"

Wyse exhaled with relief. "Sir, we have a full crew. Mostly experienced men."

At first words of ship talk, the surgeon began pacing around the cabin, a small space with a cot, a bookcase, and a chest of drawers. He removed a random book from the shelf and leafed through it.

Captain Grey inclined his head. "Excellent. Wyse, our doctor has an unusual request."

The doctor raised his head from the book, blushing. "Um... I've invited an assistant to join me."

Wyse shrugged. That was nothing unusual. The doctor, over sixty, slouched from a lifetime of bending over patients, and often complained of various aches and pains. The captain had urged him to find an able assistant. "Aye. If you're looking for a place to berth him, the lad can swing his hammock in your cabin, Doctor, or in the forecastle."

The captain pinched the feather on his pen. He had an air of amusement about him. "You see, Wyse, the surgeon's assistant is not a lad."

"Huh?"

"A well-educated, proper young lady." The surgeon put the book down and rubbed the back of his neck. "Mr. Wyse, I was hoping you would let her have your cabin."

Heat rose to Wyse's head. His tooth gave such a pang, he almost screamed. *A woman on his ship! Never again!* He wanted to cuss or pick up a heavy paperweight from the desk and throw it against the bulkhead. Instead, he drew air into his nose as he addressed the captain. "You're going to allow this... sir? It's bad luck to have a woman on a ship."

Captain Grey shuffled papers on his desk. "I don't believe in superstitions. The young lady is Dr. Pesce's choice. I believe in giving people chances, *all people,* as you know, Wyse." The captain gave him a meaningful look. "This may be taking my conviction further than I intended, but I'll let it stand. So, will you let Miss Ella Parker sleep in the comfort of your cabin?"

The irony in the captain's voice was obvious. Wyse's cabin was dark, tiny, and certainly not comfortable, but it was *his* cabin. He would not give it up to some skirt.

"Is that an order, sir?" Wyse stammered with his fists clenched.

"No. Only a request."

Wyse threw back his shoulders. "Then no. If this doesn't suit the woman, she doesn't belong here." She would never belong here anyway; he was shocked the captain would believe otherwise.

The doctor uttered a weak protest, but the captain clicked his tongue. "*Neptune* isn't a pleasure vessel, and Miss Ella better understand that. But where would she sleep? Not in the fore-castle, obviously." The captain gazed at the two men as if asking them to solve this problem.

The doctor adjusted his glasses. "She could have my cot. I'll swing a hammock somewhere."

The captain nodded. "Splendid. Glad this's settled. Do you still have objections, Mr. Wyse?"

A clay figurine of some woman caught Wyse's gaze, and he picked it up from the table without thinking. "Well, yes, sir. A lady... We have men... Uh confound it, I don't know how else to say this. The men could have their way with her." His fist squeezed the figurine so hard that it shattered. Wyse gasped and rushed to pick up the pieces.

The doctor gasped and put a hand to his heart. "No, this can't be."

The captain slammed his fist on the desk. "That would be a matter of honor for me and the ship. Wyse, I order you to ensure her safety. I don't care what you do, but I don't want so much as a hair to fall off her head due to any action by our men. And that was my daughters' gift, by the way. I'm sure they worked hard on it," he added with his mouth tight.

Wyse stifled a groan and apologized. In addition to all his other responsibilities, he'd have to mind some spoiled girl who wanted to play doctor. But an order was an order, and there was only one answer to give.

"Aye, aye, sir."

***

A seaman with his hair in a ponytail offered Ella a hand as she stepped off the boatswain's chair onboard *Neptune*. She asked him to help her with her heaviest bag, but he only shrugged and said through his teeth that it wasn't his job. Ella dragged her valises and sacks onto the deck and gazed around. There was no Dr. Pesce in sight, but the ship was full of activity. Men swabbed the deck, painted the hull, and did other jobs, some of which she didn't understand.

Her mood was jovial. Just before leaving the inn and heading for the ship, she received two letters. The postman handed her a letter from Matilda. Her friend wrote that she arrived at her cousin's house, but was sure she wouldn't tolerate the quiet life for more than two months. She then promised to follow news of the *Neptune* in the naval papers and to meet Ella when she would return to port.

Before the postman left, Ella had a chance to give him a letter she wrote the night before, addressed to her medical school friend Oli Higgins. She gave him a full account of her problems with finding work and her hope to learn from Dr. Pesce on the ship. Her friend's last letter updated her on his life in Chatham with his parents and numerous siblings. His family talked him out of joining the army. His father, a naval agent, was trying to use his influence to get Oli a position in a naval hospital.

The second letter, delivered by a messenger, was Robert expressing concerns for her safety and wishing her a smooth voyage. The last few lines made her grin like a fool: he had thanked Providence for their chance encounter and mused that they may see each other sooner than she expected.

"Look at your smile, sweet thing. Whose wife are you?" A redheaded man, with many teeth missing, interrupted her daydream. "Are you so happy to jump into the hammock?" The seaman hooted at his own wit.

"I..." Ella stammered.

The man's loose manner frightened her. His friend, a man with cold blue eyes and ink tattoos on his arms, sneered. "I told you she's no wife. I know them all. Come, lass, you'll have some fun with us. If you're good, we'll pay well." He pulled her by her arm, and she screamed.

"What's going on here?" An officer approached. His uniform was like Robert's but wrinkled and with a button missing.

The men leaped back from Ella and saluted. "Nothing, Mr. Wyse," the redheaded man mumbled.

Wyse glared at them. "Then get below where you're supposed to be. Can't you tell this woman is not for the likes of you? Consider this your only warning."

The seamen nodded and hurried away.

Ella gave the officer a grateful smile. He was about thirty or thirty-five, had a crooked nose, and a thin scar on his forehead. He had a look of a bold, savvy sailor. His eyes were shrewd and piercing, as he looked her up and down. "Thank you, sir. This must have been a misunderstanding. I'm Ella Parker, and I believe I'm expected. Where do I go?"

"Back home." Wyse sneered at her gaping mouth and strode away.

Ella drew air to calm her nerves. *You knew there would be no welcoming assembly*, she reminded herself. Gazing in all directions, she remembered her first cruise. She had traveled in a first-class cabin, and it was *aft*, at the *stern*. Those words were like a foreign language to her. Leaving her bags on the deck, she made careful steps in the direction opposite to the one the rude seamen had gone. The deck heaved under her. Walking even a few steps required concentration.

"Miss, may I help you?" A young officer of about twenty with auburn hair descended from the quarterdeck, gliding as if he were walking in a park. By his uniform, Ella assumed him a midshipman, a junior officer. In her mind, she gave herself a pat for knowing *something* of the ship life.

"That would be most kind. My name is Ella Parker. I'm looking for Dr. Pesce."

He bowed his head. "Of course. I'll let him know you're here. Your things..." He glanced at her bundles spread behind them.

"Is there something I can take to the hold? I'm afraid all these bags won't fit in your cabin."

She bunched her skirts and returned to her luggage. "Oh dear, I didn't think of that. I suppose the extra clothes may go to the hold. My books too. I've wrapped them with many layers of fabric to protect them. I'll keep this valise with my necessities, and this one with medicinal herbs."

"What about this one?" He pointed to her leather medical case.

"Oh, I need that. It has my surgical set."

He flashed her a smile. "Hope you won't have to use it much. I'm Midshipman George Stafford, by the way."

"I appreciate your assistance, Mr. Stafford." She bobbed a curtsy, and almost lost her balance.

He gripped her elbow to steady her. "You better hold onto the railing, Miss Parker." He lifted the bags intended for the hold and disappeared into the hatchway.

Minutes later, Ella heard her name, and her heart quickened at the voice she had sorely missed. Dr. Pesce's thin frame and hunched back gave her a twinge of worry. Yet his eyes were bright, and a smile lit his wrinkled face. She flew into his embrace.

"Ella, please, let my old eyes look at you." He stepped back to admire her. "My dear, you were a lovely girl of fifteen when I met you, but you have grown into a beauty. The short hair suits you, makes those green eyes stand out."

She instinctively touched her chin-length hair. "It's so good to see you, Doctor. I brought the cures you asked for, and Matilda added some herbs. I also have a new set of surgical tools." She decided not to tell him of her unpleasant meeting with the vulgar seamen and the curt officer to avoid sounding like a bemoaning woman.

"Let's get you settled, and then I would love to hear about your medical school adventures."

He lifted Ella's remaining bag; his face tensed, and he grunted. Concerned, Ella took the bag from him. "Is your backpain getting worse?"

The doctor made a dismissive gesture. "Getting old can't be helped. Let me show you the cabin so you could rest."

Ella had low expectations of cabins, yet when she observed her surroundings, she gasped. *I'm inside a tomb.*

She walked around, careful not to trip. The cabin lacked natural light; a couple of lanterns poorly illuminated the spartan place. Ella found a cot, a basin with a cracked mirror above it, a sea chest in the corner, and nothing else. She stood to her full height, with the ceiling two inches above her, while the doctor had to crouch. The smell of mildew irritated her nostrils. "This is my cabin?"

The doctor wrung his hands. "Yes, of course, it is. This cot is a decent size, and I had the blanket washed."

There was hesitancy in his voice, and Ella gave him a sharp look. "Do you mean this is *your* cabin, and I'm putting you out? Absolutely not."

He looked down at his shoes. "I considered sharing the cabin with you, but I see how inappropriate that would be. I'm used to thinking of you as a mere child, and... a daughter."

A lump in her throat pained her. She cupped his face, caressing the stubble on his cheeks.

The doctor sighed. "I'll be fine sleeping among the men, Ella. It's no trouble. I've slept in the hammock before."

"With your backache? No, I won't hear of it. You keep your cot, and I'll find another place to sleep. Not among the men, of course. Would any officer be gallant enough to offer his cabin?" She giggled, playing with a strand of her hair.

The doctor sighed. "This's a small ship, and the only cabin besides this one and the captain's belongs to Lieutenant Wyse. I tried to persuade him to offer his, but he refused. He's not fond of women on the ship." He was quiet for a moment. "I'll hang my hammock here, and a curtain for privacy."

She mustered the vigor in her voice to reassure her mentor. "I'll sleep in the hammock. It's a sea adventure after all."

The doctor sat on the cot, exhaling with relief after stooping too long, and beckoned her to sit next to him. "Ella, it's not too late to change your mind. You are starting to see why this's a terrible idea. One word from you, and the coxswain will get a boat ready to bring you back to shore."

Ella imagined the humiliation of being lowered into the boat while the men laughed at a woman who couldn't last fifteen minutes on their ship. Giving up wasn't something she allowed of herself.

She stood, her hand on the bulkhead for balance. The undulations gave her slight queasiness. "Remind me, what is it you love about this life?"

The doctor chuckled. "The views of the emerald sea and the sapphire sky, the freedom to do what I want, the friendships I've built over time. Few would understand why I abandoned my practice, but when in London, I felt like a fish out of water. I would start coming to the port to watch the ships. My heart would ache, beckoning me to the sea."

She flipped her hair with a touch of bravado. "I'll keep in mind that I'm here to hone my skills as a surgeon, to treat patients without anyone telling me what a woman is not allowed to do, and to live a life of adventure like no other girl could boast. Where I sleep matters little."

Dr. Pesce gave her an affectionate smile. "I've loved that daring spirit in you from the day we met, when you insisted on holding that seaman's hand during the amputation. Listen, this cabin has more advantages than meets the eye. We're near the captain's cabin, and he has his own privy we can use. Trust me, it's a big advantage over the head at the forecastle, where all the men go."

Ella nodded, slightly embarrassed.

"Also, we would occasionally dine with the captain. Grey doesn't like ceremony, but he enjoys company now and then. And we can use the galley to cook from our own stores to have variety from the ship's food. Just try not to get in the way of the captain's steward. He's a disagreeable fellow. But don't you worry, we eat quite well here."

Ella doubted the doctor was telling the truth, seeing his emaciated figure. She would have to keep an eye on him to make sure he was eating and resting enough.

"Are there patients to see?" she asked, lifting her instrument case.

"Ready to get started?" The doctor chuckled. "I must disappoint you. All seriously ill and wounded have been transferred to the hospital onshore. I saw one man today with syphilis lesions—such complaints are common when visiting port—but after treatment, I sent him back to work. A ship boy complained of a bellyache, for a second day in a row. I administered an enema. He didn't like it very much, but he's feeling better. Don't worry, you'll have plenty of practice here for your skills. I'm glad to have a chance to hear your stories of medical school."

"There's so much to tell, but first, I'd like to show you my new instrument set." Ella opened her medical case and revealed a black leather case with scalpels, catling knives, needles, and many other gleaming instruments. "This is the best set from J.H. Savigny's shop in London. There's even the circular drill for trepanning."

The doctor beamed. "I've done a successful trepanning once. And look how polished your tools are! I can't scrub off the dried blood from my scalpels anymore."

"There's more. I brought the obstetric forceps that got me into trouble."

"Since you're the only woman on this ship, we won't need them." Dr. Pesce chuckled. "Oh, what's that you have?"

She demonstrated a syringe with a rubber tube. "Have you heard of the stomach pump? It can save a patient from poisoning."

The doctor raised his eyebrows. "No one died from arsenic around here, thank goodness. Not even the rats."

Ella laughed. "It proved effective in various accidents. The inventor, Dr. Physick, saved an infant dying from a laudanum overdose."

The doctor gazed in admiration at her tools. "This is exciting, my dear. We'll bring your instruments and remedies to the sickbay. They'll prove handy soon enough."

"All hands, to weigh anchor and make sail!" A voice thundered from the deck.

Ella clasped her palms in excitement. "Does this mean we are leaving?"

The doctor grinned. "Yes. Your first sea adventure is now underway."

They rushed to the deck to watch the sailing preparations. Her heart fluttered as she gazed up at the men climbing the rigging to the great height of the mast. Sail canvas became taut in the fair wind. The busy Plymouth port, the clutter of buildings, and other ships grew smaller and smaller until they were nothing but dots on the horizon. Cool breeze made her skirt flap and disheveled her hair. A cold spray hit her face. Giddy with laughter, she stuck out her tongue to taste the salty-bitter water. Her lungs couldn't get enough of the cleanest air she ever breathed. Even the nausea she felt inside her stiff cabin quelled.

She beamed at the doctor. "This is incredible."

There was sadness in his smile and in his wet eyes.

She gripped his hand. "Dr. Pesce, are you alright?"

"Of course, my dear. This will be an exciting voyage. You and I working together, caring for the patients. I know you've mastered much at the university, but I'll teach you what I've learned by experience." He wiped his eyes.

"Set the course for Brest," a commanding voice came from the quarterdeck. A tall, middle-aged man in a navy uniform and triangular hat peered into the telescope.

Ella assumed him to be Captain Grey. The first lieutenant was next to him, marking numbers on the board.

"Helmsman, steer South by Sou'west," Wyse boomed.

The man at the helm echoed the command and spun the wheel.

"Brest? That's in France, isn't it?" she asked the doctor. *Not a long voyage to West Indies or Africa, but still exciting.*

"That's right. Our ships keep the French from entering the Channel. We'll not let Bonaparte and the Frogs reach England!" He shook his fist, and his cheeks flushed with vigor. "As Lord St. Vincent said to the House of Lords: 'I do not say they cannot come. I only say they cannot come by sea.'"

Ella giggled at an absurd image of the French army flying in giant balloons over the Channel. Exhilaration traveled through her nerves. Their ship and crew had an important purpose in keeping her homeland and its people safe, and she was part of that mission. She glanced towards the port to whisper a goodbye to the city and the life she knew, but it had almost disappeared from view.

Chapter 5

When Ella awoke, she hesitated to rise in the dark cabin. The hammock swayed like a child's swing. The ship's timbers squealed and groaned against the gust of wind. Anxious, she called out to Dr. Pesce, but there was no answer.

Her feet found the deck, and she gripped the bulkhead for support. Her brain registered the novel words she learned. Bulkhead was the wall, deck was the floor, deckhead was the ceiling. Her eyes adjusted, and she made out her scarce belongings. Her stomach roiled with the plunges of the ship. After washing herself with some water in the basin, she dressed and opened her bag of herbs, searching for ginger, spearmint, and black horehound—Matilda's remedy for seasickness.

With hesitant steps, she walked through the underdeck, searching for the galley, where she and the doctor made tea yesterday. After stumbling into various storage rooms with piles of sails and rigging, she recognized the familiar space. It reminded her of an ordinary kitchen, with a stove, pots, and utensils, all stored in proper places. There was no table, but two stools allowed a seat for a cup of tea.

She lit the stove and filled the kettle to boil the water with the black horehound. The herb gave off an unpleasant smell of rotting mushrooms. The leaves needed to brew for a few minutes before she would neutralize the stench with ginger and spearmint.

As she was cutting the ginger, a short, stocky man with flaxen hair entered and gave her a vexed look. "What are you doing with my kettle?" he hollered.

"I'm... boiling herbs to ease my seasickness."

"Get your own cauldron to brew your potions. I'm to make tea for the captain, and it better not stink to high heaven of whatever you put in there." He grabbed the kettle and emptied the brew into a basin before she could object.

Too stunned to protest, she watched as the man washed the kettle and put water and tea leaves to boil without giving her another look. She pondered a barb, an insult, but nothing came to mind. *A lady can put a man in his place without a foul-mouthed word,* her governess Madam Samson used to say.

Visualizing how her governess would behave if she were there, she drew herself up, straightened her shoulders and set her voice to a cold and peevish tone.

"What's your name, sir?" When properly said, even a simple question can burn with ice.

The man turned and stared. "Tom Black," he mumbled.

Ella kept her eyes on his face, staring him down with contempt.

"Captain's steward," he added with pride.

"Well, Mr. Black, you've forgotten your manners. I hope I don't need to mention your discourtesy to the captain in the future."

She glared at the steward, waiting for him to apologize. He stared back with confusion, as if wondering what kind of creature she was. Ella scorched him with her furious gaze, determined to win this staring contest, but a young man rushed in, calling her name.

"The doctor asked me to bring you, Miss Parker," he said, breathless, and she hurried after him, putting the incident in the galley out of her mind. "I'm Sully Horton, a loblolly boy." He looked about eighteen, tall, and with a mop of red hair.

"Loblolly boy? What's that?"

"We feed the sick and carry the wounded during the battle."

"Is someone ill or hurt?"

"Just a fist fight. Olson has got blood gushing out of his nose."

They arrived onto the deck, and he pointed to the two seamen who slumped near the mainmast. Dr. Pesce was there with his instrument case, holding a bloodied cloth to Mr. Olson's nose.

The bleeding seaman's skin was dark brown. Ella tried not to stare, but her lips parted. She had never spoken to a colored person before, although she glimpsed a few in London.

"Is he from the colonies?" she whispered to Sully.

"Aye, a runaway slave. When a slave escapes to a Royal Navy ship, he's free. His real name is something none of us can pronounce, so we call him Owen Olson."

Her eyes grew wide. Whoever told her that seamen come from all walks of life did not exaggerate.

"Ella, there you are." Dr. Pesce called to her, jarring her from her wonderment. "Could you check Mr. Simkin's wrist? He complains about spraining it. And then I'll have you set Mr. Olson's nose."

Ella stepped towards the first seaman, in his forties, too wide for his height, his blond hair in a long braid. He gave her a gaze full of fury.

"A woman? I don't want her touching me. She'll spread ill luck."

"If only I had such powers," Ella replied as she reached for Mr. Simkin's arm, but the man withdrew it.

"First this bugger accuses me of shirking my duties, and now a lass is here. What the devil's going on?"

He breathed hard as he spoke, and Ella smelled rot from his mouth, but not only that.

"He's drunk, this early in the morning," she exclaimed.

Dr. Pesce chuckled. "On a ship full of spirits, most men are rarely sober. Simkins especially likes a helping of grog early on."

"And it's not any of your damn business." Simkins exhaled into her face, making her cringe from the stench. He stormed away, holding his wrist.

Her mentor shook his head, still holding the cloth to the other sailor's bloodied face. "Never mind him. We need to tend to Mr. Olson."

Ella asked the seaman if she could touch his nose, but he didn't answer or look at her. His eyelids drooped as he stared at the deck.

"I gave him laudanum," the doctor explained. "Go ahead and examine the fracture."

Ella carefully felt the swollen nose and found the break in the bone. She'd never set a broken nose on a patient, only on a cadaver. Corpses suffered no pain, and the dissection room didn't pitch and roll. Constant motion and the fear of a mistake were making her ill.

"Maybe I'll watch this time?"

Her mentor put his hand on her shoulder. "You can do it, Ella. It's a minor injury. You'll have much more severe cases than this. Didn't you save a young man with a bullet wound, or was that only a story?"

Ella's cheeks heated. Dr. Pesce referred to her first surgery, and she was proud of it. With a long breath out, she stiffened her fingers and maneuvered the bone into its place. She half expected the patient to cry out in agony, but the doctor must've been generous with the laudanum. Mr. Olson gave only a weak moan.

Dr. Pesce palpated the patient's nose and clapped her on the back. "Nicely done. Now, we plug the nostrils with this cotton, smeared in sweet oil, to keep the bones in position."

She took the cotton and packed the patient's nose. The doctor ordered Sully to take Mr. Olson underdeck when he came to, and to make sure the seaman would rest and drink fluids.

"I'm ready for some hearty breakfast." Her mentor patted his belly. "How about you, Ella? Fancy some fried eggs and black pudding?"

"I—"

The thought of greasy food twisted her gut, and she barely made it to the railing. Sully chuckled behind her as she retched overboard.

***

Ella wanted to meet the captain, wanted to get acquainted with the sickbay and take stock of medications, wanted to gaze on the boundless sea. Instead, she moaned and twisted in her hammock from seasickness. Dr. Pesce checked on her periodically and offered her water and tea with ginger. The few spoonfuls of gruel he fed her came back up. He washed her face and neck and assured her the illness would pass in a week. She doubted she could endure that long. Yet, as days and nights passed, little by little, her suffering eased.

One morning, a week since they sailed, she made it to the privy and back without faintness. After her breakfast of porridge and biscuits stayed inside her, and a long nap restored her energy, she took a stroll on the deck. The sea reflected the sun's rays as golden ribbons leading into the horizon. With her seasickness conquered, Ella felt light and free; her body moved with the tempo of the ship's rolls as she promenaded the length of the deck.

All around, men busied themselves in their various jobs. The topmen scaled the rigging while the midshipman she met on her first day, Stafford, bellowed commands to raise the topgallants. Ella followed their apelike climb with her gaze. A man stood on one of the highest points of the ship, holding a glass, looking out onto the sea in all directions. The height was frightening, but she envied him. The view must be breathtaking.

She came towards the quarterdeck. A man held the helm in a powerful grip. Next to him stood the officer who told her to go home when she boarded the ship. Noticing her, he scowled, and his lips moved like he was cussing under his breath. Ella turned her back to him and walked to the railing, her head held high.

Dr. Pesce came out to the deck and waved. "You found your sea legs, Ella!"

"Yes, I'm much better. Thank you for tending to me. I hope you weren't too busy with patients while having to nurse me as well."

"Not at all, my dear. I just checked on Mr. Olson. His nose is healing well. A few men complained of sea sickness, but they're on the mend. You haven't missed any vital cases."

While the doctor spoke, Stafford approached, made a courtly bow to Ella, and nodded to the doctor.

"Miss Parker, Doctor, the captain sends his compliments and invites you to dine with him."

Ella beamed at his civility. It was good to see some men here behaved as gentlemen.

"Are you well enough, Ella?" The doctor inquired.

"I would be delighted." Her appetite returned, and a square meal sounded heavenly. She also wished to make a positive impression on the captain.

"Ella, this is midshipman George Stafford," the doctor introduced. "I used to serve under his uncle, the captain of the *Seagull.*"

George made the same polite bow as he had at their first meeting and smiled at Ella.

The doctor tapped his forehead. "George, I meant to ask. How's your uncle's health?"

Stafford lowered his eyes. "I've had a disagreement with him, and we're not on speaking terms at the moment. He insisted I transfer to his ship, but I refused." He lifted his chin. "I don't want favors I didn't earn."

Sensing the young man's embarrassment, Ella changed the subject. "I saw you issue orders to the men as they worked on the sails. Quite impressive how you commanded them despite your youth."

The young man threw back his shoulders. "That's nothing unusual in the Royal Navy. Midshipmen may be as young as twelve. Learning to oversee the crew is part of our training. I hope to take the lieutenant's exam after this voyage."

"So many things are new to me. Are there one hundred and sixty men or so on this ship? How do they all fit?"

"The men are divided into two watches, larboard and starboard. One watch rests and performs exercises or tasks below such as washing or mending, while the other watch completes various jobs on deck. Every four hours, or two when it's dog watch, they change. Of course, there are moments when all hands work together."

Ella was about to ask more, but the lieutenant at the quarterdeck called to George, and he excused himself.

"Who is that officer calling George?" she asked the doctor. "I'm not sure what I did wrong, but I fear he doesn't like me."

The doctor gazed towards the helm and frowned. "That's the First Lieutenant, Jack Wyse. As I mentioned, he disapproves of women aboard the ship."

"He's quite rude. The officers I met at Plymouth were gallant even when appalled by my occupation."

The doctor looked at her with a twinkle in his eye. "Ah, did you meet some officers at Plymouth? I hope no one stole your heart. Many officers come from prominent naval families, like George, or are sons of various professionals. Mr. Wyse, however, is an oddity. He worked his way up from the lower deck."

Ella gazed into the distance. "That's admirable, but I don't see why he finds a woman on the ship offensive."

"According to the superstition, a woman brings bad luck. We are at the mercy of the sea and wind, and the men believe their safety is a matter of fortune and old rituals."

She shook her head. "So odd to hear that in our time. Science explains how the weather behaves."

The doctor's lips curved, as if suppressing a laugh. "Ella, you've studied in a university while many of these men can't even sign their names. You're of different worlds, and you will never convince them that science plays a bigger role in their lives than the sea spirits. Just accept that's how it is."

She ran her hand on the railing, thinking. "How much time do we have before dinner?"

"We have about half an hour," the doctor said, checking his pocket watch.

Ella wrung her hands. "I better hurry."

The doctor's mouth rounded in surprise. "Hurry where?"

"To prepare for dinner, of course." *Men have no idea what we ladies do to get ourselves ready.*

In the dim light of the cabin, she undressed fully, and washed herself with a wet cloth dipped into the water from the basin. Water dripped and splashed as she struggled to keep her balance. After donning a fresh chemise and her knee-long drawers, she squeezed herself into a corset that nicely supported her growing bosom. Then she raised one leg up on the sea chest in the corner to pull on her silk stockings.

The door squeaked and opened. The doctor strolled in with another man behind him. "My dear man," the doctor was saying, "you must apply the salve regularly. It would make a noticeable difference."

Ella's muscles tightened like drawn bows. The curtain divided the cabin but did nothing to prevent the view from the door. Embarrassed, she couldn't breathe, let alone speak.

The doctor stepped past her, taking no notice. He dragged his sea chest from under his cot and rummaged through his things. "Now, where did I have it?"

The other man, gray-haired, with a patch over his eye and large muscular hands, was more observant. He ogled Ella and whistled. "You found yourself a fine-looking lass, Doc."

Ella shrieked and hugged herself, hiding as much of her half-exposed bosom as she could. Heat burned her from her neck to the small of her back.

The doctor still combed through his chest. "Where is that darn jar? I swear it was in here. What did you say, Mr. Morgan?"

Rage broke the stilling spell, and Ella found her voice. She scoffed at Mr. Morgan. "Sir, please stop gawking at me. I do not care for what you've implied."

Mr. Morgan clapped. "Oh, a spirited lass. Those are the best ones. What's your name, darling?"

The doctor jumped and slapped himself on the head. "Ella, my apologies. I forgot you are here." He put his hand on his chest. "Mr. Morgan, you better see me at the sickbay later. I must keep in mind that I now share this cabin with my assistant."

The sailor continued studying her, chuckling. "Assistant, eh? What do you assist with, lass?"

Ella stomped her foot. "Please leave, Mr. Morgan. Can't you see I'm getting dressed?"

The sailor doubled over, hooting. "Doc, I owe you one for this show," he said walking out.

Her pulse beat in her burning ears as she peered at Dr. Pesce. "Doctor, I told you I need to change for dinner. Why did you enter with this man?"

The doctor averted his eyes. "I'm so sorry, Ella. Force of habit. I'm an old, forgetful man. Please forgive me."

Ella turned and donned her petticoats with sharp motions, wrinkling the delicate fabric. "That man took me for a harlot."

She pulled the ivory gown that she wore to Veronica's wedding over her head.

Dr. Pesce sighed. "Morgan's a jokester. He won't hurt you. I better let you finish changing."

He trundled to the door, but Ella called. "Um, Doctor. Since you are here, could you help me with the buttons on the back? This is not the easiest dress to put on."

"Oh... of course. Not that I'm used to such a task."

The tension in her back relaxed. She couldn't stay mad at the doctor for long.

Dr. Pesce fumbled with the buttons and hooks. "Sure is much effort for this dress. But the effect is worth it, I'm sure."

She sucked in her stomach to help the fabric connect. "Yes, I want to make a good impression. But to be honest, I'm rarely in the mood for this finery. When I disguised myself as a boy, I longed for puffed-up skirts. Now, I miss the comfort of trousers."

The doctor shrugged. "It must be human nature to pine for what we lack."

Ella nodded. "Or to crave more than one option. Thank you, Doctor. I can reach the rest of the buttons myself. Maybe you want to shave before dinner?"

The doctor touched the stubble on his cheeks with surprise. "I thought I shaved yesterday, but it must have been longer. Days can bleed together on the voyage."

She gave him a stern look. "I hope you aren't forgetting to eat as well."

Dr. Pesce shifted his feet. "I promise I'll clean my plate tonight."

"I hope so." She stepped away from the basin to let the doctor use it for shaving.

Finished with their preparations, Ella and Dr. Pesce soon strode into the great cabin. A pearl necklace draped about her neck, and matching earrings dangled from her ears. She hoped to look sophisticated.

The cabin's dining room, next to the captain's sleeping quarters, was of a moderate size. An oak table covered by a white tablecloth stood at the center, set for five. Charts and ship sketches adorned the walls. Port holes and candelabras offered a cheerful glow.

Dr. Pesce introduced her to Captain Thomas Grey, who shook her hand. A man in his mid-fifties with salt-and-pepper hair, and blue-green eyes to match the sea, he wore a blue frock coat with gold buttons, and epaulets upon each shoulder. As they exchanged pleasantries, Wyse and Stafford approached the table as well. Stafford beamed at her, but Wyse had an air of aloofness.

The captain introduced them and mentioned that his two other officers, Second Lieutenant Van Horn and Midshipman Collins were on watch. Meanwhile, the steward who vexed Ella at the galley, Mr. Black, placed dishes with mutton, rice, and vegetables upon the table. The mutton smelled of sage and mint, making her mouth water.

The captain pulled out the chair for Ella, inviting her to sit between him and Dr. Pesce, across from Wyse. Ella beamed at the captain, and he smiled back. "Miss Ella, please tell me you play Whist. We desperately need a fourth player. The doctor and Mr. Stafford play, but Wyse can't figure out the game."

Wyse gritted his teeth, but the captain looked at Ella for an answer.

Ella tucked a curl behind her ear. "I play Whist and a few other card games as well."

The steward poured wine, and they toasted to King George III. Then, to Ella's joy, they helped themselves to the food.

"Would you like some bread, Miss Ella? It's dry, but quite edible." Not waiting for reply, the captain waved to Black. The steward placed a square biscuit onto her plate. Everyone's eyes went to her. *This must be a test to see if I'm too fine to eat the sailors' diet*, she guessed.

"Captain, I have no problem eating plain foods. This doesn't look bad at all." She grinned and lifted the biscuit to her lips, about to sink her teeth into it, but then dropped with a scream. It split in halves on her plate, and two worms wiggled from the broken pieces. The men chuckled.

"They're weevils. You're supposed to hit the hardtack on the table, so they come out before you bite." The captain picked up her biscuit, showing how to shake off the worms. "We just wanted a bit of a laugh. I hope you didn't lose your appetite." He motioned to Black, who placed a roll of white bread on Ella's plate. "We still have some bread, but when it runs out, hardtack will be our staple at dinner."

Recovering from her shock, she cracked a laugh. *Apparently, men enjoy pranks even after they've reached respectable ages and positions.*

"My appetite's intact," she replied, biting the roll. "I've seen worse. Compared to leeches, for example, these little fellows are lovely."

Captain Grey, Wyse, and Stafford paused eating, while Ella and Dr. Pesce grinned at each other.

"Leeches! Those foul black worms with teeth! You've handled them?" the captain exclaimed, waving his fork.

Ella cut her meat into small pieces. "Yes. We used them often at the university hospital. I'm not sure how much the doctor told you, but I have medical training."

Wyse muttered something inaudible, the captain examined her curiously, and Stafford beamed with admiration.

The doctor regarded her with fondness as he adjusted his glasses. "Miss Ella was the best in her class at medical school. She has also passed the naval board exams. I plan to teach her all I can, giving her experience with wounds and illnesses that often occur on the ship. When she's ready, I would like her to take over for me as the ship surgeon."

"That's ridiculous!" Wyse snapped. The captain glared at him, and the man reddened.

"Please pardon Mr. Wyse," Captain Grey said. "His manners are obviously lacking. But I must say that few women find ship life tolerable." He rested his chin on his pinnacled palms. "Why is it you want to be a ship surgeon?"

Ella sipped water and considered her answer. She decided a thorough explanation of her story would convince the captain of her sincerity. With her eyes focused on the captain's curved smile, she began. "In medical school, I disguised myself as a man and received acceptance among prominent professors. When my trick was revealed, I became an outcast. Despite my qualifications, I couldn't find a job in my profession. No doctor wanted a female assistant. I turned to midwifery, but I found myself in a difficult position. I had the skills to save a patient, however, I wasn't supposed to use them. Instead, I was expected to wait for the male doctor to arrive, even if the delay would be fatal for the mother and baby. Faced with such poor prospects and impossible choices, I beseeched Dr. Pesce to take me on as an assistant. I understand your men mayn't be used to a female surgeon attending to them, but in time they will see their care is in capable hands."

Ella glanced at the men. The doctor beamed with pride while Stafford forgot his food and gaped in awe. Wyse picked his teeth, his eyes squinted, and brow knit. The captain, who through the speech kept his gaze fixed on Ella, turned to the lieutenant.

"What do you think now, Mr. Wyse? There's a shortage of skilled surgeons in the navy, and some captains appoint carpenters to care for the wounded. Here we have a woman who's educated in medicine. Do you still believe she shouldn't be here?"

Wyse shrugged. "I complied with your orders, sir."

"I'm asking for your opinion."

The lieutenant tightened his lips into a line. "If you want to hear my opinion, and the opinion of the men, the woman brought trouble already. The lower deck is abuzz with stories about a witch who brewed potions and cursed Mr. Black with her stare."

Ella scoffed. "I was brewing tea, and the steward was quite rude when he poured it out, but I assure you I've no powers to curse the man."

"Also, she touched Mr. Simkin's hand, and it swelled twice the size."

"He complained of pain before I touched him. He wouldn't let me see to it."

"The men are anxious, saying the woman will bring bad weather and other misfortunes."

Ella bunched her napkin into a ball. "This is superstitious nonsense!"

The captain furrowed his brow. "Thank you for bringing your concerns, Mr. Wyse." He shifted his gaze back to Ella. "Miss Parker, you are in a precarious position here. I want you to fulfill your duties of treating the men, but I'm also concerned for your wellbeing. I've ordered Mr. Wyse to see to your safety, but he has many other responsibilities. Please behave sensibly and don't stir up trouble. Do you understand?"

Ella stared down at her dress. "Yes, sir."

"Also, you speak like a Londoner, but I hear a hint of a dialect. And such expensive clothing and jewelry... You are mysterious, Miss Ella. What did you do before medical school?"

If the crew learned of her wealth, she'd never fit in. "I grew up near Newcastle." That was a safe answer.

The captain raised his eyebrows. "Ah, I thought I recognized the Geordie speech even though you hide it well. My wife came from those parts. Do I know your family? Parker, from Newcastle. There was the late Earl of Greenwoods with that name, but no, that couldn't be... wait."

She maintained her face expressionless, but the captain's eyes bulged.

"You are the earl's daughter who went missing?"

Ella cringed. "Please keep this in your confidence. I escaped my father. He's dead now. My lawyer and my estate caretaker oversee my inheritance."

The captain's eyes sparkled, and he cracked a mischievous grin. "Wyse, Stafford, we are speaking to one of the wealthiest, eligible ladies in England. Will you try your luck? If you marry this woman, you'll never worry about money again."

Stafford pinked, and Wyse tightened his jaw.

Her cheeks on fire, Ella pursed her lips. "This is one of the reasons I keep my parentage secret. I don't entertain hasty marriage proposals."

The captain raised his palm in a peaceful gesture. "You have our confidence, Countess. Your secret will stay in this cabin."

She bowed her head, letting tension ebb from her shoulders.

The other midshipman stepped in and saluted his superiors.

"What is it, Mr. Collins?" the captain asked.

"Sir, we sighted a ship two points off the starboard bow. She hasn't shown her colors, but we believe her to be French," the young man replied with excitement in his voice.

The captain rose. "Stafford, come with me." He and the two midshipmen left the cabin.

Wyse rose to leave as well, but Ella stepped in his way. "Mr. Wyse, I'm here to stay. We should come to an understanding."

His eyes bore into her. "We have an understanding. You are not to cause trouble, and I'm to protect you from your own foolishness. While I'll see to your safety, I don't care for your wants or comforts. You don't belong on this ship, and I hope you leave it once we are back in England."

The doctor cleared his throat, but no one paid him any mind.

Ella crossed her arms. "Then the battle lines are drawn, Mr. Wyse." A drumbeat rapped, making her shudder.

"And we beat to quarters. You are to go to the orlop, and don't stick your nose out of there until you're told to do so. The doctor will show you." With that, he hastened from the cabin.

The doctor took Ella's hand. "Time for work. We go below to care for the wounded."

Chapter 6

As Ella and the doctor emerged on the deck, they witnessed men rushing to their positions as the drumbeat sounded '*Heart of Oak*', the anthem of the Royal Navy. The officers yelled commands to load and run out the guns. A group of marines loaded their muskets and climbed up to the platforms on the masts. A couple of boys hastened past them with boxes in their hands.

"Who are these children?" Ella asked the doctor.

"Powder monkeys. They bring gunpowder to the gunners. Or some of them will sand the deck, so the men don't slip in blood." He pointed over to a group of seamen and three boys spreading white sand from heavy sacks.

"But they could get hurt."

"Sometimes." The doctor sighed. "War's an ugly thing where even children die."

Ella sucked in her breath. She did not want to imagine a child perishing from a battle wound.

"Chin up, my dear. You wanted to be a ship surgeon. Are you ready to go to work?"

"I'm ready," she answered, glancing down at her ivory dress. It would likely become crimson with blood, even if she donned an apron. "Could I run to our cabin and change?"

"Absolutely not." The doctor led her into the hatchway. "Cannon fire can shatter cabins completely. We stay down in the orlop, the second lowest deck of the ship, above the hold. We'll be as safe as we can be down there."

When they entered the orlop, Ella looked around, inhaling the stale, musty air. Lanterns provided only dim lighting in the narrow space. The creaks and groans of timbers reached their ears, but the steps and yells of the men above were barely audible.

The berth contained a few mattresses, cots, and an operating table. Sully, along with another young man, laid out the instruments. The doctor inspected their work. "Please pour more sand around the table and fetch more bandages."

Ella lifted one of the scalpels to examine it near the light. "Could you also please bring lye soap and a basin with water? I want to scrub off the dried blood. We'll scrub with sand as well."

The other loblolly, a bespectacled dark-haired man of about twenty, stared at the doctor. "Who's this?"

"Oh, I forgot to introduce you. This is my assistant, Ella Parker. Ella, this is Tyler Monk, my second loblolly boy."

Tyler gave Ella a look of discontent, then glanced back at Dr. Pesce. "You've hired a woman instead of me?"

The doctor cleared his throat. "I did. Now be so kind as to do what she asked."

"Yes, sir." Tyler stomped away.

Dr. Pesce clicked his tongue. "Pay no mind to him. He asked to be my assistant, but I have neither time nor patience to instruct an untrained man. I considered sending him to medical school, but you know how expensive that is. Now that Matilda lost her shop, she'll need my savings."

Ella's throat constricted. "It's my fault. I offered Matilda money, but she refused."

Dr. Pesce patted her shoulder. "You did nothing wrong. My stubborn sister will start anew and succeed."

Tyler returned with the basin filled with water. "Why do you want to wash the knives?" he asked as he set it on the table.

She began washing and scrubbing the amputation saw as she spoke. "When I was in medical school, a friend of mine showed me a paper by Dr. Alexander Gordon which argued that cleaning the instruments prevents childbed fever. I'm applying the same theory to prevention of festered wounds."

She lifted the saw to the light, admiring how it shined, and started cleaning the next instrument. The loblolly boys stared without making a move to help.

“She went to medical school,” Sully said to Tyler under his breath.

The doctor nodded. “That’s right, gentlemen. Medical progress is exciting. Please assist Miss Ella with the rest of the instruments.”

The loblollies shrugged and complied. For a few minutes, they worked in rhythm—washing, scrubbing, and wiping scalpels. Sully’s face relaxed; he seemed to enjoy the work. Tyler still gave her annoyed glances but did his part. Ella wondered if these fellows might become her friends. If Tyler was keen on medical school, she could lend him some books.

The boom of cannon fire made them all shudder. Ella gasped and dropped the catling knife she was cleaning.

“It’s started,” the doctor muttered.

Another boom pounded, and the deck heaved. Ella’s heart palpitated, making her dizzy. She gripped the table for support. Screams and shouts echoed from the deck. Sully and Tyler exchanged glances, grabbed a stretcher, and rushed out.

The doctor handed her an apron. His face brightened, and eyes glittered. “Prepare for a bloody mess, Ella.”

She didn’t share his glee. Her gut twisted like tight coils. She rubbed her belly to ease the discomfort.

The doctor gave her a sympathetic glance. “It’s only nerves. The new men feel the same. There’s a bucket in the corner if you need it.”

She shook her head. “I’m fine.”

"I'll let you do an amputation. After performing one, you won't be fretting."

"By myself?"

He tilted his head. "You've done amputations on cadavers, right? You are better prepared than I was for my first operation."

Ella chewed her lip. Cadavers didn't scream or thrash in pain while students maimed them.

The loblollies carried in a man who was bleeding from his leg. The doctor ordered the lads to put the patient on the table. The injured man groaned as they moved him.

"Do you have laudanum?" she asked the doctor.

He pointed at his bag, and Ella rushed to retrieve a brown bottle.

When she returned to the table, the doctor clicked his tongue. "His wound is full of splinters. We'll need to remove them and apply sutures. Ella, let's see you do it. Tyler will help you."

Tyler twisted his lips and looked away.

Seamen brought several more injured, and the doctor hastened to see to them.

After administering laudanum, Ella picked up the forceps and, one by one, removed the sharp wooden debris. The patient shouted and twisted in Tyler's arms, his screams paining her chest. She suspected that despite her efforts the inflammation would still come.

She pointed to Tyler. "Swab here. I need to see if there's more."

Tyler obeyed without a word. She inspected the wound and threaded the needle.

"I'm almost done. Just the stitches now," she said to the patient. She wished she knew his name.

Dr. Pesce touched her hand. "Ella, I'll finish with him. You tend to Mr. Stafford."

She whipped her head about. "Stafford's hurt?"

The doctor pointed to a cot where the midshipman lay bleeding. She gasped and hastened to inspect his injury. Stafford's left arm was a bloody mess of shattered bones poking through the skin. A choking tightness closed her throat as she comprehended what she must do to the nice young man.

"It's all right, Miss Ella. I know you must remove my arm," Stafford said, cringing with pain. "The cannon ball flew in through the gun port. Collins got the worst of it. He's dead."

Amputation would be necessary, but she had to halt the bleeding first. Ella brought over bandages and scissors and tightened the tourniquet below his shoulder. "We'll take good care of you. And I'll give you something for the pain," she added as Stafford winced, his face a mask of agony.

She looked around, trying to spot the brown bottle she used before. Unable to find it, she called to the doctor. "Where's the laudanum?"

Dr. Pesce held up the bottle. "Used up. We've more in the dispensary. Sully or Tyler will bring it when they have a chance. You can give him rum."

"He's in great pain. I can't let him suffer."

Ella called to the loblolly boys, but they hastened away with a stretcher. George made a heart-wrenching moan. Seasick all week, she'd had little chance to explore the murky underdeck. Earlier, the doctor showed her the hatchway that led to the sickbay and dispensary. There was probably a way to reach it underdeck, but she'd be wandering inside the dark passages, wasting precious time.

It's been quiet for a while, and I'll be quick. She gave Stafford's good hand a gentle squeeze. "I'll be right back."

***

From his vantage point on the quarterdeck, Lieutenant Jack Wyse stared through the glass. The captain stood beside him. Blood and debris stained the sanded deck after the cannon exchange. The French corvette was coming into the firing range of their starboard twelve-pounder guns. The Frogs may respond with the same. Such a shot made a heaving mess of Collins, a simple and quiet lad. A lump pained Wyse's throat.

The captain touched his arm, and Wyse returned his glass. "We are back in range, sir."

"Fire!" The captain bellowed into the horn.

All officers yelled the same command to the men, and the deafening boom thundered from the gun deck. The fog permeated the air, and the stench of sulfur hit his nose. His eyes stung as he struggled to see if the cannon balls found their target.

"A hit!" the men cheered.

A good hit. The corvette's mizzenmast fell. This will prevent the Frogs from escaping. One or two more hits like this, and they will be ready to jump onto the French ship for some sparring, unless the Frogs see sense and give up. The closeness of victory quelled his toothache, but the battle wasn't won yet.

"Down!" Wyse bellowed to the men, anticipating return fire.

A cannonball whistled as it shattered railings on both sides. Debris hit several men, but all rose to their feet. And then his heart jumped as he noticed a figure in a dress slumped on the deck. Before he knew what he was doing, he rushed down the steps to her. He almost yelled *her* name, not Ella, but the name he forbade himself to say for many years.

Ella was wide-eyed and pale as a ghost, but he discerned no blood or damaged limbs. "Are you hurt?" he yelled.

The girl sat up slowly and shook her head. Splinters stuck to her clothing, and her face was fixed with terror, but she appeared unharmed. He yanked her to her feet and dragged her into the hatchway. Once there he pushed her against the bulkhead and brought his nose to hers. "I told you to stay in the orlop. Don't ever come out of there until you're told it's safe to do so."

He released her and gave her a nudge to keep going down the stairs. Ella made an unsteady step, then turned around.

"We're out of laudanum. I must get more from the dispensary," she said in a small voice. When he did not respond, she stared for a moment, then started up the stairs until he blocked her way. "Mr. Wyse, please let me through."

Stubborn fool, he thought. *Almost having her head blown off by a cannonball not enough for her.*

"Are you hard of hearing?" he roared.

She straightened and shot him a look of fury. "Are you? Do you want me to amputate Mr. Stafford's arm with nothing to give him for the pain?"

He swallowed bile. A jolt from his toothache made him wince. Over his years as a sailor, he carried many men down to the orlop, and nothing revolted him more than seeing the surgeon sawing off limbs. A woman doing such work doubled his disgust.

"You can get to the dispensary without going on deck."

Ella threw up her hands. "I don't know the ship. It's a maze down there. I'll get lost."

He huffed and rolled his eyes. "Then send the loblolly boys."

"They are carrying the wounded. Please, I must fetch it now."

Wyse inhaled through his teeth, then ascended to the deck. The girl was on his heels, but he barked at her to stay where she was. When a ship boy ran by, he called him to approach. Tobby, his face and hands covered with grime, looked a little devil. The child saluted him by bringing his fist to his forehead.

"Tobby, run to the dispensary and bring ..." he turned to Ella. "What is it you need?"

"Laudanum. It's a brown liquid in a bottle. Do you think you can find it?" she asked the boy.

Tobby blinked and swallowed.

Wyse gave him a light slap on the back. "Don't just stand there. Run like the wind and bring it to the orlop. And don't dilly-dally after that. The men need powder."

The boy straightened. "Aye aye, sir." He hurried away.

Ella took a long breath; her hands shook. Her face was a mask of determination and fear, the expression new men wore before the battle.

"Thank you, Mr. Wyse," she said over her shoulder and marched down.

He thought to holler back something heartening, like he would to the men, but stopped himself. She didn't need his encouragement. If today's near miss was not enough for her, he'd make sure she would receive plenty of reasons to get off this ship at the first opportunity.

***

Back in the orlop, the wounded occupied every cot and more sat or lay on the deck. Grunts and moans echoed in the crowded space. The metallic smell of blood assaulted her nose. Dr. Pesce and the loblollies scurried among the patients, applying tourniquets and bandages.

Ella checked on Stafford. He hovered on the edge of consciousness. Soothing him with her quivering voice, she reapplied the tourniquet to staunch the bleeding. Her insides still trembled after that cannonball hit so near her. She made herself focus on the wounded. A man moaned from a nearby cot, and she approached to view his injury. Nothing to do for the poor man but ease his death. Without laudanum, she couldn't even do that. After a moment, she moved on to another patient.

She bent over a seaman with a gruesome wound to his leg, a bone perforating the skin. There's another limb to amputate. She didn't know where she'd find the strength to help them all.

"Doctor!" A small voice behind her called. She turned and pointed to Dr. Pesce, who was working with Tyler on a patient with a head wound, before realizing Tobby meant her. A warm sensation spread through her body at the child's simple word. No one had ever addressed her as 'doctor' before.

He handed her a bottle. "Sorry, I kept getting lost. Is that it? I can't read that well, so I brought other bottles just in case." He pointed to half a dozen bottles of assorted sizes he had put on the table.

She checked the label on the bottle in her hand. "This is what I need. Thank you. " She beamed at the child, but he cringed and grabbed his abdomen.

"Are you all right?" She bent down to him.

"My belly hurts."

Ella touched his shoulder. "Why don't you find a place to sit? When I get a chance, I'll give you something to make it better."

The boy straightened. "No, I must carry the powder." With that, he hurried away, still holding his stomach.

Ella shook her head with amazement at a youngster with such a resolve to do his duty.

Now I must do mine.

She measured out the dose of laudanum and hastened to the dying man whose moans had turned to quiet rasps. Sully attended to a man next to him.

Ella called the loblolly boy to her. "Hold up his head while I give him the laudanum."

Sully gave her an incredulous look. "You know he's almost gone. Why waste the medicine?"

Sweat ran down her neck as she froze in thought. She didn't know how many more men would need medicine today and in the coming days. The first bottle ran out so fast. The idea of operating on a patient without opium in his system was preposterous to her, but letting the man die in pain churned her soul.

"I'll give him twenty drops," she said.

Sully shrugged and lifted the sailor's head. She administered the dose, knowing it would give more relief to her conscience than to the patient.

She returned to Stafford's side with a dose of laudanum in a cup and brought it to his lips. When his eyes closed and he didn't respond to his name, she called Sully to strap the midshipman to the operating table.

I've trained for this; she rallied her vigor.

Drawing the stale air into her lungs, she picked up the scalpel and sliced the skin. Stafford moaned and thrashed, but Sully held him down. The long, double-sided catling knife came next, as she cut the muscle tissue. The coppery smell of blood filled her nostrils. Gagging, she hurried to tie off the artery with a catgut, a misnamed cord made of sheep intestines. Fearful that he lost too much blood, she felt for a pulse on his neck, and exhaled with relief on finding a steady beat.

"Saw," she said to Sully.

He handed her the amputation saw, and she braced herself for the next part. Flexing her arms, now strong after many months of practice in the dissection room, she sawed through the bone. Sweat rolled down her face, irritating her eyes, but she worked until the arm came off. Then she threaded the needle for suturing. Her jaw ached from the tension.

"The French struck their colors!" A man announced, pumping his fist as he barged in.

"Is that good?" Ella asked Sully as she finished applying the stitches to the skin pulled over the bone.

The loblolly snickered at her ignorance. Since the men who were awake cheered and clapped, she assumed that it meant victory for their ship.

"George, can you hear me? It's all over now." She peered into the patient's half-closed eyes.

His speech slurred. "The battle?"

"That too. The surgery as well."

Dr. Pesce came to her side and inspected the stump as she bandaged it. "That looks good. Mr. Stafford is lucky. That cannonball was inches from killing him. And it's only his left arm."

"I noticed he's left-handed," Ella said.

"Ah, tough luck. When you finish, please review the journal with me. We must record the number of dead and wounded. I've counted at least eight dead...

Ella's vision swam. "Please give me a moment."

She staggered towards a basin and washed off the blood from her hands and sweat from her face. Bent over the cool water, she expelled a quiet sob to relieve the tightness in her chest. *At least eight men died.* And more may perish from their wounds. These men were full of life before the battle. Lives cut down much too early. The whistle of the cannonball still sounded in her ears. She could've been dead or maimed as well.

When her breath steadied, she assisted Dr. Pesce in recording the casualties. They counted ten dead. The doctor gave orders to the loblolly boys which patients to move to the sickbay and discharged the other men with light wounds.

"What about the dead?" she asked, closing the fixed eyes of a young man no older than her.

"The men will sew the bags for the funeral. The bodies will be committed to the sea."

The memory of the sailor wives she met sank her heart. "Shouldn't their families receive their bodies and give them a burial?" she said, still staring at the young man's face.

Dr. Pesce stepped behind her, sighing. "Ella, think how fast the bodies would rot in this moist environment, the horrible stench that would spread. The French and the Spanish navies keep their dead in the hold until those could be buried on land, as Catholicism mandates. Such practice brings diseases. No, the families will receive some keepsakes from the men's belongings and a pension."

She turned to face him. "And a mention in naval papers of how bravely those men fought and died." Her voice was hollow. She read many such articles in the last two years, scouring for any news of the *Neptune*, dreading to find her mentor's name among the dead.

The doctor patted her shoulder. "You'll get used to this life, Ella. Or maybe you shouldn't get used to it. My heart is not as tender as when I was a starry-eyed young man, exhilarated by my first voyage. But a doctor shouldn't be too coarse either."

Ella closed her eyes and nodded. “My head is so heavy. So much to do, yet I could sleep where I stand.”

He nodded in sympathy. “Soon we’ll rest. And sleep soundly, knowing we did our jobs.”

They ascended the stairs. Dr. Pesce cringed and held the small of his back as he climbed. Ella inhaled sea air into her lungs. It was a joy to see the sun. Some of the men swabbed blood off the deck while others repaired the damaged railings. Marines climbed down from the fighting tops, holding their muskets. The enemy ship appeared severely damaged; its mast broken like a lightning-struck tree. A warm feeling of contentment spread through her. *We won the battle!*

“Mr. Thompson, let me see that cut,” the doctor called to one of the seamen fixing the railing. The man looked up. Blood seeped from a nasty gash on his forehead and trickled down his face.

“It’s nothing.” He returned to his work.

“That man would do anything to avoid me,” the doctor said to Ella. “Once he had a bad lesion and still wouldn’t see me. He ended up in the hospital.”

“Looks like he didn’t learn his lesson.”

“Stubborn fool,” the doctor muttered. “Mr. Thompson, do you want to die of inflammation? Let us suture the gash. It will take only a few minutes.”

With the urging from other mates, the man put down his tools and walked over to the doctor and Ella. The doctor examined the wound. "Ella, please get the needle and thread from the orlop. You'll stitch him up here on the deck. The light is good."

"Wait a minute," the seaman piped. "I want you to do it, not the girl."

Ella crossed her arms. "Mr. Thompson, I'm quite proficient." She was exhausted, but she didn't want Dr. Pesce to kneel over another patient. The doctor's face betrayed his discomfort and fatigue.

"You can sew petticoats, darling. For my head, I want the doctor." His mates nodded in agreement.

Dr. Pesce made a dismissive gesture. "It's all right, Ella, you'll get your chance. Just bring me all I need."

Ella hastened to the orlop. The loblollies already moved most of the wounded to the sickbay and prepared to carry Stafford. "I'll check on you soon, George," she reassured the midshipman. A weak smile spread across his blanched face.

"Please give water and broth to the patients," Ella reminded the loblollies.

Sully nodded, but Tyler peered at her with his mouth tight. "We know our job. You don't need to tell us what to do."

"And you don't need to talk back," she snapped, turning her back on him.

Black spots danced before her eyes, and her head throbbed. An empty cot in the corner beckoned her to repose for a few minutes. Or an eternity. She rubbed her forehead and focused on collecting supplies. Once she found needles, thread, scissors, as well as gauze and vinegar to clean the cut, she shuffled back to the deck.

The men stood about, shirking their work, their faces turned in one direction. Someone's holler of agony hit her senses, stilling her breath. Ella struggled to see where the cry came from. Her heart hammered when she viewed a group circled where she left the doctor and Mr. Thompson a few minutes ago. The men parted as she pushed her way among them.

Dr. Pesce was slumped on his side, howling in pain, and cradling his right arm. A stream of blood flowed from it. Mr. Thompson stood a few feet away, his eyes wide, holding one hand to his cut and another covering his mouth. A marine with a musket crouched before the doctor.

"I'm so sorry, Doc," he mumbled. "Such rotten luck."

"What happened?" Ella rasped.

The marine held his head in his hands. "The ratline parted under my foot as I climbed down. I stumbled and dropped the musket. It discharged when it hit the deck."

Ella gasped and knelt to examine the doctor's injured hand.

"Ella," Dr. Pesce mumbled. "I'm sorry. You'll have to take over for me."

She shook her head. "Hush. The bones are whole, and the musket ball exited. You will heal."

"I can't work without my right arm."

She carefully removed his coat, and poured vinegar on the wound, making the doctor gasp. "We'll take diligent care of your arm, and you won't lose it." She bandaged the wound. "Please don't worry about me or our patients. All will be well."

Ella found Tyler and Sully among the faces in the crowd. Both stood frozen, eyes wide with shock. She beckoned them and asked them to take the doctor to the sickbay. This time Tyler didn't snap at her instructions on how to make the doctor more comfortable.

The doctor leaned heavily on the lads as they led him. The crowd dispersed, making way for them. Ella looked for Mr. Thompson to stitch his cut, but he had disappeared. Unable to find him, she trudged towards the hatchway with leaden legs. By the stairs, her legs buckled. A calloused hand grabbed her before she fell.

Wyse pulled her up. "You're falling off your feet."

"Can you blame me?"

"Well, no rest for the wicked. If you finished bandaging the doctor, you're to see the captain."

She stared down at her dress stained with blood, sand, and splinters. "May I change first?"

"When the captain calls for you? You're not to keep him waiting. Go as you are."

She trudged towards the captain's cabin along with Wyse. When they approached the door, a uniformed man rushed out, his face red as a radish.

"Captain of the marines got a thrashing for his man's recklessness," Wyse muttered, knocking.

Captain Grey bid them to enter. He was writing at his desk. Waiting, Ella observed the charts and the compass the captain studied as he wrote, his neatly made cot, and the large portrait of a handsome woman with two smiling girls right above it.

The captain raised his eyes at her and chuckled. "You are a mess, Miss Ella. Seeing you, one would imagine you were in the thick of battle, not in the safety of the orlop." His own uniform was crumpled, but not soiled with blood.

Ella curtsied. "I congratulate you on your splendid victory, sir. I'm sorry for my appearance. Mr. Wyse said it's urgent I speak with you, and I did not have an opportunity to change."

The captain glanced at Wyse. "You could've given a lady two minutes to fix herself."

Reddening, Wyse lowered his gaze. Ella fought an urge to stick out her tongue at the lieutenant.

The captain opened a new page of the journal he was writing in. "Can you speak to Dr. Pesce's injury?" he asked her, his eyes still on the page.

She inhaled. "The musket ball penetrated his right arm. The wound is not life-threatening but will take months to heal. His unsound health may slow the recovery."

"And Mr. Stafford?"

"Lost his left arm. He should recover in time, if no inflammation occurs."

Captain Grey drummed his fingers. His lips turned down. "Rotten luck. I'm sad for our friends, but meanwhile, the men need a surgeon to tend to their injuries. From what you said yesterday, you want the job and have the training for it. Will you accept the position, at least until Dr. Pesce recovers?"

Ella's heart pumped. The battle showed her how difficult the work would be. Yet, she was the only person onboard capable of performing it while Dr. Pesce recovered. She had to succeed for his sake and hers, and for the men who'd need her help. "Yes, sir. I won't disappoint you."

Wyse walked over to the captain's side, his eyes on the journal. "Sir, do you mean to put the woman's name into the roster? The Admiralty won't stand for it."

Captain Grey inclined his head. "That would be an easy problem to fix. Miss Ella, what was your name when you disguised yourself as a medical student?"

Ella picked at a splinter stuck in her skirt. "Alan Parker. That's the name on my certificate from the navy board as well. But isn't it deceitful to enter a false name into your book?"

The captain laughed and winked at Ella. "No ship book can be read as gospel. Ours is cleaner than most. You won't be the first woman written in under a man's name, but as far as I know, you are the first female ship surgeon."

Ella beamed. Being a pioneer swelled her with pride.

The captain wrote down her alias and asked her to sign. She almost wrote 'Ella' but caught herself and signed 'Alan Parker' with elaborate letters.

The captain studied her signature. “Beautiful penmanship. You should teach the ship boys to write with Mr. Doolittle. Although I doubt any knowledge stays in their heads.”

He glanced at the lieutenant. “Mr. Wyse, please make sure the purser knows to pay wages and a share of prize money to our new surgeon.”

“Prize money?” Ella asked. The new phrase piqued her interest.

The captain raised an eyebrow. “Of course. The French ship will be sold, and we all receive a share.”

Her delight was short-lived, as Wyse coughed into his fist. “I must point out that Miss Ella disobeyed my orders by venturing onto the deck.”

The captain’s smile faded, and he rose from his chair. “I asked you not to cause trouble, and you disobeyed me and Mr. Wyse already. You are not to step on the deck during a battle or foolishly risk your life by other means. Is that clear?”

Ella stiffened and jerked back. “I had a good reason.”

Captain Grey slapped his desk, making her flinch. “From now on, you’re to answer with ‘aye, aye, sir’ or ‘no, sir.’ I don’t give a penny for your reason. In the service, we obey orders. You care for the sick as you see fit, but you never defy me or Mr. Wyse.”

Her knees weakened. “Yes... I mean, aye, aye, sir,” she stammered.

His sea-green eyes bore into her. "It's settled then. Please give me a report on the wounded later today. We'll have the funeral, and then you can get some rest. You look like you need it." He turned to the lieutenant. "Mr. Wyse, please assign a prize crew and tell Mr. Van Horn to take the French ship to Plymouth."

Wyse saluted and left to fulfill the orders.

"Oh, the French ship!" Ella exclaimed. "What about the wounded there?"

The captain sat, tension ebbing from his face. "Most likely they have a surgeon attending to them. If not, we'll have you minister to the poor devils. My second lieutenant and his men will sail the ship as our prize and the Frenchmen as prisoners. After fixing the damaged mast, the prize crew will bring their ship to England, where the Frogs will be taken to jail, and the ship sold."

"I see. Is there anything else, sir?"

He scrutinized her with his gaze, gears shifting behind his calculating eyes. "One more word, Doctor."

Ella beamed at him calling her by that word.

The captain cracked a smile. "Yes, you are to be addressed as 'Doctor' from now on. Insist on it."

His face grew serious. "Mr. Wyse doesn't approve of you, as you can tell. He'll obey my command to protect you, but I can't order him to like you. The men are suspicious of you as well. Wyse is much closer to the lower deck than me, and I value him for that. If you convince him you belong here, it will be good enough for everyone else. Understood?"

Ella fidgeted... "All right. I mean... Aye, aye, sir."

The captain waved, dismissing her. She shuffled out, her back and legs groaning with soreness. Her head swam with thoughts. She had no idea how to befriend Mr. Wyse, but if he were a key to her success, she would find a way.

Chapter 7

Wyse marched towards the forecastle, taking time to observe the hands at work. He saw from a distance who toiled their hardest, and who idled. Those who slacked got his worst; he was in a foul mood after the meeting with the captain.

The girl would now raise her proud chin even higher after receiving the surgeon's position. His heart still thumped off-rhythm after seeing her sprawled on the deck. *No, this madness won't go on after this ill-fated cruise. As soon as they reach an English port, she'll be running back to her estate.*

Sully and Tyler passed him, arms full carrying blankets and sheets. He called after them. "Are you two ready to congratulate your new superior?"

They halted and gaped at him.

"Miss Ella got a promotion. You are reporting to the uppity girl now."

Sully reddened while Tyler glared at the deck, chewing his lip.

Wyse gestured for them to move closer. The loblollies exchanged looks and leaned in. Wyse lowered his voice. "Well, the captain's orders must be followed, but I tell you what, fellas," Wyse continued, giving his voice intimate notes, "respect must be earned. You don't have to be her friends. Trust me, she doesn't want to be friends with the likes of you. I'm not supposed to talk about this, but she's of high and mighty birth, well above us. Make her earn her place here, if she wants it. I bet she'll run home at the first opportunity, and good riddance."

The lads nodded thoughtfully, and Wyse walked away, whistling a tune. Before descending to the lower deck, he removed a flask from his pocket and took a long swig. Most officers would assemble the men and give them their orders, but he made a point of going down to their place, speak to small groups, and look each man in the eye. And he would choose his words carefully.

The starboard watch was resting below. Most of the men reposed in their hammocks, some were up mending their clothes, or playing cards. This place was once home to him. He glanced to the left, where his own hammock hung years ago, next to Olson's. He always got along well with the man as long as he didn't ask him of his past. Now his old friend jumped to his feet and shook his sleeping mates, telling them they must get up and salute the first lieutenant.

"I just have something quick to say, and you can get back to your respite," he started. "You all did well in the battle and will get an extra tot of rum, a special treat from the captain and me." The men cheered and clapped. Captain Grey allowed him to reward the men as he pleased, and he liked a happy crew, so he stocked the extra spirits from his own pocket.

"Now, you likely saw or at least heard of the woman who was helping with the wounded. She's now the surgeon. The captain charged me with her protection. If anyone puts a finger on her, I'll cut off their whole hand. If it's more than a finger, I'll watch his neck stretch in the noose."

At sea, the captain and he were the law.

"Don't give me cause for suspicion," he added. "If you are going to the sickbay, you better be gravely ill or bleeding. I don't want anyone seeking the woman's company."

"Why are Simkins and Black saying she's a witch? Can it be true?" a gunner asked.

Wyse paused and scanned their faces. He lowered his voice, and they all leaned in to hear. "Look, fellas, I've been at sea since I was a boy, and I believe in omens as much as anyone here. Any woman on the ship can bring ill luck, and raven-haired ones are the worst. Not only that, but she's also doing work unnatural to women, cutting off limbs and such. She removed Mr. Stafford's arm, poor chap. Just the thought makes me sick. I'm warning you, stay away from her. Better for her, and better for you."

The men exchanged wide-eyed looks and whispered to each other. His burden lightened. The men would stay away from Ella.

***

“All hands! All hands!” The command called from the deck.

Ella finished changing the dressing for one of the injured in the sickbay and hurried to the deck.

Men left their jobs and gathered around the quarterdeck. Once again, their number in such a small space surprised her. They parted, giving way for the captain to ascend the steps. As he passed Ella, he motioned for her to climb with him.

“You’re an officer too. You get a place on the quarterdeck.”

Glad that she donned a clean dress, she lifted her skirts as she climbed the steps, and stood next to Wyse, among other officers. The sunlight beat upon her, heating her dark hair. Her body screamed with fatigue. Eyes scrutinized her, and the glances of most men showed suspicion and dislike. *They think I’m too young and inexperienced to stand here. They’re likely right.*

A gray-haired man with shiny blue eyes, handsome despite his age, stepped forward. Ella guessed him to be the chaplain. The men removed their hats and bowed their heads. Ten bags lay in front of them to be offered to the sea. Ten lives lost.

"We commit these bodies to the deep," the chaplain began, "in certain hope of the resurrection of the body, when the Sea shall give up her dead ..."

As his melodic baritone spoke of heaven's promises, a velvety warmth enveloped her tired muscles and weary soul.

A loud yawn near her ear disrupted her trance. Wyse took an inconspicuous sip from a flask. "That holy man, Mr. Doolittle, puts me to sleep every time."

Ella bristled. "He has a beautiful voice and speaks with passion."

"Don't tell him that, or he'll blab even longer. The Sunday service is already more than I can stand."

Captain Grey stepped forward and announced the name of each deceased.

"John Taylor."

Wyse muttered, "He got married a year ago. The wife's in a family way."

Ella swallowed, picturing a pregnant woman weeping over a naval paper.

"Rodger Smith."

"He hoped to retire to his farm after this voyage," Wyse explained.

Ella bit the inside of her cheek.

"William Ward."

Wyse continued to eulogize under his breath. "Young chap. Cared for an ill sister."

The heaviness in her chest increased with each comment.

The captain finished announcing the names, midshipman Collins being the last one. The men slid the bodies off a board into the sea. The sailcloth bags sunk under the weight of the cannonballs pulling them to the bottom. Ella swallowed bile.

Everyone but Wyse and her dispersed. She stood in a stupor, leaning on the railing. The losses weighed on her despite hardly knowing the deceased. After getting to know the crew, losing someone would become even harder. Wyse took another swig from his flask, then handed it to her. "You can't watch these things sober. Have some."

The pungent smell of alcohol hit her nose. Morsels of food she ate that day threatened to come back up. She shook her head and returned the flask.

Wyse scoffed. "The princess is too fine for a sailor's drink."

"I'll keep my head clear, since my skills may be needed anytime. I should also discuss the drinking rations with the captain. Spirits harm health and provoke fights."

Wyse stared at her with his mouth open. "Odds bodkins! You do whatever you bloody want, but if you try to take away our rum, I'll make you swim back to England."

Her body flinched, but she held her gaze. "And then what? Who's going to care for your injuries and maladies?" She meant the crew in general, but Wyse blanched and held his cheek. With a look of fury, he stomped away.

***

Ella walked between cots, amusing her patients with her story from medical school of a fellow student getting drunk and messing up badly in his lesson the next day. A week passed after the battle, and she discharged everyone but Dr. Pesce and Stafford from the sickbay. Both were weak and needed diligent nursing.

The sickbay was a healthier environment than the orlop. Located a short distance from the head, the bay had gun ports that admitted fresh air and light. It also boasted a desk for writing notes and the dispensary cabinet with various remedies.

Sully and Tyler, seated together on an empty cot, chortled loudly. Loblollies often gave her the silent treatment. A laugh was a positive change.

Making her expression serious, she sat down at the desk and picked up Dr. Pesce's work journal. "You may laugh, but I have proof of how damaging drinking is. It's all here in the book. September 15th of last year, Mr. Green and Mr. Small found unconscious from drinking. Next day, Mr. Small died." She leafed through several pages. "January 7th, Mr. Morrow, inebriated, fell to his death off the rigging. April 21st, Mr. Long and Mr. Keech fought with knives, both severely inebriated, and sustained lacerations that required sutures." She looked up at her mentor. "Besides that, in the last couple years there were three deaths from suspected cirrhosis of the liver, and two patients suffering from the same disease. Oh, I don't know if I should read the next one aloud as it involved you, Dr. Pesce."

The doctor protested, but loblollies and Stafford pleaded with her to go on.

"June 3rd, you, Doctor, had burning in the esophagus and abdominal pain. Overindulgence in spirits suspected."

The doctor waved his good hand. "That was nothing. Someone treated me to a home brew, and it didn't agree with my stomach."

She peered at him. "According to your own notes, you were ill for two days. What if some crisis happened?"

He shrugged. "Doctors are human too. We get sick sometimes."

"And drunk, apparently. Since lives depend on us, we should do our best to stay well. No more home brews, or other spirits, for you."

Dr. Pesce huffed. "Ah, the zeal of a new doctor. Ready to change the world and believe yourself infallible. Do you plan to report your observations to the captain and ask him to reduce the drinking ration?"

Ella rose, her chin high. "I do. He and Wyse supply more than assigned by the Royal Navy, dipping into their pockets, but it's causing more disease and accidents."

The doctor shook his head. "Don't do it, Ella. You will make Wyse your enemy. And the men won't stand for the decrease. Drinking is one of the few joys they have."

"Yes," Sully piped. "You shouldn't give the men another reason to dislike you."

Her body jerked. "They dislike me?"

Tyler smirked. "Can't you tell?"

Ella tapped her foot, thinking how the men reacted to her. When she ventured on deck to enjoy the view, the men avoided looking in her direction. She tried to strike up small talk or ask about their work, but they answered only 'yes' or 'no'. The only people who conversed with her were the doctor and Stafford, and the captain, when she gave her reports. Once again, as it had been in medical school, she found herself lonely and isolated, even when surrounded by people.

"All right, I won't recommend the changes to the captain. But if anyone asks me for medical advice, I'll give my opinion."

Tyler bared his teeth. "Except no one is asking."

Hiding her frustration, she approached Stafford to check his bandages. The greenish pus with acrid smell seriously concerned her.

He gave her a smile as she cleaned the wound. "Don't fret about the men, Ella. They will come around."

"George, how do you command men who are older and likely more experienced than you?"

He furrowed his brow. "I try to look serious and confident, but the men have no choice but to do as I say. They must obey an officer. I never worry about them liking or disliking me."

"That's true, Ella." Dr. Pesce raised a finger. "You don't want to make enemies, but you don't need to worry about being liked either. You have a job to do, and those who really need you will come see you. Let those worries go."

She gave a weak smile to the doctor. "Thank you."

A man shuffled in, gazing around. This was the man who injured the escaped slave, Mr. Olson, and who refused her help. She recalled his name, Simkins. While she disliked him, she wanted to help. The seaman must have changed his mind about her since he came for treatment.

"Ah, Mr. Simkins, what can I do for you?"

The seaman scratched his head. "I suspect I'm ill and need to be off work for a while."

Sully tightened his lips trying not to burst out laughing, but Tyler brought a finger to his lips. The doctor gave her a worried look and motioned her to approach, but she took no notice. If she helped one man, it would be a start. Patients would trickle in.

She led Simkins to an empty cot to conduct her exam. "What ails you?" she asked, as he sat down.

"Oh, you know, a bit of everything. Some mornings my back hurts, or sometimes my shoulders, and after a day of work my whole body aches like I took a beating. Also, a toothache won't let me sleep."

His tone was friendly, and Ella relaxed. "Let's see."

She examined his back and shoulders and checked the range of motion. Then she had him open his mouth, and trying not to wince from the foul smell, prodded the blackened tooth in the back. After a thorough exam, Ella cleared her throat. “I have good news, Mr. Simkins.”

He looked up at her with interest.

“I don’t see anything wrong that would require you to be off work. I’ll give you warm compresses that can help with muscle aches. As for the tooth, I will extract it.”

Dentistry wasn’t part of her training, but she was confident of her ability. She selected the forceps for the job, asked Simkins to open wide, and gave the tooth a forceful yank.

“Ahh!” Simkins screamed and jerked. The tooth didn’t budge.

Ella chewed her lip. “Sorry, let me try again.” Digging in her heels and flexing her muscles, she tugged on the tooth one more time. Simkins yelped louder, but the tooth stayed put.

Hooting, Sully grabbed the forceps from her. “Ha, you’ve never done this before. You rock the tooth back and forth to loosen it. Here.” With what seemed like little effort, he pulled out the tooth.

Her cheeks heated. To hide her disappointment, she busied herself searching for gauze for the patient’s bleeding gum.

“That’s it, Mr. Simkins. Please stop by in the evening for the warm compress,” she said as he bit down on the gauze.

"What about days off?" he managed to say with his mouth stuffed with cotton.

"There's no need. Your toothache won't bother you anymore, and the compresses will loosen your tense muscles."

He grunted, rising to his feet. The meanness of his piglike eyes took her aback. "Go to the devil and be buggered."

Ella shrank back. Her scalp heated. No answer to the insult came to her shocked mind.

"Mr. Simkins, apologize to the lady," Stafford ordered from his cot, but the seaman snorted and stormed out of the berth.

Her eyes flooded with tears. Sully turned away, repulsed.

"Oh, Ella," Dr. Pesce motioned for her to approach. "I tried to warn you. Simkins and a few others like to shirk their duties sometimes and have days of rest."

Her chin trembled. "But you didn't let them, right?"

The doctor looked away. "I did. Especially Simkins. He's a mean bully. I know it's wrong, but... there are dangerous men among the crew. Better let them have their way. And you'll get better at tooth extractions. It takes practice."

She collapsed on the edge of Stafford's cot. The young man reached for her hand.

"I'm glad you didn't give in to Simkins. Tell Wyse, and he'll wipe the deck with him."

"Thanks George, but I won't." She wiped her eyes with a handkerchief. "I prefer the men loathing me for standing up to a malinger than for telling on him."

His reddened face gave her a start. “How are you feeling?”

“Oh, just fine. You’ve been taking diligent care of me.”

She put a hand to his forehead. It was much too hot. “You’re burning up. Why didn’t you say something?”

“Oh no,” the doctor muttered.

“So much for washing instruments,” Tyler barbed.

Stafford sighed. “I know how it ends, and you can’t do a thing about it. I don’t want you blaming yourself. You did all you could for me.”

She jumped to her feet and rushed to the dispensary. “We should have willow bark for the fever.”

Dr. Pesce’s look told her that he doubted its effectiveness. Inflammation that came after surgery was often fatal.

Ella found the powder and other ingredients to mix into the medicine. Her gaze lingered on the laudanum bottle. *It was full this morning. Who used it?* She dismissed the thought for another time. The wounded midshipman was her priority.

By nighttime, Stafford’s fever rose. Ella cleaned his wound with vinegar every hour and made him drink water and the medicine for the fever until he fell into restless sleep. Her own eyes closed as she sat on the chair next to him.

She startled when he cried out, “I don’t want to be buried at sea. I won’t be food for the fish.

He’s delirious, Ella realized.

He sat up and grabbed her hand.

“George, calm yourself. You had a bad dream.”

"Ella, please, do this for me. Ask the captain to send me home."

Ella stroked his cheek and shushed him. Her fingers seared from the heat of his skin. "You're not going to die. Please lie down."

"We both know the fever will kill me. If another British ship delivers me to port, maybe I'll see my mother before I die. Or at least she'll bury me in the family plot."

Her heart ached for him, and for his mother. A transfer by boat in his condition would be agonizing for him, and his chances of reaching Plymouth alive were minuscule. *At least his mother will say goodbye,* she thought. At the first chance, she'd speak to the captain.

***

The Sunday service lasted nearly two hours. The chaplain, Mr. Doolittle, had the orator's fervor, praying for the success of their voyage, and for the recovery of George Stafford, who was transferred to the hospital ship traveling towards Plymouth. Her heart weighed as a heavy rock as she prayed for the midshipman's healing.

Ella stood on the quarterdeck, watching the chaplain's animated profile, repeating prayers after him. Several times, Mr. Doolittle made eye contact with her and gave her an encouraging smile. When the men glanced at her, she read blame in their faces. *They think Dr. Pesce would've cured Stafford, or that I brought the young man bad luck.*

She caught Wyse staring at her, taking sips from his flask when the captain and the chaplain were looking elsewhere.

"What?" she hissed.

"Did you ..."

"Look, I tried my best! No one knows why wounds fester."

Wyse shrugged. "I just wanted to ask if you needed anything for the doctor."

Ella's face burned.

Captain Grey turned his head towards them. "You two bicker like an old married couple. And always at an inappropriate time."

"Sorry, sir," both said at once.

The captain stepped forward and announced four hours of leisure time for everyone who did not have indispensable duties. The ship's crew dispersed.

"I'm sorry, Mr. Wyse," Ella whispered. "This was a difficult week."

"There're no other kinds." He sipped from his flask. "You still don't drink?"

"No. I promised myself I won't."

"We'll see how long you can hold such a vow." His lips curved into a crooked smile, and his eyes flashed.

Ella trudged to the sickbay to check on Dr. Pesce but found him sleeping. Tyler was with him, reading a thick book. She tiptoed to the table with the journal to compose her notes. After finishing with the journal, she walked over to the dispensary to take inventory. There was enough fever and cough remedies, as well as purgatives and emetics. The mercury for the syphilis lesions was plentiful as well. Ella made a mental note to prepare more salve for burns. Her gaze fell on the laudanum bottle. She opened a new bottle when administering the last dose to George. Now it was only three-quarters full. *Who took the medicine?* With his right hand bandaged and in a sling, Dr. Pesce would not uncork the bottle or measure the dosage without help. The loblollies didn't administer medicine without the doctor's or her permission.

She called Tyler in a whisper, and he approached. "Did you or Sully give someone laudanum?"

The young man flinched. "No."

"The bottle was full two days ago."

"Are you accusing us of stealing?"

She put a finger to her lips. "Shh, you'll wake up Dr. Pesce. I'm not accusing you, but I want to know what's going on."

"I don't know what you're talking about."

She wanted to believe Tyler. The loblolly boys did their job well, and she admired their loyalty to Dr. Pesce. Her priority would be to prevent more medicine from disappearing. Laudanum consisted of opium powder mixed with alcohol, an addicting mix. Dr. Pesce always kept the dispensary cabinet unlocked. If someone wanted the laudanum badly enough, he could sneak in when the doctor slept, or she and her assistants were busy.

She opened the desk drawer and withdrew a small silver key. "Is this the only key to the dispensary?"

"Dr. Pesce has another one in his cabin."

"I believe I've seen it. From now on, the cabinet will stay locked, and I carry both keys. Call me day or night if you need to open it."

"Fine." He looked at her for a moment like he wanted to add something, but then shrugged and walked back to his chair.

Ella glanced at the doctor, who snored. He should have improved by now, but he rarely left his bed, brooding about his injury rendering him useless. She hoped sleep would benefit him.

With her immediate tasks finished, and no patients knocking, she sauntered to the deck to enjoy the view and lift her spirits. It was midday, and the sea churned with foam. The sails bellied out above her, and the seagulls, following the ship, screeched gayly. At the bow, a group of four ship boys sat on the deck, and Mr. Doolittle, in front of them, spoke in the ringing voice of a master storyteller.

"Then the Lord sent a great wind on the sea, and such a violent storm arose that the ship threatened to break up." The chaplain waved his hands, showing the terrible storm.

"Did they throw the cargo overboard to lighten the load?" A curly-haired boy of twelve asked.

"Which sails did they furl?" An older boy inquired.

Ella gave an amused laugh at the children's eager faces. Mr. Doolittle smiled back at her and invited her to join. She knelt among the group and spread her skirts upon the deck.

The chaplain waved to get the boys' attention. "Children, that's not the point. If you'd listened without interrupting, I would have told you how a whale swallowed Jonah. Now you'll have to wait till the next lesson to find out."

The boys groaned and whined, but the clergyman folded his arms.

"No, it's too late. Instead, you're to work on mathematics."

He passed around writing boards with chalk and gave them a few problems to solve. When the boys bent their heads to work on addition and subtraction, using their fingers and toes to count, the chaplain motioned for Ella to approach him.

"At last, I meet my lovely listener. Miss, I cannot tell you how heartening it is to see a captivated face at my services. It's such a rarity on this ship."

She bent her head. "I find your sermons uplifting. This voyage has been trying so far, but my heart lightens at your services. I wanted to get acquainted with you, but I was busy with patients and a bit shy to speak with you in front of everyone."

His eyes glistened and he clasped her hand. "Oh, my dear, it's such a joy to be appreciated. The men here are heathens, from the lowest sailor to the first lieutenant. I can't walk three steps without hearing someone making an oath and saying the Lord's name in vain. At least the boys are purehearted. Do you like children?"

"I do. When I worked in the children's ward at the hospital, they gave me much joy."

Mr. Doolittle beamed. "That's right, you are the new surgeon. How extraordinary! A well-bred and educated lady is an invaluable asset to this ship. You'll benefit the crew with examples of polite manners and piety. I see the hand of the Lord in sending a healer and a faithful daughter of the church to us."

A pleasant warmth spread down her spine. It was nice to feel so appreciated.

The chaplain gazed towards the boys, who were peeking up from their boards. "Let me introduce you to my class. I hope you befriend them. They are unschooled rascals, but teachable and curious. This is Ben," he pointed to the curly-haired redhead. "Next to him is Digby." The dark-haired older boy scowled at her.

"And that's Jimmy, and there's Johnny." He indicated twin boys, who answered with a shrill laugh.

"You mixed us up again!" the one on the right said.

"We don't look the same. I'm much more handsome," the other yelled and received a thump on the head from his brother.

"No fighting, children! Oh, and please tell Tobby that if he misses class again, I won't spare him the rod. Idleness is a deadly sin."

Ben piped. "But sir, his belly hurts again."

"Likely story. I suspect he gets a bellyache when it's time for class or worship, but never at meals. The rod cures such sickness quite effectively." He chuckled.

Ella pinched her chin. Children feigned illnesses at times, but she'd prefer to make sure the boy wasn't truly ill.

Mr. Doolittle turned back to her. "How should the children address you?"

She smiled. "Doctor Parker. Or Doctor Ella is fine."

He introduced her to the boys and asked her to check their answers. She reached for Digby's board, but he hugged it to his chest and turned away. Ben stared at her, so she took his board. He made a couple of mistakes, and she explained how to fix them. Soon enough, Mr. Doolittle dismissed his class. The other boys left, but Ben sat working with her for a few minutes longer. The chaplain complimented their extra effort and excused himself.

"Is Tobby your friend?" she asked Ben.

The boy nodded. "It's not fair if Mr. Doolittle takes a rod to him. He can't help his bellyaches. He misses meals all the time."

Ella shook her head. "I'm glad you told me. Your friend needs to see me."

"He won't. I even offered to come with him. He still won't."

Ella gazed up at the sky, willing the heavens to send her patience. *Do men get their aversion to doctors in infancy?*

"Well, if he won't come to me, I'll go to him." She rose and extended her hand to Ben. "Please show me where he is."

The boy led her down to the lower deck. The berth was full of men using their hours of respite for mending clothes, playing cards, or dozing. Ella followed Ben among the hammocks, catching inhospitable glances. A couple of men whistled or made lewd gestures.

"Are you looking for me, lass?" someone yelled. "Come under my blanket."

"Remember what Wyse said, you dimwit," his mate answered.

That seemed to quiet the taunts, but the glances she received became even more hostile. She ignored them, keeping her face stern, and her back stiff, reminding herself of her purpose. Ben pointed to the hammock on her left.

A child cringed in a fetal position, his knees near his chin, his hands hugging his belly. He was the same boy who fetched her laudanum during the battle. He complained of a bellyache that night as well. In her mind, she scolded herself for not checking on him.

"Tobby, do you remember me?"

The boy turned to her, and his pale face contorted. "Aye."

"I heard you've been having bellyaches. Why didn't you come to see me?"

He sighed but didn't answer.

"Would you let me feel your belly?"

He grunted, then lifted his shirt. His ribs showed through his thin stomach.

"Where does it hurt?"

He put his hand on the lower abdomen, below his navel. "It hurts but then goes away."

"We don't want it hurting at all.

Her fingers palpated the firm stomach, and Tobby winced at her touch. She checked for fever, asked him about vomiting and his bowels, and ensured there was no pain on his right side. After ruling out appendicitis, she rubbed his belly in a circular motion, encouraging his stiff muscles to relax.

A weak smile curved his lips. "This feels nice."

"Good. How long has this been going on?"

Tobby frowned. "A few months. Started at the orphanage."

"A few months! Why didn't you see me?"

He cringed again. "I saw the old doctor."

"Dr. Pesce? What did he say?"

The boy squeezed his eyes. "He gave me an... what did he say... an enemy? I didn't want it, but two lads held me down."

"An enema. I'm sorry they forced you. Did it help though?"

"For a day or so. Then my belly hurt again, and I came back. This time the enema had hot smoke. I screamed and fought, and again they made me. I didn't come back anymore."

"Tobacco enema. I see why you don't want to visit the sickbay." She tousled his hair. "Let's make a deal. You'll come with me to the sickbay now, and any time your belly or anything else hurts. I'll make you comfortable and ask your permission before I do anything."

She extended her hand, but the boy gave her a skeptical look.

"I will keep my promise if you keep yours," she assured the boy.

"Deal." He sighed but shook her arm.

Chapter 8

When Ella entered the sickbay with Tobby, Tyler was feeding Dr. Pesce his dinner, holding it for him on the tray.

"Ah, Tobby," the doctor said between the bites. "Belly hurts again?"

The boy nodded solemnly and glanced at Ella.

"We know how to fix that," the doctor continued after Tyler brought a cup of water to his lips. "Tyler, I can't eat anymore. Why don't you get the enema ready?"

Tyler removed the half-full plate and cup and went towards the dispensary. Tobby's eyes widened. He made a leap for the door, but Ella caught him.

"Dr. Pesce, let me handle this." She helped the boy onto the cot. "He doesn't want a clyster. I'll make him chamomile tea and give his belly a good massage."

The doctor clicked his tongue, motioning for her to approach. "Ella," he lowered his tone and took her hand. "An experienced doctor to a new one. Children don't know what's good for them. That's what adults are for. I love children, but when a boy needs an enema, he gets an enema."

Ella squeezed his hand. "Doctor, I appreciate your mentorship, but I barely talked him into coming here. Some gentler treatments can be effective and less distressing to a child. If needed, I will persuade him to let me administer a clyster, but only if nothing else works."

"Persuade him?" The doctor shook his head.

Ella turned on her heel and unlocked the medicine cabinet to select herbs for the tea. While the tea steeped, she massaged the boy's belly in a circular motion. The boy's tense body relaxed. He closed his eyes with a smile on his lips. His ribs showed through his pale skin.

"Have you always been so thin, Tobby?"

"Aye. But now I make the belt tighter, so my breeches don't fall."

"What do you eat?"

He shrugged. "Same as everyone. Salted meat, rice, tack."

Dr. Pesce chuckled. "Who wouldn't get closed bowels from such a diet."

Ella propped the boy up with pillows and brought him tea to drink. "What about beans and vegetables?"

"I give them to Ben. He likes them."

"Please eat them too. And drink water. It tastes stale, but we must drink it anyway. Also, you don't indulge in sweets, do you?"

"Sweets? You mean raisin duff or molasses on the bread? I like them when I can get them."

"Be careful with getting too much. When I was your age I gave myself a wicked stomachache once. Want to hear the story?"

"Yes, please." He sipped his tea and laid down again, letting Ella caress his belly some more.

She continued the massage, while chatting. "Well, I was a silly girl at times. On my tenth birthday, I ate too many sweets throughout the day: scones, crumpets, cream puffs and such. By evening I was in bed, moaning and groaning, and my birthday celebration had to be canceled. Didn't even get to have my birthday cake, which looked so good."

He widened his eyes. "What kind of cake was it?"

"Two-tier, with cream roses and cherries on top. Just the smell was to die for. I ate it when I was better, but... you know... it wasn't my birthday anymore."

Tobby looked at her in wonder. Then his face crumbled. "I've never had a birthday cake."

In her mind, Ella kicked herself. Why was she prattling about the fancy sweets when it was obvious the boy never had such things?

"When is your birthday?"

"Don't know. We never had birthdays in the orphanage."

She tickled his cheek. "Then you can have a birthday whenever you choose. When we return to Plymouth, we'll celebrate your birthday with the other boys, and I'll get you a cake."

His face lit up. "You will?"

"I promise. But we must cure your belly first."

"It's not hurting now. The tea helped."

She palpated his belly again. It was soft, and the boy didn't wince. "Well, that's good. See me if it aches again. And start eating those vegetables."

Tobby nodded and grinned at her. "Thank you, Doctor," he mumbled.

When he left, Dr. Pesce shook his head. "Ella, you're too indulgent. Children don't get to decide their treatment. He needed a good cleanse of his gut."

"If that's the case, he'll be more comfortable letting me do it next time. Now, let me see how my other patient is doing."

The doctor glanced around. "Did someone else get sick?"

She rolled her eyes, approaching. "I mean you, of course. You've been in bed for ages. Why don't you enjoy the view from the deck for a bit?"

The doctor drew the blanket to his chin. "I was going to nap."

"You'll sleep better after getting fresh air. Tyler, would you please help the doctor to his feet?"

Tyler raised Dr. Pesce, and Ella draped a coat on his slumped shoulders. She ushered him to the stairs, as he leaned on her arm.

Tyler was behind them, carrying a chair. As the doctor struggled with each step, she noted his heavy breathing and sweating. He was becoming weaker.

They came to the stern, and Tyler helped Dr. Pesce into the chair.

"How do you feel?" Ella asked the doctor.

He gave her the look of a capricious child. "Brr... it's windy. I may catch a cold."

A pleasant breeze cooled her neck. "Why don't I bring you a blanket?" Ella offered.

He agreed, and she left for the sickbay to retrieve one.

As she descended, a rustling sound coming from the sickbay gave her a start. Concerned a patient might be awaiting her, she hurried.

Click.

There was something familiar about that click and the squeak of the door. Suspicious, she proceeded with caution, her heart thumping. Since Sully was at the forecastle, and Tyler with the doctor, someone uninvited was opening the dispensary, probably hoping to help himself to the laudanum. The locked cabinet should stump the intruder. With any luck, she'd catch him.

She crept inside. Someone bent over the desk.

Her cry pierced the silence. "Aha, you're the one stealing the laudanum!"

The man dropped something with a thud.

"Shame on you," she continued. "When the captain hears of this..."

He straightened and turned to her with his hands raised. To her shock, it was Mr. Olson. He stared down, and his lips trembled.

"Mistress Augustina, please... I didn't steal your bracelet." His voice quivered.

Ella froze. The man may be delirious or mad, but she suspected something else.

Olson quaked through his whole body. His eyes were wide and dazed.

She touched his arm and made her voice gentle.

"Mr. Olson, I said nothing about a bracelet. Why don't you sit down?"

She led him to a cot. When he lowered himself, she checked his forehead. No fever, as she suspected. She considered offering him something calming, but chose brandy instead, as it seemed to be the most respected remedy for nerves on the ship. As she removed the bottle from the dispensary, she checked on the laudanum. The level of the liquid had not changed.

Olson needed no coaxing to empty his glass. His hands stopped shaking, and he blinked, as if waking after a dream. Then he moved his gaze to Ella, and his eyes focused. "I'm sorry, Miss. Did I say something?"

Ella gulped. "You spoke of a bracelet. Were you accused of stealing it?"

The seaman sighed. "Yes. Mistress Augustina had me and a few other slaves whipped for it, then she found it in the garden."

"How awful... Did I do something to remind you of her?"

He sat silently. When she thought he wouldn't answer, he whispered. "When you hollered about... whatever you are missing, you had the same shriek in your voice. And you carry yourself in the same manner with a stiff back and shoulders. Please... I try not to think about my past."

Ella shifted her feet. "I didn't mean to pry. And I'm sorry if my manner brought back those memories you want to forget. Please be assured that I abhor slavery. You're extremely brave for running away."

He shrugged. "Thank you, Miss. I didn't mean to disturb. I'll get going."

The sailor rose, but Ella took his hand. "What were you doing when I came in?"

"Oh, nothing to trouble you. I just wanted to borrow the tweezers."

"For what?"

He turned the back of his left hand to her. A thin piece of metal was sticking out of his skin.

Ella winced. "Is that a fishing hook? Why didn't you say so?"

"I hoped to catch a fish but caught myself instead." He gave a self-deprecating laugh. "It's a small one. If you let me use your tweezers..."

She tilted her head. "Mr. Olson, you're a carpenter, right?"

"Yes, Miss."

"Do you lend your tools to everyone and let them do whatever they wish with them?"

He frowned. "No. The tools are for my job."

"As the forceps are for mine. Please, let me extract the hook. That's *my* job."

The sailor had reluctance in his gaze. "I don't know, Miss."

"Do you believe me such a poor surgeon that you can't trust me to remove a hook?"

Olson lowered his eyes. "I can't trust myself not to cuss as you do it."

Ella laughed. "Go ahead, Mr. Olson. I'll learn to swear like a sailor. When Mr. Simkins cussed at me for not letting him have a day of rest for no reason, I couldn't retaliate."

Olson clenched his fists. "Simkins is a real shit. Oh, I'm sorry for my language."

Ella raised an eyebrow. "I'll count it as my first lesson. Now please sit and relax your arm. You may close your eyes if that helps."

She let Mr. Olson's arm rest on a pillow and prepared her tweezers. The tension in his shoulders remained, so she spoke soothingly.

"You see, Mr. Olson, small hands and thin fingers, like mine, are advantageous for some surgical tasks." She pushed on the eye of the hook. Olson flinched and grunted.

Her tweezers grabbed the hook and rotated it. "I've built my muscles to saw large bones, but my dexterous fingers are great for delicate jobs like this." The barb stuck out of his skin, and she cut it off.

Olson opened one eye. "That didn't hurt too bad."

Ella removed the barb. The hook easily slipped out the same way it went in. She cleaned the punctured skin with warm water and vinegar and wrapped a bandage around his hand.

"All done. Good luck with fishing. By the way, I'm glad your nose healed well. You were barely awake when I set it and mayn't remember."

He touched the bridge of his nose. "Yes, it mended. I thought Dr. Pesce set it. Thank you, Miss. Or should I say, Doctor?"

A smile touched her lips. "Yes, I would appreciate that. By the way, do you want me to call you something different? I heard Olson isn't your birth name."

"No... My old name's from my past."

She lowered her gaze. "I understand. I also have a name that I prefer not to use. Please don't tell the others, but I was once called Eloise Parker of Greenwoods. When I remember that name, I feel as if I should ring for a maid to brush my hair or iron my dresses."

The man narrowed his eyes. "That name suits the woman who walked in and yelled about me stealing from her. It doesn't suit the one who removed the fishing hook."

"Right, that's not who I am now, at least most of the time." She put a hand on his elbow. "Mr. Olson, would you help me? Someone's stealing the laudanum. If you learn who, can I count on you to tell me?"

Olson shook his head. "I'm not a snitch."

"But laudanum can be dangerous."

He cocked his head. "What will you do if I name the thief?"

"I would... tell the captain to punish the offender."

"Do you know what punishment the man will receive?"

Ella shrugged. "I'm sure the captain will choose something like peeling vegetables or an extra watch."

"Ah... Don't be so sure. The Articles say the punishment is death, unless the captain says otherwise. Most captains would hang the man."

Her veins iced. "I wouldn't want that, of course. What if I promise not to tell the captain?"

Olson shook his head again. "I'm not snitching. It took me a while to belong among the crew. I'm on their side."

She opened her palms. "But there are no sides. I'm just here to help."

He rose, looking aside. "I'm sorry to tell you, Doctor, but the men don't want you here. I thank you for removing the hook and fixing my nose, but I won't be telling the others you've done it. Their friendship means much to me, while you are new here. Good day to you."

Ella stared as he walked out of the sickbay. Disappointment stung her. *What will convince these men that I fit in here?* She shook herself and fetched the blanket for the doctor.

***

A crackling noise came from the door of her cabin, and Ella opened her eyes. She shifted on the cot, stretching her stiff back. Since Dr. Pesce slept in the sickbay, she took over his cot, an upgrade from the hammock. While the new arrangement was more comfortable and private, she wished her mentor back in his cabin. He, however, insisted that he slept better in the sickbay, with loblollies attending to him at night.

"Tobby, is that you again?"

"Yes, just me," came the boy's small voice.

"Wait, let me put something more on."

Yawning, she threw a robe over her dressing gown, lit a lantern, and unlocked the door for Tobby. Dr. Pesce insisted she kept the cabin locked, especially at night. She thought him too cautious; no one seemed to give her any mind.

"You know, a proper lady doesn't entertain gentlemen alone in her cabin, especially this late at night." She mimicked the stern tone and haughty expression of her governess.

Tobby stared, gaping. "I... I'm sorry."

She cracked a smile. “It’s all right. I’ll make an exception for you. Belly aches again?”

“Mmhmm.”

He plopped on her cot, while she sat on the edge. Tobby lifted his shirt. He reminded her of Dash, a pup she owned in childhood, who would lie on his back and beg for belly rubs.

Her hands caressed his distended belly in circular motion. “Goodness, Tobby, this is a second night in a row. Have you been eating vegetables and beans?”

“Aye. I eat all the vegetables they give me. And I drink water with drops of lemon juice. Not the grog.”

She shook her head at the thought that boys imbibed spirits. While she chose not to pursue a temperance campaign, she had at least convinced the boys to refrain from drinking. Since the battle three weeks ago, she spent most of her free time with them, teaching them to read and write, telling them stories, or just playing games.

“And your bowels were normal?”

“Aye.”

That’s what he said last night as well. Dr. Pesce insisted earlier that Tobby just needed a purgative or an enema. Fatigued from interrupted sleep, she was ready to follow his advice.

“I’ll make you tea and a warm compress, but we must try something different in the morning. This can’t go on.”

He closed his eyes and nodded. “Alright.”

She patted his disheveled hair, no longer greasy since she gave him soap and taught him how to wash properly. He was one patient, besides Dr. Pesce who trusted her, and she yearned to help him.

In the morning, she brought Tobby to the sickbay. Dr. Pesce shook his head at her.

"I told you the bellyache would come back. Did you stay up another night with him?"

"Yes, but we'll do something different today. I'm going to give him castor oil."

The doctor snapped his fingers. "Now you are making sense. Give his system a thorough cleaning. I also recommend grains of calomel for the next few days to keep the bowels open."

She poured the dose of the oily liquid and gave it to Tobby. He smelled it and winced.

"Sorry to tell you, it tastes even worse than it smells, and you will spend the morning at the head."

The boy shuddered. "No... My belly doesn't hurt anymore."

"Think of the birthday cake I'll get you when you get better."

Tobby drew air through his front teeth, closed his eyes, and emptied the cup in one gulp. His cringe made Ella laugh. She had him relax on the cot and caressed his belly until he clenched it and sped to the privy.

"Now, my other patient." She brought a chair over to Dr. Pesce's cot. "Shall we go up to the deck today?"

The doctor's lips turned down at corners. "Again? Yesterday was too hot. I got tired walking up those stairs."

She unwrapped the dressing and inspected his wound. The white pus with no foul smell didn't worry her. She brought a clean bandage.

"You used to say that watching the sea was your reward that restored you after a difficult day."

"Doesn't seem to work anymore. I must be getting old. Where are the loblolly boys? Oh right, I sent Sully to get me breakfast."

"Good. You need to eat better and keep up your strength. Speaking of Tyler and Sully." Ella shifted in her seat. "I've noticed something. The laudanum in the dispensary is disappearing a little bit at a time. Do you think they take it?"

The doctor knit his brow. "No. I'd see something if they did."

"Signs of opium habit are subtle. Do they seem moody to you? Do you hear them complain about closed bowels or poor appetite?"

"Definitely not about a poor appetite. They eat like hungry wolves." The doctor chucked.

"Perhaps they take it for someone else?"

The doctor shook his head. "I trust the lads. They never gave me a problem. Are you sure you are not imagining something?"

Ella jerked back. "No! I wouldn't..."

He patted her hand. "You took on a big job that's giving you much angst. Life on the ship isn't easy. Your sleep has been disturbed for a couple of nights. Under such circumstances, the mind plays tricks. You need to give yourself a respite."

Sully came in with a breakfast tray for the doctor.

"More porridge," the doctor grunted. "I suppose it's good for me."

Sully set the tray down on the table and addressed Ella. "The captain asked for you."

Ella rose. "I better see what he wants."

Dr. Pesce nodded. "And then get some rest. Sully will check on Tobby and call you if you are needed."

The sun reflected in the froth and foam of the sea. A great ship, much larger than the *Neptune*, plunged in the bobbing waves on the horizon. The French coast appeared in the distance.

On the deck, the men went about doing their jobs. After more than a month on the ship, Ella knew a bit of what their work entailed. On the larboard side, a group pounded oakum into the deck, fixing the gaps. This job was taxing on the fingers. On the starboard side, a man heaved the lead—tossed in the line to measure the depth. Others were tarring the rigging through the full height of the mainmast under the watchful eye of Mr. Wyse.

Despite the early hour, Ella's skin singed with heat and her brow was drenched with sweat. The August day would be a hot one. Good thing the doctor declined to come up. She glanced again towards the men who climbed aloft. *How hot was it for them, working under the scorching sun?* Concerned, she approached Wyse.

She greeted him with a polite smile. "Good morning, Mr. Wyse. Sweltering day, isn't it?"

Wyse grunted. "Save your pleasantries for the captain. When he calls, you go without stopping to flap your tongue."

Her cheeks heated. "I wanted to say that in this weather the men need frequent breaks and plenty of water. Even better to defer the work for a different day, if possible."

"That's right, lass," one of the men called from the rigging. "Tell him we shouldn't be working today." The other men responded with laughter.

Wyse's nostrils flared and his face reddened. He grabbed Ella's arm and pushed her against the railing.

"What are you thinking, undermining my authority in front of the crew?" He hissed.

"I..." Ella trembled under his raging glare. "I'm concerned for the men."

"The captain or I decide around here. Our orders aren't questioned. Especially not where the men hear you." He breathed into her face.

"Wyse, why are you detaining the doctor when I called for her?" The captain's voice boomed.

Wyse stepped aside. "Sorry, sir. I needed to explain something."

Captain Grey shook his head. "Save your explanation for another time. I prefer not to go out to fetch her myself when I need her."

Ella gave him a curtsy. "Sorry you had to wait, sir. I'm at your service."

He offered his arm. "Hot day, isn't it, Doctor?"

"Indeed, sir."

As they promenaded to the captain's cabin, she turned her head to peek at Wyse. The lieutenant stormed back to his men, his scowl darker than a thundercloud.

"I hope you can save me." Captain Grey closed his cabin door behind them. "Do you know anything about oysters and mussels, and other sea filth like that?"

She gasped. "Oh no, if those are not fresh, they may give a terrible poisoning. But you look well, sir."

He gave a hearty laugh as he walked to his desk. "I wouldn't touch those abominations at free will. My friend Weston, the captain of the *Crown*, employs a French chef. I know how that sounds when we are at war with his country, but the fellow has been in England for ages, although he maintains that pretentious accent. Last time he served those oysters, and brace yourself for this one, lobsters."

Ella laughed. "I love lobster. It can be quite tasty with a tangy sauce and some lemons. I had a French tutor when I was a child. He introduced me to his native cuisine."

The captain cringed. “They’re sea cockroaches. When I tried breaking the shells, the juices splashed everywhere. Weston had a good laugh at my expense and now wants to have another one. His invitation specifically mentions the sea-inspired menu.”

Weston. Captain Weston is Robert’s father. A current spread through her on mere mention of the name.

She restrained her lips from spreading into a silly grin. “Would you like me to teach you how to eat such dishes?”

“Yes, I’d be obliged. More than that, you’ll accompany me. You must’ve noticed the ship of the line by us—that’s the *Crown*. We’ll take a boat tomorrow night. Do you have another dress like the one you wore at our last dinner?”

Ella clapped her hands. “I do. It would be an honor. Might the captain’s son, Robert Weston, attend?”

“I hope he does. The lad beat me at Whist, and I must have my revenge. Wait, how do you know the younger Weston?”

Her cheeks warmed. “We met at Plymouth before the sailing.”

“I see.” Captain Grey pursed his lips. “Well, keep your pretty nails off him. My daughter Bella has mooned over him since she was ten.”

“Oh.” Ella’s throat closed. Her arms fell to her sides. “I didn’t realize he and your daughter are betrothed.”

The captain gave her a side glance. “They’re not. Bella’s dowry is too small to marry into the Weston family. It’s just her silly dream. I was jesting when I said you must keep away from Robert."

"We've only met once. He probably forgot me."

"I'm sure he hasn't. Does he know in what capacity you are on my ship?"

"I told him I was planning to be Dr. Pesce's assistant."

The captain rubbed his chin. "If he's interested in you, he'll keep this from his father. Captain Weston wouldn't react well to hearing of a woman meddling in the sickbay. I don't want him slipping something to the Admiralty about me hiring you. I'll introduce you as Dr. Pesce's relation."

She was about to respond, but a knock at the door halted her.

"Come in," the captain said.

A young seaman stepped in. Sweat poured down his forehead. He panted. "Sir, and you... Doctor. There's been an accident on the deck."

"Go see to it," Captain Grey commanded Ella.

With her heart palpitating, she hastened out of the cabin.

Chapter 9

A group of sailors gathered by the mainmast. As Ella neared, they let her pass through. A twisted body sprawled before her, his head a mess of blood.

He must be dead, she thought.

Slowing her breathing, she kneeled and checked for a pulse. To her shock, she found a faint beat. The man moaned at her touch.

"Did he fall off the rigging?" she asked.

Wyse loomed over her. "Odds bodkins, yes."

Bile burned her throat. Her mind reeled. What could she do for such a gruesome injury? The man's legs must be fractured, maybe even a broken back, but she needed to tend to his head first. She wiped the blood with a handkerchief to view the gash, then pressed on the depression above the unmoving right eye.

"I need my instruments. Mr. Wyse, please ask these men to step away. I don't need an audience."

Wyse gave orders; the men retreated a short distance. That gave her some relief, but the lieutenant's eyes bore into her, making her heart pump.

She pressed on the sailor's head. The skull was a swollen mess. Inside there would be blood accumulating and pressing on the brain. With horror, she realized: she'd need to trepan the skull—drill a hole to access the brain and relieve pressure from the internal bleeding. She'd give her fortune to have Dr. Pesce guide her, but by the time the doctor got up here, it would be too late. The moment to find the source of the hemorrhage and halt it would be fleeting.

Sully appeared with the surgical tools. "What do I do?"

"Have you assisted with skull trepanation before?" she asked him, trying to sound calm.

He shrugged. "I passed the instruments to the doctor."

That's what I did, back in medical school, she thought. *And then I watched the postmortem after the patient expired.*

The injured man rasped. She clenched her jaw, reminding herself that she possessed the required knowledge for this surgery. Trepanation of the skull was the earliest operation ever performed. If unskilled primeval people did it, so could she.

"Scalpel," she commanded Sully. Her trusted blade in hand, she cut along one of the lacerations, then asked for the circular drill. After choosing the place, she bore into the skull with a mighty effort. *Just a little more,* she told herself as she worked her fingers to make a hole about one inch in size. Sweat rolled off her forehead. The bulging dura of the brain emerged. Now, to cut through the membranous fibers and staunch the bleeding...

"He's dead," Sully stated.

"No! I just need... Oh, yes, he is," she echoed when she registered that the undulations of the man's ribs stopped. Her mouth went dry. She considered looking for the source of bleeding to expand her knowledge, but her energy had depleted. With a sigh, she closed the incision, suturing the skin over the bones.

Was I too slow? Did I drill in the wrong place and cause his death? She may never know the answer.

"Lost another one," Wyse muttered.

Ella put down her instruments, straightened to her full height, and stared at the lieutenant with indignation. "That one was not on me. That was on you." Her voice rose with each word.

Wyse blanched, then reddened. "What did I say about undermining my authority?" he bellowed. "The men hear you," he added through his teeth.

Ella looked around. Much of the starboard watch were steps from her, keeping some pretense of work while watching her and Wyse. "Let them hear. It was preposterous to make them work in the hot weather, when I said it was dangerous."

"What's going on here?" the captain's bellow made them startle.

"Sir." Wyse saluted. "Peter Hart, topman, fell to his death."

Ella's heart pinched as if from a puncture. She met his wife Nancy before the sailing. The newlywed wept that she wouldn't see her husband again. Her premonition turned out true.

The captain stared at the body. "Poor man. What work was he performing?"

"Tarring the rigging, sir," Wyse answered.

The captain knit his brow. "That could've waited for a more opportune weather."

"That's what I said," Ella interjected, but both men glared at her. "Sorry, sir."

Wyse went on as if he didn't hear her. "Hart and others were performing the work as punishment, sir."

"Punishment for what?"

Wyse glowered at Ella and whispered into the captain's ear.

Captain Grey's mouth twisted. "I see. Next time, when it's this hot, ensure the men get water and breaks, but the punishment fits the crime." He turned to the seamen. "Men, take the body below and clean up the blood."

Several men hastened to follow the order. The captain stepped towards his cabin.

"Sir, but the man died. This weather was too hot to work," Ella stammered. "I... I tried to perform the trepanation of the skull."

The captain pivoted. "No one's expecting miracles from you. I've never seen a man break his head and live. I support Mr. Wyse in assigning this task. Men must be ready to perform work in all conditions. Good day, Doctor."

Captain Grey marched away. Ella stood like a statue with her shoulders slumped, staring at the blood on her hands.

"You alright?" Wyse asked.

Ella fell to her knees. "Of course I'm not alright. I haven't slept in two nights. A man died as I cut into him. I met his wife before we sailed. I couldn't help him. I can't help anyone!"

Wyse grunted. "You'll make yourself sick if you don't start drinking. Here."

He offered her his flask, but she sniffed and winced.

"Drink. It's good rum."

She gagged from the stench of alcohol. "I don't drink spirits, especially before breakfast."

Wyse grabbed the flask from her hand and sipped. "Why aren't you sleeping? Nightmares? That's why you need the rum."

She ran her hands over her dress. "It's not nightmares. It's my patients. One of the ship boys has bellyaches."

"Tobby?"

"You know about him?"

"I keep an eye on the boys. It's not anything bad, is it? I hate it when the boys die."

Ella hugged her knees. "I don't believe it's serious, but he's been suffering for weeks. I'm doing all I can to make him better. Why are these boys on the ship? It's not a place for children."

Wyse gave her a hand to rise. "It's a better life than working at the mill. I was about Tobby's age when I started on the *Neptune*."

"You've been here since boyhood?"

"Aye. That's why I know this ship like the back of my hand."

Ella wanted to ask him more about his childhood on the ship, but Wyse whipped his head towards the seamen. Their snickers were audible as they pounded oakum. His face darkened.

"Why are you standing around doing nothing?" he bellowed at her. "Don't you have work to do?"

"I..." Ella hunched but then sucked in her stomach and straightened her back. She wouldn't let this boorish man scare her. "Don't speak to me in such a tone, Mr. Wyse. I'm a lady and you are a gentleman, or at least your rank suggests so. Mind your manners, if you have any. Or are you in need of etiquette lessons?"

With that, she spun on her heel and promenaded to her cabin.

***

The men watched her amble, whispering to each other as they worked. Wyse spat overboard as the girl walked with her chin up, like the queen of this place. *Damn her and all women!*

When he gave her his hand and told her of his childhood, he overheard them murmuring about the girl and him looking sweet together. He showed some pretend anger to make them stop staring. The hussy, in turn, attacked his underbelly, his manners.

He advanced toward the men. They stopped their chatter, stood up, and saluted him.

"The funeral for Hart will be in an hour," he announced. "I repeat, for anyone who needs another reminder, stay away from the woman. There are worse deaths than falling off the yard."

The men winced.

"Dismissed. Get below and drink some water."

The deckhands staggered away. One young fellow remained. "Sir, may I ask?"

"What is it, Williams?"

"Can I keep Hart's fiddle? I don't have the money to buy one."

"Oh right, he was our merry fiddler." Wyse's eyes rested on the men washing the blood off the deck. His heart squeezed. "I'll check his sea chest to see if he left any wishes on what to do with his things. If not, you may keep it." The rest of his belongings would be auctioned among the men; the proceeds saved for the widow.

"Thank you, sir." The lad made a step to go, but Wyse halted him.

"Do you play well, Williams?"

"It's been a while since I played, sir, but I used to be good."

Wyse snapped his fingers. "Let's try you out tonight. It'll be a proper sendoff for Hart."

***

Ella scanned the boys gathered in the passageway by the captain's cabin. She chose the place to be away from the men who might distract or taunt her and her young students. The twins shifted from one foot to another, Digby was wiping his nose with his hands, and Ben was scratching his neck. Tobby's cheeks were pale after the castor oil treatment, but he was the only one who expressed eagerness about the etiquette lesson. The idea came to her when she tutored the captain ahead of the dinner with Captain Weston. She would teach the ship boys good manners, as her mother and governesses once taught her.

All five gaped at the clothes she was wearing: men's trousers, a shirt, and a jacket.

"Why are you dressed like that, Doctor Ella?" Tobby asked.

She grinned. "Because it's easier to show how a gentleman bows when wearing trousers. Digby, please don't blow your nose into your hands. Do you have a handkerchief?"

The lad gaped at her. "A what?"

She removed her lace hankie from her pocket and offered it to Digby. "A gentleman always has a clean handkerchief in case he needs to blow his nose. If he notices a lady who's crying, he offers one to her."

He frowned, twisting the delicate fabric with his fingers. "For me?"

"Yes. You'll all get one. Ben, why're you scratching your neck?"

"It's itching. Some fly bit me," the curly-haired boy replied.

"Don't scratch, or you'll make it worse. I'll bring you a salve later. Now, pay attention. I'll show you how a gentleman bows to a lady and offers her his arm."

With her back straight, she made several steps and bowed in front of Ben. The boys snickered.

"The lady, in turn, makes a curtsy. Let's pretend you did one, Ben. And now the gentleman offers his arm, and they walk together." She demonstrated this with the boy, whose cheeks pinked. "Let's pair up so everyone can try."

The twins practiced with each other, Ben picked Tobby, and Ella approached Digby while she kept an eye on everyone. "Very nice, gentlemen. Those of us playing the ladies must keep our backs straight when we curtsy. The trick that my mother taught me was to pretend I have a sixpence clenched between my buttocks and don't want to lose it."

The comment made the boys double over with laughter, and she had to give them a break from the practice. When they caught their breath from chortling, she led them to the captain's dining room, where white china plates and elegant silverware adorned the table. The salted beef and mushy vegetables looked palatable in ivory serving dishes. The boys froze.

"We'll eat here, from the captain's plates?" Tobby marveled.

"Yes, but please be careful. The captain was kind to let me use them."

The boys sat at the table, and she served the cold beef and vegetables for everyone but Tobby.

"Sorry, Tobby, you're getting broth today to go easy on your belly. You'll learn how to eat properly with a spoon, while the rest of you will work with knives and forks."

The boys grabbed their utensils in their fists, but she demonstrated a proper grip. "This is how you hold your fork. No elbows on the table, Digby."

The boy obeyed at first, but then spread his elbows and gave her a defiant gaze. "Why're we doing this? We'll never eat with the captain or anyone else important."

The other boys' smiles faded, and they stared down at their plates.

"Don't be an ass, Digby. This is fun," Tobby said.

"It's bunkum. The seamen don't eat holding their forks all proper. We eat with our hands or jackknives. We're not the officers."

Ella gave him a piercing stare. "You *can* be one day. Lieutenant Wyse came onto the ship a boy like you. Now he's the second most important person on the ship, after the captain." She wanted to barb about Wyse's poor manners but held her tongue.

"I don't believe that story," Ben said with his mouth full. "It's seamen's yarn."

"You should swallow first, then speak. Mr. Wyse told me the story himself. He said it was better than working at the mill."

Jimmy nodded. "Johnny and I worked at the mill. The ship is better."

"And better than the orphanage." Ben elbowed Tobby. "Right?"

Tobby bobbed his head. "Oh yes, by miles. The other children were so mean."

"I guess it's better than jail," Digby added.

Everyone quieted and stared at him, forks frozen in the air.

"What? My da's there. My ma visits him. She thought Da got a better lot than me."

"And what do you think?" Ella asked.

He shrugged. "The ship's not so bad. I got friends here."

I wish I had friends, Ella thought.

"Doctor Ella, where's your mother?" Tobby asked.

Ella suppressed a sigh. "She died while giving birth to my brother three years ago."

Tobby stared at his plate. "Do you have a father?"

"No. My father died soon after my mother passed. He ruined his health and mind with his drinking, and then suffered a horse-riding accident."

The boys chewed in silence, until Tobby spoke. "You're an orphan like us. Well, almost all of us, because Digby has parents."

"Is that why you don't like that the men drink? Because of how your father died?" Digby asked.

She hugged herself. "That's one of the reasons. As a doctor, I know the health problems too much drinking can bring. Poisoning, accidents, cirrhosis of the liver."

"There's going to be lots of drinking tonight," Ben mused.

"Music and dancing too," Jimmy added.

"But it's such a sad day. Poor Mr. Hart died." Her throat thickened at the memory of the seaman's shattered body.

"Hart played merry tunes on his fiddle. He'd want his friends to remember him with music," Johnny explained.

Ella glanced at her clothes. "Then I better change. Or maybe... Yes, I'll go as I am."

The boys stared at her. "Why would you wear trousers when you have pretty dresses?" Jimmy asked.

"I'm hoping to fit in this way."

The boys kept staring without comprehension in their eyes. She changed the subject. "Let's enjoy raspberry jam for dessert. Help me clear your plates. Johnny, you barely ate."

"My tooth is wiggling." The boy pointed into his mouth.

"He's not Johnny," his twin snickered.

Ella snorted. "Yes, he is. I've no problem telling you two apart. Johnny, I can remove your tooth."

The boy hid his mouth behind his hands.

"As you wish. Tobby, please don't suck your fingers, it's a bad habit."

After removing the dinner plates, she brought out the jam, saucers, cups, and spoons and poured the tea.

"Sorry, Tobby, only tea for you. But I'm saving another jar of Matilda's best jam for when you can have it. How's your belly?"

"Good. I think I can have a couple of spoons of that jam."

"No more than two. All right, everyone, enjoy the tea. Hold your teacups by the handle and don't cradle them. I'll get that salve for Ben. Johnny, are you sure you don't want me to extract your tooth? You'll be able to eat meat again."

"Fine," Johnny said in a small voice.

"You promised hankies for everyone," Ben reminded her.

"Yes sir. I'll be back."

She made her way to the sickbay, where she found Tyler feeding Dr. Pesce his dinner. The two men gawked at her clothes.

Ella turned in a circle to demonstrate her attire. "Don't look so surprised, Doctor. These are the clothes that you gave me before I left for medical school."

The doctor frowned. "Right. But why're you wearing them? With your hair almost to your shoulders, you don't resemble a boy anymore. And you look ... womanly... in other ways as well."

Ella's cheeks heated at the last comment. "I'm trying to fit in with the crew. Besides, I'm tired of washing blood and dirt off my skirts. These clothes are more comfortable and freeing. Maybe I could even climb the rigging in them."

The doctor waved his hands. "Don't even think of it. Too dangerous. But I admit you do look handsome."

"That's not the point, doctor. All right, I'm here to fetch the salve and the forceps. Then I need to get back to my class."

"Your class?"

"I'm teaching the ship boys good manners."

Tyler snorted. "What do they need them for?"

"To grow up into decent people and not barbarians. Let me know if you want a lesson, Tyler."

The loblolly scowled at her.

"It's nice that you're watching over the children," the doctor said. "But don't indulge them. These rascals need a firm hand, or they spoil faster than fruit in the sun. Today you made Tobby drink the castor oil, and he's better."

"Let's hope. I doubt if I addressed the underlying problem."

The doctor rubbed his abdomen. "The ship's diet makes everyone costive. I used to have an iron stomach, but now I suffer from closed bowels."

Ella threw up her hands. "You should've said something. That's why you've been eating poorly. I'll brew some senna leaves for you."

Dr. Pesce groaned. "Please Ella, I don't need you ministering to me. Tyler will give me an enema. That's all that can be done for this capricious old man whose bowels refuse to work."

"Maybe after you feel better, you'll come up to hear the music for a little while?"

The doctor huffed. "That's the last thing I want. Go enjoy yourself, Ella. Don't dwell on what happened with Hart's surgery. I suspect the pressure from swelling built up so much that the brain hemorrhaged through the foramen at the base of the skull. In that case, he was beyond saving."

She sighed. "That makes me feel a bit better. Poor man. And his poor wife."

"You did your job. The outcome is not up to you. Now go, have a little fun to lift your spirits."

After bidding Dr. Pesce good night, she unlocked the dispensary and collected the forceps for Johnny's tooth and the salve for Ben's neck. The laudanum jar caught her attention, and she brought it to her eyes. The level of the liquid inside hadn't changed from that morning.

Chapter 10

The seamen, seated in a circle around the musician, clapped their hands and tapped their feet to a jolly tune. Wyse stood near the railing and sipped his flask. The purser poured grog from the wooden tub into the metal cups. The men lined up to drink and then rejoined the circle to enjoy the music. Williams proved to be an excellent fiddler. After some sad tunes to reminisce about the dead topman, he switched to the happier song, *Spanish Ladies*. Hart played that song often. He was a decent fellow who enjoyed harmless pranks. Except his last prank, to collect bets on who'd be the first to bed Ella, went too far. Wyse shook his head.

Damn that woman. Such folly because of her.

He was about to order the men to rest when she put her nose into his business. After she declared that the men needed a break and water, he had to keep them working, or it would look like she commanded him. And then, ten minutes after she sauntered to the captain's cabin and likely complained to Captain Grey about his rude lieutenant, Hart lost his grip and fell.

Men died at sea. On every voyage, the captain would mark '*D.D.*' for 'Discharged, Dead' by someone's name. An empty space would emerge where someone once sat at meals. The men would whisper about the dead, choosing their words carefully, as if their ghosts lurked nearby. And when the death struck because of an officer's blunder, the men would remember. The crew would enjoy the music and the extra grog, but in their hammocks they'd whisper that it was Lieutenant Wyse who caused their friend's death. *Unless...*

He advanced towards Simkins, who sat with his cronies. The song Williams was playing had words unfit for polite company, and that group bellowed them the loudest. Wyse disliked Simkins, but the bully's big fists and an eager tongue attracted a large following. If one wanted to start a rumor, he'd tell it to Simkins, and by morning every man would hear it.

When the song finished, he motioned for Simkins to approach. The seaman stared with apprehension, and Wyse offered him tobacco for his pipe and a sip from his flask. He winked at the seaman. "Enjoy. It's home-brewed."

Simkins smacked his lips. "Thank you, sir. Your drink tastes like cider, but I hear it goes right to the head if you aren't used to it."

"It's applejack. My friend makes barrels of it all winter. Warms up the blood and makes any sad business easier to bear. Like poor Hart. One moment a healthy fellow going about his work, and the next, dead as a doornail."

Simkins rubbed his chin. "Sad business for sure, but the hot day..."

"And suspicious too. I get goosebumps thinking about it."

"I heard..."

Wyse slapped the seaman's shoulder. "About the woman, right? Hart didn't mean any harm, but she took offense at his prank. Next thing we know, he fell."

Simkins gaped and crossed himself. "She must've cursed him! The moment I saw her, I knew she was a witch. Bloody hell!"

"Tell your friends not to go near her."

"Right. Have you heard that she's giving lessons to the ship boys on how to be gentlemen? Who knows what she'll teach them next."

Wyse's face heated. *That's her trick to spite me. She's doing this to show everyone that even the ship boys have better manners than me.*

"Golly! Look at her over there, dressed in trousers." Simkins pointed. "Shameless hussy. No god-fearing woman would do such a thing."

Wyse scanned for Ella. He hadn't noticed her until the seaman indicated. With short hair and men's clothing, she blended in from the distance.

Odds bodkins! What is she thinking?

He strode in her direction.

Ella crouched among the ship boys, Olson and a few others. Rogers, one of the men punished with Hart, was telling her something. Wyse strained to hear.

"Hart's bet was only a joke," the lad said. "We meant no harm."

Her cheeks flushed. "All right. But how would you feel if someone made such a bet about your sister or your sweetheart, if you have them?"

Rogers stared down. "I have both, and I wouldn't like it. I'm sorry, Miss... I mean Doctor. We didn't think. Please don't be mad at us."

Ella gave a small nod. "I'm not mad, only shocked. But poor Hart is dead. Saving him was beyond my skill."

"Err... Your tools gave us a scare. What were you doing?"

Olson rolled his eyes. "I told you, lad. It's surgery. I've seen Dr. Pesce use that drill when a fellow broke his head. That man never walked or talked again, but he lived."

Ella's shoulders slumped. "Dr. Pesce has decades of experience. I have a lot to learn."

Wyse was surprised at her admission. Perhaps the guilt of her failure consumed her, prompting her to share her feelings with the men.

Rogers scratched his head. "If you ask me, I'd rather die quickly than lay like a log my whole life."

Wyse silently agreed. Few things scared him more than the prospect of being bedridden. No one would care for him.

An upbeat tune jarred him from dark thoughts. The men stomped their feet to the jig. Ella rose and offered her hand to Digby, inviting him to dance. The boy drew in his neck like a hermit crab. She then turned to Olson and clasped his hand. He stepped back, stunned. Wyse didn't expect her to ask a colored man to dance. He admired her in that moment.

Rogers wrapped his arm around Ella's waist and brought her into the middle of the circle. Both were light on their feet and made an impressive series of hops and turns. The crew cheered. The girl's cheeks reddened and beads of sweat glistened from her forehead. Some of the men stopped dancing and stared at her bosom, which bounced with her leaps.

She's having too much fun for her own good, Wyse thought.

After the music stopped, she returned to the boys and asked them something. Digby, Tobby, and Ben scrambled to their feet and hurried away. Wyse crouched down where they sat a moment ago.

"I sent the boys for water," she panted. "Not just for me. The men should drink."

"They are drinking grog," Wyse answered, not liking where this conversation was headed.

Ella frowned. "They seem merry enough without the extra spirits. And the boys shouldn't drink anything stronger than watered-down wine."

He scoffed. "I told you not to put your nose where it doesn't belong. What do you think you are doing, dressed in men's clothes like a freak?"

Her lips turned down. "I want to fit in. The men should see me as a friend."

"You can't have friends."

The words spurted instinctively because he repeated them over and over to himself the first year he became a lieutenant. After promotion, he severed bonds with all his chosen brothers. As an officer, he was above them, and it was his duty to work them, to reward them, and to punish them. He took on a conspiratorial tone to get information out of them, but he was no longer their mate.

She stared towards the dark sea. "That's so lonely."

"Then go back to your palace and dance at the balls."

She squeezed her eyes shut, like he hit her, but then composed her face and raised her chin. "You won't be rid of me so easily, Mr. Wyse. Now, since the boys aren't back, I'll find water for myself. Or maybe you'd be a gentleman and bring me some?"

He glared at her. "I'm not your errand boy."

"Or a gentleman."

She muttered the words under her breath, but he read her lips. Red spots flashed before his eyes. His arm itched to slap her. Seized by an idea, he offered her his flask.

"Here."

She gulped with greed. Her face squeezed, and she doubled over with a cough. "That wasn't water," she rasped after catching her breath.

"Don't look at me with such horror. It's only cider. Or is it not good enough for you?"

"Cider suits me fine. I thought it was something stronger." She took another sip and returned the flask. "Thank you, Mr. Wyse. I was quite thirsty after dancing. It's time I head back to my cabin."

She made a couple of unsteady steps, then turned back. "The waves must be picking up. I'll sit down for a spell."

He shrugged. The sea was as calm as it was all evening. He raised the flask to his lips, but only a few drops came out. He was unsure how much he had in there before giving it to her. Maybe half the flask. He winced, anticipating the headache she'd wake up with the next morning.

Good. Enough of her acting like she's better than everyone.

"Sail ho!" the lookout yelled. The music and songs halted.

"Where?" Wyse jumped to his feet.

"Three points on the larboard, sir."

Wyse turned to the remaining ship boys, the twins. "Jimmy, run and get my glass, next to my cot in my cabin. Johnny, knock on the captain's cabin door. Tell him the lookout spotted a sail."

"Aye aye, sir," the boys answered in unison and ran off.

He went to the side and peered into the darkness. A wonder the lookout discerned a sail with only a sliver of the crescent and sprinkling of stars giving faint light. If proven right, Wyse would reward him for his sharp eye.

"Sir." Jimmy saluted and handed him the glass.

His brother wheezed next to him. "Sir, the captain's coming."

Johnny took out a lace handkerchief and wiped his sweaty face. Wyse's jaw fell open. *What's Ella doing to the boys? Soon she'll have them bowing like princes.*

Putting the boys out of his mind, he adjusted the glass. Nothing resembling a sail loomed in the black vastness.

"Call the lookout here," Wyse said to the ship boys.

The captain approached. "What do we have here, Wyse?" He was in his undress uniform, without the gold braid and epaulets, ready to give the signal to prepare for a battle.

"Sorry, sir, but I don't see a sail. I sent for the man who spotted it."

The captain opened his telescope. "I don't see it either. Either our man has the eyes of a hawk, or his vision played a trick."

The lookout approached with wobbliness in his gait. Wyse recognized Perkins, an experienced and cheerful seaman. Judging from his way of walking, he partook in the drinking before going aloft.

"Where did you see the sail, Perkins?" Wyse asked.

The man pointed. "I thought I saw a sail show itself over there but only for a moment."

"You're not sure?"

"No, sir... I saw white. Maybe a bird. An albatross."

Perkins exhaled. Wyse smelled grog on his breath. An experienced man like Perkins could climb the rigging in his sleep, but the captain winced and shook his head. "Had some grog, didn't you? We already lost one man today because of a fall. Wyse, send someone up who's clear-headed enough to distinguish between a sail and an albatross. I'll wait at the quarterdeck."

After saluting the captain, Wyse advanced to the lingering men who gathered by the foremast. When the entertainment stopped, some went below, but most stayed to learn about the sail, excited about a potential battle. None of them looked fully sober. He glimpsed Digby with a jug of water and called for him.

"Sir." The boy put down the jug and saluted.

"Do you have good eyes, Digby?"

"Aye, sir. I used to hunt rabbits with my da."

"Can you run up the rigging?"

He gave an eager look. "Aye, sir."

"Did you drink tonight?"

The boy continued to stand at full attention. "No, sir. The lady doctor won't let me and the other boys drink nothing but water."

Wyse nodded, satisfied. "Then I want you to climb up to the topgallant crosstrees with my glass and see if you can spot a sail. It would be on the larboard, if it's there at all."

The lad's face lit up. "Aye, sir."

Digby accepted the glass reverently, put it in the pocket of his wide trousers, and scaled the rigging with the agility of a baboon. Wyse watched with admiration as the boy cleared one yard after another. When he reached the crosstrees, he was no bigger than a dot to Wyse's eyes.

"No sail. There's a flock of birds flying about," Digby yelled from above.

"You sure?"

"Aye."

"Get down." *The boy would make a good topman*, Wyse thought, watching Digby climb. He sent a relatively sober man to take his place as lookout, and another to report to the captain that there was no ship. Digby ran over and handed Wyse his glass.

Wyse clapped him on the back. "Good job, lad. We'll make a topman out of you. Or since you've been learning proper manners, we could make you a midshipman, or a young gentleman, as we call them sometimes." Wyse grinned saying the last part, intending it as a joke. He made a step towards the quarterdeck to report to the captain, when Digby's voice stopped him.

"Would you, sir?"

He whipped his head around. "What's that?"

"Would you make me a midshipman, sir?"

Wyse cursed himself for the jest. He turned to the boy, who stared at him like a worshiper before a deity. "Digby..."

"Doctor Ella said you were a ship boy, and now you are the first lieutenant. If I become a midshipman, then I could be lieutenant too, and then a captain one day."

Wyse sighed. Years ago, he would tell the boy to stump out any dreams of walking the quarterdeck. Now, after Captain Grey gave him an opportunity he never dreamed of, he struggled to think of what to say without sounding like a hypocrite. "Lad, you can't read or write or do mathematics."

The boy swallowed. "I've learned to write my name. The lady doctor showed me."

"You know that's not enough. Midshipmen read charts, study navigation, copy notes for the captain. They must serve six years at sea and be nineteen years old before they can take the examination for lieutenant. A difficult examination, given by three captains."

Digby hung his head.

"Forget it, son. Topman's a decent job, you'll like it."

Digby raised his eyes and thrust forward the stubborn lower lip. "I can ask Doctor Ella to give me extra lessons."

Where is Ella? Wyse thought with a start.

In the commotion with the sail, he forgot about her. He scanned the men gathered near the bow. Ella wasn't with them. Most likely, she was soundly asleep in her cabin, but he had to make sure. This made for a delicate situation. Disturbing her this late or entering her cabin if she didn't answer would breach propriety. On the other hand, the captain ordered him to ensure her safety.

When he thought he'd have to go knock and risk a complaint from her, his eyes rested on the boy. "Digby, does Doctor Ella let you boys come to her cabin at night if you are sick?"

"Aye, sir. Tobby goes to her when his belly hurts."

"Check if she's in her cabin and doing alright."

"Aye, sir." He scratched his head. "What if she doesn't answer and her door is locked?"

Wyse wrinkled his forehead. He didn't like giving such a mission to the boy, but better make sure that Ella didn't pass out from the drink. "Do you know how to pick a lock?"

"Aye, sir." The boy gave him a look as if he asked him if he knew how to walk.

"If she doesn't answer, pick that lock as quietly as you can, and see if she's sleeping. Also, check the sickbay, but quietly. Don't wake Dr. Pesce. Then find me and report." He chewed his lip as he gave the command. Sending the boy to the woman's cabin wasn't exactly proper, but the boy seemed... only a boy.

Digby sped away. Wyse hurried to follow up with the captain, who paced the quarterdeck.

"No sail, sir. Perkins made a mistake," Wyse said, climbing the steps.

Captain Grey halted pacing. "So I've heard. Maybe it's the darkness to blame, but I prefer to see the men more coherent when going aloft. Let's not give our doctor another skull to fix."

Wyse shivered remembering the nightmarish tools Ella used on Hart's head. How the girl operated with them was beyond him.

"Sir." Digby shifted from one foot to another by the quarter-deck stairs.

Wyse cursed silently that he didn't ask the lad to wait for him somewhere out of the captain's eye. While he pondered what errand to send him on to cover his mistake, the captain piped. "What is it, boy?"

"Doctor Ella's not in her cabin or the sickbay, sir."

"What's that, Mr. Wyse?" the captain rounded on him. "Are we missing our doctor?"

"Aye, sir. She drank too much. I wanted to make sure she made it to her cabin."

Captain Grey winced. "How shameful. I thought better of her."

"Look, she's over there!" Digby bellowed.

Their eyes followed the boy's finger to the mizzenmast, where a small figure climbed the ratlines. Even though she wore trousers, Wyse was sure it was Ella. He cursed under his breath.

The captain gaped. "Good heavens! She may fall. Wyse, get her down."

Wyse and Digby hastened towards the mast. The boy pulled himself up onto the rigging and in a heartbeat was next to Ella. Wyse, swearing with every step, climbed behind him, glad that the darkness covered his clumsy ascend. He was a swift climber as a boy, and a skilled topman in his twenties, but now his joints ached, and his muscles protested the exercise.

"What are you doing, Doctor Ella?" Digby asked.

She giggled. "I'm climbing. This is fun."

"Get down right now," Wyse rasped.

"No! I want to get to... whatever that's on the top."

Digby piped. "It's late. You should go to bed."

She hiccupped. "I won't! I'm a daredevil seaman."

Ella scrambled upward, and Wyse struggled after her, his side aching, and his lungs burning. He was sure the men by the bow were watching him and sniggering at his clumsiness. None would help him without a direct order. Maybe they even hoped the sea gods would send him to the same fate as Hart suffered. His heart skipped a beat from such a dark notion.

The girl was under the fighting top, and Wyse considered whether he should talk her into getting on it. He'd talk some sense into her while she rested there. Digby must've had the same idea, as he pointed out the lubber's hole to Ella. The girl's arms reached for the platform, but her fingers missed their grip. One foot slipped off the ratline. She tumbled down a step with a piercing shriek. Life-preserving instincts kicked in, and she found her footing. Wyse reached for her; his arm found her waist.

"Steady now. You're fine."

The jolt must've sobered her. She gazed about, wide-eyed, her mouth gaping. A shiver passed through her as he held her under his arm. A gasp left her lips when she glanced below. Her voice quivered. "It's so high. What have I done?"

"Don't look down. Never look down."

He accidentally peeked down, and his stomach dropped. Out of practice, he forgot how startling it was to perceive the deck from above. The man at the wheel and the captain at the quarterdeck were mere insects from this height.

"Digby, you get down. Don't need you in the way," he told the boy, who clung to the ratlines right under the platform. He expected Digby to descend the same way they came up, but the lad raised himself to the platform and then swung his lean body onto a shroud. In a moment, he slid downward, his hands and knees wound around the cable. Wyse cringed at the memory of rope burns from such feats.

"Now we climb down," he said to her.

Moonlight shone on Ella's face. Tears glistened as they ran down her cheeks. "I can't."

"You can't bloody stay here. You got yourself into this mess, you get yourself out of it. Rest on the platform for a bit."

He helped her up to the platform. Sighing, she leaned against the mast and closed her eyes.

When she didn't move for a few minutes, he nudged her. "No sleeping. Climb down. One foot at a time, and then one hand at a time. Hold on to the shrouds, not the ratlines. Those can part."

With a deep breath, she tiptoed to the lubber's hole. After a pause, she took a hesitant step down, then another.

"Yes, yes, you're doing fine," he yelled as he climbed behind her. Descent required more care than climbing up because it was easier to misstep. His knuckles whitened as he gripped the shrouds.

Many heart palpitations later, the girl's feet touched the deck, and she made a beeline to the railing. Relieved to be on the deck as well, Wyse mourned the waste of good applejack on a girl who couldn't hold her drink. Shame, but that's the payback for strutting around like a princess and prattling about good manners.

When Ella finished retching, he gave her a hand to rise. The captain approached, shaking his head. "I can't believe what I see, Doctor. What would happen if you fell? We don't have another doctor to tend to you or anyone who may need you. I'd forbid you from leaving your cabin, but you have your duties. See that you are fit to perform them by morning."

Ella's head slumped low; she resembled a broken doll.

"Do you have anything to say for yourself?" He continued.

The girl sighed and yawned.

The captain wrinkled his nose from her breath. "And you, Mr. Wyse?"

Wyse tensed. *Did the captain guess that I got her drunk?* "Sir?"

"I thought you'd tell her that you don't appreciate having to climb after her. You're not so fit anymore to enjoy such an exercise."

Wyse cleared his throat. "That's right. Climbing the rigging isn't for landlubber women."

Ella yawned with her eyes half-closed and leaned on Wyse's shoulder. Her curls tickled his neck.

Captain Grey rolled his eyes. "Take her to her cabin, Wyse."

With Digby's help, he dragged her insensible body to her cabin. When they reached the pathway, Tobby was waiting there, shifting from one foot to another. Wyse wondered if the boy needed Ella's ministrations. Guilt pinched his chest.

Wyse was glad Ella had men's clothes on, and he wouldn't need to consider what to do with her corset or petticoats. He pulled off her jacket and boots, leaving her in her loose shirt and trousers. The boys fluffed her pillow and covered her with a blanket.

"Maybe she has a fever? Digby, check her forehead," Tobby said.

Digby touched her face with great care. "She's not hot."

Wyse grunted. "She's not sick. She's drunk. Let's put a jug of water by her cot so she relieves her thirst and washes her face in the morning."

Tobby stared at her closed eyes. "She can't be drunk. She wouldn't drink grog."

"It's strange," Digby answered. "She was fine till she went dancing. Then she got thirsty and asked us to fetch water."

Wyse's tooth gave him a pang. "Lads, I'm telling you, she's fine. Everyone gets drunk sometimes."

Digby shook his head. "She's different."

Tobby had tears in his eyes. "She's like a princess from a story where everyone bows and curtsies, and talks without cussing, and eats cakes."

Wyse sneered. "Then she should get back to her fairytale palace. We don't need her to tell us how to live. Right, boys?"

The boys looked down and didn't answer. Wyse sighed. An uncomfortable sensation was poking his chest, telling him he was betraying the children, including the child he once was.

"It's late, boys. Go to sleep."

Tobby thrust his chin forward. "I'm staying with her."

"Me too," Digby echoed.

Wyse chewed his lip. The girl could be sick again or fall off her cot. He allowed them to stay.

The events of the night gnawed at him, and he had no more liquor handy to drown his gloom. He spent the rest of the night walking the deck, barking commands at the sleepy men, and cursing all women.

Chapter 11

Tears streamed down Ella's hot cheeks and fell into her tea. Her headache finally subsided by the afternoon, but the weeping brought it back with full force. She was thankful to run into Mr. Doolittle in the galley. The chaplain sat her down on the stool, made tea for her and coffee for himself, and urged her to share her troubles.

Her voice quivered. "I'm as wretched as my father, who drank and acted recklessly. And just like him, I barely remember what happened. I don't even recall what I drank and when."

Mr. Doolittle shifted on his stool as he stirred molasses into his coffee. "What an unfortunate incident. I must say I'm surprised, although I shouldn't be. Life at sea tempts the stoutest of souls into sin. You should reconsider wearing men's clothing. I see a connection between your unladylike appearance and your shameful behavior."

Ella stared down at the trousers she was wearing. "These clothes are easier to care for and to move around in. They can't be the reason I overindulged."

The chaplain clicked his tongue. "Remember what the Bible says. 'A woman shall not wear anything that pertains to a man, nor shall a man put on a woman's garment, for all who do so are an abomination to the Lord your God.'"

She bit her lip to stifle an argument that in Biblical times neither men nor women wore trousers. Her religious upbringing forbade her from arguing with clergymen.

"I'll think on it, Mr. Doolittle. I will wear a proper dress to dinner on the *Crown*."

The chaplain smiled with approval. "The captains and their officers are more suitable company for you than the coarse sailors. The ship's crew is a bad influence on you."

Ella sipped her tea, salty with her tears. "I was mortified to hear of my conduct from the boys. Yesterday I gave them a lesson in good manners, and then I showed the most despicable example. I woke up with a splitting headache and a parched mouth. Tobby and Digby thought me ill and nursed me."

Mr. Doolittle clicked his tongue again. "I'm happy you befriended the boys, but I don't approve of you letting them visit you at night. Digby, at fourteen, is almost a man. And Tobby may be more after your attention than your bellyache remedies."

She shook her head. "He's suffering, and I feel useless because I can't cure him. I thought myself ready for the job, but... Mr. Hart died during my operation, my dear mentor Dr. Pesce is growing weaker, and the men avoid me even when they need my help. Only the boys trust me."

The chaplain nodded with understanding. "You are kind. The lonely children are drawn to you."

With a deep breath, she wiped her tears and composed her face. "I was thinking... if I can't figure out what's wrong with Tobby, I should bring him to London to see an esteemed physician."

Mr. Doolittle's eyes rounded. "That would cost a fortune. Surely your salary doesn't allow such expenditure."

"My salary, no, but I have the means."

"Is that right?"

"It's a long story." She gave a small smile. "The money won't be a problem. It would be worth it to cure the poor boy."

The chaplain fingered a cross on his neck. "You're a generous soul. I'll pray that Tobby and Dr. Pesce get better, and that you'll find purpose and happiness. Why don't you spend the time before dinner reading from your Bible? That should make you feel better. And remember, I'm your friend and happy to talk."

He beamed at her, and she returned his smile. Her soul lightened already.

***

Ella had little time to read the Bible per the chaplain's suggestion because she needed to dress for the evening. Splinters and blood ruined her ivory gown, but she had a velvet burgundy dress for the occasion. After a half-hour of tightening herself into a corset and wrestling with the mother-of-pearl buttons, she wiped the sweat off her brow. Her reflection in the glass showed sallow cheeks. She pinched them till they reddened. Her headache eased as she admired herself dressed in her finest, and jitters spread through her body. *Robert may attend the dinner.*

When she stepped onto the deck, the men stopped their work to stare. Suspicion and even fear were in their eyes. Ella desperately tried to recall the events of last night. She remembered vaguely that some seamen chatted and danced with her. She smiled at the men standing around, but the officer on duty yelled to them to stop gawking.

It's the dress, she told herself. *It sets me apart. Mr. Doolittle upholds that I must wear women's clothing, but the men were friendlier to me when I wore trousers. I can't please everyone.*

Under the coxswain's commands, the seamen lowered the captain's gig into the water. Ella, wrapped her shawl around her shoulders to keep warm, watched as they worked. The wind tugged at her skirts. Fresh sea air cured the ill effects of her indulgence.

Tobby ran up to her and whistled to call the other boys. They grinned as they studied the details of her dress. Ben bowed, and then the rest of them demonstrated their lesson in greeting a lady.

She smiled at them and checked on Ben's itchy neck, which was much improved, and she reminded Digby to wash behind his ears. She was going to ask Tobby about his bellyache, but the captain emerged in his full uniform, his sword fastened to his side. The ship boys saluted him and scattered when he waved them off.

Captain Grey bowed to her with a smug expression. "Now there's a lady I can bring to a fancy dinner."

Ella smoothed her dress. "I'm sorry for my conduct last night... It won't happen again."

"You don't sound sure."

She sighed. "It's just that I can't recall what I drank and how much."

He chuckled. "I suspect a good amount if you can't even remember drinking."

Ella's cheeks heated, and she stared down. "I'm so ashamed."

The captain gave her his arm. "Cheer up, Doctor. These things happen. I'm sure you wanted a little fun and didn't know your measure. Not to encourage you, but your climb was impressive."

Her eyes went towards the mizzenmast platform. The thought of being up so high made her flinch, although a little part of her wished that she remembered the view more clearly. "I've made a fool of myself. Do the men know of my behavior?"

He puffed. "Plenty of them saw you on the rigging. I'm afraid you're the subject of the day."

"Oh bloody hell." She covered her mouth with her hand. "I don't know what's wrong with me. Now I'm cussing."

The captain shook his head. "I hope I can count on better behavior at dinner."

The boat was ready for them, and they stepped onto the boatswain's chair, and then into the boat. Coxswain Morgan ordered the men to row towards the *Crown.* The boat bobbed on gentle waves in the twilight. Ella touched the surface of the water and found it cool and refreshing.

The *Crown* grew larger; Ella gawked at its enormous size. The ship had two gun decks. Three magnificent masts seemed to touch the sky. An elaborate figurehead of a bare-breasted mermaid, wearing a crown, decorated the bow.

Ella ogled at the indecent mermaid, then averted her eyes when the captain snickered at her curiosity.

"Didn't mermaids supposedly tempt sailors to jump into the sea and drown?" Ella asked, giving her face a serious expression to mask her embarrassment.

The captain inclined his head. "True. But as figureheads, they are believed to calm the seas. What do you think of the ship? It's a giant compared to the *Neptune*."

"It's impressive. How many men and guns does it have?"

"She's a ship of the line. Seventy-four guns, about six hundred and fifty men."

"Goodness. Their surgeon must have his hands full."

Captain Grey rolled his eyes. "If he'll be at dinner, please don't speak of medicine. I don't want to hear about leeches again." He shook his finger. "Oh, that reminds me. I received another note from Captain Weston. He requested that I bring Dr. Pesce's niece to this dinner. Seems like you're impatiently expected."

A warm sensation pulsed through her. "Robert."

"I told you he didn't forget you. He must've told his father you are Dr. Pesce's relation and my guest, so play along."

She fidgeted on her shaky seat and smoothed the velvety fabric of her gown. "You said to dress my best for the dinner. A doctor's niece, probably a girl of modest means, wouldn't own a dress like this."

Captain Grey shrugged. " I'm sure you'll think of an explanation. More importantly, don't show off your medical knowledge above what a doctor's niece may know."

Ella nodded, and they stepped onto the chair to be lifted to the deck of the *Crown.*

***

The captain's dining room on the *Crown* could've enclosed three of the *Neptune's*. The table, covered with a lace tablecloth, was set with white china plates with the emblem of the ship, a gold crown. The silver candleholders illuminated the space. The room boasted Persian rugs, Chinese vases, and figurines made of elephant tusks. If not for the ship's pitches and rolls, Ella could pretend she was visiting a wealthy Newcastle neighbor with an exotic taste.

Captain Weston, a handsome man in his fifties, his hair all white and his face aged with frown lines, bowed elegantly after her curtsy. The gold ribbons and medals on his uniform swayed as he did so. Other officers bowed as well. Ella beamed, spying Robert among them.

"When my son asked me to invite the doctor's niece, I wasn't expecting a princess of such beauty to visit us. How did you come to Grey's humble ship, my dear?" Captain Weston asked.

Ella had the story prepared. "My uncle, Dr. Pesce, is my only family. I've missed him dearly, and after much persuasion, he agreed to let me join him for a voyage. He believes the sea air would benefit my health."

"I know Dr. Pesce as one of the finest surgeons in the service. Since you look so splendid, the remedy must be working wonderfully for you." He winked at his friend. "Grey, how do you keep such a treasure safe?"

Captain Grey chuckled. "I gave that job to Mr. Wyse, and he has his hands full."

The host feigned shock. "To Wyse? In that case, the lady must be in dire need of polite company."

Some of the officers sniggered at their captain's jest. Righteous anger beat at Ella's chest. *Must everyone laugh at his poor manners, especially behind his back?* She had no chance to speak to him about the events of last night, but from her vague memories, the lieutenant saved her life.

She gave the officers a stern look. "Mr. Wyse is a brave man and my protector."

Captain Weston cocked his head. "Well, if there's ever a need, we'll find you even better protection on the *Crown* and more comfortable accommodations as well. Let me introduce you to my officers. Mr. Brown, the first lieutenant, Mr. Sawyer, the second lieutenant." He gestured at the two men by his side, and they bowed their heads. "And you've met my third lieutenant. My son, Robert Weston." The captain's voice was full of affection and pride.

Robert stepped forward. He looked as dashing as she remembered him. His thoughts must've been about their first meeting as well. After his bow, he took her hand, brought it to his lips and whispered, "I dreamed of seeing you again."

Captain Weston introduced the other men: the four midshipmen, and the ship surgeon Dr. Martin. The doctor and the lieutenants gave her looks of admiration and complimented her beauty, while the young gentlemen gawked and blushed. Ella basked in their attention.

Such a pleasant change to be marveled at instead of loathed, she thought.

Meanwhile, the steward completed his last touches to the table setting. The host invited everyone to sit, offering Ella his arm. He seated her between Captain Grey and Robert, across from the *Crown's* surgeon, while he took a seat at the head of the table. A freckled thirteen-year-old midshipman, following the tradition, gave a toast "to the King," and everyone raised their wine glasses. Then, like a conductor starting a concert, Captain Weston waved his hand for the steward to raise the silver lids and reveal the dishes: lobsters, cooked whole; a dish of oysters, and a seafood stew, bouillabaisse.

The young midshipmen stared unhappily at the meal. The freckled youth, who gave the toast, whispered to the other lads, "Can't we have beef?"

"I agree with him," Captain Grey muttered.

Captain Weston beamed at the selection and the effect it was producing. "My chef slaved over this menu to please us. Are my friends not brave enough to try these dishes? I bet our charming guest is ravenous for something better than salted pork and hardtack."

Ella beamed. After last night's adventure, she drank cups of chamomile tea to settle her stomach. The aroma of butter and fresh fish made her mouth water. "This is a treat, captain."

"Allow me to serve you," Robert said. "What would you like to try first?"

“The bouillabaisse.”

Captain Weston nodded. “Great choice. My chef lived in Marseille and learned the authentic recipe.”

Robert filled her plate, and the other guests helped themselves as well. Captain Grey observed what utensil she picked up and copied her. Ella found it endearing that the captain was fearless in battle but anxious at a formal dinner.

A man with a curled-up mustache added another dish to the table. Ella guessed him to be the French chef.

“What did you bring us, Jacques?” Captain Weston asked.

“Please let it be chicken,” Captain Grey piped, folding his hands together as if in prayer.

“Frog legs, sir,” Jacques answered and, with Ella’s permission, put one piece on Ella’s plate.

Doctor Martin’s fork slipped out of his hands and fell with a thud, making everyone glance in his direction.

Weston gave him an annoyed gaze. “You’ve been dropping things all over the place, Doctor. Is your hand not steady enough to cut the food?”

Doctor Martin clasped his hands together, covering a tremor. “I’m simply surprised by the exotic dish, that’s all.”

Ella tried to distract the others from the surgeon’s blunder. “It’s prepared expertly. *Délicieux. Compliments au chef.*” She hoped Dr. Martin’s tremor was nerves and nothing more.

“Do you speak French fluently, Miss Parker?” Robert asked.

"Yes and Spanish as well. I…" Ella halted as she realized such erudition might be unusual for a doctor's niece. "I translated medical texts for my uncle."

Captain Weston turned his lips down. "That sounds tedious. I hope your uncle doesn't expose you to his gruesome work. Although, I suppose that can't be helped during battles. How frightening it must be for you to hide in the orlop with the wounded men, where your uncle's cutting off their limbs."

A couple of midshipmen shivered at the image. Mr. Sawyer lowered his fork.

Dr. Martin piped. "My wife joined me on one voyage and was a great help with the wounded. Maybe Miss Parker inherited her uncle's interests in medicine?" His hands trembled again when he raised a spoon to his lips.

Captain Weston waved his arm. "Please, no woman should be interested in blood or other bodily fluids. It goes against their nature. Am I right, Miss Parker?"

Ella drew air through her teeth. Arguments about her abilities and accomplishments were on her tongue, but she stuck with her role of a submissive doctor's niece. "Well… I help my uncle. Bring the wounded water, give them encouragement."

The host beamed. "Such compassion is most womanly. The *Neptune* crew is lucky to have you. Still, I'm glad my daughter is safe at home. Have any of you heard of what happened to Captain Fitzharris's daughter? The sad story happened on the *Neptune*."

Captain Grey frowned. "Fitzharris, my predecessor? I received the command after he died. Never heard of his daughter."

"Oh, it was ages ago, but the naval wives spoke of nothing else for months. The foolish young woman ventured onto the deck during a battle and died from the enemy fire."

"How awful. I'm surprised Wyse never mentioned her. Let this be a lesson to you, Miss Parker. Please stay out of harm's way." Captain Grey gave her a meaningful look.

The memory of the booming shot and the flying splinters unfolded before her eyes. The room spun. Ella gulped water to keep the nausea down.

"Are you all right, Miss Parker?" Robert inquired. "You've gone pale. I'm sorry the tragic tale affected you."

"Women are such delicate creatures," Mr. Brown muttered.

Ella warmed from their concern. "I'm fine, but let's talk about something more pleasant. Captain Weston, you've mentioned your daughter. I'd love to hear about her."

Captain Weston beamed. "Like Robert, Lydia's my pride and joy. She will soon be married to Samuel Bathgate, the son of Admiral Bathgate."

Chuckling, Captain Grey raised one eyebrow. "Is that right? Then I wish her all the *wealth* in the world."

"Ha!" The host snorted. "You should talk when you have *two* daughters. Will you let Miss Bella and Miss Cecilia marry for such a vague notion as love?"

Captain Grey sipped his wine. "What else could I expect when their mother and I set such a terrible example? We married for love, and when we see each other, we're blissfully happy."

Ella grinned at her captain. His feelings for his wife and daughters were obvious in his voice.

"Young people, don't listen to this madman!" Captain Weston shook his finger and gave a comically stern look first to the midshipmen, and then to Robert and Ella. "Marriage is a serious business. Any money or property a woman possesses becomes her husband's. My daughter learned in her cradle that she's to marry a wealthy man. And my son," he glanced at Robert, "also knows that his future wife must increase the family fortune. Right, my boy?"

Robert reddened and glanced at Ella. Her breath quieted as she waited for an answer. "I hope to be blessed to marry a woman who's wealthy not only with money, but with intelligence and beauty."

He beamed at Ella, and her heart jumped.

Surely, he means me. Is he considering marriage already? Ella wondered. Her wild excitement surprised her.

"And what do you think, Miss Parker?" Robert asked her.

Her mouth went dry. Everyone's eyes were on her as her mind raced for what to say. "I... I believe a wife is more than a dowry. Women are given minds and hands to do good."

A pause ensued. Captain Weston furrowed his brow. Ella bit her lip at her forwardness. Then the captain of the *Crown* clapped. "Right you are. An officer's wife is his ally and his guardian angel. My wife befriends all the right people at the Admiralty and heads several charities. Her efforts contributed to my career rise as much as my achievements. Gentlemen, let's drink to steadfast women who are the beacons of our stormy lives."

The men clinked their glasses. Robert's hazel eyes shined, and he gave her an admiring look. Captain Weston gazed from Ella to Robert and scratched his cheek.

The host pushed away his plate. Most of the food was consumed by this time. "The dinner and conversation were marvelous, but it's time to discuss battle strategy. I don't want to bore our lovely guest. Robert, would you take Miss Parker for a stroll on the deck? I'll fill you in later. Bring her back soon for dessert and a game of Whist."

Ella rose, nodded to the gentlemen who rose as well, and left the dining room on Robert's arm. As she stepped out, Captain Weston asked, "Grey, where did you say Miss Parker's from?" She prayed silently that her captain would keep her confidence. As she said to Captain Weston, she was more than a dowry, and hoped to prove it.

They came out to the main deck, expansive compared to the *Neptune's*. A veil of darkness spread over the ebbing sea. The wind whispered a secret and gulls screamed in answer. Robert led Ella towards the bow. The men, who holystoned the deck, saluted their lieutenant as he passed.

"Ever since we met in Plymouth, I dreamed of bringing you here," Robert said.

"You anticipated this meeting, Mr. Weston?"

He leaned onto the railing, studying her. "Please call me Robert. I knew there was a chance, since our ships previously fought together, and my father is fond of dining with Captain Grey. You cut your hair since I last saw you."

Ella touched her shoulder-length locks, recalling the wig she wore to Veronica's wedding. "Yes. It's hard to properly wash hair on the ship. I collect rainwater when I can."

"Short hair looks good on you. How are you faring on the *Neptune*?"

"Not as well as I'd hoped."

He gave her a worried look. "Are you safe? No one's hurt you?"

She gazed at the *Neptune* heaving a short distance away. "I'm safe. It's that instead of coming to me for help, the men avoid me."

"I'm not surprised. Men don't like to see the surgeon in general, and a woman surgeon is too much of a novelty to them. Does this upset you, Miss Ella? "

The sound of her name on his lips made her giddy.

Her eyes found his. "Most days I'm lonely and unhappy, but I'm having a wonderful time tonight."

Robert held her chilled hands, spreading a warm sensation into her chest. "You deserve to be showered with attention. You're a mysterious firefly that has brightened my life."

Ella gave a soft laugh. "Mysterious? I imagine your father is mystified by me. Not the modest doctor's niece he expected."

"He's most impressed by you, I'm sure. And that's splendid, because his approval is vital for our future."

Her knees grew weak. "What is our future?"

He lowered his gaze. "Hopefully, a happy one. I'd like you to have this."

Something smooth and cool fell onto her palm. She wished for more light to inspect the unanticipated gift. In the moonlight the gems shined brilliantly, framing a small picture on a chain.

"It's a cameo pendant my mother gave me to present to a woman who captures my heart. I want you to have it."

Her breath caught as he pulled the necklace around her neck and fastened the lock. "Robert, are you sure? We're only meeting for the second time. Don't you need time to get to know me?"

The silky notes in his voice made her apprehension ebb. "I'm sure, Miss Ella. We're at war, and I want to be worthy of my father and build a successful navy career. Such life comes with risks. No matter what happens, I want you to have this token of my affection."

She clasped his palms. "I'm honored to receive it. I wish I had something to give you in return, to bring you luck."

Robert smiled, making her very soul sing. "I know what you can give me to bring me luck in battle."

He raised her chin, brushed his finger along her neck, then leaned in to kiss her. The sensation of his warm lips touching hers gave her a tremor, and her back arched with pleasure. Ella's heart fluttered like a swallow's wing. Her first kiss. Unexpected, and yet, long-awaited. And perfect.

Robert pulled away. "We're supposed to come back to play Whist," he said, breathless.

Her head was in the clouds. "I forgot the rules."

"So did I."

The infinite sky, peppered with stars, beckoned her to spread her arms and soar into the night. They stayed on deck, speaking of trivial things that took on special meaning in her mind, until Captain Grey emerged and ordered the men to prepare his boat. He studied them and shook his head. "Mr. Weston, your father requires you. We've assigned you a special role in our plan."

The young man beamed; his eyes flashed like two flares. He bid them a quick goodbye and hastened to the great cabin. Ella wished he would turn and give her another smile, but she sensed that his thoughts were already far from her.

***

Back on the *Neptune,* she tiptoed to sickbay, eager to talk to her mentor. She brought a lantern to descend the stairs safely.

I can wake Dr. Pesce this one time. He sleeps much of the day.

The doctor's chest rose and fell in even rhythm. Deep breaths of the loblollies sounded from other cots. Ella sat on the edge of Dr. Pesce's bunk and caressed his face.

"Dr. Pesce, I'm sorry to wake you," she whispered. "If I don't talk, I will burst. When I was younger, I sneaked into my mother's bedroom at night and told her about boys that caught my eye. Now you are the only parent I have. I want to tell you about Robert Weston. You may know his father, Captain Weston. Do you hear me, Doctor?"

"Mmm." Dr. Pesce's eyes opened. Ella raised the lantern to view his face. His gaze was unfocused and pupils unnaturally small.

Words gushed out of her. "I met Robert at Plymouth, before the sailing. We danced the waltz. It was so... sensual." She giggled. "Today, after we dined, we walked on the deck, and he kissed me. It was my first kiss. Everything I hoped it to be. When we talked, I felt like I've known him all my life. And then he gave me this gorgeous pendant. He even hinted about our future together."

"Yes, yes," the doctor mumbled.

She wrung her hands. "It's not too soon? I was afraid you would disapprove. I think I love him. My intuition wouldn't let me fall for an unworthy person, would it?"

"Mmmhmm." The doctor blinked.

She patted his hand, exhaling. "I'm so glad you understand. Are you happy for me?"

"Water! Lindsey, fetch me water."

"Oh." Ella's head dropped when the doctor murmured the name of his deceased daughter. "I thought you were awake."

Tyler raised his head. "Would you shut it? We are trying to sleep."

"I'm sorry. It's just... never mind."

She brought Dr. Pesce water and gave him a sip to drink. Her excitement gave way to regret for bothering him. "I'm glad you sleep soundly. We'll find another time to talk. I hope your dream about Lindsey is a pleasant one."

She kissed him on the cheek and smoothed his blanket.

Chapter 12

The ship rocked with such a force that Ella flew face first into the bulkhead of the orlop. The timbers moaned. The operating table fell over with a thud, and surgical instruments scattered onto the sanded deck. Dr. Pesce gasped, and the wounded groaned and cussed. Through this horrible night, several broadside hits jostled them, but this last tilt made Ella fear the ship would capsize.

"What was that?" she yelled, massaging her nose and cheeks.

"I bet we hit a reef. I can almost hear Wyse's cursing," one of the wounded said from his cot, cradling his broken fingers. "More than one ship was lost on the rocks by the Goulet."

Ella's breathing quickened. She had three wounded men with her, as well as Dr. Pesce. "Would we sink? Are there enough boats?"

Another seaman rubbed his injured shoulder. "You look ready to soil yourself, lass. I don't feel us sinking. The carpenters can fix small leaks."

"Phew," she exhaled. "Sully, Tyler, please pick up the table and wash the instruments again. We may need them at any moment."

Tyler scowled. "Wash them again?"

"They have blood and sand on them. Please do as you're told."

The third patient muttered something indistinct. Ella rushed to his side, relieved that he was regaining consciousness after a fall. She peered into the red-haired man's bewildered eyes, accessing his head injury. This was the man she met when she boarded the *Neptune*; he mistook her for a whore.

"Can you tell me your name and where you are?"

The seaman groaned. "I'm the King of England, and that's my castle. And you must be my fair wife."

She pressed on his skull, looking for swelling. "Please, no jesting. I'm checking if you hurt your head. Do you remember what happened?"

"Uh, I was... We were firing at the frigate..."

"Yes?"

"He hit his head too hard," the seaman with the broken fingers piped. "We weren't firin' on the bloody frigate, or she would've blasted us to the smithereens. The *Crown* was duelin' with the Frog's frigate. It had an escort, a brig of sixteen guns, and that ship fired on us."

Ella cleared her throat. "Thank you for the information, Mr. Cooper, but please don't interrupt."

Her voice was strict, but she was thankful for the insight. This must've been the plan the captains discussed on the *Crown* two weeks ago. Not only her ship's crew were risking their lives, but Robert as well. Her chest tightened. In her mind, she recited a quick prayer for Robert.

Meanwhile, her patient's eyes snapped wide open. He sat up abruptly but grunted and grabbed his temples. "I know who you are. You're that witch!"

Ella pressed on his shoulders. "Please lie down. You need rest."

"Don't touch me!" He swatted her hand away. "Simkin's hand swelled from your touch, and Hart fell to his death from your curse. I'm not stayin' here." He scrambled to his feet.

She blocked his path and grabbed his arm. "Sir, I'm trying to help you. You must stay in bed."

The man spat in her face and stumbled away. The seamen and the loblollies hooted as she wiped her face on her sleeve. She inhaled through her nose to prevent herself from bursting into tears.

"That was a fast cure," the seaman with an injured shoulder said. "Lay like dead one minute and went back to fightin' the next."

"You alright, Ella?" Dr. Pesce called.

"I'm fine." She came to his side and adjusted his pillows. "It's just so vexing. I try to help people, and they loathe me for it. Even Tobby. Since nothing else worked, I administered him an enema as you recommended, and he's been hiding from me ever since."

The doctor gave a dismissive wave. "Children are silly."

"Adults as well." Ella rolled her eyes. "I suspect Mr. Wyse has a toothache, but he won't admit to it."

"Why would he ask for your help? You can't pull teeth," Tyler piped.

She placed her hands on her hips. "For your information, I extracted Johnny's and Mr. Morgan's teeth. I'm getting better. Now, how's your hand healing, Doctor?"

Dr. Pesce sighed and showed her how his fingers refused to bend. His expression was mournful.

"We both know I'll never wield a scalpel again."

Ella kissed his knitted brow. "Perhaps you'll join Matilda in the country and enjoy some quiet life."

The doctor cringed. "Matilda's a merciless caregiver. She'll make me walk for hours to gather herbs and drink her horrid teas, all while listening to her barbs."

Her hand caressed his arm. "Sounds like the perfect arrangement. You'll get stronger."

"I don't want to burden her with my uselessness."

"Nonsense!"

The boom of cannon fire and taps that sounded like rain halted her arguments. As her limbs paralyzed, she strained to hear moans or cries from the deck. Time stood still for several heartbeats, then the steps pounded from the stairs.

"Doctor Ella, help!" a thin voice wailed. The voice belonged to a boy. Her legs trembled as she bolted to the operating table.

"Go," she commanded the loblollies.

They hurried away, while she brought more light to the operating table and donned a fresh apron to cover her shirt and trousers. Her mind conjured gruesome injuries. Her pulse raced. Unable to wait, she mounted the stairs. Ella shuddered seeing the loblolly boys carrying Tobby on the stretcher. Digby was behind them, his face drained of blood. Her breath froze in her chest.

"It's his leg," Digby said.

She ushered them into the orlop. Tobby whimpered as the loblollies lowered him onto the operating table.

Ella grabbed Digby by the shoulders. "What happened?"

"Got hit by the debris."

Tobby sobbed. "My belly hurt again. I couldn't run."

Ella stroked his head. "Poor dear. We'll take care of you."

She cut his breeches and stockings with scissors to expose the wound on the right leg. Tobby shrieked. When moving the fabric aside, she found a deep laceration through the calf, full of splinters. Blood gushed from the wound. Her heart in her throat, she tied a tourniquet above the cut.

"It hurts," Tobby whimpered.

"Tyler, bring me laudanum."

The loblolly gave her an uncertain look but then hastened to fetch the bottle. She counted out the drops, considering her patient's small size. When the boy's eyes drooped, she dug out the splinters with the forceps, then proceeded to clean the wound with vinegar and apply sutures. Her lips shook, but her hands remained steady. Tobby moaned weakly as she worked.

He will heal, she promised herself.

After bandaging the wound, she helped Tyler and Sully carry the injured child onto a cot and covered him with a blanket. Digby, blanched and soundless, watched her. She hugged the lad's tense shoulders. "He needs rest. You can sit with him if you are quiet."

Digby raised his head. "I need to get back. Mr. Wyse may let me stand on the quarterdeck with him."

Tyler snorted. "You must be thicker than you look. Do you really think he'll make you a midshipman?"

"Tyler!" Ella crossed her arms. "If Digby wants to be a midshipman, he'll be one. It's nothing to taunt him about."

She embraced Digby again and kissed his cheek. "Be safe. We'll tend to Tobby. You can visit him in the sickbay after the battle."

Digby hastened away with his face red as a cherry. An injured man stumbled in, leaning on Sully, and cradling his arm. Ella sped to help him.

"There's more wounded," Sully said. "The French hit us with a carronade. That's a canister filled with hundred fifty musket balls," he added for Ella's benefit.

Ella soon found herself moving from one patient to another, examining injuries, cleaning, suturing, bandaging. She didn't know how many hours had passed, one or ten. Sully and Tyler obeyed her orders without argument. A large, bearded man had a musket ball stuck in his arm; she prepared her instruments to extract it. He asked for rum for the pain, but she gave him and others laudanum. She had yet to learn of the thief's identity, but since she carried both keys, the medicine had stopped disappearing.

After removing the musket ball and finishing all other required ministrations for the seaman's injured arm, Ella prepared a makeshift bed. When she glanced at Dr. Pesce's cot next to it, she was surprised to find it empty. She spun around and spotted the doctor bent over Tobby, his hands palpating the boy's abdomen.

Dr. Pesce caught Ella's eye. "Poor boy. Injured leg, and his stomachache's back."

She bit her lip. Laudanum should've alleviated his suffering, but the boy was grimacing in pain.

"Don't worry." Dr. Pesce massaged Tobby's belly like she often did. "I'll tend to him. Take care of the others."

"Thank you," she mouthed as a patient called for her.

She adjusted a bandage on a seaman's shoulder when she heard her name again and looked up to see Wyse next to her. Blood was running over his ear down to his collar. He seemed slouched from weariness.

"Mr. Wyse, that's a nasty gash. Please sit so I can suture it." She pointed to a cot.

"What, this scratch? I'm not letting you poke me with your needles. The captain's asking you to see him when you can. It's safe for you to go. The battle's over."

She fetched the gauze. "Please let me tend to your ear first. You saved my life when I foolishly climbed the rigging. It's the least I can do in return. And don't you have a tooth that's been bothering you?"

He shrank away from her. "I don't need your tending."

"Fine." She dipped gauze into vinegar. "Press this to your cut while I'll see what the captain needs. Why don't you sit? You look exhausted."

To her surprise, Wyse complied. She scanned the orlop to check if anyone needed her. Satisfied that her patients were resting, she sped up the stairs.

On deck, her eyes squinted in the daylight. While she worked, the time passed faster than she anticipated. The *Crown* plunged and tossed a short distance away, its masts and sails intact. The French ships were gone.

She found Captain Grey on the quarterdeck. His uniform was dusty and crumpled, but with no bloodstains.

He beckoned her with his finger. "What's the butcher's bill, Doctor?"

"Excuse me, sir?"

"How many dead and injured?"

"Ten wounded, including a ship boy. All expected to live."

He nodded. "Good to hear. The *Crown* must've been less fortunate. They've signaled a message asking for Dr. Pesce's assistance."

Ella's hands clutched. "They must need another pair of hands. I'll go in his place."

Frowning, the captain cocked his head. "When Captain Weston learns that you're the surgeon instead of Dr. Pesce, he'll object to your presence. He may forbid his son from seeing you. I won't force you to go."

Energy ran down her spine, giving strength to her tired muscles. "The wounded can't be neglected. Captain Weston will see sense, and Robert will support me. I need a few minutes to get ready. Also, Mr. Wyse has a cut on his ear I need to tend to."

Captain Grey nodded. "Go prepare while we lower the gig into the water. I'll accompany you, as I need to speak to Weston. If Wyse gives you trouble, tell him that I order him to submit to your treatment."

Dismissed, Ella descended the steps to the orlop. The loblollies were mopping up the blood. The wounded reposed; one was conversing with Dr. Pesce. The doctor's face was animated as he patted the seaman on the shoulder.

Tobby sucked on his fingers as he slept, his face pallid but calm. She checked his bandages; he stirred but kept sleeping.

Wyse sat where she left him. His eyes were half-closed. He hunched over, risking falling forward. Shaking her head, she selected a long needle and catgut for the suture. Her hand tapped the lieutenant's shoulder. "Mr. Wyse, the captain ordered me to care for your cut."

He muttered an oath. Unperturbed, she wetted a cloth and washed the blood from the wound. Wyse winced at her touch.

"This'll be quick. Only a couple of sutures."

He groaned. "Just get this over with."

She made the first stitch, and Wyse grunted.

"What did the captain want of you?" he asked.

"We're going to the *Crown*. I'm needed there," she answered without pausing her suturing.

He winced from another stitch and gazed about. "What about your patients here?"

"I'll check their dressings before leaving and give Sully and Tyler instructions. They'll move the wounded to the sickbay and give them broth."

An approving expression flicked in his eyes and disappeared. She wanted him to praise her efforts, but he said nothing.

She suppressed a sigh. "I'm finished, Mr. Wyse. I advise you to rest."

He snorted. "I must be on deck in the captain's absence. And there's hull and rudder damage to inspect."

When he left, she checked on each patient and inspected their wounds. Then she filled her instrument case and gave instructions to the loblolly boys on how to care for the patients.

The bearded seaman with the injured arm groaned. "That nasty stuff you gave me was good for nothin'. I asked for rum."

Ella licked her dry lips. The dose of laudanum she administered should've been enough even for this large man, but he seemed unaffected by it. "I'm sorry, but I can't give you more laudanum or rum. It's dangerous."

The seaman groaned. "You doctors are worse than the Frogs."

"Easy there, friend." Dr. Pesce approached. "Doctor Parker's doing her best. I'll bring you some tobacco to chew on."

Ella wrapped her arms around the doctor. "It's so good to see you up and about."

"I couldn't stay away, even though you hardly needed me."

Her palms rested on his shoulders, and she looked into his face. "I'm going to the *Crown* to aid their surgeon. I'm glad you can give the patients some aid while I'm away."

The doctor smiled, but his smile didn't reach his eyes. "I'll never operate or suture again. Thinking about that hurts me more than I can say."

She kissed his injured arm, wishing her love could heal it. "If only I had a way to make it better."

Dr. Pesce waved her away. "No use wanting for the impossible. Go, my dear girl, you have more patients waiting. I'll hold the fort while you're gone." His gaze lowered. "Oh... I may need laudanum... for the wounded."

"Of course!" She handed the doctor one of the keys from her pocket. She dropped her voice. "Please watch the loblollies. I still suspect them in the laudanum disappearance."

"And I still believe your mind played a trick, but don't you worry. I'll keep an eye on the lads."

She pecked his cheek, grabbed her instrument case, and hurried up the stairs.

Chapter 13

From the quarterdeck, Wyse followed the captain's boat with his eyes, as it disappeared into the horizon. An officer rang the bell, and the larboard watch came on deck.

"Hands, get to work. By the time the captain's back, I want the deck to shine like fresh snow," Wyse ordered.

The men busied with sweeping and swabbing the bloodied sand off the deck. He nodded to himself with approval.

"Sir." Olson saluted, approaching the quarterdeck.

Wyse noted the carpenter's furrowed brows and descended to him. "Bad news, Mr. Olson?"

"Aye, sir. We repaired the leaks, but the rudder's broken. We can't fix it."

Wyse swore under his breath. Luring the French brig onto the rocks seemed a brilliant plan till the *Neptune* hit them as well. Small consolation that the enemy brig sunk. The frigate rescued their crew and escaped to the French port. The *Neptune* survived the broadsides and the carronade hit, but she was adrift without the rudder. *Another stroke of bad luck.*

He nodded to the carpenter. "We suspected as much. I'll signal Captain Grey. The ship of the line, the *Crown*, will haul us back to Plymouth. Thank you, Olson."

The seaman didn't move and gave Wyse a hesitant look.

"What?"

"Sir, it's Simkins. He got it into his thick head that Dr. Parker's a witch. That's all he talks about with his friends. Says how everything bad that happens around here's the rotten luck she spreads."

Wyse kept his face blank. "What's it to you?"

"Simkins's mean and stupid, especially when drunk. He may do her harm."

"He won't. He doesn't have the guts to do anything besides blabbering."

Olson's eyes pleaded. He lowered his voice. "I don't like it that the men are set against her. She needs friends. I'd never last here without them."

Wyse groaned. "She doesn't need to last here. She doesn't belong here. I won't let her be harmed, but I've had enough of her prancing about like some duchess. Let her go back to her mansion."

Olson lowered his gaze, but then raised it to meet Wyse's. "Is that why you got her drunk? To shame her?"

Wyse's face heated. "Now, that's insolence, Olson. You forget you are speaking to an officer. If not for our old friendship, I'd have you flogged."

Olson's eyes dulled and his lips quivered. Wyse's heart gave a pinch.

"Olson, come now, I wouldn't do that to you. Just stay out of this business with the woman. She's no one to you. And the faster she gets back to her old life the better for her and everyone."

Olson's shoulders slumped. "Sorry, sir. I'll keep my mouth shut."

He joined the other men at work.

Wyse shook his head. In all the years he'd known Olson, his friend kept his head low and never brought any concerns to the captain or officers. To question Wyse's actions was out of character. Wyse grunted. *The woman muddles men's minds.*

***

Four seamen raised and lowered their oars in unison. The boat bobbed on the waves toward the *Crown*.

Captain Grey stared at Ella's bloodied shirt and trousers. "When you said you needed time to prepare, I thought you'd change into a dress."

She shifted on the uncomfortable seat. “Sir, this isn’t a social visit. Men’s clothing is more practical than women’s when it comes to surgery.”

Questions crowded her head, straining her nerves. How many wounded did the *Crown* sustain? Was their surgeon, Dr. Martin, attending to them, or was he unable to perform his duties? Was Robert all right? She wouldn’t let herself imagine otherwise.

This is your chance, she told herself. *You can show two captains that you are a capable surgeon.*

Captain Weston approached them as soon as they stepped onto the deck, but his jaw slacked seeing Ella.

“Where’s Dr. Pesce? And why are you here, Miss Parker, and dressed in such a fashion?”

Shifting his feet, Captain Grey spoke. “Dr. Pesce sustained an injury a few weeks earlier. Dr. Parker is a trained surgeon. She overtook his duties and has been performing them well.”

Captain Weston stepped back, gaping.

Ella mustered her courage to speak with confidence. “I assure you, captain, I’m capable of caring for the wounded. How may I be of service?”

The captain of the Crown crossed his arms. “This is nonsense with terrible timing. I need a surgeon I can trust with my son’s life.”

Ella’s heart skipped a beat. “Robert? How is he wounded?”

Captain Grey grunted and gripped the railing.

"He received a musket ball to his thigh. Dr. Martin said it's in a bad place, near an important artery, or that's what I understood from his medical speak. The doctor's hands shake like aspen leaves. I won't let him cut into my boy." The captain's voice caught.

Ella wondered if Dr. Martin was allowed to perform surgery on less important patients.

The worried father's eyes pleaded, and his lips trembled. "Your uncle's known as an excellent surgeon. I need him."

I need him too, Ella thought. *But I must stay calm and brave for Robert.*

She stepped forward, inches away from Captain Weston. "I empathize with your feelings, sir, but Dr. Pesce's injury prevents him from operating. Please let me tend to Robert."

The captain looked away. "Your compassion is characteristic of your sex, Miss Parker, but the surgeon skills are not. I doubt you can do Robert any good right now, and time is precious."

I can't let him stop me, she told herself. *Robert's life may depend on me.*

She made her voice confident and clasped Captain Weston's hand. "Sir, I spent the night caring for ten injured men. Musket wounds, splinters, broken bones, head injuries. You can see the blood stains on my clothing. All of my patients survived. When I heard that your ship needed a surgeon, I didn't hesitate. Captain Grey warned me that you would object, but I ask you, no I beg you to let me care for Robert. As you said, time is of the essence."

He rubbed his forehead with his fist. "You can't have the needed experience. What if you make a mistake? My boy may lose his leg, or even his life."

"Weston, let Dr. Parker examine him and take whatever measures needed," Captain Grey interjected, loosening his collar. "If your surgeon is unfit, you have little choice."

The frantic father's eyes widened. "Grey, you are a parent. Would you trust this woman, barely more than a child, with the life of your loved one?"

Captain Grey blanched but held his gaze. "I trusted her with the lives of my men, and if something were to happen to me, my life as well. I vouch for her skill."

With a nod of his head, Captain Weston motioned for them to follow. As they walked, Ella's captain caught her elbow and whispered in her ear. "You better not be over your head. I gave my word."

Her heart hammered. "This is for Robert. He needs me."

"I rarely pray, but I'm inclined to do so now. If you blunder, Weston will never forgive us."

They proceeded to the stern, where Captain Weston ushered them inside his quarters, beyond the lavish dining room. In the roomy cabin, aired from the stern galley, Robert lay on the wide bedstead. His ashen face peeked out from under a feather quilt. The heavy velvet curtains hid the sunlight for the patient's comfort.

Ella tiptoed in, bent over Robert, and stroked his cheek. "Robert, it's me, Ella. Please say something."

The young man's eyes opened, but tiny pupils stared with dullness. He didn't speak.

"How much laudanum has he been given?" she asked Captain Weston.

His hands fidgeted with a button of his frock coat. "About a teaspoon half-hour ago. Do you want me to send for Dr. Martin to find out?"

She shook her head. Operating on Robert would be hard enough without another surgeon looking over her shoulder and judging her every move. She moved the blanket and unwrapped the bloody bandage on the young man's left thigh. The entrance hole was on the left side, three inches above his knee.

"I should call for Dr. Martin," Robert's father muttered. "At least to watch her."

"Were you diplomatic when you told him you don't want him operating?" Captain Grey asked. "The surgeon strikes me as a proud man."

Captain Weston coughed and scratched his neck. "Let's carry on as is."

Ella muted them out. Vexed that her patient was not on the operating table, she knelt to see the wound better. Captain Grey opened the curtains, letting more light into the cabin. There was no drainage or swelling, and the skin was cool to the touch. She removed a probe from her case and inserted it into the wound, listening for the click of metal against metal. When she heard it, she visualized the placement of the ball and what blood vessels it touched. Likely it lodged itself near the femoral artery, and it would be too dangerous to leave it in. A wrong move, and the ball would damage the vital vessel, causing a deadly hemorrhage. The same threat applied to the surgery. The smallest nick with her scalpel, and Robert would die from her mistake.

"You aren't thinking of amputating his leg, are you?" Captain Weston's voice quivered.

She winced, swallowing. "No, not unless an inflammation starts. But I must remove the musket ball."

"Do you want him on an operating table?" Captain Grey asked. "I'm sure we can arrange for one to be brought here."

Ella shifted on her knees. An operating table would be more comfortable for her, and the patient would be restrained properly. There was a chance, however, that the musket ball would move while they transferred Robert onto the table. She didn't want to take any additional risks.

"No, I'll operate here. Just give me a moment to think."

Captain Weston's doubting look irritated her, but she ignored it and prepared the scalpel, the catling knife, the needles, catgut, and bandages. Captain Grey offered her a silver tray that was probably part of the tea service, and she laid out the instruments. Studying the wound, she considered where she would make the incision and how she would slice through the skin, fat, and muscle. She then visualized the forceps gripping the musket ball and her bringing it out.

She gazed at the captains. "I need two people to hold him. Do you want to call someone?"

"I'll do it," Captain Weston said. "Grey, will you help?"

"Of course. Where do you want us, Doctor?"

Robert's father tightened his lips into a line.

Her calm voice revealed nothing of the tingling in her chest. "Someone should hold down his shoulders and another hold his legs. And hold him tight."

Captain Weston bent at his son's head, while his friend came to the foot of the bed. Ella gripped a scalpel, but then released it, and squeezed Robert's hand.

"Robert, I hope you won't feel much, but if you do, please don't struggle. Your father and Captain Grey will restrain you but do your best not to move."

"Ella," Robert muttered.

She kissed his hand. Then she pushed a strap into his mouth to protect his tongue. "Bite down on this."

Blood pumped in her temples. The captains grabbed Robert's legs and shoulders. She gripped the scalpel and made an incision. Blood pooled from under her blade. Robert moaned. Captain Weston moaned louder.

"If you can't watch what I'm doing, focus on his face," she said through her teeth.

Captain Weston inhaled. His complexion paled a shade as his gazed glued to Robert's closed eyes.

Her heart in her throat, she swabbed the blood. There was much muscle to cut through, and she switched to the two-sided catling knife. Struggling with the tough tissue, she cut deeper, swabbed again, and used the probe to find the ball. Almost there, but she had to be accurate. The medical school's dissection room appeared in her mind. A cadaver, whose leg she unceremoniously dismembered as a student, gave her an invaluable gift, preparing her for this moment. She pushed further with the blade, and when metal touched metal, she picked up the forceps and extracted the ball, then applied sutures to halt the bleeding. She turned the ball in her hands, inspecting it. A piece of cloth was stuck to the sticky surface.

"It's all out," she said.

"Praise the Lord." Captain Grey offered his handkerchief to drop the bloody ball in. His expression softened. "Weston, you need to breathe, or you'll faint."

Captain Weston's face was nearly as bloodless as his son's. Sweat rolled down his forehead. "I'm fine," he muttered.

Someone knocked at the door. "Sir, there's a message for Captain Grey."

"Not now," both captains snapped at once.

"The hard part is done," Ella breathed. "I'll clean and close the wound. Hold him tight."

Suturing took the longest, as she connected the tissues she sliced through. Her patient struggled and groaned as she worked the needle.

"Robert, hold on a little more. We're almost done."

As she finished stitching and dressing the wound, a tightness attacked her shoulders and back. Groaning, she straightened and stretched.

The young man murmured something, and she removed the strap from his mouth and touched his face. "Robert, all's well. You will heal."

"I love you," he whispered, his sleepy eyes fixed on her face.

His father gasped.

She laughed. "That's the laudanum talking." Heat rose to her cheeks.

"Come, Weston, let's have a drink," Captain Grey proposed. "Where's your famous brandy? Doctor, I bet you need some as well."

"Just water, please." She required a clear head to monitor her patient for fever and inflammation.

Water spilled as Captain Weston filled the glass with shaking hands and offered it to her. Then he joined his friend for brandy at his desk.

"To Robert's health," Captain Grey toasted, as they clicked glasses.

Captain Weston drained his brandy in one gulp. His face regained some color. He wiped sweat off his forehead. After draining another glass, he approached Ella.

"Miss Parker, I'm more grateful than words can say. I can see that Robert is important to you. Please tend to him as much as your time allows."

Ella stared at Robert's blanched complexion and half-closed eyes. There was nothing she wanted more than to hold his hand, soothe his pain, and witness his recovery. Captain Weston's appreciation and Robert's half-conscious admission of love was a tonic for her weary soul.

"I'd like to be here with Robert, but I have other patients."

Captain Grey approached them, filling his pipe. "I suspect the message for me will confirm that the *Neptune's* rudder is broken. We'll need the *Crown* to tow us back to port."

"Of course," Captain Weston replied. "I'll give orders to my men. My coxswain would ferry Miss Parker between the ships as needed."

Ella nodded in agreement.

"My servant will fetch you anything you need for Robert," Captain Weston added. "He'll bring you something to eat as well."

Her empty belly rumbled at the thought of food. The captains left, speaking among themselves.

"Ella," Robert mumbled and tossed in his bed.

His forehead was warm to her touch. Her chest pinched as she brushed his hair away from his unfocused eyes. It could be his body reacting to the surgery, or the start of the inflammation. The next few hours would be critical.

Chapter 14

"Miss Parker, please wake up."

Ella shifted and almost fell off the chair. Captain Weston's hand steadied her.

"I hate to bother you, but I'm unsure what to order for Robert's breakfast."

The morning light from the windows bathed the captain's cabin. She pried her eyes open and stretched her sore arms. Her sleepy gaze fell on her bloodstained, wrinkled shirt and trousers. The last thing she remembered was applying leeches and poultice to Robert's wound and a damp cloth with vinegar to his burning forehead.

"Robert!" she jerked herself awake.

Robert, propped up on his pillows, smiled at Ella. His hair was sweaty and his complexion still pale, but his eyes gleamed. "Good morning."

"His fever broke shortly after you fell asleep," the captain said. "Your remedies worked."

She exhaled with relief. "I'm glad."

"I hope you weren't too uncomfortable on that chair."

Ella arched her neck and back. The captain offered her a cabin to rest in more than once, but she refused to leave Robert's side. Slumber must've claimed her despite her efforts to keep awake.

"Please use my privy to freshen up. My steward just brought warm water for washing," the captain suggested. Ella traversed to the door at the far corner of the spacious cabin, past the mahogany desk and a bone-white statue of a half-naked woman. The thick Persian carpet muffled her steps. While washing her face, Ella caught her reflection in a large mirror decorated with a golden frame. Disheveled hair, sallow cheeks, and dark circles under her eyes blemished her look. Her clothes were dirty and damp with sweat. She shook her head at her vanity. Her grooming mattered little under the circumstances.

Freshened up, Ella unwrapped the dressing on Robert's wound and cleaned the milky white discharge and dry blood.

"How's the pain?" she asked, changing the dressing.

"Not too bad. Father said I was brave through the surgery."

"You were."

She checked his pulse and listened to his heart and lungs. Captain Weston glanced at her expectedly.

"He's doing well," she said to the captain. "He can have porridge and tea. Keep his meals light for now."

The captain called his steward to bring them breakfast.

Robert clasped Ella's hand. "Will you stay with me all day?"

She considered her patients on the *Neptune*. Sully and Tyler would tend to them, but she needed to check on their progress. Guilt pinched her chest when she thought of Tobby. The boy would pine for her.

"I have patients on my ship. A ten-year-old boy suffered an injury. I must see how he and the others are faring."

The corners of Robert's mouth drooped. "All right. But please come back. I'll miss you."

Ella grinned. "I'll miss you too. I'll return later today. Please eat your meals and rest while you wait for me."

He pulled her closer and whispered in her ear. "I'd kiss you if not for my father standing there."

Giggling, she caressed his cheek.

Captain Weston cleared his throat. "I'll order the boat for you, Miss Parker. Thank you for all you've done for Robert. We're anxious to see you later today."

The captain stepped out. Robert reached for her neck, and after burning her with a kiss, traced her necklace with his fingers. "You are wearing my pendant. Would you wear it with a nice dress tonight?"

Her eyes dropped to her wrinkled and soiled shirt and trousers. "What, you don't like my clothes?" she asked playfully.

His lips pinched. "I prefer seeing you in something finer. And cleaner." He laughed lightly.

She wanted to argue that these clothes were practical for her work and much of the blood on them was his, but let the retort go. No need to bicker over such trivialities. Besides, clean clothes sounded quite heavenly.

***

An hour later, after donning a simple but handsome blue dress, she descended to *Neptune's* sickbay.

"Ella!" Tobby cried as she entered.

The boy rested on the cot, his leg bandaged and propped on a pillow. Dr. Pesce sat on the chair next to him, reading. Only one other patient occupied the berth, a man with a wound to his shoulder. The man tossed and moaned in his slumber.

"That one is a goner." Dr. Pesce glanced towards the injured sailor. "Someone always gets a deadly inflammation. Tyler gave him laudanum to ease his suffering. Meanwhile, Tobby is anxious to see you."

She approached the boy and reached for the bandage on his leg, but Dr. Pesce halted her.

"I just checked the wound and had Tyler change the dressing. I wonder if he'll develop a limp, but it's too soon to tell."

"Hmm. How did you sleep, Tobby?" She asked.

The boy sighed. "My leg bothered me and my belly. I wished you were here, but Dr. Pesce said you were caring for patients on another ship. I thought they might need you more and didn't cry."

She patted the boy's head, checking him for fever at the same time. "You're very brave."

"How are your patients on the *Crown*?" Dr. Pesce asked.

Ella's shoulders relaxed. "I tended to Robert. He had a life-threatening wound, but he's healing."

Dr. Pesce raised his eyebrows. "The young man gave you a pendant and hinted at your future together. Now you saved his life. This sounds... like your destiny."

Ella's cheeks heated. "I hope it is. I had to convince his father that I'm a competent surgeon, but after Captain Grey vouched for me, he gave me his support. And Robert... well... I should wait for his recovery before thinking too far ahead."

The doctor gave her an affectionate look. "It's wonderful to see you happy. I hope my discovery will gladden you as well. Can you prepare this remedy?"

Ella read the list of ingredients on the paper he handed her. "Aloe? For what?"

"Tobby sucks his fingers in his sleep."

"A bad habit, but I still don't see..."

"His habit reminded me of Miss Bessy, a twelve-year-old girl I tended to on a passenger ship. One morning, a maid called me to their cabin with such an alarm that I assumed something dreadful occurred. When I entered, the shocked family pointed at a wriggling tapeworm the girl vomited. It was almost ten feet long."

"Goodness," Ella exclaimed.

"The seasick child expelled the parasite along with her dinner. Her mother told me that Miss Bessy always had her hands in her mouth."

"I have a giant worm in my belly?" Tobby shuddered.

"They could be small but many more of them. Children exposed to dirt are most likely to suffer from parasites."

Ella bit her lip. "I should've suspected intestinal worms earlier. Especially since the purgatives didn't fix the problem."

Dr. Pesce stared at his shoes. "I'm guilty of misleading you, thinking only of closed bowels. Now you will know better in the future."

Ella gathered ingredients for the recipe, glad to find she had everything needed. Matilda gave her aloe for burns, but the medicinal plant had many other uses. After cutting roots, smashing them with a mortar and pestle, and brewing in hot water, she had the medicine ready and handed a cup of it to Tobby. The boy took a tiny sip, winced, but then gulped down the drink.

"I was thinking of the cake you promised me," he said to Ella.

She fluffed the boy's pillows and put a warm compress on his belly to give him comfortable rest. "Soon we'll be back in England, and I'll buy you and the other boys that cake. Hopefully, we'll be celebrating your full recovery."

Dr. Pesce waddled to his cot. Ella approached to adjust his blanket as he lay down. His eyes expressed fatigue, and his mouth turned downward.

"Doctor, you've helped so much. Why are you upset?"

He grunted and showed his unbending fingers. "I couldn't even cut the roots for the recipe. I'm a useless piece of rubbish."

"Don't say that. You've cared for the wounded and worked out Tobby's illness."

"You would've made the right diagnosis eventually. You're on the rise, but it's all downhill for me. Enough placating this old man and let me catch some sleep." He turned on his side, facing away from her.

Ella left him to doze and checked on the wounded seaman. He was burning up with fever; his shoulder wound inflamed and swollen.

"Are you hurting?" she asked. Most likely he was beyond pain or soon would be.

"Annie, you came," the man muttered. "My boy..."

She bit the inside of her cheek. The woman with the baby at Plymouth Port was named Annie. In an hour, she'll be his widow, although she won't know it yet. Ella could be this poor man's wife for now.

"Yes, this is your Annie," Ella breathed. "The baby is... healthy and beautiful." A sob broke her voice.

She held his hand and whispered to him until his last breath escaped his lips.

***

Mr. Morgan, the coxswain, hoisted the gig to carry Ella to the *Crown*. The patch over one eye and muscular arms gave him a ferocious look.

He sneered, scrutinizing her. "Dolled yourself up for the rich captain's son."

"If you must know, he likes to see me this way," Ella replied, smoothing her baby-blue dress.

He chuckled. "He'd like to see you without your dress even more."

Ella's cheeks flamed. "How dare you, Mr. Morgan!"

Morgan slapped her on the back. "Come now, lass, it's only a joke. Drop the grand lady act. You were fun to watch when you were merry. And that one time I caught you in your cabin changing." He held his large belly as he laughed.

Her ears burned with embarrassment. She searched her memory for the cuss Olson taught her to throw back to the impertinent coxswain. When Mr. Olson emerged from the forecastle, she waved to him.

"Mr. Olson, please remind me of my lesson. What do I call a man who bothers me?"

The sailor raised an eyebrow. "Who's bothering you, Doctor?"

"Mr. Morgan is. He's making improper comments."

Both men laughed at that, upsetting Ella more.

"Ah, Morgan is a harmless jokester. Call him a 'real shit.'"

Ella inhaled. "You are ..."

Morgan doubled over, laughing. "She can't even say it."

Ella stomped her foot. "You are a real... real shit, Mr. Morgan. Please keep your lewd comments to yourself." Something loosened in her chest, and she strained not to laugh.

Morgan hooted. "That was like a dressed-up poodle trying to roar."

Olson nudged him. "Enough taunting Doctor Parker."

"What's all this merriment about? Why isn't the boat ready?" Lieutenant Wyse barked, startling them.

"Sorry, sir," both seamen said at once and busied themselves lowering the boat. When Wyse walked away, Olson pressed a small wooden object into Ella's hand.

"My birth name was Olaudah Ogogo," he whispered to her and caught up to Wyse.

Ella gaped with confusion. It took her a minute to understand why Olson shared with her his birth name. A gift of trust. She was unsure what she did to deserve it.

When Ella stepped down into the boat, she glimpsed at Wyse and Olson by the gangway in what looked like an argument. Olson was gesturing wildly, but Wyse stomped his foot, and Olson hung his head and stumbled away.

Morgan shook his head. “I’m betting that was about you, lass.”

Her intuition agreed with Morgan. “But why?”

The seaman shrugged. “Women bring trouble just by being there. My bunkmate has a wife, a daughter, and a sweetheart. All three are trouble. What did Olson give you?”

Ella unclasped her palm to examine the gift. “I think it’s a whistle.”

She put it to her lips, and it made a deafening shriek.

Morgan chuckled. “That thing will wake up the dead.”

“But I’m not a little girl to play with whistles. Why did he give it to me?”

“It has a string tied to it. I think he meant for you to wear it.”

Ella raised an eyebrow and tied the string around her neck. The whistle touched Robert’s pendant.

Twenty minutes later, Ella ascended to the *Crown’s* deck. The sentry stepped aside, and she entered the captain’s cabin. The steward kneeled next to Robert, as he shaved the young man. Ella smiled, watching Robert squirm as the razor cleaned the stubble off his chin.

The steward handed Robert a towel and stepped out. Robert wiped off the foam and beamed at Ella. “I wanted to freshen up before your arrival. The day was long with nothing to do.”

She sat down next to him and stroked his smooth cheeks, inhaling the pleasant smell of shaving soap. “I’m glad you rested. You look better.”

"And you look like a dream. What is it you are wearing next to my pendant?"

She fingered both decorations. "The carpenter, Mr. Olson, gave this whistle to me. I'm not sure why."

Robert's lips tightened. "I hope he didn't mean it as a token of love. You should've refused."

"It's a nice gesture, nothing more. I removed a hook from his arm, and I asked him to dance once."

The young man's eyes were ablaze. "You dance with the common sailors?"

Ella shrugged. "I was being friendly. We danced a jig."

Robert glared at the whistle.

"I'm telling you, it's nothing." She removed the whistle and hid it in her pocket. Then she moved the blanket to reveal the bandage and undressed the wound. The skin was pink around the stitches, but nothing that alarmed her. "It's mending well."

His smile revealed his white teeth. "How else could it be with you tending to me? If you were here all the time, it would heal in record speed. What did you have to do today that was important enough to leave me?"

Her face fell. "I comforted a dying man. And I tended to Tobby. His leg is healing, although he may develop a limp. But I'm hopeful that the treatment for intestinal worms will cure his bellyaches."

Robert cringed. "Ugh, nasty. Ella, do you like what you do?"

Ella sighed. "I love helping patients. But it's not easy when people are unkind and make rude comments."

His hand clasped hers. "Come over to the *Crown* to be under my father's protection."

"Even your father can't prevent the men from wagging their tongues. I don't like it, but it's only talk. Besides, I can cuss back at them." She giggled.

Robert crossed his arms. "Ella, you're a lady! Don't you see how harmful the ship's life is to you? No more mingling with the lower-deck men. Hold yourself apart. If you stay here, my father and I would ensure the men treat you with deference suitable for my betrothed."

She gasped. "Did I hear you right? Did you say..."

His fingers caressed her cheek. "Ella, I don't want to say the words now, while I'm bedridden. When will I be well enough to walk with you on the deck?"

She forced herself to exhale. "A week, I hope. You must continue resting, and I'll keep applying poultices to promote healing. Also, start eating more robust food to get your strength back. Does your ship have fresh meat?"

Robert gave her the mischievous smile she adored. "We have five bullocks we've been saving. I'll ask my father to slay one tomorrow. You must join us for dinner."

Ella put the back of her hand to her forehead and leaned back in a pretend swoon. "Fresh beef! I'd pay a fortune for a steak."

Robert chuckled and pulled her towards him. Did she imagine that Robert's eyes flashed when she joked about her fortune? His lips found hers. Bliss pulsed through her body, making her forget any worry.

Eight bells announced the change of watch. She pulled herself from Robert's arms.

"I must get back to my ship."

He pursed his mouth capriciously. "To tend to the ship boy?"

"He's a dear. I need to see if the treatment is working."

His expression warmed. "I love how tender your eyes become when you speak of him. You'll make a wonderful mother. I want many children."

Ella winced from a painful lump in her throat. Her mother's passing from childbirth and the deaths of pregnant patients she witnessed in medical school haunted her. But ladies hid such fears from their suitors. "I love children."

Robert brought her hands to his lips. "I want a baby for every finger I'm kissing."

How am I going to be a surgeon if I'll be raising ten children? Ella thought with amusement. The idea of raising even one child seemed foreign.

His smile made her heart melt. "The sea wants us together," Robert said. "The wind died."

"I thought it was my imagination. The world went still with our embraces."

He chuckled. “If the calm lasts, our ships will be close by even longer. Call me selfish, but the notion makes me happy.”

She caressed his chin. “I’ll be here every day.”

Chapter 15

The myriad of stars reflected in the still mirror of water, creating an illusion of infinity. When Ella reached the *Crown's* bow, her heart fluttered. Robert embraced her with one arm, leaning on his cane with another. She put her head on his chest, letting her qualms float away.

Afraid to tire Robert's wounded leg, she led him to a sea chest to sit. They squeezed next to each other, their knees touching. Robert cupped her face; his breath warmed her lips.

"This was the best week of my life," Ella said.

"When you visited me, yes. Otherwise, wallowing in bed bored me out of my mind," Robert answered.

"Sorry. I've been busy in the sickbay."

He cringed. "Tending to that boy? What did he have again? Worms?"

"I'll spare you the details. His bellyaches are gone. I'm concerned about his limp, however. It may cause him to lose his job. What if we... make him our ward?" She was planning to say, 'adopt him,' but wanted to gauge Robert's reaction.

Robert furrowed his brow. "Why?"

She made a tiny shrug. "He has no family. You said you wanted children."

"Our children, Ella. I'm sure every ship boy on the *Neptune* worships you, but we can't adopt them all. We can give him an easy job on the *Crown,* but let's not get over our heads."

She nodded, thinking of the ship boys. They were well-behaved and studious during her lessons. Digby surprised her with a kind note he wrote himself, and Ben drew a lovely portrait of her.

Robert's words jarred her musings. "Let's do this properly."

He leaned on his cane to stand and took her hand. The stars reflected in his eyes. "Ella Parker, would you make me the happiest man on Earth and become my wife?"

She gulped air like a fish caught on the rocks.

"Ella, please say something. You are making me worry."

"Yes! Oh Robert, yes."

Tears sprang from her eyes, and her heart ached, heavy with emotion, telling her she wouldn't be alone anymore. In Robert's confident arms, she would find love and protection.

"I understand Dr. Pesce is like a father to you. Should I ask his permission for your hand in marriage?"

Ella's feet drummed against the deck. "He'd love that. He's been dreading letting me go, but he wants my happiness."

"I'm sure every daughter's father feels the same. Please invite him for dinner tomorrow. My father will invite Captain Grey as well."

She clapped her hands. "That sounds wonderful."

"Say, is Dr. Pesce in charge of your trust fund?"

She raised her head in surprise. Her eyebrows met. "No. That would be my lawyer, Mr. Hastings. Why?"

He sat back down. "Well, there will be documents to sign. When do you turn eighteen?"

"Not till May."

"I don't want to wait that long. I'll contact Mr. Hastings to settle the financial matters. You don't need to trouble yourself with those things. Once we are back in Plymouth, you'll have your hands full with the wedding dress preparations and choosing the banquet menu."

Ella's head reeled. The images of elegant flower arrangements, table setting, and sumptuous dishes at Veronica's wedding appeared in her mind. The plethora of decisions that went into every step of that lavish event astounded her. An idea gave her a jolt. "What if we have our wedding on the *Crown*?"

Robert's smile lit his face. "That's a splendid idea. My father loves to display his ship. We'll have the captains stationed in Plymouth in attendance."

Ella nodded. “There’s plenty of space for dancing. We’ll invite musicians...”

“I’d love to talk to you about those things all night, but I’m starting my duties in the morning. Best we say goodnight.”

She grinned. “Parting is such sweet sorrow that I shall say goodnight till it be morrow.”

“Sorry?”

“It’s from *Romeo and Juliet*. One of my favorite lines.”

He squirmed. “They die in the end.”

“They do. But it’s so beautiful and tragic.”

“I never liked Shakespeare, except for *The Taming of the Shrew*. Now that’s a witty play.”

She wanted to ask what he liked about it, but he called for men to prepare the boat.

***

In the gig, Ella’s feet tapped, and she danced in her seat. Morgan gave her a stern look.

“Do you have pins up your arse, lass? Stop rocking my boat.”

Instead of riling, she giggled. “I’m betrothed to Robert Weston.”

The coxswain rolled his eyes. “The captain’s son? I suppose he’s rich.”

She huffed. "He's charming and brave, and it doesn't hurt that he's handsome. Above all, we love each other. That's more important than wealth."

"Ha! Says a girl who wears dresses that cost more than I make in a year. I liked how you looked that night we had music. You wore old trousers, you danced with us, and you got drunk like a green seaman. Now you are prissy again."

She crossed her arms. "I'm marrying a gentleman."

He spat into the dark water. "A gentleman who'll lock you in his house and have you knit his socks. I thought you wanted to be a surgeon."

Her back stiffened. "It's none of your business, Mr. Morgan. I won't let your grouchiness lessen my joy."

Morgan scoffed and turned away.

Ella stepped onto the gangway, the excitement buzzing through her. Sleep was impossible. Instead, she descended to the sickbay. As she entered, she listened to the even breathing of loblolly boys and tiptoed to Dr. Pesce's cot. *Maybe this time he'll be awake. My news is too important to wait till morning.*

"Who's there?" Dr. Pesce asked.

She caressed his hand. "It's me, Ella. I came from the *Crown*, and I'm too excited to sleep."

The doctor sat up and put on his glasses. "Oh, Ella, I can guess what happened. I'm afraid to awaken the lads with our chatter. Is the weather calm?"

"It's the most perfect night."

"Let's come up to the deck and talk."

Ten minutes later, after Ella helped the doctor throw on his coat, they perched on empty crates, absorbed in conversation. The doctor's expression was sentimental as Ella described Robert's proposal.

"So, you've accepted. You are now betrothed to Robert."

"Yes. We'd like you to come to the *Crown* for dinner. Robert will ask you for my hand."

The doctor shook his head. "It's too much for me. I'll cry like a baby. I don't want to embarrass you."

She wrapped her arms around him. "You'll do fine."

He patted her shoulder. "I had many dreams for you, Ella. Marriage wasn't one of them, but that's because I never found love. You should follow your heart and be happy. Are you going to stay in Plymouth after the wedding?"

Ella frowned. "No, why would I? I'll be on the *Crown* with Robert. It's a bigger ship, with more people to care for."

The doctor gaped. "Will Captain Weston make you his ship surgeon? And Robert is supportive? I perceived them more... old-fashioned."

Ella stood and paced a few steps. Needles poked her skin. She pivoted and faced the doctor. "They know how skilled I am. I saved Robert's life."

Dr. Pesce bowed his head with a mournful expression. "Hmm, I imagined you would spend time with me while Robert goes to sea, but of course you prefer to be with him."

"You'll be in Matilda's care."

He winced. "My sister's bitter teas and merciless barbs will be the end of me. You are the late gift this life gave me, my child. I hope Robert deserves you."

She sat back down and put her head on his shoulder. "He's wonderful. I think I loved him the moment we met."

The doctor tapped his foot. "I'm a skeptic when it comes to love at first sight. People need time to get to know each other. You're sure that Robert is not after your fortune, right?"

"Of course not!" Ella gave an uneasy laugh. "His father is wealthy. Why would they want my money?"

"Well… some people show off expensive things they can't afford. And those who have a taste for luxury only want more."

Ella smoothed her dress. "Robert is nothing like that." His questions about her inheritance did not sit well with her, but she trusted her betrothed. Perhaps he was watching out for her.

Dr. Pesce clasped her hand. "Tell me one more time that you are happy, and this is what you want."

She beamed. "I'm extremely happy. This is what I want."

"That's all I needed to hear. What a beautiful night, Ella. I've missed looking at the sea. If you don't mind, I'd like to stay here alone and reflect."

A pinch of concern gnawed at Ella. "I should help you down when you are ready for bed."

"My dear, I'm not that feeble. You should get some rest. Make yourself a cup of Matilda's tea if you can't sleep."

She flew towards her cabin, then returned. "Dr. Pesce, you said you never found love. Were you seeking something else?"

The doctor raised his eyebrows. "Hmm. When I gave up on love, I sought... belonging. The sea was where I belonged."

Ella nodded. "I wanted to belong. But love will make me happier."

The doctor gave her a smile that warmed her despite the night breeze. "Maybe you'll have both."

She kissed him on the cheek and sauntered to her cabin. Concerned for the doctor, she asked one of the men to help him to the sickbay when he was ready. Twice she looked back at the doctor's slouched figure staring into the dark.

In her cabin, she drank some water from the jug, pulled out a dressing gown from her chest, and collapsed onto the cot. The undulations of the waves failed to lull her to sleep. She craved to read a pleasant novel, but ship rules forbade burning candles for such frivolities. Instead, she closed her eyes, and dreamed of her future with Robert.

Their wedding on the Crown would be picturesque, but not excessive, limited to friends and family, Dr. Pesce and Matilda in place of her parents. There would be music, dancing, and toasts. She would include the boys in some way. Dr. Pesce would shed a tear, giving her away. Matilda would comfort him and to Ella she would say...

Matilda's voice rang in Ella's ears. *"I say, why so much fuss over one day of your life? What about after?"*

Ella's eyes snapped wide open. Matilda's sharp gaze bore into her brain, as if expecting Ella to conjure images of her life after the wedding flurry.

Taking deep breaths, Ella shut her eyes again, relaxing her limbs. She would accompany her husband onto the *Crown*. Her mind showed her boarding the great ship on Robert's arm, the men saluting them. As Robert's wife, she would have respect from seamen and officers. They would give her no trouble when she would minister to them in the sickbay.

Matilda's tilt of the head and eye roll made the image fade and disappear. *"Does Robert's father want you in the sickbay? Have you been summoned to look after patients besides Robert?"*

Ella turned over to her side. The thin mattress gave as much comfort as a wooden board. "*Robert's wound required all of my attention,*" she reasoned. *"Dr. Martin is still the Crown's surgeon. I'll take over after he leaves."*

Her friend raised an eyebrow. "*Are you sure of that?*"

Ella hid her face in the pillow. "*Yes. Robert loves me and wants to make me happy. His father is impressed with my skill and will let me care for his crew.*"

Matilda turned her back on her. "*Ella, for all your brains, you often miss what's right in front of you.*" The midwife marched away, fading with every step.

"Matilda, wait!" Ella's own cry jolted her.

Someone pounded on the door. She sat up on the cot, her head groggy.

"What? Who is it?"

"Ella, you must come." The voice behind the door was Sully's. "Dr. Pesce... he's dead."

Chapter 16

The doctor's face was the color of smoke, his jaw hung open. Ella's vision blurred as she closed his eyes and placed his hands onto his stomach. She wanted to pretend he was asleep on his sickbay cot, but he must've been dead for hours. The pain in her heart was a million strings breaking from tension.

Sully's lips trembled, and Tyler wrung his hands. The lads looked shocked, miserable, but also... guilty.

"Did you see him last night when he returned from the deck?"

Neither answered. Tyler stared down at his shoes. *They are hiding something from me.*

Ella stood close enough to hear their rapid breathing. She cleared her throat, and let her voice take on unnaturally low notes. "You will have to talk. If you don't, I will perform a post-mortem and learn exactly how he died. Lord help me, but I will do it."

"Don't!" Sully cried. "He was our friend."

Her jaw was set. "He was like a father to me. I need to know what happened."

Tyler's eyes were fixed on the deck. "I saw him come in. He sat at the desk and wrote. Then he asked me to give him his laudanum."

She flinched. "What? You gave him laudanum regularly?"

His voice was barely above a whisper. "Yes, and Sully as well. He took it for backaches before he was wounded. But lately, he asked for it three or four times a day."

Her hands itched to throttle them. "Why didn't you tell me?"

"He didn't want you to know."

Nausea came up her throat. The symptoms of an opium habit, like a textbook excerpt, appeared in her mind. Moodiness, loss of appetite, closed bowels, cognitive decline, small pupils. Her trust in her beloved mentor prevented her from seeing what was in front of her nose.

Her hands shook. "I don't understand. I carried the keys. And the level of liquid in the bottle didn't change."

Sully's shoulders rounded. "We picked the lock. It's easy to do. And when you noticed that the laudanum was disappearing, the doctor had us add alcohol to the bottle."

Ella trembled with rage. *Liars!* The doctor was ashamed of his habit, but the loblolly boys had no excuse for deceiving her.

Diluted laudanum was less effective for pain relief. The patients suffered from their deception.

"He wrote something!" she cried. "What did he write last night?"

Tyler staggered to the desk, but she sped past him. Three letters laid in plain view, unsealed. With pain in her chest, Ella observed the doctor's messy handwriting; crooked letters made with his left hand.

She picked up the first letter, addressed to her. Tears obscured her sight, but she made herself read.

My Dear Daughter,

I'm ashamed to tell you that I acquired a laudanum habit. I'm even more ashamed of deceiving you. There's no hope of saving me from this misfortune. I don't want to end my life in bed or worse, in an asylum. Nor do I want to burden you or Matilda with nursing me. Please don't grieve for me, my dearest Ella. I die a happy man because you found love and will soon know marital bliss. I'm immensely proud of your achievements and hope that you will not abandon medicine.

Joseph Pesce

Tyler grabbed the letter from her hands. She didn't protest and picked up the second letter, addressed to Matilda. The first line was the same as the letter to her, and she didn't read the rest. When they dock at the port, she would have to mail that letter to the Plymouth address Matilda provided. Her heart pinched as she imagined her friend receiving the news of her brother's death.

The last letter was the formal will, stating that the doctor bequeathed his possessions to Matilda.

"He said nothing about me!" Tyler exclaimed.

Ella flinched. "What?"

The young man quaked, clutching her letter. "I cared for him! I fed him and brought his medicines. He didn't leave me a penny. I thought he'd send me to medical school."

Her hands on her hips, she stared him down. "A medical student, even a new one, possesses ethics and common sense. Your deceit shows you have neither. How much laudanum did you give him last night?"

Tyler walked over to the dispensary, picked the lock with a pin from his clothing, and retrieved the bottle. Ella mentally noted that it took him less time to pick the lock than for her to fumble with a key. The bottle was about two-thirds full. Tyler's hands shuddered holding it.

"He said he needed more to go to sleep."

"But it was much more than he's ever taken, right? The bottle was almost full the last time I saw it. Even diluted with alcohol, it was plenty to kill him. Why did you let him ingest such a large dose?"

Tyler squinted his eyes. "I didn't think. He's a doctor, after all."

Sully shook his head. "That was dim-witted."

Ella crossed her arms. "It's more than dim-witted. Tyler, you've killed him. And you've assisted, Sully. Tyler gave him the last dose, but both of you are culprits."

She grabbed the three letters and hid them in her pocket. "I won't have his good name soiled. Dr. Pesce died of an apoplexy. Report the tragic news to the captain. I'll be in my cabin."

She stormed out, feeling sicker with every step. When she stepped onto the deck, her stomach heaved, and she reached the railing to empty her insides overboard.

"Look! The girl is drunk again," someone yelled, and several men laughed.

She ran into her cabin and slammed the door behind her. Exhausted, she threw herself on the cot that not long ago was her mentor's and buried her face into the pillow. There will be a funeral, and she'd sew the bag. She'd add her own words to Matilda's letter and apologize for missing the signs of the doctor's habit. But first, she wanted a quiet moment to grieve for her dear friend, the man who called her his daughter, and whom she loved like a father.

"Doctor Ella, it's us." Tobby's voice and the shuffling of feet came from the door. "We are sorry about Dr. Pesce. Can we talk to you?"

Ella's chest ached. "Not now. Thank you for thinking of me, but I need time alone."

Their steps echoed as they walked away. She wondered who else would check on her or express condolences.

Tears poured as she reminisced about meeting Dr. Pesce on the ship to London and assisting him in surgery. That day changed her life and gave her a purpose. She had so little time with the doctor, and yet each day with him gave her so much.

She was annoyed to hear another knock on her door.

"Can't I have a moment to myself to grieve?" she cried.

"Ella, help!" The scream was Sully's. "It's Tyler... He's taken laudanum. A lot of it."

She jumped off the cot and bolted for the door.

"When? How much?" she rasped as she ran with Sully to the sickbay.

"Just now. He asked me to find his book at the forecastle, but it wasn't there. When I returned, he was insensible, and I couldn't wake him up. I found the bottle of laudanum. It's almost empty."

"Bloody hell," Ella muttered, speeding down two steps at a time, her heart banging against her ribcage. Once in the sickbay, she made a beeline to her instruments and grabbed the stomach pump.

"Get a basin," she yelled to Sully and hastened to Tyler, who was sprawled on the cot. She put her head on the young man's chest to hear his heartbeat and breath.

"Is he..." Sully's voice broke.

"He's breathing. I'm going to pump his stomach."

She slid a rubber tube down Tyler's throat. *This better work*, she prayed. She didn't want to contemplate holding two funerals.

"What do you want me to do?" Sully asked.

"Hold the basin here."

She pumped the syringe attached to the tube with all the strength of her fingers. After several heart-stopping seconds, the contents of Tyler's stomach poured out from the other end of the tube into the basin. The reek of stomach acid, alcohol, and half-digested porridge made her gag.

Sully's face turned green, and he clutched his abdomen. "I may be sick."

Ella was glad that her own belly was empty.

"He'll be alright, won't he?" Sully whispered.

Ella removed the tube from Tyler's throat. She counted his pulse on the wrist, watching his chest rise and fall. Satisfied with a steady beat, she slapped his cheeks to awaken him. Tyler's eyes remained shut. She unbuttoned his collar. "He needs to sleep off the opium in his bloodstream."

"Doctor Parker." A seaman she didn't know barged into the berth. "Mr. Wyse is asking when you want to hold the funeral for Dr. Pesce. The men want to pay their respects."

Ella's chest ached at the thought of her solemn duties. "Please tell him I need to sew the bag. We can have the funeral in an hour."

She addressed Sully. "Sorry, but you'll miss the service. Stay with Tyler. When he wakes, give him water."

Her body ached as she rose to her feet. It wasn't even noon, but she was exhausted. A tiny part of her envied Tyler for being oblivious to the world and escaping responsibilities.

I have a job to do, she reminded herself.

***

Wyse stuck his jackknife into the mainmast to join about twenty more hilts. One had to strike at the right place for the wind to return. The captain laughed at superstitions and wanted Wyse to abandon them as well. But when one unlucky event followed another, Wyse clung to seamen traditions. *The sea is punishing us for having the woman on board.*

"Mr. Wyse!" Olson jarred Wyse from his dark thoughts. "May I speak with you?"

Wyse frowned. Olson vexed him recently with his demands to increase protections for Ella. "What is it?"

The man shifted from one foot to another. "It's too bad the old surgeon died. We should show Dr. Parker kindness. Tell her that we are her family."

"What?" Wyse's jaw dropped. "I told you, she's of high birth. She doesn't need kindness from us."

Olson rubbed his face. "The boys say she's an orphan. Dr. Pesce was like a father to her."

"An orphan rich enough to buy this ship. Morgan said she's getting married to that upstart Robert Weston."

"Still, she should know we are grateful for her work, and we'll protect her if needed. Simkins is planning something. He spreads rumors that she scares off the wind. He wants to test her… Some way they used to test witches."

Wyse raised an eyebrow. If nothing else convinced Ella from leaving the ship, this test would. And he would be the one to save her and oblige her plea to deliver her home, like a knight in a story.

"Simkins is too stupid to do anything dangerous," he answered Olson. "If that's all…"

Olson lowered his voice. "Come now, Jack. You owe Doctor Parker. It was you who got her drunk. And now you want Simkins to scare and shame her. This is not about her bringing bad luck. You want her gone because she reminds you of Miss Charlotte Fitzharris."

Wyse's fists balled and his vision doubled. "Don't you dare say that name! Don't you dare speak to me like this!"

The seaman met his gaze and spoke at full volume. "I knew it. You'll have me flogged for truth? Go ahead. But if you do, I'll lose the respect I have for you. And so will all lower deck."

The lieutenant swallowed bile remembering the crisscross of scars on Olson's back. The man was whipped to shreds in his old life as a slave. Wyse hated hurting him, but a public display of insolence required a punishment. Two marines and their captain stood nearby, their eyes on Olson.

"You leave me no choice!" He gestured to the marines. "Take Mr. Olson to the hold and put him in irons."

The seaman trembled but gave his detainers no trouble. He kept his accusing gaze on Wyse as he descended into the hatchway. The captain of the marines approached.

"It's been a while since we've had a mutineer, Mr. Wyse. A word from the captain, and we'll have him hanged."

Wyse cringed. His mind was showing him his friend's lifeless body dangling from the mainmast.

"What mutineer?" He feigned a laugh. "Olson's just restless from the calm. The hold will cool him off. No, we don't have mutineers among our good men."

"Are you sure, Mr. Wyse? I heard..."

"Nah, Olson is nothing to worry about. Please make sure he gets some food and water and release him tomorrow night. By that time, he'll be sorry for his temper. How would you like some brandy? Let's mourn the poor doctor."

"Don't mind if I do, Mr. Wyse."

They ambled to the wardroom. On their way, they passed by Ella, who drudged to the captain's cabin, hunched like she carried a weight too heavy for her. Her thinned face and red eyes gnawed at his chest.

Maybe Olson's right. We should offer her friendship.

He banished the strange notion. *The girl needs to be humbled, isolated, and made sorry she ever came here. For her own good and everyone else's.*

Chapter 17

Captain Grey, seated at the desk in his cabin, shook his head as he penned *'D.D.'* next to Joseph Pesce's name in the ship book.

"Apoplexy. How unfortunate. I considered him to be one of the best surgeons in the service. We were lucky to have him."

"I was privileged to have him as a mentor and friend," Ella replied. Swaying on her feet, she gripped the desk for support. Her eyes blinked fast, barring the tears from pooling.

"It's fine to cry, Doctor. No one will think less of you. And please sit."

She collapsed on the chair and sobbed. With a flustered look, he rummaged in his pockets for a handkerchief.

"Thank you, sir," she said in a faint voice, accepting it. "Is there a possibility to bury Dr. Pesce in England? The idea of him having no grave..."

Captain Grey shook his head. “Without the wind, who knows how many days it will take us to reach Plymouth. I don’t want a decomposing body in the hold. A sea burial is proper for a man who loved the sea as much as Dr. Pesce. Do you want to change before the funeral?”

Her eyes scanned her trousers, shirt, and the black scarf tied around her arm.

“Dr. Pesce gave me these clothes when he sent me to medical school. They have a special meaning to me.”

“I understand, but...” His lips turned down. “Captain Weston wouldn’t think them appropriate.”

Ella raised her head. “Captain Weston?”

“You seem surprised. I invited him and Robert to pay their respects. We were supposed to dine with them, do you remember?”

She gasped. “I completely forgot about the dinner. Robert was going to ask Dr. Pesce for my hand in marriage.”

The captain nodded. “That’s what I assumed. I’m sorry that the start of your betrothal became tragic. I wish you happiness.”

He stared down as he spoke. Ella wondered if he thought of his daughter Bella, who would be heartbroken by the news of Robert’s engagement.

“Thank you, sir.” Her voice was lifeless. With Dr. Pesce’s death, the excitement of the proposal faded. The last conversation with her mentor and the dreamed argument with Matilda echoed in her mind. She had questions for Robert.

Captain Grey offered her his arm and led her to watch the funeral. The marines gave a short ruffle on the drums; the bosun and his mates piped the side, to give honors to Captain Weston whose boat had just arrived. Captain Grey shook hands with him and Robert and led them to the quarterdeck. Robert, leaning on his cane, turned to her. She reached for his hand. His lips pursed as he gave it, while his eyes scrutinized her clothes. She considered explaining her choice of garments but decided against it. Robert didn't know she had disguised herself as a man for two years. It occurred to her that she hadn't shared much of her past with Robert, and she knew little of his past or anything beyond his current life as well.

Chairs for the Westons, the captain, and Ella were prepared on the quarterdeck. The accommodation was due to Robert's wound, but she was glad to rest her legs. Her body ached with weariness.

The men assembled on the deck with their heads bowed. Mr. Doolittle came out to read the words of the funeral service. Once again she marveled at the chaplain's magnificent baritone that made the cold formality of the words sound comforting.

When the chaplain finished, Robert squeezed her hand. "That chaplain could speak at our wedding."

She didn't return his smile.

Captain Grey stood up to speak. As he gazed at the men, he shifted his feet and rubbed his face.

"Dr. Pesce has been our surgeon and a friend on many journeys. He tended to us. We all knew his skill and dedication to his work. Um... May he rest in peace." He sat back down and blew air through his teeth.

Robert's father raised an eyebrow. "We have Cicero among us."

Captain Grey reddened. "I prefer a bloody battle over speaking on a formal occasion. Well, at least that's over."

A heavy silence followed the captain's curt speech. The sailors moved toward the bag. Another heartbeat, and the doctor's body would be committed to the sea.

He deserves more, Ella thought.

She rose and stepped to the edge of the quarterdeck, aware of the eyes on her. Her cheeks and neck grew hot, and her mouth dried.

"Dr. Pesce was one of the kindest people I've met. He was like a father to me." Her mind raced to find what to say next. All she could think of was her story. "A little more than two years ago, my mother died. My father became violent when drinking and wounded me." She pointed to the scar that ran down her neck.

"I ran away from home. I don't know if I would've survived alone. Fortunately, I met Dr. Pesce, and he took me under his wing. When he saw my conviction to study medicine, he bought me the clothes I'm wearing now, chopped off my hair, and paid for my tuition at the university. Thanks to him I've learned to save lives. And when I couldn't find employment, he gave me another chance: to be his assistant here on the *Neptune*. This voyage didn't turn out the way we hoped, but I'm forever grateful to Dr. Pesce for the opportunity no one else would give me."

She filled her lungs to strengthen her quivering voice. "He had no living relations other than his sister. His life was this ship, and you were his family. If you have a story, please come forward and share it."

She stepped back and collapsed on the chair. Robert eyed her with wonder.

Captain Weston cleared his throat. "The sentiment was lovely, Doctor Parker. Your story left me surprised... to say the least."

Ella nodded, but her eyes focused on the men. She waited for anyone to volunteer.

Captain Grey rubbed his sweaty palms. "The men are unaccustomed to speaking on such occasions. That doesn't mean they didn't love the doctor. Let's finish with the funeral and have some spirits."

He motioned for the men to pick up the body wrapped in the bag, when a thin voice rang, "Pardon me. Please let me through. I want to say something."

Tobby wedged his way through the crowd, limping on his injured leg. The men parted, chuckling at the boy's polite language.

"Help him up here," Ella asked the men. She stood up to give him a hand as he climbed the stairs.

Robert's father gave an astonished look. "A ship boy doesn't belong on the quarterdeck."

Captain Grey shrugged. "I don't see any harm if the boy says a couple of words. Except he may turn out a better orator than me."

Positioned on the front of the quarterdeck, Tobby shivered as he viewed the crowd. "This was a bad idea," he whispered to Ella.

She stooped to him. "You are incredibly brave. Speak up so all can hear you. I'll stand right here next to you, if you want."

Tobby swallowed, but then made his voice loud and clear. "I used to be afraid of Dr. Pesce. I was sick, but I didn't go see him because I hated the remedies he used. Clysters and tobacco enemas..."

A boom of laughs broke out. The boy halted. He gave Ella a panicked look. "Did I say something wrong?"

She gave an encouraging smile, snickering on the inside. "It's good to make people laugh. Keep going."

"Dr. Pesce figured out what was wrong with me. He was kind when he treated me. I learned that he was always kind, even when he was giving me treatments I didn't like. He just wanted to help me. I wish he were still with us. It's not fair that he's gone."

The boy's eyes wetted, and Ella swept him into a hug. Her own face flooded with tears.

"Tobby, that was beautiful. I'm so proud of you."

She kissed his wet cheek. The boy blushed and pulled away. She let him go, and he limped back to hide among the crowd.

A large man with tattooed arms made his way forward. "When we sailed around India, several of us caught a fever." As he spoke about how Dr. Pesce treated him and his friends, Ella crept back to her chair next to Robert. He handed her a handkerchief.

"Was that the ship boy you mentioned?" he asked.

She wiped her tears. "Yes. His name is Tobby. Wasn't he wonderful?"

Robert's lips turned down. "You became attached to the urchin. It's understandable, considering your loneliness. When we are at Plymouth, my mother and sister will bring you into their circle. You'll have many friends and diversions."

"But..." It took Ella all her will to shut her gaping mouth and not to argue while the men spoke of her beloved mentor. She gave her betrothed a pointed look. "We must speak of this later."

Robert's lips tightened into a line. Captain Weston whispered into his son's ear. Ella caught, "Be firm."

Meanwhile, the seaman finished speaking. Another one took a step forward and opened his mouth, but Captain Grey made him halt with one glance.

"You can continue eulogizing the doctor after dinner and grog. Let's give his body to the sea."

Two seamen lifted the bag. Ella averted her eyes, unable to watch. The splash told her that the body met the water's surface.

A cannonball inside the bag would sink it to the bottom. Ella's heart was full of broken glass. If the doctor had died in London, she would've buried him next to his adopted daughter, Lindsey, and ensured his resting place was cared for. With him buried at sea, Matilda or she wouldn't be able to visit his grave.

With the funeral finished, Captain Grey dismissed the men. "Weston, would you dine with me? I have nothing but salted beef, but the wine is decent."

Captain Weston rose. "With pleasure. Let's give the young people privacy to discuss their nuptials."

When they left, Robert and Ella, now alone on the chairs, glanced at each other with uncertainty. The questions that churned her soul were uncomfortable to voice. She decided to start with something neutral.

"How are you feeling?"

"Much better, thank you. And you?"

"Well..." She couldn't describe how she felt. There were no words for it. Yesterday she had no doubts in Dr. Pesce's candor or in Robert's complete devotion. She no longer trusted her heart or even her eyes. Only her work made sense and kept her mind from breaking. "We are having a shortage of laudanum. Would you send us a bottle?"

"I will arrange this. Anything else?"

She shook her head. The heavy silence stretched between them. Her intuition told her that one wrong word may rip their fragile bond, yet she had to ask questions. Her wise mentor and his sharp-tongued sister would want her to step into marriage knowing her future husband's plans.

Ella peered into his eyes and rallied herself to listen and to hear. "Will I come with you on voyages after we are married?"

He chewed his lip. "It would be lovely to have you on the *Crown*, but you would be more helpful to me and my father joining the circle of officers' wives. Building friendships with the influential women would ensure invitations into the right homes, which in turn, would lead to coveted missions."

An icy chill went through her, and she hugged herself. "I don't knit or embroider with the ladies. That's the life I left behind. I'm a surgeon."

He gave her a mischievous smile, the one that infallibly quickened her pulse before. This time, her heavy heart refused to flutter. "You'll liven up their mundane existence. We should alter your story, however, or they may swoon from shock. No need to tell them that you are a surgeon."

Ella frowned. "What do you mean?"

He stood up and paced the quarterdeck, leaning on his cane. Then he stopped by the railing, beckoned her to his side, and put his hand on her elbow. "I would tell it like this: We met at a wedding, then became reacquainted at the dinner given by my father. You nursed me back to health after I suffered a wound. The ladies would speak of nothing else for weeks."

"A story worthy of a novel, except for one inexactness." She tilted her head. "The musket ball lodged in your thigh required removal by a skilled surgeon, a better one than your father employed. An inadvertent nick to the femoral artery, and you could have died of hemorrhage. How did I perform the operation if I wasn't a surgeon?"

"They don't need to hear such gruesome details." Robert winced, leaning back.

Ella drew herself up. "In other words, you want to keep my occupation a secret, as if it's something to be ashamed of. Is my coming aboard the *Crown* completely out of the question? After your father watched me tend to you, I was sure he'd want me as the surgeon."

His eyes looked away, towards the sea. "Well... If you insist on coming aboard and tending to the sick, you could do some light work under the surgeon's supervision. My father believes that reading to the wounded or giving them water is an admirable occupation for a lady."

Heat burned Ella's scalp. She cupped his face, making him look at her as she spoke. "Even a hospital nun does more than reading and fetching water. Does he believe I mustn't soil my hands with blood?"

Robert's lips tightened. He removed her hands. "No, you mustn't. After the wedding, you must behave as his daughter-in-law, not a surgeon. Captain Grey had no right making you, a noblewoman, do the dirty work in the sickbay."

Ella stepped away and leaned on the railing, watching the *Crown* heave with the ripple. Her soul tore, and agony spread through her body. Why couldn't she have both, her betrothed and her calling? Choosing was too painful.

He hobbled over. "I didn't mean to upset you. It was a trying day for you."

She faced him, letting him see her pain. "Robert, you knew of my occupation. I proved my skill to you and your father when I saved you. Medicine is too important for me to abandon... even for you."

He caressed her curls, letting them slide through his fingers. His arm lowered to her waist. Her knees weakened.

"Wait till I'm the captain with a command of my own. On my ship, you could do as you wish."

Hope, close to dying, found new vigor. "Do you mean it?"

He stretched out his hand. "You have my word."

A weak smile formed on her face as she clasped it. "Then I will anticipate your swift promotion, Lieutenant."

"And that's where those vexing teas and dinner parties with the officer wives come in. You can be a great aid to me."

She leaned into him. "I'll do my best to befriend them."

His fingers tickled her cheek. "They will fight over having you at their card games and charity balls. I'll provide you with a monthly annuity from your assets to purchase the latest fashions. My wife will be the envy of every man and woman in Plymouth."

Her body recoiled. *I'm not a trophy to display. And what did he mean about the annuity?*

He kept smiling, oblivious to her curled lips and pinched brow.

Because that's the law, the realization dawned on her. A woman's assets become the property of her husband. Every farthing of her money; every inch of her land. If she wished for a new pin or a pair of stockings, she'd have to ask her husband to pay the bill.

Dr. Pesce's dear face came to her troubled mind. *You're sure that Robert is not after your fortune, right?* Her throat convulsed.

She stared into the water, hiding her face from Robert as he embraced her. "Robert... I must tell you... I didn't inherit my father's fortune. I have no dowry."

He stiffened and let go of her. "But... Captain Grey told my father you are one of the richest women in England."

"Captain Grey made wrong assumptions about the affairs he wasn't privy to. On his deathbed, my father changed his will in favor of his betrothed, Lady Fillips." Ella flinched, remembering her father's last night, and how he expired during the lawyer's visit.

Robert stumbled back onto the chair, falling hard on it. Blood drained from his face.

Ella hurried over, scolding herself for shocking him after his injury. *I wasn't fair. We shouldn't play games.* Her mouth opened to take back all she said a minute ago.

"Robert, I didn't..."

He covered his face with his hands. His voice was wooden. "We can't get married. I must withdraw my offer."

Ella froze, ice spreading through her. Every fiber in her chest ached as she forced herself to breathe. She leaned on the empty chair.

"You and your father are rich. Why do you need a wife with a dowry?"

He sighed and rubbed his forehead. "We have debts. I must marry a rich woman to pay them. Ella, I feel awful, but this is likely for the best. You are ... eccentric."

She laughed bitterly, hugging herself. "Oh, that wasn't the case when you believed me wealthy. I have 'faults' that embarrass you."

He reached for her hand. "My family will always appreciate what you've done for me. Let's part as friends."

Tears choked her. "Friends? You said you loved me."

"My family's expectations matter more. Since we won't be married, do you mind returning the pendant?"

She ripped at the silver chain, breaking it. The pendant slid down her neck and fell to the deck with a click; the quiet, inconspicuous sound of a heart shattering. "Too bad you can't return me my first kiss. Or my love."

With her face in her hands, she ran towards her cabin. She entered the pathway when she ran smack into the chaplain. He gasped and fell onto his bottom.

Struggling to speak, Ella gave him a hand to stand up. "Devil… I mean… I'm terribly sorry, Mr. Doolittle. Are you hurt?"

He brushed off the dirt from his clothes. "Nothing harmed but my pride, Doctor. Are you all right?"

Her head shook 'no', and she sobbed.

"There, there, my dear." He patted her shoulder. "Let's have some tea and talk."

"Doctor Parker!" Sully hastened to her, panting. "Tyler's awake."

"Thank heavens!" Ella wiped her tears with the back of her hand. "Sorry, Mr. Doolittle, but I must minister to my patient."

The clergyman clasped his hand. "Do we have a sufferer I should pray for?"

"Tyler had … suffered an unfortunate accident. I must see how he's faring."

"Of course, my dear, but don't neglect your own needs. I'll wait for you at the galley with a cup of tea and my most heartfelt sympathies."

Sully bounced on his heels from impatience, and she let him lead her away.

"He complains of a headache and a bellyache," he told Ella.

"That doesn't surprise me."

They entered the sickbay, and she took a chair by Tyler's cot. He turned on his side, away from her.

"I don't want to see you."

"I'm here to help, Tyler." She slapped him lightly on the side. "I've endured enough today without your grumpiness. Turn onto your back so I can examine you."

Grudgingly, he did as told. His lung and heart sounds improved to her satisfaction. She had him open his mouth and shook her head at his grayish tongue. When her hands pressed on his firm belly, he grunted.

She clicked her tongue. "Laudanum closes bowels, as you already know from caring for Dr. Pesce." She turned to her assistant, who hovered at her side. "Sully, fill up a jug of water and make sure Tyler drinks it by the end of the day. He needs liquids."

Tyler gave her a defiant stare. "I'm not going to drink. Let me die."

Exhausted from events of the day, she had no patience left. "Would you rather have us force you to drink? I can put you in a straitjacket."

"Bitch!"

She winced and stood up. Tears burned her eyes again. "This is the thanks I get for saving your life. You are welcome. Sully, please give him an enema to open his bowels. He's a real shit."

She punched the bulkhead as she stormed out. She raged at Tyler, at Dr. Pesce, at Robert, and most of all, at herself. Mr. Doolittle awaited at the galley. A cup of chamomile tea and a friendly chat would ease her pain.

Chapter 18

Mr. Doolittle waited, sipping his tea on one of the galley's stools, as promised. He studied her face. "Dear Lord! Is your patient dying?"

Ella collapsed on another stool and clasped her shaking hands. "He's better, but not happy about the treatment. He cussed at me, and I'm ashamed to say, I cussed back."

The chaplain sighed. "Poor dear. You give so much and receive no appreciation for the fine work you do. Why don't you tell me what happened?"

Sipping her piping hot chamomile tea with honey, Ella told the chaplain everything that occurred since she dined with Captain Weston and Robert. The words and tears poured like a flood as she described her first love that left her crushed. She hesitated before revealing the true cause of Dr. Pesce's death, but the chaplain's sympathetic eyes and supportive nods put her at ease.

After her narrative, the chaplain contemplated as he stirred his tea. "That was a heart-wrenching tale, my dear. I'm despairing for your suffering. You didn't need to hide from me how Dr. Pesce died. I'd have given him a Christian funeral no matter what. I'll pray for the young man who almost followed him. You saved not only his life but his soul."

Ella wiped a tear from her nose. "He hasn't taken kindly to my efforts."

The chaplain patted her shoulder. "I'll speak to him and make him see his error. Let's talk about your broken betrothal. I'm confused. You are a woman of means, but you let Robert believe you are penniless? Why?"

She sipped her sweet tea. It warmed her and restored some of her energy. "He loved me for my wealth. I don't want to marry someone who is after my fortune."

He narrowed his eyes. "And it's a sizable fortune?"

"Yes. Sometimes it feels like a burden."

"I imagine it's an onerous responsibility for a young woman. Does someone help you manage your assets?"

Thankful for the kind concern, Ella took another sip. "Yes, my lawyer, Mr. Hastings, and my estate caretaker, Mr. Smiley. They do a good job... as far as I can tell. Their reports aren't easy to comprehend."

Mr. Doolittle leaned forward. "Dr. Parker, I have a proposal for you. You are a special person with able hands and a burning heart. Such women are rare in our vain and immoral society. Away from the hustle and bustle of the city, there's a peaceful refuge for the stoic and devout sisters. Have you considered taking the nunnery vows?"

Tea spilled onto her lap. She shrieked. "Become a nun? But..."

His blue eyes shined with excitement. "As a sister, you'll treat patients, care for the poor. You could continue your education and teach others. Instead of insults and ungratefulness, you'd receive respect and thanks. And you would find belonging among hardworking and compassionate women. What do you say?"

Ella shifted on the wobbly stool. "I never... I imagined I'd get married one day."

The chaplain rose and poured her another cup of tea. "I understand, my dear. Girls are told they will become wives and mothers from early age. It's no wonder anything different never occurred to you, but it's well worth considering. Or are you set on marriage despite your unfortunate experience?"

Ella stared down, sipping the honeyed tea. Its sweetness coated her tongue. "I thought Robert loved me, but I was wrong. I was blind to his vanity. If I marry, all my assets would go to my husband to do as he wishes, while I may need to beg him for every little thing. And he may forbid me from pursuing medicine."

Mr. Doolittle nodded as he sat. "There are many women who escaped cruel husbands and hid themselves beyond a monastery wall. I would abhor for such a tragedy to happen to you. But perhaps you dreamt of children?"

She bit her lip. "I love children, but my mother died in childbirth. I'm afraid to suffer the same fate."

His hands folded in prayer, the chaplain blinked, as if trying to stop himself from tearing up. "May your mother rest in peace. I've given funerals to many such women, ripped from life at a young age, their children left motherless. Husbands can be deaf to their wives' struggles with childbearing. Some men impregnate their spouses despite the doctor telling them that childbirth will kill the mother and likely the child as well. A nun, however, can care for children without risking her life for the esteem of motherhood. I owe my life to the good nuns. When I was a boy, I broke my leg far from home. The sisters brought me to the abbey, set my leg, and nursed me back to health. They also read to me from the Bible, taught me letters, and instilled the spark in my soul that eventually made me a servant of the Lord."

Her soul lifted as she imagined young Doolittle comforted and educated by kind nuns. "How inspiring! But... It's such a radical idea. And there's no turning back."

"Correct. Nunnery vows cannot be broken. I recommend you become a novice to decide if such a life is for you. There's a lovely sanctuary hidden among the forests by Plymouth. I can write a recommendation letter to the abbess. What do you say to this idea?"

Her head hurt from the buzz of thoughts. *Nunhood couldn't be worse than the traps of an unhappy marriage. It could give me purpose and belonging. Why does the idea feel so ominous?*

Ella stood, contemplating. Her body screamed from fatigue. "Thank you for the tea, Mr. Doolittle. I can't give you an answer right now. I never considered this possibility before."

"Weigh your options. Talk to me if you have questions, my dearest friend."

Ella gave him a weak smile.

After the supper of predictable salt beef in her cabin, Ella fell on the cot, too tired to remove her shirt and trousers. It was still early in the evening, but she craved sleep. Drunk voices bellowed vulgar songs. Repelled, she forced herself to rise and lock the door.

A troubled dream came to her where Dr. Pesce was on the bottom of the sea, calling out to her. She bent down over the railing and extended her hand, reaching for him in the dark water. Suddenly the railing disappeared, and she fell into the abyss.

Then she was back in her cabin, but there were men standing over her. One held a lantern over her head. Their faces were familiar, but their rage altered their features, reddening their eyes and baring their teeth. She gagged from the smell of grog and sweat.

It must be another dream. I'm safe in my cabin, with the door locked. She blinked and rubbed her eyes, but the vision did not change.

Simkins threw off her blanket. "Ha! She even sleeps in men's clothing. Grab her!"

Oh God, I'm not asleep! The cold awakening hit her stronger than a spray of icy water. Her hand reached for Olson's whistle under her pillow, but someone grabbed her arms. She drew air to scream. Simkins lodged a wooden gag into her mouth.

Why have locks if people pick them?

"Wanted to curse me? No more trickery from you. We'll have a witch test and make you bring the wind back."

Simkins threw her over his shoulder. She thrashed and punched her assailant on his muscular stomach and chest. He only grunted. The cool air went through her. They were on the deck.

"It's twilight, exactly the hour," someone said.

"Let's see if she's afraid of water!" another yelled, his voice followed by laughs and hoots.

Her heart was in her throat. *What do they mean to do to me?*

Someone grabbed her legs, tied them, and lodged a heavy rock between her knees.

Simkins brought her to the railing, and it dawned on her. They meant to throw her overboard. She shivered with all her body and grabbed her assailant's collar and braid.

"Ouch! Let go, you little bugger!" Simkins roared, but she pulled harder on his braid. In a frenzy, he swung her over the railing, shaking her off himself. She was hanging in the air, holding on by Simkins' hair.

"Why are her hands not tied?" Simkins bellowed. He bent his waist over the railing and reached for Ella's elbow. His fingers circled her arm, but his palm was sweaty and slippery. The next moment, she plunged into the darkness, a lock of Simkin's hair still in her hands. Men's screams echoed and dissipated.

Like the dream.

The water's surface struck like a brick wall. A chill froze her blood. Salt stung her nose and eyes. She was sinking into the pitch-black water.

The rock pulled her down, further into the darkness. Her lungs screamed for air, as bubbles escaped her nose. Cold and fear bound her arms, threatening to still her pulse. Her body became heavy, as if preparing for a long, well-deserved respite. The water weighed on her like a blanket, lulling her into a bed of eternal sleep. Her body was ready to give in, but her mind refused to rest. Gears shifted, and survival instincts sprang into motion.

Witch or not, I'm not drowning. They forgot to tie my hands. I can swim.

She got a hold of the rope that tied her legs and pulled at the knot. It didn't budge. She wrestled with the ropes. Her blood pounded in her temples. Her arms were heavy like lead. She screamed in her head, *Don't stop!* With twisting and thrashing, she loosened the ropes and dislodged the rock between her knees.

Relax, and the water will raise you. Her mother taught her this when she was a child on a seaside holiday. *An object that's lighter than water will float.*

Her limp body slowly rose. The gag shifted in her mouth, and she spat it out. The surface opened, and the cool air hit her face. She coughed; water poured from her nose. Air tasted sweeter than the nectar of the gods. She gave herself a moment to bask in it and thank her fortune that she was wearing trousers and not a heavy skirt. The rope drifted off her legs.

"Ella! Over here!"

Her head snapped to see a boat with a few men coming toward her, and she made a few strokes to meet it. She was a proficient swimmer, taught by her mother during their seaside holidays. Morgan threw her a rope, and she gripped it. Hands pulled and lifted her. She curled into a ball at the bottom of the boat, spitting out the nasty salt water. When she caught her breath, she straightened and shook her head from side to side to relieve the pressure in her ears. A tremor went through her body.

"Here, put this on." Wyse wrapped his uniform jacket over her shoulders. "Your teeth are chattering so hard it's making me cold."

"Thank you."

He stared as if expecting her to say something else.

Her intuition told her that he wanted her to admit her terror. *He expects me to weep like a damsel in distress. I will show him that I can be as brave as any man on his ship.*

"Rather cool day for a swim," she jested. "I appreciate you bringing the boat." She made her voice cheerful to quell the thud of her pulse in her ears.

Wyse's eyebrows rose. "You weren't frightened?"

"Look at Simkins splashing!" One of the oarsmen yelled. "Funniest thing I ever saw!"

Others laughed and pointed. Gripped by the spectacle, none of them rowed. Ella squinted to discern what they stared at. The twilight almost turned to darkness, but after a moment, she saw a figure flailing his arms in the distance as the current swept him further away. His frightened scream reached her ears.

"Simkins? He fell too?"

"Sure did," Morgan answered, chuckling. "Serves him right. He must have slipped when he bent over the railing."

Her neck stiffened. "He's a poor swimmer."

"No worse than most of us. We threw him a life buoy. It's right by him."

One of the oarsmen started. "Whoa, what was that? Looked like a fin."

Simkin's shrieks became louder. "Help! For God's sake, help me! A shark!"

Ella gasped. Her breath stilled.

"Row like hell," Wyse commanded.

The men grabbed their oars and rowed to Morgan's cadence. Ella gripped the side of the boat; her knuckles whitened. "His thrashing would attract the shark. Someone must help him."

Morgan scoffed. "Swim to him with a shark in the water? That's madness."

Simkin's next wail was pure terror.

Wyse removed a pistol from his belt. "I doubt I can get a good shot."

"Impossible," Ella responded. "You'll hit Simkins instead. Who's the strongest swimmer here?"

He shrugged. "I'm not making anyone swim."

The words left her mouth before her mind considered her actions. "Then give me a knife."

He stared like a dummy. She searched the pockets of his jacket and found a jackknife.

Wyse bellowed, "No!" but she threw off his jacket and dove. Her body heated from her muscles pushing against the current. Water sprayed into her eyes and nose, stinging them.

The seaman's terrified shrieks echoed through her. A dorsal fin emerged within five strokes. It had a curvy tip and arched backwards.

Strange, that's not what a shark fin's supposed to look like.

Simkins disappeared underwater. The fin dove as well. Ella screamed in terror. She swam towards the place where the seaman flapped moments ago and filled her lungs with air, preparing to submerge. The powerful back of the sea creature rose. She tensed, preparing to attack it. It flapped its tail up and down and made a cheerful whistle. Ella released the jackknife in surprise. Simkins reappeared, propped up by the clever animal.

"It's a dolphin!" She cried with relief. "Simkins, don't be afraid."

She read that dolphins had been known to save humans by carrying them to the surface, but it was a marvel to witness. The dolphin splashed her with its tail and swam away. Simkins's flapping was weary, his eyes unfocused. She held his head, not letting his chin dip below the surface. The life buoy made of cork, with tails to hold onto, floated nearby. She thrust it into his hands, holding on as well until the boat approached. Wyse grabbed her by the arm, while other men helped Simkins. She beamed at the lieutenant as he pulled her out of the water. The daggers in his eyes stabbed her.

"What were you thinking?" he roared.

"I... saved a life."

Simkins wailed. "The witch commands the sea creatures. She made the shark swim away and called the dolphin." He moaned as his eyes rolled into the back of his head.

"Oh, for heaven's sake." Ella laughed, but the wide-eyed stares startled her. "You don't believe I'm a witch, do you?"

"How did you make the shark leave?" a young oarsman asked, his tone cold and suspicious.

"There was no shark. Simkins panicked. We couldn't see properly in the twilight. It was a clever dolphin."

"You floated," another oarsman piped. "You're a witch."

She scoffed. "This boat and our ship float as well. It's the physics of water, as discovered by Archimedes."

He crossed himself. "Is she another witch? Friend of yours?"

Ella hid her face in her hands, laughing and crying.

"Odds bodkins, the wind's back. Row faster, you devils!" Wyse boomed.

The men cheered and rowed with vigor to Morgan's count. A cold gust blew through Ella's wet clothes and hair, and her teeth rattled. She hugged herself to keep warm. In minutes they were on the gangway, climbing aboard the *Neptune*. Simkins, still in a swoon, had to be lifted by the boatswain's chair.

Captain Grey bellowed commands into the speaking trumpet. "Set the topgallants and the royals! Signal the *Crown* to get the cable ready to tow us!"

Everyone was busy at once, scaling the rigging on all three masts. Sully brought the stretcher to carry Simkins to the sick-bay. Wyse hurried past, heading for the quarterdeck.

"Mr. Wyse!" Ella yelled after him.

He whipped his head back. "What?"

Ella swallowed but made herself speak through her chattering teeth. "Will you tell the captain how I saved Simkins's life? Or maybe you'd finally acknowledge that I belong here?"

His eyes were of an enraged bull. He grasped her collar and pulled so hard her feet almost left the deck.

"I want you off my ship. When we dock at Plymouth, go back to your palace or wherever you came from."

He let go of her, and she fell backwards. He marched away. Her head pounding, she scrambled to her feet and dragged herself first to her cabin to remove her soaked clothes and change into a dress, and then to the sickbay.

"It was the Monster of the Seas, I tell you, lad," Simkin's voice rang in the hatchway. "At least twenty feet long, thousands of teeth."

"Whoa," Sully exclaimed. "A great white."

"The greatest of all whites."

Ella snorted, entering. "Great whites don't live in the English Channel. It was a harmless dolphin."

Simkins threw his pillow at her. "Get away, witch. We all saw you float and command sea creatures. Don't come near me."

She rolled her eyes and stepped over the pillow to examine him. "You should be thanking me for swimming after you, but I don't expect that much."

The sailor swore and showed his large fists. "You get closer, and I will break your nose, witch."

"If only you were this brave when you were splashing and wailing about a non-existent shark. Suit yourself. A patient who boasts and cusses is sure to live."

Ella went to her other patient, Tyler. In her absence, his face regained a healthier color; his eyes now alert.

"Don't bother me," he stammered through his teeth. "Can't you see that you are not wanted? How many times do you need to be told?"

Sully shook his head but said nothing.

Her hands, about to reach for her medicine bag, fell to her side.

How many times have these people told me I'm not wanted? Ella thought. *I risked my life to save a man who could've killed me, but I get no thanks. They all want me to go away. Why should I help?*

She grabbed her medical bag and spun on her heel. "I finally received the message. I hope to never see any of you again."

Tyler's snort, Simkin's cuss, and Sully's silence was the response.

Drained, she trudged to her cabin, barricaded the door with a chair, and fell onto her cot. Hours passed. The ship dipped and rose, as if trying to make up for the idle time. The draft blew through every gap of her cabin. Ella warmed herself under her blanket. Her throat was scratchy, and her muscles ached. In her dreams she saw sea monsters, Wyse with his raging eyes, and Dr. Pesce screaming for her again.

Then the dream changed, and she found herself in a grove. The branches, heavy with fruit, bent towards her. A lively hymn, sung by a choir of women's voices, sounded from the pinnacled church behind her. Several nuns came out, smiling and waving to her. Warmth and hope enveloped her.

A knock on the door disturbed her tranquil dream. She stirred, refusing to leave the heavenly place.

"Dr. Parker, I know it's late, but I want to make sure you are alright," Captain Grey said.

Her tongue refused to obey. A sleepy moan sounded instead of speech.

"Sir, she must be dead asleep. Drunk and exhausted... I doubt she'll be up anytime soon." False notes sounded in Wyse's voice.

What did he mean about me being drunk? her mind wondered, as she yawned, too tired to ask out loud.

Captain Grey spoke. "That's too bad. I have a busy day tomorrow. Accounts to prepare before our docking at Plymouth. Please tell Dr. Parker when she wakes that... she should resign her position upon arrival. Simkins will get his due, but her behavior was just as abhorrent. She could've died, and no one to blame but her own foolishness. I hope she thanked you for rescuing her with such haste."

"Yes..." Wyse stammered. "We've already spoken. She wishes to go home."

Ella tossed and turned, half-asleep. The voices buzzed like annoying flies. She wanted them to quiet so she could enjoy the songs in her dream.

"Let me sleep, damn you," she muttered.

"Hmm... It's settled then." Captain Grey's voice rang with finality and disappointment.

In the morning, a violent cough rocked her chest. The thought of her usual breakfast of burned oats turned her stomach. She remained on her cot, drifting in and out of sleep.

Eight bells marked the end of the afternoon watch. Someone rustled behind the door. "Doctor Ella, can I come in?" Tobby asked.

She slipped on her dress and allowed the boy to enter.

He tiptoed in, carrying a steaming cup. "I made you tea."

"That was so kind of you, Tobby. Thank you." Ella accepted the cup from him but cringed at the odor of rotten eggs. "What did you put in it?"

"Sully let me take some herbs."

"Black horehound. It's not for tea."

The boy's face fell. "I'm sorry."

"It's the thought that matters." She put the cup on the table. "Come sit with me."

Tobby smiled and clambered onto the cot next to her. She wrapped a blanket around herself.

"What are the other boys doing?" she asked.

"Mr. Doolittle made us copy lines. I feigned a bellyache and sneaked away."

Ella gave him a stern look. "Feigned a bellyache? Have you ever feigned bellyaches with me?"

"No! Well... once. I was sad and wanted to hear your stories. Tell me how you spoke to the shark and made the dolphin come."

Ella burst out laughing. "Is that what the men are saying? That I speak to sharks and summon dolphins?"

"Aha. And that you floated, which proves you're a witch. And... You and Simkins were drunk and fell overboard in a fight. That's what Wyse's telling everyone, even the captain. I heard them myself. The captain said that such behavior from a woman is disgusting."

Ella's face heated. "And everyone believes this of me?"

Tobby glanced down. "Yes, because after you fell overboard, the wind came back. Some men also say you brought Dr. Pesce bad luck, and he died. Your sweetheart learned of your powers and didn't want to marry you."

Ella's lips quivered. "How do they know about me and Robert?"

"A few men saw you return his pendant."

She hid her face in her hands. Nothing stayed hidden on the ship. When revealed, the secret took a life of its own.

Tobby patted her shoulder. "The boys and I don't believe what they said about the doctor. You loved him. I said you are the cleverest woman in the world, and that's why you could swim and call dolphins for help, but the other boys still think that you may be a witch. Mr. Doolittle said we are growing up superstitious dolts."

"That's not your fault. Here." She opened her sea chest, and after some rummaging, found a book at the bottom. "This book is about sea creatures. It shows how you can tell a dolphin from a shark. They have different dorsal fins and tails. Dolphins make various sounds, while sharks don't. Dolphins are clever, and they help their sick pod mates reach the surface to breathe. They have been known upon occasion to save humans as well."

The boy leafed through pages, marveling at the drawings. "Do you have more books?"

She smiled. "Oh yes. There's a thought. Would you please go to the hold and have someone help you to bring all my bags? I'll leave the books to you and the other boys."

Tobby's head snapped up. "What do you mean?"

"When we dock at Plymouth, I'm going to leave. I want you to keep my books and read them. Start with the novels, but eventually, you should read about science. You'll find a story about the Greek man named Archimedes who took a bath and discovered the principle that explains which objects sink or float."

The boy's eyes teared. "I don't want you to leave. Take me with you to your castle. I won't be a good powder monkey with my limp. If no one wants to marry you, maybe I will, when I'm older."

Tears flooded her eyes. She turned away from him. "I'm not going back to my estate. There's nothing there for me. No family or friends. The neighbors will snub me for becoming a surgeon and living on the ship."

"Why?"

Ella sighed. "That's how the world is. I'll never belong with the prim ladies. And I don't belong here either. That fact was made clear to me."

"You'll leave tomorrow?"

"Is that when we are expected to dock at Plymouth?"

"If the wind holds up, or so I heard. But don't leave. I don't want you to go."

A sob escaped her lips. "I'm sorry, but I must. I'll always remember you. Meeting you and the other boys was one of the few good things that happened to me on this ship."

He pulled out a handkerchief from his pocket and offered it to her. "You said to give it to a lady if she cries."

She smiled and looked the boy over, glad to note that he was a little taller and much better groomed since she first met him. His cheeks were rosy, but he was too thin. "I'll write a note to the captain asking him to give you a different job. Maybe you'll be a cook's boy and get more food to eat."

Tobby rubbed his belly. "Good. I'm hungry all the time. Oh, what about my cake? I was dreaming about it last night."

Ella chuckled through tears. "I haven't forgotten. You'll have cake. Not too much though, or you'll get a stomachache."

The boy nodded, and she threw her arms around him. Her heart ached ahead of the upcoming parting with her boys.

“Dr. Ella, are you alright?” The boy pulled away, alarmed. “Your cheeks are hot, and you are shivering. Maybe you are sick?”

“I am, but not in the way you mean. Please get help to bring my things from the hold and tell Mr. Doolittle that I’d like to speak to him.”

Tobby looked at her with uncertainty but obeyed. As he limped out of the cabin, she whispered a prayer for him to stay safe and healthy. She wouldn’t say goodbye to the other boys; it would hurt too much. And there was no reason to say goodbyes to the ungrateful seamen who ignored her diligent work, spread wild rumors, played vicious pranks, and denied her friendship.

Chapter 19

"The lass, I mean Dr. Parker, is ashore, sir," Morgan reported on the gangway. He held a round box with ribbons in his hands. Wyse had no idea what it could be.

What's done is done. Wyse congratulated himself on another deed accomplished before breakfast. The ship safely docked at Plymouth, and the girl was out of his life. The *Neptune* will go to the dockyard today or tomorrow, and then he'd reward himself with a visit to his favorite tavern. He took a swig from his flask, hoping the brandy would quiet the nagging voice in his head that told him he mistreated Ella.

Why should I care if her precious feelings are hurt? She'll go to her palace and arrange a ball.

He dismissed the coxswain, but Morgan gave him a hesitant glance and lifted the round box.

"What's this, Morgan?"

"It's... a cake, sir. For Tobby, one of the boys."

"Huh? What cake? I don't understand."

Morgan cringed and stared down. "I don't either. Dr. Parker was crying the whole time in the boat. When we docked, she asked me to go to the baker with her and ordered this cake. She gave me and the men money to enjoy a good breakfast while the baker made it. Then she waved goodbye and shed more tears. I asked her to write to me. I haven't gotten any letters in years. But she said... where she's going, there may be no writing letters."

Wyse's rotten tooth gave a sharp ache. "What is that supposed to mean? Surely there's post in Newcastle."

"Don't know, sir. Her look, when she said it, gave me chills."

Wyse took another swig of brandy, but his throat constricted, and he choked.

"You alright, sir?" Morgan asked.

"Aye."

A tingle trickled down his spine. Nightmares haunted him since the evening Simkins threw Ella overboard. Everything went wrong that night. He imagined he'd rescue the girl like a knight in a story. Broken and afraid, she would beg him to bring her home. Instead, Ella saved herself and jested about a good swim. And then, she jumped back into the water to save Simkins. Wyse died a thousand deaths watching her swim to the rescue. Learning that there was no shark gave him little relief. When he closed his eyes at night, he saw an enormous great white pull Ella under, and the water coloring rusty red. That nightmare would be followed by the one that haunted him the past ten years: his betrothed, Charlotte Fitzharris, lying in the pool of her blood.

After dismissing Morgan, he ordered himself to take his mind off Ella. Her plans were no longer his business. Captain Grey would have orders regarding the ship repairs. Wyse marched aft to the captain's cabin.

The ship boys lingered by the quarterdeck. A couple of them wept and sniffed into those fancy handkerchiefs they carried.

"Tobby, there's cake for you. Morgan has it," he said in passing.

The boy didn't react. "Sir, where did Doctor Ella go?"

Wyse shrugged. "Back to her palace."

"Something's wrong! We need to find her."

Wyse bent to the boy's level. "What are you talking about, lad? Why should you care where she went?"

"Because she cared about us!" The boy's voice rang, becoming louder. "Why did she leave behind her dresses, her jewels, even her medical things?"

Wyse's stomach, irritated with a breakfast of grog and brandy, twisted into a knot.

Seamen crowded behind the boys, listening, whispering among themselves. Olson, back after finishing his punishment, stared with his arms crossed. A few men strode towards Ella's cabin, talking with excitement about the money that the fancy gowns and the jewelry would bring, but Wyse's voice stopped them at once. "No one enters her cabin. If even one pin goes missing, the thief will be punished according to the Articles of War."

The men halted and stepped back. He gripped Tobby's shoulder. "Show me what you mean, son."

The boy hobbled aft, and Wyse followed. They stepped inside the cabin, and Tobby pointed to the cot where Ella's dresses were laid out. A small velvet bag sat next to them. Wyse pulled on the strings and found a pair of diamond earrings, a set of pearls, an emerald necklace, and a matching bracelet. Wyse gawked at the shimmering jewels, his jaw ajar.

Tobby touched his arm. "Her men's clothes are gone, but she left her dresses. Why would she leave such pretty things behind?"

"She must mean to come back for them," Wyse answered without conviction.

"There's a note on her pillow. I can't read her fancy letters." The boy handed him a neatly folded piece of paper, and Wyse brought it to the lantern to read.

The elaborate writing said: *Gift or sell, as you wish*. There was no signature, but it was unnecessary. No one else on the ship penned such neat and elegant letters.

"What's the devil?" he muttered.

"And her instruments," the boy added, pointing at a battered case filled with blades, needles, and forceps. A stack of books lay next to them, along with a journal. “There is another note on top of the books.”

Wyse read the second note in the same impeccable handwriting. *The books are for the boys. The instruments and journal are for your next surgeon.*

“Mr. Wyse, she was so sad yesterday.” There was a frantic note in his voice. “She said she can’t go home because other fine ladies won’t talk to her. Where did she go? Why did she leave all this behind?”

He stared at the sniveling boy. His gut twisted in premonition of something sinister. “I don’t know.”

“You don’t think she means... to die?”

Wyse’s heart pained like someone punched him in the chest. If the girl decided to off herself, it would be on his conscience. The captain ordered him to keep her safe, but instead he pushed her over the brink. Every few years someone on the ship took their life, and each time Wyse wondered if he had a hand in driving the man to it. This time there would be no doubt in his mind or anyone else’s.

“Maybe she has not done it yet? We need to find her!” Tobby urged.

Wyse’s mind snapped into action.

“Have you spoken to her this morning?”

“No, I was helping the cook with breakfast. I came just now to ask when she would get cake for me. I didn’t know she was gone already. I don't want that cake anymore. I want her back!" Tobby sobbed and shook from head to toe.

Devil take me if I understand women. She abandoned her prized possessions but kept some silly promise to the ship boy.

Wyse took the trembling boy by his shoulder. "Pull yourself together, son. We'll find her."

He gave the lad a reassuring look, but his head swam. *Where am I going to look for her? And when? There's work all day.*

He and Tobby returned to the deck. The boy rejoined his friends; they put their heads together, talking. The men argued, and some threw hostile glances his way. Wyse motioned for them to get closer by the quarterdeck.

"It's a strange business. I don't know why she left her things, but I will find out," he announced.

"What she left behind is ours. We can sell her things at the market and share the profit," Simkins yelled. His cronies cheered in approval.

"Do you think us fools? You'll keep the money for yourself," someone yelled.

Wyse stomped his foot. "I already said no one will touch her things. I'm putting a sentry by her door. Now, did anyone speak to the woman in a last couple of days?"

No one volunteered. Wyse was about to dismiss them when Olson piped. "Simkins, you didn't bother to thank Dr. Parker for saving your life? Or to say you are sorry for throwing her overboard?"

Simkins spat on the deck then crossed himself. "Damn me if I go near the witch who can speak to sea creatures. She's even more powerful than I feared!"

Wyse gritted his teeth. "You spit on the deck or call her a witch again, I'll feed you to the sharks myself, piece by piece."

Simkins shuddered, and Wyse nodded in satisfaction.

"What about you, Wyse?" Olson piped, pushing his way to the front. "What did you say to her?"

Wyse started. "Address me as your officer! Or should I return you to the hold?"

Olson kept his gaze leveled with Wyse, standing inches away from him. "I'm not afraid. I warned you about Simkins's plan. Why wasn't he arrested?"

Wyse winced from a lump in his throat. "The accusations had to be proven."

"Yet you told Morgan to prepare the boat. You let that vile 'witch test' happen because you wanted to scare Dr. Parker and appear as her rescuer. Instead, she saved Simkins's life."

Wyse threw up his hands. "What does this have to do with her disappearance?"

Olson quieted. After a minute of silence, his eyes cast down, his voice soft. "When I ran from my master and gained my freedom, I forbade myself from remembering the plantation. But I'll tell you what made me risk my life and run."

Everyone quieted to listen. Olson continued. "One night, I, and the other slaves, heard screams. We hurried out of our shed and saw the master's house aflame. The master, the mistress, and their daughter were outside, screaming that the young master was trapped in his bedroom. He was a mean boy of five, but only a child. I ran into the house. The smoke singed my eyes and my lungs. I carried him out. The rest of the night, I felt as light as a sparrow in the sky. I didn't even know I had burns all over my hands and legs. In my mind, my masters were thanking me on their knees and giving me my freedom. Then the next day passed, and not a word came from my masters. I was put to work as usual. At dinner, I received an extra helping of food, and that was all. All feelings left me, and I was dead inside. Such ingratitude was worse than the beatings I received. That night, I ran."

Olson raised his head to look at the men, who stood frozen, as if spellbound. A few had tears in the corners of their eyes. He walked forward and stopped a few steps aside from Wyse, facing the men. "You may wonder why I'm telling you all this. At first, I didn't care for the wealthy gentlewoman. Her walk was like the young mistress's, with a stiff back and a proud chin. Yet, I found that she's not that different from us. She toiled, she didn't complain, she wanted to make friends. It's hard to fit in when you are not like everyone else. I would know. But my friends made my life here bearable." He glanced at Wyse. Sentimental smiles softened their features, reflecting shared memories of their youth.

Olson filled his lungs before continuing. "She had no friends other than the boys. Dr. Pesce died, her sweetheart refused her. None of us said a kind word. Simkins blamed her for the calm and threw her overboard. I bet you all were cheering. When Simkins imagined himself being attacked by a shark, Dr. Parker swam to his rescue. He still didn't thank her or apologize."

"Simkins, you dirty bastard!" some yelled, and the crowd murmured in agreement.

Olson nodded. "Yes, Mr. Simkins is one of the foulest men I ever met. But what about the rest of us? You spread rumors about her being a witch, talking to sharks, bringing bad luck. None of you showed kindness or respect. I thought us better men. A crew who cares for one another. Too late to wonder what happened to Dr. Parker. She didn't say where she was going and why because none of us, except for ship boys, earned her friendship."

Tyler, pale and thinned like after a lengthy illness, stepped forward. "It's true. She saved my life. I failed to thank her as well. I cussed at her while she treated me. Sully and I taunted her because Mr. Wyse said she'd never be friends with common sailors. But she was an excellent doctor. She might've saved Dr. Pesce had we told her about the laudanum he was taking. And I don't think she counted herself above us, even if she's of gentle birth and educated."

"You tricked us, Mr. Wyse," one of the topmen said. "You started the rumor that Hart fell to his death after the woman cursed him. That was a lie. Dr. Parker asked you to give us a break to drink water."

Wyse's face wrinkled and he stooped. His mind raced for an argument that would bring these men back to his side.

Olson piped, his eyes blazing with fury. "Mr. Wyse tricked Dr. Parker as well, getting her drunk. After his applejack, she almost fell from the riggings."

The men stared at Wyse with animosity. Wyse cringed. His authority dangled on a fine string. He gave a dismissive snort. "Oh, don't look at me. You didn't like the hussy with her prim manners. If not for me, she would've asked the captain to cut the grog rations."

"Her father got drunk and wounded her," Tobby yelled from the midst of the crowd. "People do foolish things and get hurt when they drink too much."

"We liked her lessons in nice manners. She wanted us to grow up gentlemen and have a better life," Digby added next to him.

"I don't care if I get a bit less grog. I've drunk enough for two livers already," the cook, known for his love of spirits, piped.

For the second time that day, Wyse's jaw hung open. His men had rarely ever surprised him before. Spirits were what they lived for, or so he believed. There was only one thing to do to save his authority and right the wrongs.

He extended his hands, palms open. "I take responsibility for all this. Captain Grey ordered me to keep Doctor Parker safe. I protected her, but I encouraged unkindness towards her too.

We will find her and set things right. I'll ask the captain..." His voice rose with excitement.

The men straightened. Whispered conversations silenced. Their eyes were directed to Wyse's right, to the pathway that led to the captain's cabin.

Captain Grey emerged onto the deck and advanced on Wyse. "What will you ask the captain, Mr. Wyse? What's going on here?"

Wyse took a long breath, but his chest squeezed as he saluted his superior.

"Sir... I've failed to comply with your orders. You asked me to ensure Dr. Parker's safety, but I purposely endangered her life on two occasions. I must give you a full account of what happened the night she climbed the rigging and then also when she fell ... I mean, was thrown overboard. I will accept your punishment, but, most urgently, I must find her."

Captain Grey gave him a measured stare. "Yes, you'll tell me everything. She left me a note. The way she worded her goodbye gave me an ominous feeling. Find her and bring her back. You better not fail."

Chapter 20

The night breeze penetrated through Ella's clothes, damp after the rain. Her knees shook from the cold and weariness. Numbness spread through her arms from the weight of the bundles she carried. When her blistered feet refused another step, a bell tolled. Not the curt ring that marked every half-hour on the ship, but a melodic, soulful sound. A church bell of the monastery.

With the little energy left in her, she pushed on, spurring herself with thoughts of an inviting fire and a warm bed. A brick wall appeared in the distance; slanted roofs and a church pinnacle loomed beyond it. Ella reached the gate with a heavy padlock. *My ship's crew would pick this lock in moments,* she thought with amusement. Then she shook her head, chasing away the notion. *They are not 'my' crew.*

She walked alongside the wall, spied a closed window, and knocked. Voices whispered beyond it.

"I think I see a boy. Maybe a young man."

"Is he handsome?"

"Why do you, a Bride of Christ, want to know if he's handsome? What I want to know is what he's doing here late at night."

Ella removed Mr. Doolittle's letter from her pocket. "Sisters, please. I mean you no harm. I'm a woman. I need your help."

Talking seeped the last of her strength. The world spun and careened. The stars in the sky mixed with the flashes before her eyes; she fell to the ground.

***

Heat spread from Ella's aching head to her swollen toes. Her limbs were heavier than lead. She slipped in and out of sleep. In moments of clarity, she gazed around the roomy cell with its cheery fire in the corner. Spirited songs and prayers flowed in from the window.

A nun's face with a pointed chin loomed over her. A large pectoral cross hung from her chest. The sister shook her by the shoulder.

"Miss Parker, we are all praying for your recovery. But everything is God's will. Mr. Doolittle wrote that you are a devout woman with no family. If the Lord is ready to receive you, don't you want your earthly possessions to go to the Church? Please sign this document, and we'll take care of the rest."

"I'm too weak to read this," Ella whispered. "I didn't come here to die. Please bring me some willow bark tea."

The nun frowned. "No cure is stronger than a prayer, my child. Let's recite *Our Father* together."

Ella tried to sit up. Her head reeled. "Surely you have healers here. I need medicine to break this fever."

The nun turned to the cross on the wall as if she didn't hear. With folded hands, she intoned, "Our Father, who art in heaven..."

Ella's throat parched. "Get me a bloody healer... darn it," she rasped, fighting to breathe.

The nun glared down. Her mouth twisted, ready to admonish. A younger sister with apple cheeks tiptoed in, making her shift her indignant stare.

"What is it, Sister Claire? Can't you see I'm busy."

"Mother Superior, the orphanage supervisor is here. She said she can't wait long."

"Ah. Thank you. That is urgent business. Miss Marietta's baby must be well cared for. I'm coming."

When they left, another nun shuffled in, carrying a steaming cup. Gray strands of hair escaped from under her veil.

"I thought they'd never leave. Drink this."

Ella sipped the bitter taste of willow bark sweetened with honey. Her eyelids became heavy again.

An arm shook her. "No, no. Drink to the bottom. I'll bring you more tonight."

Ella finished the tea. Rough but gentle hands lowered her back onto the pillow and tucked her in like a child.

"I'm a healer too," Ella said through sleep.

The nun chuckled. "Good. That makes one of us."

***

Ella strolled through the garden, stopping to smell the yellow then pink chrysanthemums and compare their fragrances. This was her third day at the monastery, but the previous two were foggy in her mind. Recovered from her fever, she was eager to explore the grounds. Fall only started to color the leaves gold and red on the trees beyond the garden. The bees from the nearby beehive buzzed and collected the nectar. Two sisters in habits kneeled in the grass, weeding. They rose and greeted Ella and her companion, Sister Claire.

"Are you well, Miss Ella?" one of them asked, smiling. "What a nasty bout of fever. We all prayed for you."

"Yes, I'm much better," Ella replied, shifting the veil away from her eyes. "Thank you."

"Thank God!" the nun corrected, looking up to the sky. "All healing comes from Him."

"Do you have everything you need?" the other woman asked. "I can bring you more bath oil and pillows. You are our guest, and the abbess said to pamper you."

"I'm most grateful for your hospitality." Ella ran her hands over the coarse fabric. "Except I'd like my clothes back. Wearing a habit doesn't seem right. I'm not a nun, only a visitor."

"But it suits you! You look like a sister," Sister Claire declared, and the three nuns grinned at Ella.

An uncomfortable sensation gnawed in her chest. *Why? This place is tranquil, and the sisters are sweet.*

Ella addressed her guide. "I'd like to survey the infirmary. If I stay here, it would be to help the sick. Also, where is the surgical set I brought? I asked several times for it."

Sister Claire frowned. "We are looking for it. I'm sure it will be found. The infirmary..." Her expression brightened. "Oh, would you like to visit the library? It's beautiful."

Ella fidgeted. "All right. I'd like an enjoyable book to read. And the medical texts interest me as well."

The sister led her a short distance to a small brick building. Inside it, Ella found a fireplace with a vibrant fire, a divan that one could sink in, and pictured windows with Biblical designs. She'd love to spend hours in this inviting room, inhaling the intoxicating smell of old books. Except the reading selection was minuscule—a couple of stands with dusty volumes.

"Strange. Mr. Doolittle boasted a great library." Ella inspected the titles. "Only religious texts. Is that all you have?"

"Oh no, not all." The young nun winked at her and reached behind the tallest volumes to remove a couple of tattered books with pages loose and crumpled. "French novels! I can't read French but leafing through these gives me giggles. Some even have pictures, but Mother Superior ripped and burned the ones she found."

Ella raised an eyebrow. "What about science and medicine books?"

"Mother Superior burned those as well. They were full of heretic lies. And the medical books had indecent illustrations of naked bodies."

Ella's breath stilled. In her mind, her medical pursuits didn't conflict with her religious beliefs. There was nothing indecent about textbook anatomy illustrations. Part of her wanted to run from this strange place already.

"How do you heal the sick if you don't have medical books?"

Sister Claire returned the French book to its hiding place. Her expression grew serious. "With God's help, of course. Also... Sister Frances, who's in charge of the infirmary, has books on medicinal plants. Would you like to see her garden? The daisies and hibiscus are pretty."

"Why not?"

The nun led her out of the library and towards the gardens. When they passed a bench, Ella's muscles, achy after two days in bed, cramped. Her head was heavy and sluggish.

"I need to sit."

The sister threw up her hands. "Of course! Please don't let me tire you."

Ella stretched her legs, removed the veil, and shook her clammy hair.

Sister Claire gave her a disapproving look. "The veil feels uncomfortable at first, but the more you wear it, the faster you get used to it."

Ella met her gaze. "Why was I given these clothes? I'm not a nun yet. I want to learn about your life and decide if I should stay."

The sister crossed her arms. "You can't wear your shirt and trousers. Sister Charity mistook you for a man and fainted from fright."

Ella suppressed a snort. "What? You never see men?"

Her cheeks reddening, Sister Claire tilted her head. "Some of us seek seclusion from the horrors of the world. Sister Charity survived an attack by outlaws and is terrified of men. But those of us who feed the poor or tend to the sick are more worldly. Sister Frances, that's her over there, is not shy with men at all. She came here from a ... what do you call a place where the men go to meet a woman and..." The young nun snickered.

Ella's eyes widened. "You mean a house of ill repute?"

"Yes. Can you imagine? But that was years ago. Now she's a proper nun and heads the infirmary. Oh, she's coming towards us." The young sister stifled her giggles and composed her face as Sister Frances advanced at a brisk pace.

Ella recognized the nun's wrinkled face with bright gray eyes. This was the woman who brought her willow bark tea that broke her fever. Sister Claire greeted the older nun, but the woman ignored her and addressed Ella instead.

"You said you're a healer."

"Yes."

"Delivered babies?"

Ella liked her direct manner. "I'm not a midwife, but yes."

"Come with me."

Ella stood, but Sister Claire caught her hand. "Sister Frances, Mother Superior's instruction didn't..."

"Sister Claire!" the older nun exclaimed as if she just noticed her. "Don't you have carrots to pull or goats to milk?"

The young woman huffed. "I'm giving our guest a tour per the abbess's directives."

"I will take it from here and show her the infirmary. I'm sure she prefers seeing it to the chicken coop or the cow shed."

Sister Frances took Ella's palm. The younger nun frowned and grabbed her other hand. For a moment, Ella was caught in a tug-of-war between the two nuns, each pulling her in their direction. She yanked her arm from the younger woman's grip.

"Sorry, Sister Claire, but I'd like to inspect the infirmary. You can show me the rest of the grounds later."

The gray-haired woman started towards a building in the distance, still gripping Ella's hand, as if afraid someone would whisk her away.

"I trust you are feeling better," she said.

Ella grinned. "Yes. Thank you for the willow bark tea. You know your herbs."

"Not well enough."

Sister Frances glanced behind, and Ella turned as well. Sister Claire sped as quickly as her skirts allowed towards a large building by the church.

The nun snorted. "Goody two-shoes is running to Mother Superior. You just chose my side, healer."

Ella's legs froze. "What side? I don't want to be caught in some dispute."

The sister stopped as well and placed her hands on her hips. "I thought a healer would want to relieve the suffering. I'll send you to shovel manure if you prefer."

Ella flinched. "I want to help the sick. But what do you mean about taking sides? Don't you all work for the common good?"

The nun balled her fists. "There are things going on here that I don't support. I need allies."

She turned from Ella and sped forward. Ella caught up, wiping sweat off her brow.

"Please tell me about the infirmary. Mr. Doolittle said you have a big hospital with many beds."

The sister gave her a sharp look. "Did Mr. Doolittle send you here? He's Mother Superior's old friend. I wonder what his game is. But if he boasted about our hospital, you'll be disappointed. I received the infirmary assignment last month, and I won't tell you how I got it. The sister who had it before me believed in healing by prayers only. No medicine."

Ella's jaw slacked. "But..."

A shadow crossed the nun's face. "Yes, some people died while sisters prayed. I'm putting a stop to that madness. We planted medicinal herbs and bought remedies from the apothecary. Right now, we have only one patient, a pregnant woman. The baby's position seems wrong to me. I have your surgical set. Sorry, I took it without your permission, but I wanted it hidden. You may need it."

Her heart pumped as it always did when contemplating a delivery. The set she brought with her contained scalpels, needles, catgut... forceps. *I packed the obstetrical forceps, didn't I? I left Dr. Pesce's old instruments for the Neptune's new surgeon, but I brought my tools.*

When they neared the building, Sister Frances grabbed Ella's shoulder and gave her a conspiratorial grin. The nun's eyes twinkled. "What ship did you come from?"

Ella's eyebrows rose. "You know about me?"

"Sister Claire gossips like a fishwife. I bet she told you that I worked in a brothel. Well?"

"The *Neptune*."

The sister gave a gleeful shriek. "Is old Morgan still there?"

Ella smiled. "Yes. He was nicer than most. Brash, but kind."

The nun ran her tongue over her lips. "Well, he's a seadog, not a prince. He visited me when he was allowed ashore in Plymouth. We had fun. But enough prattling, we have a patient to help. Poor girl, she's been here for three months, and does nothing but cry. Her sister as well."

A prickle went through Ella's skin. "Why do they cry? What's going on here?" She tossed her head. "Listen, Sister Frances, I will examine this mother and help with the delivery, but then I will go. This place is not the paradise the chaplain described. Power struggles, book burning, healing by prayer. I don't want to be part of any of it."

The older woman sighed. "You think I like it? And leaving may not be so easy."

Ella's eyes bulged. "What do you mean?"

The nun didn't answer and ushered her into the rundown stone building with a cracked façade. The sobs and wails reached Ella's ears as she stepped into the gloomy corridor. Not the shrieks of a woman in active labor, but heart-wrenching moans of someone's despair. Ella gazed around. The ward ahead of her had several beds, but all were empty.

The sister pointed at the door. "She's in confinement."

Unsure what to expect, Ella stepped inside. Dim light from the curtained window illuminated a small chamber with a bed, a basin, and a large cross on the wall. The cell was hot from the fire in the wood stove and reeked of sweat and urine.

The young woman on the bed lay on her side and clutched her pregnant belly as she cried. A slightly younger woman in a habit patted her shoulder while wiping her own tears with the other hand. Ella's jaw dropped when she recognized their faces, and they in turn gave shrieks of surprise.

"Marietta! Henrietta! How are you here?" Ella squealed, shocked to find her childhood friends whom she last saw at Veronica's wedding.

"Eloise!" Henrietta, who stood by her sister's bed, flew into Ella's arms. "Please save us! Take us away from here! Or are you a nun too?"

Ella hugged her tightly. "No, I'm not a nun. Why are you so upset?"

Marietta sat up, rubbing her belly, her expression pained. "Eloise, please, will you help me?"

Worried, Ella came to her side. "Of course, I'll help. You know I'm a doctor. How do you feel?"

"No... Help me keep my baby. The nuns will take the child away from me."

"Surely not."

Sister Frances approached the foot of the bed. "They will take the baby to the orphanage. The unwed mother will remain here and take the nunnery vows."

"I want to go home with my baby!" Marietta wailed, her hands clutching her abdomen, as if protecting the life inside it.

Henrietta sighed and stroked her sister's shoulder. "You can't come home. Mother forbade it. But I won't leave you."

Ella's heart flipped. She stared down Sister Frances. "You won't allow these atrocities to happen, right? These women can't be forced into monasticism. The baby must stay with its mother."

Sister Frances raised her arms as if in surrender. "Not much I can do. I only have a couple of sisters on my side. My best hope is to learn what orphanage the abbess will send the baby to and find it later."

Marietta covered her face with her hands. "My baby will be gone."

Ella caressed Marietta's hair, soothing her friend. "I'll do all I can to take you, your baby, and your sister away from here. But first, you must give birth to a healthy child. Calm yourself for its sake and tell me, what are you feeling?"

Marietta rubbed her swollen stomach. "It's been making a ruckus inside me all day."

"Ah, maybe it's ready to break for freedom, like its mother. Have you felt painful cramps?"

"Only pinches. They don't hurt."

"Good. Relax and let me examine you. Hold your sister's hand, Henrietta."

Ella put her hands under Marietta's nightgown, examined the cervix, and then palpated her firm belly.

Baby's kicks pounded at her touch. She smiled to reassure Marietta. "It's a very active baby." Except, the kicks were lower than where she expected them. She looked for the head. "Oh..." her hand stilled.

Marietta gasped. "What is it?"

Ella chewed her lip. Her temples squeezed, but she steadied her voice and relaxed her face. "The baby is in the breech position, pelvis first. I suspect the ruckus you felt was the baby turning."

"Goodness!" Henrietta cried.

Sister Frances groaned. "As if their troubles weren't enough. I've never delivered a breech baby."

Me neither. If only Matilda were here.

Ella's palms sweated. As usual, thoughts of childbirth made her insides coil. She addressed the nun. "Could you find an experienced midwife?"

Sister Frances wrung her hands. "It would require Mother Superior's permission. I doubt she will grant it."

Marietta sobbed. "Eloise, please save my baby. If I die, so be it, but I want my child to live."

Ella drew in a deep breath. "Stop this nonsense. There's no need to fret. Many infants are born breech, but the headfirst delivery is optimal. I suspect you have a few days before your labor starts. Use them to help the baby turn. Stay calm and relax your stomach muscles. Eat well so you have strength to push this baby. Walks in the garden will do you a world of good."

Marietta's eyes widened. "A walk? The nuns don't let me leave this room!"

"What?" Ella lifted her head to address Sister Frances, but three nuns entered, their habits swishing. With so many women in black, the chamber seemed overrun by crows.

A woman with a pointed chin and a pectoral cross on a gold chain gave Ella a wide smile and extended her hand. "Miss Ella, you were unwell at our first meeting and mayn't remember me. I am Mother Superior. We are overjoyed you've recovered from your fever. Our prayers have been answered."

Ella recognized the nun who wanted her to sign a document. She didn't accept the hand. "Why do you want to separate this mother and her baby?"

Mother Superior's smile widened. "Goodness, this must be a misunderstanding. Let's talk in my chamber over dinner."

"Don't listen to her, Eloise," Marietta shouted.

"She's a monster," Henrietta warned, hugging her sister.

The abbess shook her head in an arch. "Poor dears don't know what they are saying. Come, Miss Ella. We have much to discuss."

Marietta clutched her abdomen and sobbed. "Eloise, our mother was awful to you. We did nothing to help you when your parents passed. But if you can forgive us... Promise you will save my child!"

Ella turned to Marietta and met her tearful gaze. "I promise. I'll do everything I can."

The abbess and sisters pulled Ella towards the door.

Chapter 21

Lieutenant Wyse wheezed as he walked along the busy streets, passing by taverns and inns favored by seamen. Merry music and songs boomed from hospitable dining rooms, warmed by burning hearths. The smell of roasted meat made his mouth water. He had spent all day searching for Ella, without stopping for breakfast or dinner.

"Mr. Wyse, did you find Dr. Ella?" a thin voice called behind him, and he spun around. Tobby was limping towards him, his eyes shining with hopefulness. The limp and that revering gaze halted the bout of cussing that came up Wyse's throat.

"What are you doing here, lad? Everyone is supposed to be helping with the ship repairs. I only let ten men go ashore, and you weren't one of them."

"I sneaked away from the dockyard. I wanted to find Dr. Ella, but no luck."

Wyse sighed. “I had no luck either. The constable assured me that no dead women turned up in the last three days. But... I’ve been everywhere. She didn’t hire a coach, or buy a horse, or board a ship. No one noticed her at inns, taverns, or... the houses you are too young to know about.”

“The whorehouses? Why would she be there?”

Wyse cleared his throat. “Never hurts to check. The point is, no one saw her in Plymouth, but I can’t see how she left the city.”

The lad scratched his head. “She could’ve walked somewhere to hide. And then waited to see if we’re looking for her.”

Wyse was about to respond that adults don’t play hide-and-seek but stopped himself. He already admitted that he didn’t understand women, especially Ella. Every possibility, even a strange and unlikely one, should be considered.

He bent down to the boy. “Son, you were the last person, besides Morgan, to speak to Dr. Ella. The best help you could give me is to remember that last conversation and any hint where she went.”

Tobby squeezed his eyes in concentration. “She said she won’t return to her palace because the rich people would snub her. Then she sent me to the hold to bring her things. And... oh, how could I forget! Mr. Wyse!”

Wyse grabbed his shoulder. “What? What is it?”

“She wanted Mr. Doolittle to visit her.”

"The chaplain? He resigned the same day Ella left. I saw him at an inn earlier. He was eating a roasted pig at..." Wyse rubbed his forehead with his fist. "Hmm, where was it? At the Cooked Goose? That's it!"

Wyse sped up the street with Tobby at his heels. The three-story red brick house attracted visitors with its large sign depicting a goose and tempting smells of roasting poultry. Wyse and Tobby stepped inside. The noisy dining room was crowded with sailors, laborers, and a few women enjoying their supper with spirits. He scanned the diners, but the chaplain wasn't among them.

"Are you hungry?" He asked Tobby.

The boy swallowed. "Yes, sir."

Wyse crooked his finger to call a voluptuous young woman who whirled among the tables, serving mugs of beer and ale.

She had to shout to be heard. "Hello, Mr. Wyse. Do you want a table? Or a bed for the night?"

"Jenny, please bring this lad something to eat. Also, I'm looking for a man. A gray-haired, smooth-talking chaplain named Doolittle. I saw him here before."

The server rolled her eyes. "Ahh yes. He devoured the whole leg of a pig, drank three pints of beer, and asked if I wanted to pray with him in private. Then he left, his legs barely holding him."

"Did he say where he was going?"

The thud of broken glass jolted Jenny. At a table in the corner, an older woman in a simple dress and bonnet covered with road dust was shouting at two sailors. The men's faces were flushed, their movements clumsy. One put his arm around her, but she swatted it.

Jenny groaned. "Oh dear, those ruffians are bothering the good lady. She came from afar to find her niece. Mr. Wyse, would you help me drive them off?"

"Stay here with the boy while I deal with these fellows. How far do you want me to throw them? Back to their table or out of this place?"

"The further the better. They've caused enough trouble for the night."

"I'll help you, Mr. Wyse!" Tobby yelled and stepped towards the ruffians, but Wyse caught him by the collar. Jenny grabbed the boy in a bear hug as he squirmed.

One of the sailors attempted to give the lady a smooch on the cheek. She smacked him in the face with her fan.

"I'm a lady and won't be treated this way!"

With a measured step and a crack of his knuckles, Wyse advanced towards the drunks and grabbed them by scruffs of their necks, one in each of his muscular arms. "Fellows, get back to your ship before your captain hears of your behavior. Let me show you the way."

They gave him little fight as he dragged them to the door.

Jenny appeared in front of them and stretched out her palm, holding Tobby's shoulder with her other hand. "Payment! Six pints and the broken mug."

"You heard the lady." Wyse shook them.

Their hands trembling, the men fished in their pockets and gave the server their coins.

Propping the door open with his foot, he threw the ruffians out. They landed on the street and scrambled away. Jenny blew him a kiss and led Tobby towards the kitchen.

With a pump of his fist, he returned and approached the woman to see if she was all right. The woman smoothed her dress and adjusted her bonnet to tuck in her gray hair. No tears marred her face, only turned down lips and a fierce expression in her eyes.

"Thank you, sir." She sipped her water. "How sozzled those fellows must be to want an old hag like me. My blood boils thinking how they must treat young women like my Ella."

Wyse leaned in. "Are you speaking of Ella Parker?"

The woman drew up. "Yes. Do you know her?"

"I do." He sat down. "I'm the First Lieutenant of the *Neptune,* Jack Wyse. I ensured her safety on the ship."

Her face brightened. "Glad to hear it, lieutenant. I'm Matilda Pesce. Ella and I had an agreement to meet at this inn when she'd return to Plymouth. I got more than enough of the country and my cousin and arrived here much earlier than the *Neptune's* planned docking date. Then I learned that the *Neptune* returned early due to some damage. But instead of Ella, her letter waited here for me. A very sad letter… informing me of my brother Joseph Pesce's death." A shadow crossed Matilda's face. "Would you escort me to Ella?"

The woman's keen eyes unsettled Wyse. His pulse quickened. Beads of sweat formed on his forehead.

"She … disappeared after we docked at Plymouth. I'm searching for her."

The woman's wrinkled hands balled into fists. "You let a despairing girl go off alone into the city full of ruffians and drunks? Didn't you say you ensured her safety? Fine job you're doing!"

Swallowing, Wyse wiped sweat from his brow. "Madam, I've been searching for Dr. Parker for three days. I've spoken to the constables, and there's no reason to believe she came to harm. The last person she spoke to was Mr. Doolittle, the chaplain. He may know where she went."

"Where is he?"

"I came to find him here, but he left. I'm planning to check more taverns and inns."

"There's no need for that, Mr. Wyse." Jenny handed him a beer mug. "Have supper on the house for your help with the louts. One of the servers saw Mr. Doolittle staggering into Madam Moss's."

"Ha!" He slapped the table. "The holy man isn't so holy. My supper will have to wait, Jenny. Take care of the boy. If he gets sleepy, find him a bed."

Jenny nodded. He rose and checked his pockets to ensure nothing went missing during the skirmish. With her joints cracking, Matilda rose as well and put the payment for her supper on the table. "How far does this Madam Moss live?"

Wyse stared in shock but remembered that Matilda was new to the city. "I can't take you with me. Madam Moss's is a brothel."

Her eyes piercing into him, Matilda lifted her bag. "I'm not letting you out of my sight until we find Ella. Lead the way, Lieutenant."

***

Nuns flanked Ella while the abbess marched in front. They strolled to the largest building, next to the church, passing by an apple orchard. Sisters sang a spirited song as they gathered fruit.

Blissful haven if one doesn't look beyond the surface.

In the abbess's chamber, a couple of novices, no older than thirteen, arranged dinner on a round table set for two. Ella's mouth watered from aromas of roasted chicken with rosemary, golden potatoes, buttered peas, and fresh bread.

The abbess dismissed the nuns and the novices then grinned at Ella. "Our food comes from our toil and God's will. We grow vegetables and fruit, care for the livestock, and bake bread. There's great satisfaction in consuming the fruits of your labor. Don't you agree?"

Ella shrugged. "I'm not a farmer or a milkmaid. I'm a surgeon."

"You are a landowner as well." Mother Superior tilted her head. "What do you and your tenants grow? How is this year's harvest?"

Ella furrowed her brow. "You are well informed."

"Yes, and I look forward to learning more about you. But let's celebrate your safe arrival and recovery first." Mother Superior opened a small cabinet by the wall, selected a bottle, and poured a small amount into two glasses. "Cherry cordial. A gift from our mutual friend, Mr. Doolittle."

Ella made no move to accept the glass. "Thank you, but I don't drink. I want to speak about Marietta and Henrietta Fillips. Why are they being held against their will?"

The abbess sat and said grace, then put a forkful of chicken into her mouth. "Please sit and sate your hunger. This chicken is particularly good. I must reward the sisters who cooked it."

Ella sat, resting her chin on her palms, but didn't touch the food. "You haven't answered my question."

Mother Superior swallowed another mouthful. "Miss Marietta's labor pains may start at any moment. Where do you want her to go?"

"Her baby is breech. She needs to walk, so gravity may help the baby turn. And her chamber must be cleaned and aired while she's out."

"Hmm," the nun chewed with a thoughtful expression. "I suppose there's no harm if she takes supervised walks in the gardens. And tidiness is next to godliness. I'll have the novices clean the chamber and change her linens."

Ella gripped the table. "What will happen after she delivers her baby?"

The abbess sipped her drink and licked her lips. "You still haven't eaten. The sweet cordial compliments the spices in the chicken. Try some."

Ella leaned forward and waited for the abbess to speak. The nun wiped her mouth with the linen napkin.

"Miss Marietta made unfortunate choices. Instead of marrying her respectable suitor, she fell for a simple farmer, her mother's tenant. When she told him she's carrying his child, he abandoned her and ran. The foolish girl kept her dishonorable secret from her mother for almost six months, and her sister covered for her. Lady Fillips finally learned the truth during their visit to Plymouth. She wisely brought her disgraced daughter to this monastery, far from their home. Miss Henrietta came willingly with her sister. Lady Fillips paid the nun's dowry for both. At the monastery, they will cleanse off their sins and find forgiveness and support."

"This is not what they want."

The nun pushed her plate away. "Then they should've obeyed their mother. She's protecting her daughters from scorn. You, an earl's daughter, must know how society treats disgraced women."

Ella crossed her arms. "You are well-informed of my parentage and my assets."

The abbess grinned; a habit that gritted Ella's nerves already. "Yes. Mr. Doolittle wrote a detailed letter. My heart ached on your behalf as I read. You are orphaned and burdened with a vast estate that you have no training to manage. You wasted your healing talents on lewd sailors who loathed you. How fortunate that the good chaplain shepherded you."

Ella drummed her fingers. Mother Superior and Mr. Doolittle showed great interest in her fortune. Let it be her and her friends' ticket to freedom. After all, a problem that could be solved with money is not a problem, but an expense.

She raised her chin. "I decided that monastery life isn't for me. I'll help with Marietta's delivery, and then the Fillips sisters, the newborn, and I will leave together. I wish to make a charitable donation for your hospitality. You name the sum."

Mother Superior's eyes glistened, and her smile bared her teeth. "Your donation will do much good."

"Splendid. How much?"

The abbess emptied her glass and smacked her lips. "All of it, my dear."

"I beg your pardon?"

Mother Superior stood and removed a piece of paper from her writing desk. "If the list of your assets is not entirely accurate, I'm sure your lawyer, Mr. Hastings, will make corrections. All I need is your signature at the bottom." She handed the paper to Ella.

Ella's eyes rounded as she skimmed the document. "You want all of my money and land? Bloody hell! You must be mad."

"Not at all, child. And please watch your language. Don't you know of the Vow of Poverty every nun must take? We give all we have to the church." She put a hand on Ella's shoulder. "Think on it. You won't carry the burden of overseeing your estate and tenants anymore. Your money will go towards this monastery and other worthy cloisters. The church will manage your assets with wisdom and fairness. Our friend Mr. Doolittle was particularly interested in the assignment at your estate. Shall I bring you a pen or would you like to eat first?"

"Go to the devil with your paper. I can rule my estate and do charitable deeds without you." Ella ripped the document into pieces.

Mother Superior clicked her tongue and opened the door. "Daughters, in here!" Six sturdy-looking nuns walked in, blocking the exit. "Miss Ella earned punishment for vulgar language, defiance, and greed. She's to be confined to a penance cell. Her sustenance will be hard bread and plain water. The detainment will end when she's ready to speak to me with deference and sign the document." She glanced at Ella, smiling. "My dear, you should've eaten. Now your belly with churn from stale bread. If you are sorry, I'll forgive. I'm in a benevolent mood after a scrumptious meal."

"Hunger won't break me." Ella snorted. "I ate salted meat and tack for three months and survived."

The abbess shrugged. "Well, if not hunger, then loneliness. Breaks stubborn spirits like nothing else."

Ella flinched and sprang to her feet. Her eyes searched for where to run. Five nuns circled her, while the largest one obstructed the only door. One tried to grab her, but Ella dodged the nun's grip and swung the chair in her direction. The woman fell with a scream, but other nuns grabbed Ella from behind. She struggled, but her assailants were too many and their hands held her tightly.

Accepting that she couldn't win by strength, Ella tried reason. "Marietta's baby is positioned breech. It's a complicated delivery. Sister Frances needs me to assist. The mother and the baby could be in peril."

The abbess shook her head. "Like most healers, you overvalue your importance. It's up to God to save the mother and her baby or take them into eternal life."

Ella's heart wrenched at her last memory of her mother, who died in childbirth with her brother. The doctor did everything possible to save them. "I believe in eternal life and the power of prayer. But every patient deserves a chance to survive with medical care. Let me deliver Marietta's baby. Or find her a midwife."

The abbess played with the cross on her chest. "I'll consider a midwife. You, however, must endure your punishment. When you gift your assets to the church, I will acknowledge your readiness to help Miss Marietta. I suggest you pray for guidance in the penitence cell. And I hope to see you soon, ready to be my respectful and humble daughter."

The sisters led Ella into a maze of corridors. After shepherding her from one gloomy pathway into another, they pushed her into a dark cell. The lock clicked and steps quieted.

Ella inhaled musty air to steady her nerves. Her empty stomach groaned, and her head ached. She screamed from frustration, and that scream loosened her chest. Her next scream was a warrior's cry. She would use isolation to contemplate breech deliveries and strategize her escape with the new mother, a newborn, and the mother's sister in tow. *The abbess will swallow her words and choke on her greed. No one breaks Ella Parker!*

Chapter 22

Wyse and Matilda trudged to the end of the street, passing by more inns and taverns. At the screech of an out-of-tune piano, he quickened his step in rhythm with the merry melody. Matilda rasped and grumbled about the hardships she had to endure for Ella.

He stomped into the dim main room of the brothel and searched the faces of the customers at the tables. Many had a girl or two sitting next to them or on their lap. The place hadn't changed much since he was here years ago. The musty aroma of perfume, the broken furniture, the velvety lounges and pillows that looked inviting at first glance, but a closer inspection revealed their age, grime, and wear. The same could be said for most of the women in this place.

His companion tightened her lips into a thin line. "Women like these came to my shop to buy herbs that prevent pregnancies or cure female maladies. Some were the sickest sufferers I've treated. Look at that child. She can't be more than fifteen. Good thing her customer is too tired to fondle her."

Wyse glanced at the couple and chuckled. The man, asleep on his chair with his head hung back and his jaw slack, was Mr. Doolittle. The girl was familiar to him as well: the bosun's daughter, Wendy. He advanced towards them, but the proprietress, Madam Moss, in her translucent black dress, stepped into his path.

"Mr. Wyse, it's been a while. I'm afraid Wendy is occupied. If slender girls interest you, I can offer you Rosie."

He handed the woman a few coins. "I need to talk to the gentleman and the girl. After I speak to Wendy, she's to go home."

Madam Moss counted the change faster than a banker. "Give me more for the girl. She came in rags. I bought her a clean chemise and a pretty dress. If you have a problem with the man, talk with your fists outside. This is a fine establishment. We even have classical music."

Wyse gave her another coin, alarmed how quickly the wages he received a day ago were disappearing. "This'll be a peaceful conversation between friends. Bring two more chairs and some water."

The proprietress obliged. Wyse offered a chair next to Wendy to Matilda, while he sat by Doolittle, who snored loudly in his sleep.

He gave Wendy a stern look. "I'll start with you. What the devil are you doing here?"

The girl stuck out her bottom lip. "Trying not to starve. If I lift my dress, I'm nothing but skin and bones."

She grabbed her skirts and moved them up her scrawny frame. Matilda gasped. Wyse reached over and grabbed the girl's hand. "Stop that. The Madam won't allow a free show, and I paid enough for you already. You are going home."

The girl straightened her dress and swallowed a sob. "I can't. Father lost his wages in a card game, and Mother has a fever. I must earn some money for medicine and food."

Matilda crossed her arms. "And what will you do if you get a baby in your belly? Or catch the French disease? Here, take these herbs to break the fever. Now go home and boil them for your mother." Matilda pulled out several dried leaves from her bag.

The girl accepted the remedy with a tearful smile. Wyse gave her a couple of coins and made a mental note to talk to the bosun.

"Here's something to tide you over. When your mother gets better, go to The Cooked Goose, and ask for a job. Tell them I sent you. Now, what did this man and you talk about before he fell asleep?"

"He came in already drunk. After he tickled and kissed me, he asked if I attend church. He promised to give me a good whipping to absolve my sins, but he fell asleep before we got to that."

Matilda shook her head. "What disgusting behavior from a clergyman. Was Ella on good terms with him?" she asked Wyse.

"She admired his sermons. And she..." Wyse cringed, "had few friends other than him."

"Did you say Ella?" Wendy echoed. "He mentioned that name."

"What did he say?" Wyse and Matilda asked together.

"He said something like, 'now that Ella is at the nunnery, I'm getting off that stinkin' ship and will live like a lord. The bishop will forgive me and send me to Newcastle.'"

"Goodness! Ella's estate is near Newcastle. He's out for her wealth!" Matilda exclaimed.

Wyse nodded. "He must've talked her into going to some nunnery and hopes to be rewarded for it."

The midwife clenched the table; her knuckles turned white. "The nuns would want Ella to donate her assets to the church. This must be his plan."

Grunting, Wyse gave Wendy a light tap on the shoulder. "Time for you to go home. Don't let me catch you at this place again."

Wendy dashed towards the door, but then came back, threw her arms around him, and kissed his cheek. She sped away, smiling. Meanwhile, the chaplain gave another loud snore. Wyse seized his collar, shook him hard, and doused him with water from the glass. "Wake up your holiness."

"What the hell is this!" Mr. Doolittle said in a drunken voice.

Leaning back, Matilda crossed herself. "If this is how the chaplain speaks, what can be expected of the sailors?"

Wyse gave him another shake. "Tell us where you sent Ella."

"The girl went ... far ... where you won't find her." Mr. Doolittle closed his eyes and yawned.

With a snort, Matilda rummaged in her bag till she found a small vial. She emptied the contents into the remaining water in the glass. "If we can make him drink this, it'll sober him a bit."

"Not a problem." Wyse thrust the man's jaw open and poured the drink down his throat. The chaplain coughed and spit as he gulped.

"How fast does this remedy work?" Wyse asked Matilda.

"It's quick. You better take him outside."

"Ah." He grabbed Mr. Doolittle around his shoulders and dragged him onto the street. In two steps, the chaplain's hearty feast gushed out of his mouth. Wyse made a mental note not to consume anything Matilda would offer him.

When the chaplain finished retching, he attempted escape on his wobbly legs. Wyse caught him and threw him against the wall. "Not so fast, your drunken excellency. Where did you send Doctor Parker?"

The clergyman panted, and Wyse gagged at the stench on his breath. "To the nunnery. She will be a great asset to the church."

Wyse's fist came dangerously close to the chaplain's nose. "Yes, an asset with many assets. You're after her riches."

With his arms raised, Mr. Doolittle dropped to his knees. "For the church! To benefit the poor and struggling."

"You hoped to reap rewards as well. Tell me where Ella is."

Rasping, the chaplain stood up slowly, holding onto the wall. "She went ... this way!"

When Wyse looked the way he pointed, the chaplain raced the other way. A moment later, he screamed as he slipped on his own vomit, and landed with his face in the dirt. "My ankle!" he cried.

Wyse put his foot on the man's back. "Thought you could run. Start talking before I break a bone."

"Have mercy. The monastery is beyond the forest. The best way to get there is on foot. There's a path that leads to it. It starts behind the cemetery, and if you follow it for half a day, you'll come out to the clearing and the nunnery."

"You'll show the way."

"I've sprained my ankle. And the forest is dangerous at night."

Wyse grunted. The man was right; they better set out in the morning.

He raised Mr. Doolittle by his shoulder and stuck his head back through the brothel's door to call Matilda.

"She is in the monastery beyond the woods. We'll spend the night at The Cooked Goose and go with the chaplain at dawn. Can you bandage a sprained ankle?"

Matilda nodded, and they shuffled towards the inn with Mr. Doolittle, who cried and moaned with every step.

Chapter 23

Wyse watched Mr. Doolittle toss and turn through the night at one of Cooked Goose's upstairs rooms. He didn't sleep a wink, suspicious that the chaplain feigned his injury, even though the man's misery seemed genuine.

Matilda examined the swollen ankle the next morning. Her lips turned down. "It's worse than I thought. I suspect the ankle's broken."

The chaplain wailed. "That's the same ankle I broke as a boy. What have I done to deserve this suffering?"

"I think we all know what you did," Wyse said. "You're lucky. There're worse places to be laid up with a broken leg than the Cooked Goose. Here's Jenny with your breakfast."

Jenny entered with a plate of eggs and sausage on her tray. Tobby was on her heels, carrying a steaming cup of tea. Mr. Doolittle dug into his meal.

"We need to summon a surgeon or a bone setter. This injury is beyond my skills," Matilda said to Jenny.

"Leave it to me. I'll send for a healer and feed this gentleman while he recovers. His appetite didn't suffer a bit," she observed as Mr. Doolittle shoved a forkful of sausage into his mouth.

"Your kindness will be repaid, dear lady," the chaplain said while chewing.

Jenny gave him a smug look. "I hope you mean in money. I'm keeping a tab."

Tobby handed him the tea. "I'm sorry you broke your leg, Mr. Doolittle. You didn't believe that I was sick until Dr. Ella started treating me, but I believe you. I hope you get better."

Mr. Doolittle stared at the boy. "Thank you, Tobby. You are kind. I've been unfair to you. I'm sorry."

"Why did you tell Dr. Ella to go to the monastery? Did you think she'd like it, or did you want something for yourself?"

The chaplain put down his fork. "I used to run a church with a great following. Then I... did something I wasn't proud of, and the bishop assigned me to the *Neptune* as a punishment. I hated that ship. I thought if I convinced Ella to take the nunnery vows and donate her assets to the church, I would gain forgiveness from my superiors. Maybe even assigned to manage her estate."

"Selfish clergyman." Matilda piped. "You cared nothing for a grieving and lonely girl."

Mr. Doolittle bent his head. "I deserve this. When convincing Ella, I painted a rosy picture of the monastery life and purposely omitted the Vow of Poverty from my explanations. I encouraged her to explore the monastery as a visitor, but the abbess could be forceful in getting her way."

Tobby put a thumb in his mouth, but then removed it. "You lied to Ella. Didn't you teach that we must treat others as we want to be treated ourselves?"

The corners of Mr. Doolittle's mouth trembled. "I'm a weak man. Yet you've learned a great lesson in my classes. Maybe not all is lost. I'll contemplate how to teach not only by words, but by examples. After all, I'll have nothing better to do for weeks."

Wyse tapped his foot. "But where does this leave me? I need to get to this monastery and find Ella. I don't trust you, Doolittle. How do I know you won't send me the wrong way?"

The chaplain folded his hands in praying position. "I swear on my life, Mr. Wyse! I wouldn't dare cross you, especially when I can't run from you. Just follow the road beyond the cemetery and follow it. It's quicker to go on foot than by horse or coach, as those would require taking the road around the woods."

Wyse pulled on Mr. Doolittle's collar. "I'll remember you swearing on your life. If you're lying, I'll return to deal with you."

"He's telling the truth," Jenny said. "I had a friend, Fran, who... had a troubled life. She became a nun in the monastery, and I visited her once. The hike was lengthy and scary at times, with bogs nearby and animals howling, but I managed fine. I'll pack you some provisions, Mr. Wyse."

Matilda scoffed. "Not just for him, of course. I'm coming as well."

"I'm goin' too," Tobby said.

"Your limp," Matilda countered. "Won't walking hurt your leg?"

"Nah. Dr. Ella said walking won't make it any worse. She's my friend and treated me when I was ill."

"I'm glad she has such a loyal friend. You can waddle with me then, while Mr. Wyse speeds ahead on his long legs." She tied her shawl around her shoulders. "Shall we go, Mr. Wyse?"

Wyse gazed at his potential companions: an old woman and a limping boy. A poor crew, but better than none. His men stayed with the ship at the dockyard, helping with repairs. A few were off visiting their families. Pulling them in for the rescue would waste time. "Let's go."

***

The trio struggled through the woods for most of the day. Wyse strode ahead, Matilda and Tobby hobbled far behind him. Their slow pace unnerved him. On their way, they got stung by nettles, heard the howling of wild animals, and waded through marshes. More than once, Wyse's heart froze in his chest as he imagined Ella being sucked in by the bog or attacked by wolves.

When Tobby recalled that Ella seemed feverish during their last conversation, Wyse's anxiety grew another notch.

A high-pitched scream made Wyse's knees lock. He turned, but his companions were out of his sight. Cursing, he raced back to find them. Most likely, the woman fell stepping over a fallen tree and hurt herself. If so, they would walk even slower, or worse, he might have to carry her.

He exhaled with relief when he saw Matilda and the boy standing, visibly unhurt, by... a berry bush. He was about to holler at them for screaming for no reason but stopped himself. Matilda was gesturing wildly.

"Don't you know anything about wild berries, boy? Children have died from eating them!"

"What happened?" Wyse asked, coming closer.

The woman's chin trembled. "Tobby ate poisonous berries."

Wyse shuddered.

"I didn't." Tobby protested. "You screamed and I dropped them."

"Thank God. You scared me, child." The midwife exhaled and put her arm around the boy's shoulders. "Don't ever eat wild berries if you don't know what they are."

"I thought they were blueberries."

Wyse glanced at the berries. If he weren't in such a hurry to find Ella, he might've tasted some as well.

Matilda shook her head. "This is black nightshade. There's an even more poisonous variety, deadly nightshade, or belladonna. They look like blueberries, but poisonous to eat."

Wyse's tooth ached as he added another danger to the fast-growing list of forest perils. In his mind, Ella, weary and feverish, reached for the berries to relieve her thirst. *No, the girl knows all about the herbs and plants,* he told himself. *She wouldn't eat wild berries unless she was sure they're safe.*

He threw the boy an apple from his sack and gave another one to Matilda. "Are we going to stand here all day? Eat this as you walk."

Eager to find the cloisters before darkness, he sprinted ahead. As he jumped over another fallen tree, he considered what he'd do once they found the monastery. If they asked for Ella, would the nuns allow them to speak with her? He hadn't met many nuns, but he perceived them as kind, honest, and somewhat naive. Certainly not dangerous. When the stone buildings and the church pinnacle came into his view, he told the others to stay behind the bushes. Then he threw his shoulders back and puffed his chest as he advanced to the gate.

The heavy lock on the gate was beyond his skill to pick. The walls were tall and likely difficult to climb.

This place looks like a fortress. Or a prison.

He rubbed his chin. If he broke the lock, or scaled the walls, then what? Where would he find Ella? Shrewdness would get him further than brute strength. When he spotted the caged window on the wall, he knocked, humming to himself.

Hushed voices from behind the wall reached his ears. The women on the other side seemed to argue over who should answer.

"Get Mother Superior!" one voice urged.

"What if it's a beggar?"

"You find out what this is about, and I'll call her."

An apple-cheeked woman in habit stuck her head into the window and flashed him a smile. "Hello. My name is Sister Claire. How can I help you, good sir?"

Wyse forced a grin. "I'm looking for a young woman named Ella. Has she come here? I'm her... cousin."

The nun frowned. "I'm not sure. Why don't you wait for the abbess? She knows everyone. Maybe I can get you something to eat or drink while you wait? I imagine your journey was long."

An older nun shouldered Sister Claire away from the window. She panted like she ran here. "I'm Mother Superior. And your name?"

No reason to lie. "Jack Wyse."

"A Royal Navy Lieutenant, judging by your uniform. May the Lord keep our ships and the brave seamen safe."

Wyse bowed his head. "Thank you. I'm looking for Ella Parker, my cousin. Is she here?"

The abbess twisted her lips. "I can't confirm or deny the presence of any woman who found shelter here. You say you are her cousin, but how do I know if you were good to her? Some women come here seeking protection from their relatives. I'm sorry that you've made a fruitless journey. If you wait, Sister Claire will bring you food and water for your trip back. The forest is treacherous at night. You better walk a mile north and find lodging at the nearby village."

The abbess turned from the window. Wyse despaired how to halt her. An idea, like a flash of lighting, came to him. "Mother Superior!"

The nun turned with a scowl but forced a smile. "What is it?"

"I have a rotten tooth. Now this gumboil appeared. It hurts bad. My cousin is skilled at extracting teeth. That's why I need to see her." *I may have to go through with this and let her pull my tooth,* he thought with a shudder.

The abbess gave a sympathetic nod. "Oh dear. I still can't let you see your cousin, even if she's here. And I don't believe my healers know dentistry. There's a barber in the village who can remove the tooth. I'll pray that the procedure goes well. Have a good night."

The abbess disappeared from the window. A minute later, Sister Claire opened the gate and handed him a sack of food and a bottle of water. He considered pushing past her to get inside the grounds but rejected the idea. Searching blindly for Ella among those buildings would lead nowhere.

He pretended to head towards the village, then came back around to find Matilda and Tobby in their hiding place. While

Tobby bit into the warm loaf from the nun's sack, moaning with pleasure, Wyse shared what happened. With each sentence, Matilda's dismay increased.

When he finished, she put her hands on her hips. "Was that your plan, to ask for Ella? A simpleton would've done better."

Heat rose to his head. "Why not? They're only dimwit nuns."

Matilda scoffed. "What made you call them dimwit? That they survive in a remote place? That they run their own society? Or was it ... that they are all women?"

Wyse hung his head. "What do you think I should've done?"

"Not mention Ella's name, of course. The aching tooth excuse was a good one, but you already made the abbess suspicious. We are worse off than before, Lieutenant. We've learned nothing and spooked the opponent. This round is lost. Time for me to take over."

He bit the inside of his cheek. "Do you mean to get inside?"

"Yes, and I'm sure to get further than you without raising suspicion. I'm only an old woman, looking for shelter, and considering nunhood. Once inside, I'll explore what I can. But don't leave me there. Unlike you, I don't underestimate these nuns. They may suspect something and lock me in some cell, as they might have done with Ella."

Wyse nodded. "Tobby and I will go to the village. If we don't see you there by noon tomorrow, we'll gather our men to free you and Doctor Parker. That may be a desperate plan, but I can't produce a better one."

She put her hand on her chest. “My heart tells me there are many secret places inside those walls to hide a woman, whether she wants to be hidden or not.”

Tobby stopped chewing, and his eyes grew wide. “Please be careful, Mistress Matilda.” He offered her the rest of the loaf.

Waving away his polite offer, she gave the boy a hearty embrace, and extended Wyse her hand. Wyse shook it with the same respect he’d give a fellow officer leaving on a daring mission.

Chapter 24

It was mid-morning when Matilda wobbled into the dining room of the inn where Wyse and Tobby spent the night. Wyse was groggy; his toothache kept him awake all night. To pass the time, he taught card games to Tobby, who proved himself a quick student. The midwife leaned on a stick with one hand and fanned herself with another as she approached their table.

Wyse winked at Tobby, then raised an eyebrow at the woman. "I was ready to gather the men to free you."

The midwife scoffed. "The sisters couldn't wait to get rid of me. But I saw Ella."

Nonchalant, the woman sat and ordered a tankard of beer. Wyse nudged her, impatient to hear her account, but she shrugged and waited for the serving girl to bring her drink. After satisfying her thirst, she wiped her lips with a napkin and spoke.

"What a strange, eerie place. The nuns were all smiles. They showed me their gardens, their mess hall, and their kitchen, but I didn't see Ella anywhere. I feigned a pain in my leg and asked for a healer, but they prayed for my recovery instead."

"Get to the part about Ella," Wyse said through his teeth.

"Right. When the sisters escorted me to my cell for the night, I saw Ella at the end of the corridor. She wore a habit and was surrounded by four nuns, all as large as grenadiers. I think they were moving her to a different cell. She walked slowly, and once gripped the wall, as if she were lightheaded."

Tobby gasped. "She's sick. We must help her."

Matilda nodded. "We must. After overcoming her dizzy spell, she turned and saw me. She showed no recognition, but her lips moved. I believe she mouthed the word, 'help.' Then she looked towards a building in the window."

"Did you see where they led her?" Wyse gripped the table.

"No. I wanted to search for her once everyone had gone to sleep. But then the sister locked my cell for the night, claiming it was for my own protection."

Wyse drummed his fingers. "That's too bad, but still, we've learned much. Ella's inside. She may be ill, but well enough to walk and to use her wits. She's held prisoner, and she wants to be out. This round is won."

Matilda gave him a smug look and extended her hand to shake. Wyse took it, but instead of a handshake, he kissed it.

Matilda's eyebrows rose with an ironic expression. "Oh my, the age of chivalry isn't over."

Wyse chuckled. "And now I call my fellow knights, and we raid the place."

"No!" The midwife tapped her hand on her forehead. "Can't men think with their brains and not with their muscles? While you raise havoc, the sisters will hide Ella somewhere you won't find her. We must do something that would force the nuns to bring her to us. But I don't know what."

Wyse rubbed his forehead. Riddles were not his strongpoint.

"What if I get sick? They'd bring Ella to heal me," Tobby suggested.

Matilda shook her head. "We've tried that already. They'll either pray over you or send you to the village healer."

"But what if it's something serious, like I could die? What if I break my leg or eat those berries that looked like blueberries?"

The midwife put a hand to her heart. "Heavens, don't even think of doing something like that, child."

"I'll pretend. I've feigned sickness before."

"Later I will tell you about the boy who cried wolf. But the idea is worth considering."

Tobby beamed. "What if it's not just me who is ill, but all five ship boys? Like we all ate the poisoned berries."

Matilda gulped her beer. "The notion of five gravely ill children makes my heart race. Even an experienced healer may be overwhelmed in such a situation."

"Not Ella. She stayed calm in a berth full of wounded," Wyse said. "The sisters would need her. This is an excellent plan, Tobby. Our men will disguise themselves as a hunting party who found five ill boys near that poisonous bush. The men will make an uproar and demand that the nuns save the children. In such an 'all hands on deck' situation, the sisters are bound to summon Ella."

Matilda nodded. "We'll practice, so everyone knows their part."

"Like we drill for a battle," Wyse confirmed.

He checked his pocket watch. If he hurried, he could bring his men to this village before nightfall. They'd practice through the night and execute their plan tomorrow morning. Ella must hold out one more day.

***

Ella chewed her meager breakfast of stale bread and washed it down with water. The bed she sat on was the only furniture. The window overlooked the cow shed, and the stench of manure made her eyes water. She would've tried escaping through the window, hoping to land on the shed roof, but the window had bars like a prison cell. Restless in her confinement, she pined for the boundless green sea, the salt residue on her face, the gull screams.

The boys. She regretted not saying goodbye to them. If only Mr. Wyse acknowledged her work, or the men showed some friendliness... She understood her mentor like never before. *The sea is where I belong.*

To pass the time, she assembled in her mind everything she knew of breech deliveries. The textbook explanations, the lectures in medical school, Matilda's teaching. Whenever a sister brought her food or took her to the privy, Ella inquired about Marietta, and learned that her friend was allowed daily walks in the gardens. She dared not ask about Matilda. Their meeting couldn't be serendipitous. Her friend must be here searching for her or tending to the mother-to-be.

Sister Claire burst in, rasping, her apple cheeks flushed. She wasn't large like the other sisters that guarded her. Ella rose, prepared to run. The nun's words stopped her impulse.

"Miss Ella, come with me to the infirmary. Please hurry."

Ella stepped to the door. "I'm glad you saw sense."

The nun walked at a brisk pace along the corridors, and Ella struggled to keep up. The diet of bread and water seeped her strength.

"When did the labor start?" Ella asked the sister as they emerged into the windy morning.

Sister Claire blinked rapidly. "What? Oh no, it's not Marietta. Other sisters are attending to her."

"Then who?"

The sister opened her mouth to answer but was interrupted by another nun's wailing. "The outlaws! It's those outlaws!" the nun cried and fell into the arms of other sisters.

Ella stepped towards her, but Sister Claire grabbed her by the elbow. "Forget Sister Charity. She faints whenever there's a man about, and she just saw a whole hunting party. There are five dying children to tend to."

Ella's heart jumped to her throat. "What's wrong with them?"

"Sister Frances isn't sure. The abbess... Well, I don't care what the abbess will say. Save them if you can."

Several nuns were rushing in the direction of the infirmary, speaking rapidly to each other. Ella caught the words 'hunters' and 'berries'. The doors of the infirmary flew open, and Sister Frances stepped forward holding a heavy book in her arms.

"How can we help, Sister?" a nun asked her.

"What good are you to me? Go to the chapel and pray since that's all you know. I need Ella."

Ella waved her hand. "I'm here." Sister Frances grabbed her elbow and pulled her inside. High-pitched shrieks sounded from the confinement chamber. "Marietta's in labor? Is she attended by a midwife?"

The nun tugged Ella's sleeve, not letting her slow down. "Sisters are caring for her. They believe she has a few hours before delivery. You must help the boys."

Men's shouting drowned Marietta's cries. "When will you bring your healer? The children are at death's door!"

Sister Frances drew a breath. "These hunters found five half-conscious boys lying by the berry bushes that look like blueberries. I've been looking through this book on poisonous plants for what to do."

Ella rubbed her temples to ease tension as she stepped into the ward. Every bed was occupied with a young patient. The nuns and the men crowded the space. The nuns were praying; the men with muskets and hats that hid their faces demanded that the nuns do something besides praying.

"Look up the black nightshade and the deadly nightshade in your book," Ella ordered Sister Frances. She wedged herself between the nuns and the men to approach the first bed. Her hand covered her mouth to quiet her gasp. Tobby, white as a sheet, lay motionless in a fainting spell. On the other cots, Ben and Digby were in a similar state, and the twins clutched their bellies and moaned.

Maybe this is a ruse to rescue me. She dismissed the hopeful theory as she bent over Tobby. He didn't respond to her touch. Sweat drenched from his forehead. His breath reeked with vomit. *This is no pretense.*

Sister Frances leafed through her book with trembling hands. "They show symptoms of black nightshade poisoning. Sweating, vomiting, abdominal pain, drowsiness. No fever though."

"It may come later," Ella muttered.

"Then it gets worse." Sister Frances's voice caught. "Hallucinations. Difficulty breathing. Death."

Ella put her ear to the boy's chest. To her relief, the heartbeat was steady, although rapid.

"Do you have a stomach pump?" she asked the nun.

The woman stared like she never heard of such a thing. Ella groaned. She left hers behind, thinking it would get more use on the ship than in the monastery. Her mind raced to make a new plan. She straightened and gave strength to her voice.

"You two," she gestured to the sisters that prayed at Tobby's bedside, "bring them water. Sister Frances, find the chapter about antidotes. There must be one for this poison."

Sister Frances frantically searched through her tome, while the two nuns hastened to fetch water.

"Tobby, answer me." Ella spoke in a gentle voice as she caressed his cheeks. "Please, wake up." Focused on her patient, she ignored the commotion around her.

Mother Superior stormed in waving her arms, her eyes full of fury. She stopped next to Sister Frances. "I'm not allowing this! Take Miss Ella back to her cell. Whoever disobeyed my orders will be locked up too."

"We don't listen to you anymore," Sister Claire shouted. "We'll help Miss Ella save these children." Cheers from other sisters erupted.

A large man with an eyepatch pointed his musket at the abbess. "Fran, should I shoot her?"

Sister Frances pummeled the abbess on the head with her volume. The chief nun fell like a sack of potatoes. "I'm Sister Frances to you, Morgan. And I can handle this lunatic myself, thank you very much."

Through all this uproar, Ella stroked the boy's face, trying to awaken him. Then the noise died as quickly as it started.

"All the nuns secured?" a gruff voice said.

Ella looked up at Wyse, who removed a scarf that obscured his face. Around her, each man held a sister in his grip, pointing their muskets or knives at them. Only Sister Frances stood free, studying Morgan, while he clutched his musket like he was unsure what to do with it.

"Dr. Ella, don't worry, we aren't sick!" Tobby squealed and rose to hug her.

"I didn't give the command yet!" Wyse roared.

Tobby froze. "Sorry, sir."

"Joke. The dying may rise." The lieutenant winked.

The laughing boys jumped off their beds and surrounded Ella. She embraced them one by one.

"You scared me to death. I believed you were all gravely ill."

Tobby gave a chuckle. "That was Matilda's trick. She deemed us too rosy-cheeked and healthy-looking for the part, so she gave us a medicine that made us retch."

Ella shook her head. "Goodness. I can't believe Matilda would do this."

Wyse put his arm on her shoulder. "The boys are fine. What do you want us to do with the nuns? Or do you wish to remain here?"

She snorted. "No, I won't be a nun. Please take the sisters to the chapel, except for Sister Frances. Post men to guard them till we leave. Don't harm anyone. If Matilda's about, bring her here. There's a woman in labor we must tend to. Also, do you have any food? I'm bloody starving!"

The men laughed and a couple of them threw her their sacks with food. Ella's fingers trembled as she undid the knots to find fresh bread, fragrant cheese, and apples. She stuffed her mouth full.

Morgan approached with a flask. "Do nuns drink wine?"

Ella chewed and swallowed before responding. "Not now. I have a patient to tend to."

"I'll have some, Morgan," Sister Frances piped. "Is that the sweet wine you used to bring me?"

"Same one, Fran. You remember?"

She took a delicate sip, and then a hearty gulp. "Mmm, the taste of my old life. And I still crave another taste." Pulling Morgan into an embrace, she gave him a sultry kiss.

Ella chortled with amusement, but a piercing shriek from the confinement chamber jolted her.

"Enough." Ella rose. "Marietta's labor progressed. Sister Frances, bring my instrument case. Mr. Wyse, please choose a few men and come with us."

His eyebrows rose. "For the woman in labor? Why do you need my men?"

"The nuns who are with her want to take her baby away. We can't let them."

Wyse signaled to two men to follow him. A minute later, the men brought out four nuns.

"I'm her sister and the baby's aunt," one of them protested.

"Let that one go," Ella said, recognizing Henrietta.

Wyse and his men led the nuns away, while Ella, Sister Frances, and Henrietta rushed into the room. Ella was pleased that the floor shined after mopping. Marietta's sheets were now clean, and the air had a whiff of flowers from the garden.

Marietta's brow was hot to Ella's touch. "How are you holding up?" Ella asked her friend.

Sweat and tears drenched Marietta's face. "I walked every day, but I don't think the baby turned. But even if the birth goes well... Mother Superior said she arranged to take my baby to the orphanage. I'd rather die than let her."

Ella patted her trembling hand. "Don't talk like that. The abbess is no longer a threat to you."

Wyse stuck his head into the door. "Madam, my men are guarding the room. No one will come in but your friends."

Marietta exhaled a long breath. "Thank you, sir. Whoever you are."

His cheeks reddened. "Jack Wyse. I'll be outside the door."

Ella examined her patient's abdomen and cervix. The baby was still breech, but it was ready to be born. *The baby chooses the birth, not the mother or the midwife,* Ella remembered Matilda's teaching. She longed to hear her friend's calm voice, but they had to start without her. Ella washed Marietta's face and helped her sit up to push. She then asked Sister Frances to stand next to her at Marietta's feet, and Henrietta at her sister's side. Positioned to catch the newborn, Ella encouraged the mother-to-be to push with each contraction. The young woman gripped her sister's hand, concentrating.

Three hours later, Marietta was still pushing. Sweat doused her body, but her eyes stayed bright and focused. Time stood still. Wyse's pacing echoed from the hallway.

"Another push." Ella commanded.

Marietta grunted and gripped her sister's arm.

"Ouch!" Henrietta yelped. "That hurt."

"What's wrong?" Wyse's voice boomed from the door.

"Sorry, that was me. My sister just about crushed my arm," Henrietta squealed.

Wyse entered. Sister Frances's eyes widened. "Sir, it's improper for you to be here."

Marietta gasped and tried to cover herself.

Reddening, Wyse averted his eyes. "I won't look at you. Grip my arm as hard as you want."

Henrietta stepped aside for him.

"Where's Matilda?" Ella asked Wyse.

"I sent men to bring her. Not sure what's holding them up."

Ella drew breath. *I know what to do. If the baby's head won't fit, I'll use the forceps. I've done it once, and I can do it again.*

"The baby! I feel it coming!" Marietta rasped, gripping Wyse's arm.

Ella talked Marietta through another series of pushes. "So close, my friend."

After another push, Marietta screamed her loudest cry yet. Ella's hands gripped the baby's slimy pelvis, which came first. With several more pushes, she delivered the baby's legs and trunk. Her chest lightened for a moment, but no longer. Delivering the head would be the hardest part. As she feared, after the baby's neck appeared, the head wouldn't move further. Marietta pushed till her face turned purple, but the head wouldn't budge. The baby required assistance to be born.

Supporting the infant's body in her arms, Ella hollered, "Sister Frances, hand me the forceps."

"The forceps?" The nun glanced around. "There were no forceps in your case."

"What? Where are they? Oh, confound it."

Ella wanted to hit her head against the wall for her stupidity. She must've placed the forceps into the wrong case and left them on the ship.

"What do I do now? How do I free the head?

She closed her eyes and forced herself to think of what Matilda would do. Her friend's voice was in her mind: "*You are well aware midwives can't use the forceps, only surgeons can.*"

Ella's mind raced to remember Matilda's teaching. Forbidden to use the forceps, Matilda delivered babies without them, including breech births. Ella visualized the Mauriceau maneuver she used.

"Sister Frances, I will need you to press on her uterus, here." Ella showed the spot on Marietta's lower belly.

The nun inhaled and pressed. With the baby lying on her right hand, Ella slid her left hand into the birth canal. Marietta's eyes bulged. She clenched Wyse's arm, gasping. With bated breath, Ella found the baby's cheekbones and positioned her fingers on them.

"Sister Frances, press hard. Marietta, be strong and push," Ella commanded. "One, two, three."

As Marietta gave a push, Ella, with her heart in her throat, pulled the slimy fetus towards herself. Marietta screamed like a banshee. The lieutenant groaned as she dug her fingers into his arm. With another push and pull, the head squeezed through. The infant gave its first shrill cry. Everyone in the room exhaled a collective sigh of relief.

After cutting and tying off the umbilical cord, Ella examined the pink, rather large baby boy in her arms, with chestnut hair, like his mother and aunt. His head was conical in shape, and his eyes gray and shiny.

Ella helped Marietta deliver the afterbirth, while Sister Frances washed and wrapped the baby. Swaddled into a tight cocoon, the baby boy met his mother's waiting arms. Wyse stepped back and leaned on the wall. Concerned by his paleness, Ella wondered if she should find smelling salts.

Marietta wept as her sister embraced her.

"What will you name your son?" Ella asked.

"My son?" Marietta's jaw fell. "I was sure it was a girl. I wanted to name her Eloise."

"You need a new plan, my friend."

The new mother tilted her head and gazed at Wyse. "What did you say your name is, sir?"

Lieutenant straightened. "Jack Wyse. At your service."

Beaming through tears, she turned to her sister. "Jack Fillips. What do you think?"

"Sounds like a rascal." Henrietta snorted.

Ella peered at the baby's twinkling eyes. "With the birth he chose, I say the name fits. He's a rascal all right."

Still leaning on the wall, Wyse coughed. "You wish to name your son after me, Madam? I don't deserve the honor."

The new mother frowned. "Why not? You are the brave, noble officer who came to our rescue. I can't imagine a better example for my baby boy. Would you like to hold him?"

Wyse accepted the bundle with reverence and stared at the infant's precious face.

At that moment, Matilda entered and gazed at the baby. "Looks like I'm not required."

Ella threw up her hands. "Matilda, where were you? I needed you."

The midwife shook her head. "You didn't. The sailors said you wanted my help to deliver a baby. I was about to go when I thought, 'What would Ella do if I weren't here? She'd stop fretting and deliver without me.' Joseph and I taught you all we could. We sent you to medical school to learn things beyond our knowledge. Out in the world, you need to use your skills without depending on me."

"The world doesn't want a woman surgeon," Ella said, her head lowered.

Wyse handed the baby back to the mother and stood across from Ella. He raised her chin with his fingers. "There's at least one place where you are wanted. "On the *Neptune*. Please come back, Doctor Parker."

Chapter 25

The large group hiked through the forest on the carpet of gold and ruby leaves. The men took turns carrying the makeshift stretcher where Marietta and baby Jack reposed. Wyse walked in front, warning of any obstacle that could disturb the precious load. The rustle under their feet, the song of nightingales, and the tap of woodpeckers combined into the first lullaby for the newborn.

Morgan gave Ella a hand as she stepped over branches that threatened to catch her skirts. "I'm glad you are not wearing the habit anymore. I was afraid to speak to you," he said.

The boys brought her a dress, and she was thankful for their thoughtfulness. "I'm glad to be rid of it too. Things may be different in other monasteries, but I don't want to find out. I was shocked by sailor superstition, but these nuns were worse, burning science books and denying patients medical care."

The coxswain sighed. "Yet Fran chose to stay...Sister Frances, I mean. I asked her to come with us, but she said she has important work to do."

"Right. Mother Superior slipped away in the commotion, and good riddance. Sister Frances hopes to become the new abbess and make the monastery the healing place it's meant to be. Except I have a strange feeling that it's not the last I will see of the old Mother Superior."

He cleared his throat. "I asked Sister Frances to write to me. I like receiving letters, even though I can't read. She wants me to write back. Would you help me?"

Touching her face, Ella gave him an uncertain glance. "I'd love to help, but I'm not sure if I'll return to the *Neptune*."

"But why not? The men will tell you how sorry they are for mistreating you. If you want someone flogged, just say so."

She covered her gaping mouth with her hand. "Heavens, no. You all redeemed yourself by rescuing me and my friends. It's just...I don't fit in on the ship. I've tried, but I guess there's too much of a gentle lady in me to behave like a sailor. Although, strong expressions slip in now and then." A giggle tickled her throat. "Anyway, I hope you will find someone to help you."

His head shaking with disappointment, he walked away. Matilda caught up to her. The midwife put her arm around Ella, who leaned on her friend.

"Oh, Matilda. I'm so sorry about Joseph. I should've known what ailed him."

Matilda groaned. "Ella, who made you responsible for my pig-headed brother? Why are you bearing the guilt for the habit he hid? He died on his own terms, at the time and place of his choosing."

Tears welled in Ella's eyes. "I miss him."

Her friend wiped her own tears. "As do I. But we must go on. Let's start new in Plymouth. We'll open an herb shop and deliver babies. From what I saw of the city, we'll be busy. Will you partner with me?"

Blinking away tears, Ella shook her head with a small smile. "Only as a financial sponsor. My first day as your assistant was disastrous for you. Not again."

"I doubt Mrs. Kelley and her children would view that day as disastrous, but as you wish. I hope you won't be far from Plymouth. I will look after Marietta and her baby and search for a suitable spot for my shop." Baby Jack made a demanding cry, and Matilda went to assist his mother with nursing.

While the party stopped to allow Marietta to feed the baby, Henrietta approached Ella and took her hand. "Thank goodness for Matilda. I'm going to ask Veronica to house us until Marietta recovers. Why don't you join us as well? The embroidery circle will be together again, and without our mothers and governesses there, we'll be free to talk about whatever we wish as we needlepoint."

Ella snorted. "Not the embroidery circle. After we decorate the baby's shirts, what will we do?"

Henrietta lowered her voice and glanced towards Wyse, who ushered the men away from Marietta to give her privacy. "Sew Marietta's wedding dress. I predict Mr. Wyse will propose. He's so attentive to my sister."

"Wyse to marry? I'd never... But you may be right. He seems besotted with her."

The girl's lips curved into a dreamy smile. "He doesn't care that she's an unwed mother with no dowry. Isn't it romantic?"

Ella rolled her eyes. "Romantic... I didn't take the nunnery vows, but I'm over romance and marriage."

"But..." Henrietta gawked. "Without them, could you be happy?"

"I believe so. Marriage doesn't guarantee happiness. It's often the opposite. A husband would possess all my assets and may forbid me from practicing medicine. Why should I ever get married? Matilda seems happy as a spinster. She raised a child and ran a successful shop. My work will fulfill me. But maybe I'm different than you and your sister. I want Marietta to be happy. How does she feel about Wyse?"

"Marriage would save her reputation, but she wouldn't marry for that reason only. She's charmed by Wyse despite that horrible gumboil on his face. I must say, he would be handsome, if not for it." Henrietta snickered.

"Pff, that gumboil came from his rotten tooth. That stubborn man spent the whole voyage suffering from a toothache, yet he won't let me help."

Henrietta winked. "Maybe he'll ask now. He's approaching." She went to her sister's side. The men raised the stretcher, and the party resumed their way.

Ella smiled, walking next to the lieutenant. "Mr. Wyse. I never expected you to come to my rescue, but I'm glad you did. Thank you."

Wyse scoffed. "What did you bloody expect with the way you left your things? The boys imagined you were going to off yourself, and the men were ready to rise against me."

She drew in air. "I thought, as a nun, I wouldn't need my jewelry and fancy dresses, so I left them for you to sell. And since I had my own instruments, I left Dr. Pesce's behind. I wanted to benefit the ship's company even if they didn't like me. I apologize for the trouble I caused."

The lieutenant sighed. "I'm the one who owes you an apology. I did everything I could to ruin your life on the *Neptune*. I turned the men against you and ordered them to avoid you. Instead of keeping you safe, I put you in danger, first by tricking you into drinking, and then by allowing Simkins to do the 'witch test.' Others mistreated you, but it was from my example and permission."

Ella swallowed. "Why did you do those things? Do you dislike women that much?"

Wyse took a long swig from his flask. This time it didn't smell of alcohol. "No. I'm scared to see a woman die on my ship. It happened once. And it broke my heart."

"I'm so sorry. What happened? If you wish to tell me."

He cringed, as if in pain. "Her name was Charlotte. Captain Fitzharris's daughter. I was a lower-deck hand, but we fell in love. We were young. She told me stories of brave knights and fair princesses. I promised her to learn to read and write. Earn promotions so we could wed."

He cleared his throat. "Anyway, I got a scratch in one battle, nothing serious. I refused to see the surgeon. A loblolly blabbed that he saw me bleeding to death. Charlotte left the orlop and ran onto the deck to find me. Like you did when you needed laudanum for Stafford. A musket ball hit her square in the chest. Right in front of me."

Ella covered her mouth. "How horrible. I'm so sorry."

Wyse sniffled air. "Captain Fitzharris made me learn to read and write. Said it was his daughter's wish that I better myself. I did it, first for her, then because I liked learning. I became a master, the best job I could hope for. Then Captain Grey received command. He asked me if I wanted to rise higher, to a lieutenant. He gave me a chance to pass the exam. Which I did."

Ella nodded. "I admire you for that. The ship boys look up to you." She glanced back at the boys, who walked as a group, engrossed in a discussion.

"They are good lads. I hear you are planning a celebration for them. Does that mean you are staying?"

She tilted her head from side to side. "I haven't decided on my future yet. Like I told Morgan, I don't fit in on the ship."

He scratched his chin. "You don't need to fit in. You're from a different world, but that's not a bad thing. We all come from various places, but at sea we become one crew. And you are part of that crew. You proved over and over that you belong."

Ella gave a sideways glance. "I don't know. Only a few days ago men accused me of witchcraft and threw me overboard. Is everyone eager to accept me?"

"Not everyone, but enough. Simkins and a couple of his cronies transferred to another ship. The others are ready to make amends and welcome you back. They'll tell you so."

"I appreciate that, but there's something else I want you to do."

He frowned. "What's that?"

"You'll let me remove your rotten tooth. In front of the crew." She gave a smug look.

Wyse froze. "Odds bodkins, no. Anything but that."

She shook her head. "Wyse, that tooth must go. Be an example to your men and show your trust in my skills. You may drink all you wish beforehand."

Wyse grabbed his cheek and winced. "Fine. But first, please tell me as Miss Marietta's friend... Would she want to marry me?"

Lost in thought, Ella tripped on a root and grabbed Wyse's arm for balance. "Are you serious?"

Wyse reddened and turned away. "No. Of course she won't have me."

"What? No. I meant that you hardly know her. I think you should court her. Her sister said that she finds you charming."

"Charming is not a word for me." He hunched his back. "With my bad manners, I'm not good enough for her. She was in labor pains and didn't curse even once. The way she said she'd rather die than give her child away made my heart break. I'm dirt compared to a woman like that. I could never court her."

Ella scoffed. "Wyse, stop putting yourself down. Marietta named her child after you. You are worthy of her. You taught yourself to read and write, to navigate the ship. How hard could it be for you to learn polite manners? Find a moment and ask her, 'Would you allow me to call on you sometime, Miss Marietta?' If she agrees, we can discuss how you should behave when visiting her."

Wyse chuckled. "Aha, that means you're staying."

She crossed her arms and turned her body away from him. "I didn't say that."

He returned to his lookout position upfront, his lips silently forming the phrase Ella taught him.

They came to Plymouth with several hours of daylight left. The smell of sea salt left a familiar taste on her tongue. Her lungs gulped air with greediness.

As they neared the port, The *Neptune* emerged in the distance, seaworthy after repairs. Cradling Baby Jack in her arms, Marietta whispered to him about the magnificent ships and the bobbing sea. Henrietta's eyes sparkled; her neck twisted left and right as she smiled at the uniformed officers.

"Ella, I can't believe you are forsaking romance with so many handsome men about," Henrietta gushed. "They are ignoring me because I'm dressed in this awful habit, but you are attracting gazes. That handsome officer can't take his eyes off you. Too bad he lost his left arm."

Ella gazed at the officer and stumbled. "He lost his arm because I amputated it. My goodness, he lived. I must talk to him."

"Please tell him I'm not a nun," Henrietta whispered.

Ella sped in the young man's direction, her heart jumping with every step. "George Stafford! You've recovered!" Ella squealed and threw her arms around him.

The midshipman put his good arm around her. "Thanks to you, Doctor Parker. The surgeons in the naval hospital said that if not for your expert care, I would have died."

Ella's eyes watered. "Oh George. Seeing you well makes me happy. Are you returning to the *Neptune*?"

"No. I've transferred to my uncle's ship, the *Seagull*. My wound reconciled us. He promised to show no favoritism and treat me like any other officer under his command. How did the rest of your voyage go?"

Ella played with a stray curl. "It was ... adventurous."

He peered into her face. "If those adventures weren't to your taste, my uncle will welcome you onboard. I'll vouch for your skill as a surgeon."

She tilted her head. "Thank you for the offer. I'm weighing my options."

"Please come to dinner at my mother's house tomorrow. My parents would love to meet you."

"That sounds nice. May I bring a friend, the young woman who is standing over there? Her name is Henrietta Fillips, and she wants you to know she's not a nun."

Henrietta giggled and covered her mouth with her hand. His cheeks reddened.

"Any friend of yours is a friend of mine. I'm intrigued why she's wearing a habit. She's more than welcome."

They bid each other goodbye, and Ella raced back to her group. The men, except for Wyse, Tobby, and a few who carried Marietta's stretcher, went to the boats that would take them to the *Neptune*.

Near Veronica's house, Ella indicated a bench for Marietta. Rocking her yawning baby, the new mother rested in the shade of a large oak. Matilda stretched her legs next to her. The men grouped under the tree and opened their sacks with food. Tobby grabbed a large apple.

Wyse stood by Marietta, watching her and the peaceful infant.

He rubbed his trembling hands and took a long breath. "Would you allow me to call on you sometime, Miss Marietta?"

Marietta kissed her son on the temple. "We both would like that very much."

The midwife cracked an amused smile and found another bench, giving them privacy.

Ella and Henrietta knocked on the door of Veronica's house; tiny compared to the estate that Veronica grew up in. Yet the brightly painted door sign, the swing on the porch, the flowers on the windowsills made Ella believe her friend was enjoying her new life.

Hurried steps sounded. Veronica opened the door and gaped at them.

Henrietta spoke first. "My dear friend, we come uninvited, but I hope my sister, her newborn baby, our new friend Matilda, and I can count on your hospitality. Our circumstances are dire."

Veronica stared for a moment at Henrietta's habit, but then she beamed. "We're the embroidery circle friends, but our bond is stronger than silk threads. Stay as long as you like."

Ella embraced both friends in turn. "I'm so proud of us. We've grown into women who can count on each other."

"I would love your help as well, ladies," Veronica said. "Ernest is away on a voyage. In my idle time, I've sewn a couple of elegant ball gowns. It made me think, why don't I open my own dress shop?"

"What will your parents say? And your husband?" Henrietta raised her eyebrows.

Veronica shrugged. "Ernest won't object. My parents think that a lady shouldn't work, but I'm a grown woman and can decide for myself."

Henrietta shrieked with glee. "Then put me to work! We'll start with Marietta's wedding dress, and I hope we'll sew mine soon enough."

Ella rolled her eyes. "Don't count on me ordering a wedding gown."

"Veronica, can you talk some sense into Ella? She's denouncing love and marriage!" Henrietta threw up her hands.

The hostess shifted her gaze from one friend to another. "Ella is denouncing marriage, but you're the one wearing a habit? I'm confused."

Ella shrugged. "It's a long story. I don't want to get married. I choose my freedom and my work. But let's discuss this some other time. Marietta needs to feed her baby and rest."

When Ella called, Wyse lifted Marietta into his arms and carried her into the house. Matilda followed with the baby. Ella bid hearty goodbyes to her friends and promised to see them tomorrow, when she would collect Henrietta for dinner with George Stafford and his family.

"Are you coming onboard, Dr. Parker?" Wyse asked after they left Veronica's house. His expression was dreamy after a goodbye to Marietta.

Tobby pulled her hand. "Doctor Ella, you must come. You promised another cake."

Ella laughed. "That's true. I did promise a celebration for you and the boys." She led Tobby to the bakery and told him to order anything he wanted. After a long consultation with the baker, the boy asked for the largest cake that could be made in one day with cream roses, tart currants, and most importantly, a blueberry filling. With a grave face, Tobby added that the blueberries must come from the market, and not the forest. The baker scratched his head and promised to have his assistants deliver such a cake to the ship by evening.

***

As Ella stepped onto the gangway of the *Neptune*, the ship company erupted with clapping, whistles, and cheers. Wyse gestured to the men to shout even louder before running off towards the captain's cabin. The men waved their hats in the air and stumped their feet. The boys were in the crowd, yelling at the top of their lungs. Ella nodded at the familiar faces, who smiled and nodded back. A small group of Simkin's remaining cronies gave Ella hostile looks and booed, but their discontent drowned in the storm of cheers.

Right in front were Olson, Sully, and Tyler. When the noise died down, those three surrounded her.

The carpenter spoke first. "Doctor Parker, I'm so happy you are safe. The trick Simkins and his friends played on you was wicked. I wanted to stop it."

"Is that why you gave me that whistle?"

"Yes. I hoped you would blow it if in danger, and me or my friends would hear. I was in irons when Simkins and his men attacked you. I heard how heroic you were. And I understand better than most how ingratitude drove you away. I hope you'll forgive us and stay."

Ella beamed. "I happily forgive, and I will always wear your whistle around my neck from now on. But I don't know about staying. There are days when I want to wear trousers and cuss like a sailor, and those when I would rather swish my skirts and speak like a gentle lady. I'm Eloise, the earl's daughter, and I'm Doctor Ella Parker, the surgeon. I can't separate the two and fit in. Although Mr. Wyse said that I belong."

Olson chuckled. "I reckon he's right. I'm more than one person as well. I'm a free man and a skilled carpenter Owen Olson, but I'm also Olaudah Ogogo, a runaway slave. I spent years closing my mind to the memories, but now I wish to tell my stories."

"And do both Owen and Olaudah belong here?"

"Yes, they do. And if a former slave can belong among the British sailors, so can a woman on a ship full of men. Belonging is a funny word, isn't it? So many meanings. When my master would say that I belonged to him to do as he wished, my knees would buckle with fear. When two people get married, they are said to belong to each other, which could be a wonderful or a terrible thing. But when we speak of belonging to the crew, warmth spreads through my chest. Without such belonging, people suffer."

Ella squeezed his palms. "I understand. I thought I should change and fit in, but instead I can be myself and belong. That's a crucial difference."

Tyler tapped her shoulder. "Dr. Parker, please accept my apologies for my rudeness. I was unwell and didn't know what I was saying. I'm most grateful for you saving my life."

She cupped his face, peering at him. "You look well. How do you feel?"

"Fully recovered, and ashamed of my stupidity. I was wretched with guilt for giving Dr. Pesce the deadly dose of his medicine and with disappointment for being left out of his will. It was my only chance to afford medical school. I don't deserve it."

"You got that right, friend. Not after what you've pulled," Sully muttered.

"Oh, Tyler." Ella sighed. "I'm afraid it's my fault the doctor had no money to leave you. His sister closed her shop because of my actions, and she needed funds. But I have the means to pay for your education."

The young man gasped. "You'd do this for me after how I treated you?"

Ella nodded. "Dr. Pesce paid for my education when I couldn't afford it. I want to follow his example. Let's start with a new page. I will tutor you for medical school. We'll consider if you have the resilience as well as the knowledge needed to succeed."

Tyler beamed. "I'd be honored to learn from you."

"As would I," Sully echoed.

"I have much to learn as well," Ella said. "Dr. Pesce isn't here to guide me. I must rely on books and my limited experience. Sometimes doctors make mistakes, but they learn painful lessons that help them grow and save more lives. And having loyal assistants by my side would be invaluable."

Sully and Tyler shook hands with her.

"Dr. Parker, will you stop prattling and give your attention to the captain?" Wyse's voice boomed. "He asked you to come to the quarterdeck."

Ella cringed. "Sorry, I didn't hear."

Captain Grey offered her his hand as she ascended the steps. "There she is. Men, three cheers for Doctor Parker!"

"Hip hip hurray!" The ship's company thundered thrice.

When the cheers dissipated, the captain spoke. "By now everyone's heard the full account of Doctor Parker's brave actions in saving Mr. Simkins' life. I want to acknowledge her valor. The Admiralty forbids women from serving in the Royal Navy. I'll submit a detailed report about the valiant surgeon Alan Parker. Some details would be altered or left out, but we'll remember the true account of the events and retell them on Yarn Sundays as some of the greatest stories that happened aboard this ship."

The crew clapped and cheered. Ella beamed, overwhelmed with emotion.

"This must be the longest speech I've given." The captain wiped sweat from his forehead. "I'm letting Mr. Wyse take over."

With his shoulders squared, Wyse stepped forward. "Despite our ill-treatment, Dr. Parker wanted to be our surgeon. While none of us want to be sick, we are lucky to have her to care for us. I apologized for my behavior, and I want to do it again on behalf of everyone who was unkind to Dr. Parker. Please forgive us, doctor, and stay. We care about you, as you cared about us."

As the men yelled and stomped, Wyse crept towards the stairs.

"Not so fast, Mr. Wyse. You have a promise to fulfill," Ella reminded.

"I was hoping you'd forget."

"Not a chance." Ella called the loblollies to bring her instruments and a chair to the quarterdeck. Then she addressed the men. "Many diseases start as a nuisance but get worse if not treated in time. Mr. Wyse's tooth is a perfect example of that. He should've let me extract it months ago, well before it caused a gumboil. I hope you take my warning to heart and see me for any concerns about your health."

The seamen clapped and yelled encouragements to Wyse. He gulped down his flask. Whiffs of alcohol came from his breath as he collapsed on the chair.

"High time to get that tooth taken care of, Wyse," the captain said. "I'll hold you down, so you don't jerk."

Ella tapped the lieutenant's shoulder. "Open wide."

The dental forceps, steady in her able hands, gripped the tooth. Her flexed muscles pulled with all her strength, but it surprised her how easily the tooth came out. Her skill and confidence advanced by miles since the beginning of the voyage.

"That's it?" Wyse marveled.

She gave him gauze to bite down on and held up the rotten tooth. The men cheered. With the procedure finished, the captain dismissed them.

"You should rest." Ella rubbed the lieutenant's shoulder. "I'll make a remedy to treat the gumboil and check on you later. You did well. Didn't even curse."

Looking dazed, Wyse staggered towards the stairs. Ella called on Sully and Tyler to support him as he stumbled to his cabin.

After wiping her instrument, Ella took a moment to look around. The men dispersed and picked up their numerous jobs, some giving Ella a smile. The boys started a game by the bow, their faces shining with excitement. The tide beckoned the ship back to open waters and Ella with it.

Captain Grey's steps jarred her from her thoughts. He invited her to his cabin. Inside, he gestured for her to sit, while taking the other chair at his desk.

"Would you like to dine with me? Wyse said you had nothing but bread and water in the monastery."

Ella smiled. "The endless salted pork and the hardtack with weevils became a fond memory. I'm sorry, but I must decline, sir. I'm dining in the forecastle. We are celebrating Tobby's birthday."

The captain offered a bemused smile. "Ah, Tobby. I made him the cook's helper, as you requested. And I'm inclined to promote Digby to a midshipman in a few years, provided you tutor him in reading and writing. Are you engaged tomorrow?"

"Yes. I'm dining with George Stafford and his parents. He recovered from his wound."

"And transferred to his uncle's command. They aren't thinking of recruiting you, are they?"

Ella shrugged. "I don't know. I'm a woman with many options, or so it appears. But I've been convinced that I belong here. I already committed myself to helping Morgan write letters, preparing Tyler for medical school, and teaching Wyse good manners. And I'll be schooling Digby and the other boys, on top of performing my job as the surgeon. Great responsibilities on my plate, sir."

Captain Grey punched his desk with his fist. "I dare say you are indispensable, and I won't lose you to another captain. We have another voyage ahead, likely to last over a year. While I can't reveal details, we'll be sailing in a tropical climate, where men may catch yellow fever and malaria. There will be battles as well. I need a skillful surgeon, and I hope it will be you. Not everyone of the crew wants you aboard, but you've changed many minds and won many hearts. Just look at this stack of notes for me. And this is just the men who can write."

The captain handed her clutches of paper. The handwriting was crooked and many of the words misspelled, but the message in them was clear. The men asked the captain to bring Ella back as the surgeon. After all the arduous work, the lack of comforts, cruel pranks, and isolation, the men respected her skill, steadfastness, and resolve to help them. Her heart swelled with joy.

I belong among these rough but hardworking and decent men. I've earned my place on this ship.

"I'm happy to accept. There's much to do. I must purchase Jesuit bark to fight malaria. The sickbay should be expanded to accommodate more patients. We need to improve the men's diet with fresh meat, vegetables, and fruit to prevent scurvy. The grog—"

The captain raised his hand. "I won't prohibit the grog, Doctor. I don't want a mutiny."

"I was going to say we'll need enough grog to last the voyage, as the lemon juice prevents scurvy as well. But we must employ strict rations."

"I'll be happy to listen to your recommendations another time. I have another letter for you. It's from Robert's mother."

He handed her a letter from a pile on his desk. Ella glanced at the neat handwriting with some blotches that spoke of the writer's tears. Mrs. Weston's words rang with heartfelt gratitude, while her husband's postscript was a courtly regret of the broken betrothal and a reassurance of amity despite it.

Ella put the letter into the pocket of her dress. "They are offering their friendship. But after how Robert treated me, I'm not sure I want it."

Captain Grey cocked his head. "I suggest you stay on good terms with the Westons. They are a powerful naval family, and you never know when you may need them. Still, I'm disappointed in Robert. It's the parents' job to arrange an advantageous marriage for their son, and the son's job to rebel and stand together with his love. That's what I did, and I don't regret it. My wife and I are happy, and we are blessed with two daughters about your age. I told them about you, and they wrote you a message."

He removed a piece of paper from his breast pocket.

"Dear Doctor Ella Parker,

While you sail the seven seas, my younger sister Cecilia and I are trapped in a pitiful existence. Our mother drags us to sewing meetings and dance classes where we are wilting from boredom. Cecilia resorted to playing melancholy songs on her violin, driving me mad. Please rescue us at the first opportunity you could spare by dining with us. We must hear your fantastic stories.

Bella Grey

Dear Dr. Parker,

I want to add that my older sister is little fun and speaks of trigonometry at every chance, which is why I retaliate with my music. Yes, please, please, please come visit. We promise to be on our best behavior, however low standard that is.

Cecilia Grey

Captain Grey shook his head. “What do you think of these vixens?”

Ella clapped her hands. “They sound wonderful. I’m free the day after tomorrow to visit. We’ll get along splendidly.”

The captain chuckled. “I agree. May I suggest that you avoid revealing your brief engagement to Robert Weston? Bella is still besotted with him, foolish girl. Tell her you removed a bullet from his leg, and she’ll worship the ground you walk on. It’s settled then. Enjoy your cake with the boys.”

Ella saluted as she rose and left the cabin. Back on the deck, she admired the sunset. The sun dipped into the sea, painting the sky burgundy and scarlet. Mesmerized, she headed towards the bow, but the ship boys met her by the mizzenmast.

“Are we having cake?” Tobby asked. “The men from the bakery just brought it.”

Ella disheveled his hair. "Yes, but I want to do something first. Digby, can I borrow some clothes from you? I'm not sure what the nuns did with my trousers."

Digby shrugged and dashed below. Five minutes later, he threw Ella a set of faded clothes. She changed in her cabin and emerged in a shirt that was too long, and the breeches she fastened with a belt.

"It'll do. While Mr. Wyse is dead asleep after his tooth extraction, I want to climb the rigging with you. I wouldn't attempt that trick in a skirt."

The boys whooped and gathered by the ratlines.

"The last to the top eats dirt," Digby yelped.

Ella shook her finger. "That's no way for a young gentleman to talk. But you can go first and show how it's done."

Digby, Ben, and the twins scrambled up. Like salty sailors, they used shrouds to pull themselves onto the platform. Tobby and Ella took their time climbing and ascended through the lubber's hole.

The six of them stilled for the magnificent moment, watching the scarlet sun sink into the purple sea. For a heartbeat, the world was a picture of peace and beauty.

Dr. Pesce would love this view, Ella thought. *Sunsets were his reward after a difficult day.*

"*They still are*," his voice sounded in her head. "*I watch all the sunsets and the sunrises, the tides and the ebbs, the calms, and the storms. The birds above, the fish below. All the beautiful ships with their proud masts and taut sails. And all the people who sail in them, from the admirals to the ship boys. You don't have to wonder where my resting place is, Ella. It's everywhere around you. When you are at sea, I'm only a gust of wind away.*"

"This is where I belong," Ella said.

Digby raised an eyebrow. "Then why did you leave?"

"Sometimes you leave so your true friends can show themselves. And you can also learn who you are."

The boys scratched their heads and shrugged.

She chuckled. "That's enough philosophy. Time for cake."

They clambered down the ratlines. Most of the ship crew was waiting for them below.

Tobby gave her a concerned look. "Will there be enough cake for all of us?"

Ella chewed her lip. "How many people did you invite, Tobby?"

"Everyone, of course."

"Everyone? The cake was for your friends."

"But everyone on the ship is my friend. Yours too. And if anyone gives you trouble, just tell me and the other boys, and we'll take care of him."

She laughed. "In that case, friends always find a way to share. Cake, troubles, victories, whatever comes."

Hands reached to help her down. She waved them off, jumped, and landed on her feet to everyone's cheer.

"She's a seadog after all," Olson declared.

"Can a girl be a seadog?" Digby asked.

Ella tilted her head. "Some may say it's no job for a woman, but I would prove them wrong. *Any* job is a job for a woman."

***

Ella rejects romantic entanglements and dedicates herself to her profession. What will she do when her friends are captured by the enemy and imprisoned in a French fortress? Read A Surgeon and a Spy – Book 3 of Hearts and Sails Series.

***

Also By Alina Rubin

A Girl with a Knife—Hearts and Sails Book 1

Women could not be surgeons. She did it anyway.

After the heartbreaking loss of her mother and a cruel attack by her drunken father, Ella Parker decides that dishonesty is fine when it serves her needs. At a time when wealthy young ladies do little more than embroidery, Ella escapes her luxurious but lonely life, disguises herself as male medical student, and finds her footing in the university.

But when she brilliantly saves a patient and gains the approval of a famed professor, she must choose between truth and lies, and distinguish between real and false friends, before her pretense is discovered.

A Surgeon and a Spy—Hearts and Sails Book 3

On turbulent seas of the Napoleonic Wars, Ella Parker dedicates herself to healing the sick and wounded, resolutely dismissing the idea of romantic entanglements. Her commitment is tested when her childhood friend, Jamie Flowers, is captured by the enemy and imprisoned in a French fortress, along with other sailors for whom she deeply cares for.

When Ella is presented with a chance to journey to the prison, her mission is twofold: to rescue her friends and to complete a covert assignment. As she embarks on this perilous task, she must navigate a labyrinth of treacherous alliances, fend off bandits, and outwit a cunning prison commander.

As Ella's journey unfolds, she uncovers a sinister secret. But is she too late? Despite Ella's burgeoning affections for Jamie, she's unaware of his possible heart condition that may cut his life short. With time running out, Ella must confront her deepest fears to prevent a tragedy and save her friends.

Hearts by the Sea: Hearts and Sails Prequel

An innocent game brings unforeseen consequences

In the idyllic setting of the English coast in 1800s, Jamie Flowers experiences his first infatuation when he meets Ella Parker, a mysterious girl with a troubled past. As the two rehearse *Romeo and Juliet* together, they decide to sneak out for a midnight swim. But their plans are abruptly halted by a shocking revelation, and Ella is soon gone. Heartbroken, Jamie searches for her... and himself. With unexpected twists and turns, Hearts by the Sea is a story of friendship, secret codes, and self-discovery.

New Series with Familiar Characters!

Abigail's Song—Hearts and Harmony Book 1
When your world is out of tune, can music heal you?

Cast out from her home after her mother's death, orphan Abigail Jones wanders around her English town on Christmas Eve of 1809. Desperately trying to suppress her cough—the same that killed her mother—Abigail begs for coins on the freezing cold streets. With the help of the medical student, Oli Higgins, she recovers and avoids being sent to the cruel orphanage. Oli then reveals his secret: he is hiding his Jewish identity and his birth name, David Fridman, to pursue his chosen profession. He brings her into his devout, loving Jewish home. Over time, she embraces her found family and discovers her talent for music.

When she grows up, Abigail is caught between two worlds; not Christian enough for the Gentiles, but as a non-Jew, she has no hope of marrying David, the man she dreams of. While she is recovering from a deadly illness, David's brother Moishe inspires her with music to rise from her sickbed and to begin her journey of converting to Judaism.

Her attempt to capture David's heart fails when his true love appears in town. Heartbroken, Abigail hastily accepts another man's marriage proposal and plans a double wedding with David's bride. On the big day, guilt and misery drive her to take drastic actions.

Friends Don't Let Friends Read Boring Books!

Thank you for reading No Job for a Woman!

Leaving a review is like recommending a book to hundreds of friends. Please share your thoughts at:

Amazon

Goodreads

BookBub

Join the crew! Be the first to know of new adventures by subscribing to the newsletter at alinarubinauthor.com

I love hearing from my readers! Please connect with me!

Instagram: Alina.Rubin.Author

Facebook: Alina Rubin Author

Email: alina@alinarubinauthor.com

Historical Notes

No Job for a Woman continued my excursion into 18th-19th century medicine. One of the most compelling stories that I found was the history of the Chamberlen family, the inventors of the obstetric forceps. They were Huguenots who fled religious persecution in France and settled in England.

Peter Chamberlen the elder (or possibly his father William) invented the forceps in the late 16th century but kept his life-saving find a secret. He, and later his descendants, attended women in labor and brought a closed, gold-colored box. They asked all other attendants to leave the room and blindfolded the mother, ensuring she didn't peek at their instrument. They even employed people to make noise to prevent eavesdropping while they used the forceps to deliver the babies. Their secret stayed in the family for five generations, a timespan of about 150 years.

The Chamberlen family made several attempts to sell their secret to other doctors. In 1670, they approached the French doctor Francois Mauriceua, who was disgusted that they hid such a lifesaving invention from the medical world and refused to purchase. He became known as one of the founders of the breech delivery maneuver (Mauriceua-Smellie-Velt maneuver) that Ella used to deliver Marietta's baby. William Smellie, one of the other founders, learned of forceps after the secret was finally leaked around 1730. He improved on their design, as did several other doctors. Science advances when more great minds contribute.

The stomach pump that saved Tyler's life was invented by Dr. Philip Physick and used by him in 1812 to save three-month-old twins who were given laudanum and went into coma; one survived and fully recovered. Dr. Jukes in 1822 took ten ounces of laudanum and used the pump on himself as a public experiment, which he survived.

According to archeological evidence, skull trepanning dates to 6,500 BCE, the oldest surgery ever performed. The modern scientists don't know if the goal was to alleviate suffering or to perform religious rituals. Archaeologists discovered more than 1,500 trephined skulls from the Neolithic period around the world. Evidence showed that about forty percent of people who had undergone the procedure survived.

In my research, I scoured the journal written by Thomas Logan, the ship surgeon of the *Albion*, written in 1828. His entries included drunken fights and accidents, a shark attack, a near drowning and revival, and a girl expelling a seven-foot-long worm. These accounts sparked some of my stories.

Fiction, including this book, often portrays that women were unwelcome on ships. The British Admiralty had rules against bringing women on voyages, but many wives of officers followed their husbands to sea. These brave women shared their husbands' trials and assisted surgeons in the sickbay. A picture from *Nautical Miscellany* depicts a woman helping a wounded seaman during a battle while supporting a baby on her hip.

Many people of color served in the Royal Navy (researchers don't say how many as ship books did not specify the sailors' origins.) Some were runaway slaves from the colonies, but also crewmen from other countries. One of the bronze reliefs at the base of Nelson's column in Trafalgar Square, depicting that battle, portrays a Black seaman.

I don't know where I got the idea for Ella to be tested for witchcraft, but one of the methods used in the 17th and 18th century was a 'swimming the witch' test by tying the supposed witch's hands and dunking them into water to see if they would float. According to researcher Russell Zguta, this 'trial by water' approach was based on the religious belief that water was a sacred element.

The waltz came to England in 1813. Since this is a work of fiction, I allowed it to appear early. It was often considered to be too 'forward', in that couples were holding each other.

The monastery Ella visited was of my imagination. Mr. Doolittle would be Anglican, like all chaplains of the Royal Navy. From my research, most Anglican convents were established during the Oxford movement that started in 1830s. Possibly, there was no Anglican convent Ella could join in her time, only Catholic. I claim 'creative license' for this part. It wasn't easy to find books about 19th century convents in England, but I found one: *Nuns: A History of Convent Life* by Silvia Evangelisti. Nun's dowry paid for the Fillips sisters by their mother, and Sister Frances's rise from prostitution to nunhood were inspired by that book.

When composing my first manuscript, I envisioned Ella as a respected and beloved ship surgeon. Because she lived at a time when women couldn't practice medicine or hold official jobs on a ship, it took me two books to manifest her destiny. The life on the Age of Sail ship added a new layer to my research. I read fiction by C.S. Forester, Philip Allan, and others, non-fiction by N.A.M Rodger, John Harland, and others, and sea journal books, such as *Two Years Before the Mast* by Richard Henry Dana.

I also took my family on a one-hour cruise on the sailing ship Windy, a not-to-miss experience in Chicago. My favorite non-fiction is *Nelson's Navy: The Ships, Men and Organization* by Brian Lavery. My beloved sea fiction books are *Captain Blood: His Odyssey* by Rafael Sabatini and *The True Confessions of Charlotte Doyle* by Avi.

Book Club Questions

1. When delivering Mrs. Kelley's baby, Ella knowingly breaks the law using the forceps. Do you think she acted in the best way? What would you have done in her place?

2. On the *Neptune*, Ella is met with rudeness, indifference, and distrust. Have you ever entered a new environment and found yourself unwelcome? What did you do?

3. When the captain's steward pours out Ella's remedy for seasickness, Ella responds by lecturing him on his manners. Did Ella create more problems with her primness?

4. Jack Wyse wants Ella gone from the moment she stepped foot on his ship. At the same time, he fulfills his orders to protect her. How does he steer between his duty and his feelings? Have you been in a situation when your assignment opposed your desires? What

did you do?

5. Dr. Pesce displays the signs of laudanum addiction Ella should recognize, yet her trust in him prevents her from seeing the obvious. Have you ever been blind to someone's behavior because you trusted them?

6. Ella's romance with Robert Weston dissipated. Did you hope for their marriage, or did you see the signs that he was ill-suited? If Ella married him, how do you envision her life?

7. After the broken proposal, Ella swears off romantic love and marriage. Do you think her work and friendships will fulfill her? Can one choose not to fall in love?

8. At times, Ella wears men's clothing and cusses like a sailor. Jack Wyse, on the other hand, wishes to acquire better manners to court Marietta. What do you think of their transformations?

9. Ella often says that she can fit in on the ship. In the end, Wyse and Olson tell her that she belongs there. How does belonging differ from fitting in?

Acknowledgments

First, I want to thank YOU for reading. You could've watched Netflix, or knitted a sweater, or read a different book. Despite all those options, you chose to read *my* book and stayed with my characters to the end. This means the world to me. If you could give a few more minutes of your time and send me a quick email or leave a review on Amazon or Goodreads, you will make me smile for an entire day. Thank you to all the wonderful readers who've reached out. I pinch myself whenever I hear from someone far away.

I can't thank enough my beta readers. The draft they receive is messy and raw, but they patiently critique and share knowledge. Timothy J. Spadoni, the author of *The Final Run/Stories of Suspense and the Supernatural*, thank you for performing the hard job of being my first reader and saving me from "jumping the shark." Kester J. Bathgate, the author of *Perilous Beginnings*, thank you for your expertise in naval history and fixing my numerous terminology mistakes. S. Lee Fisher, the author of

The Women of Campbell County Saga, thank you for your great insight and support. We love giving our heroines strong voices and able hands. Lindsey S. Fera, the author of *Muskets and Minuets*, thank you for your help with the medical scenes and historical accuracy. Finally, Becky Paroz, the author of *Words of Bek: Leadership Confidence Resilience*; thank you for your perspective that good fiction must be believable.

Writing is a solitary pursuit, but being an author is a social occupation. Tamara Palmer, R.W. Biga, Becky Smalley, Christy K Lee, Jess Kotzer, Teresa Raymond and CTZ Moms Who Write, Niles Library Writing Club, All American Speakers Toastmasters, the community of 20 Books to 50K, and especially Paper Lantern Writers, thank you from my heart. The rising tide lifts all boats.

Special thank you to my work colleagues for their support. Must be weird working with someone who could put your name into her books. Michelle Ross, you are the best fan in the world! Inna Levina, Michael and Olga Goldenberg, Jamie, Michael and Karina Rubinshteyn, thank you for reading, discussing, and promoting my books. Sending love to the wonderful book clubs that hosted me: Russian-American book club, Read Between the Wines, Park Ridge Moms, North Shore Moms, Marina in Niles, and especially the Rolling Green Book Club. All the best to podcasters and interviewers: Ivonne Wolf (Glenview TV Off the Shelf), Colin Mustful (History through Fiction), Niles Library Podcast, Deanna Kuempel (Label-free Podcast), Eri Nelson (She Shed Studios), Frank Brichetto (Ukrainian-American Magazine), History Bards Podcast, and The Authors Show.

Thank you to my terrific editor Kirsten Rees for taking my work to another level. The talented designers at GetCovers, it's a privilege to collaborate with you again.

The people who never get enough appreciation: teachers. Thank you Mr. Kevin Hickey, Mrs. Barbara Fryzel-Marquette, and Mrs. Barbara Schuman, among many other wonderful teachers from Prospect High School.

My eleven-year-old head of marketing, The Young Writer, Elanna. Your creativity, curiosity, and kindness inspire me every day. My dear Vitaly, thank you for your patience while I do "that author thing". Sunny, The Writer's Cat, we all miss you and hope you are enjoying the rainbow bridge or wherever our sweet furry companions go.

Lastly, thank you to all medical professionals everywhere for your dedication and compassion.

About the Author

Alina Rubin is an IT professional and a mom, who, during the pandemic, wrote her first novel. Writing became her passion, and her characters took her on a journey beyond her wildest dreams.

Alina's debut novel, *A Girl with a Knife,* has won the Illinois Soon to be Famous Author Competition. Since publishing, Alina has been interviewed by Glenview Off The Shelf TV program, Ukrainian-American Magazine, History through Fiction, and many other programs and podcasts, as listed on her website alinarubinauthor.com.

Alina obtained a B.S. and M.S. in Business and Information Technology from DePaul University. She lives in Chicago with her husband and daughter. When not working or writing, she enjoys yoga, hiking, and traveling.